"[An] **EXCITING THRILLER**
that the **COVERT-OPS** crowd will relish."

—*BOOKLIST*

"**CLEVER** plotting and solid prose."

—*PUBLISHERS WEEKLY*

"Don your hazmat suit,
PROP UP YOUR FEET, and **ENJOY** a good yarn."

—*KIRKUS REVIEWS*

Praise for the Novels of Brad Taylor

The Widow's Strike

"Clever plotting and solid prose set this above many similar military action novels."
—*Publishers Weekly*

"Don your hazmat suit, prop up your feet, and enjoy a good yarn."
—*Kirkus Reviews*

"Taylor, whose background in Special Forces gives his work undeniable authenticity, delivers another exciting thriller that the covert-ops crowd will relish. Get this one into the hands of Vince Flynn fans."
—*Booklist*

Enemy of Mine

"The story moves along at a rapid clip . . . satisfies from start to finish."
—*Kirkus Reviews* (starred review)

"Few authors write about espionage, terrorism, and clandestine hit squads as well as Taylor does, and with good reason: He spent more than twenty years in the army before retiring as a Special Forces lieutenant colonel. His boots-on-the-ground insight into the situation in the Middle East and special skills in 'irregular warfare' and 'asymmetric threats' give his writing a realistic, graphic tone."
—*Houston Press*

"Taylor gets exponentially better with each book, and if someone is hunting for a literary franchise to turn into a film, they need to be looking at this series."
—Bookreporter

"Action-packed. . . . Those who prize authentic military action will be rewarded."
—*Publishers Weekly*

"Pike Logan returns in another stellar effort from Taylor, a retired Delta Force commander. . . . Readers of novels set in the world of Special Forces have many choices, but Taylor is one of the best. His obvious insider knowledge, combined with a well-constructed narrative, make all his work—and this novel in particular—a delight for fans of the subgenre. The added female viewpoint here provides a fascinating perspective on a primarily male-dominated world."
—*Booklist*

continued . . .

All Necessary Force

"Fresh plot, great action, and Taylor clearly knows what he is writing about. . . . When it comes to tactics and hardware, he is spot-on." —Vince Flynn

"The first few pages alone . . . should come with a Surgeon General's warning if you have a weak heart."
—Bookreporter

"The high violence level and authentic military action put Taylor, a retired Delta Force officer, solidly in the ranks of such authors as Brad Thor and Vince Flynn."
—*Publishers Weekly*

"Terrorists plan to strike America with a vicious blow, and it's Pike Logan's job to stop them. This fast-moving thriller poses the dilemma: Must he obey the law, or must he use all necessary force to thwart the enemy? Well written, edgy, and a damn good yarn." —*Kirkus Reviews*

"Fill your lungs before you start *All Necessary Force*, because it will leave you breathless." —*Suspense Magazine*

"Told with unparalleled realism informed by Taylor's decades of experience in the U.S. Army Infantry and Delta Force, *All Necessary Force* takes readers on a terrifying journey that ends at our own front door."—Fresh Fiction

One Rough Man

"Taylor's debut flows like the best of Vince Flynn and Brad Thor. An intense and intriguing character, Logan is definitely an action hero to watch." —*Booklist*

"An auspicious, adrenaline-soaked rocket ship of a debut novel. Taylor's protagonist, Pike Logan, is one rough man who is one bad dude—as a superhero, Pike ranks right up there with Jason Bourne, Jack Reacher, and Jack Bauer."
—*New York Times* bestselling author John Lescroart

ALSO BY BRAD TAYLOR

THE WIDOW'S STRIKE

A PIKE LOGAN THRILLER

BRAD TAYLOR

A SIGNET SELECT BOOK

SIGNET SELECT
Published by the Penguin Group
Penguin Group (USA) LLC, 375 Hudson Street,
New York, New York 10014

USA | Canada | UK | Ireland | Australia | New Zealand | India | South Africa | China
penguin.com
A Penguin Random House Company

Published by Signet Select, an imprint of New American Library, a division of
Penguin Group (USA) LLC. Previously published in a Dutton edition.

First Signet Select Printing, June 2014

ISBN 978-0-451-46766-9

Printed in the United States of America
10 9 8 7 6 5 4

To Taz, for protecting our way of life

Greater love hath no man than this, that a man lay down his life for his friends.

Throughout history, no human interventions have managed to stop a pandemic once it starts . . .

> Dr. Margaret Chan, Representative of the WHO
> Director-General for Pandemic Influenza

We recognized that . . . the information is going to get out. But . . . if we can slow down the release of the specific information that would enable somebody to reconstruct this virus and do something nefarious, even for a while, then that was a good thing.

> Professor Paul Keim, Chairman of the US National
> Science Advisory Board for Biosecurity, on why
> he was recommending the censorship of research
> on genetically mutated H5N1 virus

By making the leap [to humans], the virus had satisfied two of the three conditions for a pandemic. It was novel—no one had been exposed, so no one had immunity—and it had proven it could infect people. Now it just had to show it could get around.

> Alan Sipress, *The Fatal Strain:*
> *On the Trail of Avian Flu*
> *and the Coming Pandemic*

1

The technician thought the sign on the door said it all. WARNING: BIOHAZARD LEVEL IV—H5N1 RESEARCH ONGOING. It looked official enough, the universal biohazard symbol followed by a host of precautions proclaiming its authority, but it was listing a bit to the side, the tape holding it in place losing adhesive in the humid air. An indicator of the less-than-perfect nature of the work beyond the door.

Takes more than a sign to make a level-four facility. The technician thought again about telling someone what they were doing. Perhaps preventing a tragedy. He knew he wouldn't, though, because the money was too good, and there just wasn't anywhere else to do the research.

Singapore had only one level-four biosafety facility in the entire country, and it was owned by the government at the Defence Science Organisation laboratory. No way was his employer going to let them in on the action. Too much profit at stake. Not to mention the red tape involved.

He clocked in on the computer and pushed through

into the anteroom, seeing the old BIOSAFETY LEVEL III warning mounted in a frame on the wall—what this facility had been rated before they used some tape and a new sign. He waited for the outer door to snick closed, then entered the lab, still empty at this hour, and continued on, through another double-doored anteroom and into the animal housing facility.

He moved straight to two isolator boxes, ignoring the large cage at the back of the room teeming with European ferrets. Before he even reached the first box, he could see through the containment glass that the vaccine had failed. The ferret lay on his side, a small bit of blood seeping out of his eyes and nose. Golf Sixteen had lasted as long as Golfs One through Fifteen, which is to say about four days. Three healthy, and one day of agony before his body quit.

He turned his attention to the other containment box and was surprised to see the ferret sniffing the glass, patiently waiting to play.

The door opened behind him, and he heard, "Another female lived, huh? That's going to be a blow to the weaker-sex theory."

He smiled at his partner, knowing she secretly liked the fact that all the males croaked no matter what the scientists did. "Good morning to you too, Chandra. And it remains to be seen whether the vaccine took or if she's just an asymptomatic carrier like the others. We'll get the sample from Golf Sixteen in a second. Help me with Sandy Eight here."

The Sandy side of the house had fared better than the

Golfs. Seven of the initial eight had lived after being given the vaccine, but in so doing had forfeited their lives anyway. The vaccine had prevented the virus from gobbling them up whole but had not created the antibodies necessary to destroy it. The end result was a biological truce, with the virus living inside the host without attacking, patiently waiting to be unleashed on another victim. Which meant the first seven Sandys had gone into the incinerator just like the first fifteen Golfs.

He struggled into another set of surgical gloves, his third, while his partner put on a flow-hood respirator. Once he had his own hood in place, she unsealed the top hinge of the containment box. She reached in and pinned the ferret behind the skull, using her other hand to trap the animal lower on the spine.

Before it could get antsy, he used a syringe to extract a small amount of blood. As the needle bit, the ferret writhed violently, twisting out of Chandra's grip. They both ripped their hands out of the box, and he lost the syringe as Chandra slammed the lid down to prevent Sandy Eight from escaping.

Taking in great gulps of air from the flow hood, the technician felt the sweat rolling down his face, the forced air making his skin clammy. He leaned against the box and said, "Man, I like it better when they're dead. We need more sophisticated containment boxes. Biosafety cabinets designed for this instead of the makeshift stuff we have. Real equipment intended for the work."

Chandra's face was chalk white.

"What's wrong with you?"

She began backing toward the door.

His first thought was that she'd been bitten, and he knew the consequences of that. He held his hands up to calm her. To keep her from running outside the containment zone. And noticed the needle of the syringe hanging from the back of his left hand, a faint ribbon of blood visible.

THREE DAYS LATER the first symptom appeared. A simple headache. When he looked in the mirror, his eyes were bloodshot. The whites crisscrossed with a latticework of red. He felt his stomach clench in fear, wanting to believe it was coincidence. But he knew he was dead.

Inside his quarantine room they began administering massive amounts of Tamiflu in an effort to stop the progress. Like the nurses feverishly cramming him full of intravenous injections, he understood it was futile. The virus had been genetically engineered to be resistant to Tamiflu, and true to its nature it continued to ravage his body from the inside out, exploding his cells in a furious haste to replicate.

By day four he was on a respirator, with all manner of drugs funneling into him to slow the assault. He turned cyanotic from the lack of oxygen, his skin almost translucent, his lips looking like his meals consisted of grape popsicles.

He made it to day five before he began to weep blood

from his eyes and nose, his body drowning in the excretions created by the battle raging within.

Doctors from the laboratory hovered around him in pressurized biohazard suits, but they could do little to help him. It had been almost one hundred years since the great influenza pandemic of 1918, when the very existence of viruses was still unknown, yet the doctors from the lab were just as powerless as their predecessors. They might as well have put leeches on his body for all the good the leaps of modern medical knowledge did them.

On day six, at 0436 local time, his heart stopped beating. The cadaver sat inside the quarantine room for an additional eighteen hours while his employer decided what to do with it, the virus boiling away inside, desperate to find another host.

At 2230 three men entered his room dressed like they were about to walk on the surface of the moon. One carried a roll of thick plastic sheeting. Two sported cordless bone saws.

At 0100 local time his body was fed into the incinerator in ferret-sized chunks.

At 0800, Golf Seventeen and Sandy Nine were inoculated.

2

Dressed all in black, the man blended in completely with the masonry on top of the wall. Someone would be able to see him if they were interested enough to look closely, but there was little fear of the caretaker guard's doing that without a reason. Movement was the killer at this point, so the man simply lay atop the wall, waiting.

The guard continued on his route, no longer in sight, but his footfalls echoed on the paving stones. The man looked at his watch, waiting until the sound was overshadowed by the tooting horns of the endless Bangkok traffic.

Seven minutes to get inside.

He pulled up the knotted rope and set the grappling hook on the opposite side of the wall, the rubberized cleats making not a sound as it gripped the ledge. He dropped the rope on the near side, then rolled off himself, hitting the soft grass fifteen feet below.

He remained crouched where he had landed, not moving a muscle, all his senses straining for a break in the rhythm of the night. He saw no movement and heard nothing but the traffic from Luk Luang Road. Convinced he was safe, he slowly rose to get his bearings.

He had been inside the compound on four different occasions, but each one had been during daylight, coming through the front gate on official business. It was a little bit different at night, climbing up an outside wall between two buildings.

Orienting himself, the man took one step before his earpiece came alive. "Freeze, freeze, freeze. Knuckles, you got a four-man element headed across the lawn toward the front gate."

Knuckles faded back into the shrubbery. What the hell was someone doing working this late? His watch told him he had five minutes before another guard came back through on this route.

"Decoy, I'm running out of time. What are they doing? Coming or going?"

"Going. They just came out of the secretariat building and are now standing around talking on the lawn."

"I can't wait. Give me a clear path."

"Stand by."

Knuckles scanned the night sky, straining to see if he could detect the Wasp drone overhead. He came up empty, as he knew he would. The thing weighed less than three pounds and had a minuscule three-and-a-half-foot wingspan. With an electric motor, it was damn near soundless. Invisible—especially at night.

"Knuckles, this is Brett. You want to roll over? Try again tomorrow night?"

Brett was his exfil, sitting in a van on the corner of Luk Luang and Ratchadamnoen Nok Roads, right outside the United Nations offices. Knuckles considered, but ultimately decided against it. Just getting inside the compound had been a chore.

He said, "Maybe. Give it a couple more minutes. If I abort, I'll be coming over the same way. Pick me up on Luk Luang, canal side."

"Roger."

"Decoy, what do you have?"

"I'm looking. Outside of the four unknowns, I've got bodies right where we expected them. Hang on."

Knuckles shook his head, still a little aggravated that his team had been called to do the mission. On the surface, it would appear a strange choice to risk so much by breaking into the Thai Ministry of Education, but his goal wasn't inside this compound. It was the Metropolitan Police Bureau across the street, on Phitsanulok Road.

Another team on the ground had found getting inside that place was just too risky but had learned something interesting in the process: The fiber-optic data cable for the police department also serviced the Ministry of Education. All they needed to do was slave into it, which is where Knuckles came in.

The Ministry of Education's National Museum division was responsible for all archeological work in the country, a convenient arrangement that had given Knuckles's team a plausible reason to conduct the four reconnaissance missions earlier. As far as the Thai government knew, he worked for a company called Grolier Recovery Services that specialized in facilitating archeological work.

The team he was helping was in Thailand under a different cover and couldn't simply switch hats to accomplish the mission, so he'd been called forward. He had never linked up with them in-country and didn't even know who they were tracking. Just that they needed access to the Metropolitan Police database. His mission and theirs were completely firewalled.

He waited in the brush, eyeballing the route he had planned earlier and feeling the time slip away. The compound was about two hundred meters across, but his target building was only one hundred meters away. Tucked between two larger buildings, it was smack-dab in the middle, at the apex of the lawn.

He'd planned this route specifically because it was threaded through the myriad of CCTV cameras, but that was predicated on slipping in between the guard force patrols. He considered simply waiting where he was and letting the guard pass again but didn't like the odds of discovery. He was hidden well enough in the darkness, but nothing was a sure thing when other human beings were involved. Murphy would raise his head at the worst possible moment. While he felt sure he could get out clean, the mission would be a failure. No way would they attempt another break-in after a compromise.

"Okay, Knuckles, I got a route, but you're not going to like it."

"What?"

"Well, you got bodies in front of the building, cameras on the corners, and the guard shack in back. You got nothing on top."

"Are you kidding me? You need a UAV to tell me to climb to the roof? I could come up with that using a paper map."

"I know, I know, but the secretariat building runs lengthwise and butts right up to your building. The roof is sloped, so you could go the whole distance without being seen from the front. And I can track your progress."

"Do I look like a monkey? The secretariat is three stories tall."

"So you can't do what the chicks do?"

Knuckles knew exactly whom he was talking about, and the jibe didn't help his attitude any. He was about to call an abort when Decoy came back.

"Just kidding. I'm looking at a fire escape ladder on the northeast corner. It's inside the shadows. Can you climb a ladder?"

He clenched his teeth, biting back what was about to vomit out of his mouth. "Roger. I can climb a damn ladder. Is it locked?"

"Can't tell from the video feed, but you need to make a decision quick. Guard is coming down the path. You got about forty-five seconds."

"Moving."

Knuckles sprinted in a crouch across the open area to the shrubbery on the near side of the secretariat building, then scampered down the wall to the northeast corner, underneath the cameras. He heard the guard's footsteps at the same time Decoy called.

"Freeze, freeze. Guard has stopped walking."

Knuckles tried to become the wall, breathing in a shallow pant, straining to hear if anyone came toward him. *This was stupid. Only way out is through the guard. Which means compromise.*

"He's moving again. You're clear."

Knuckles duck-walked as fast as he could, finding the ladder right where Decoy said it would be. And a chain with a padlock sealing a cage at the base of it.

Damn it.

"Decoy, it's locked with a cage that goes up to the second floor. It's going to take me some time. Stay sharp. I need serious early warning."

"Roger."

"Brett, Brett, you copy?"

"I got you."

"I get compromised, same plan; I'm going to deal with the initial issue, then come straight over the wall back to Luk Luang. I'll need you there immediately."

"Roger that."

Knuckles pulled out a red-lensed penlight and studied the lock. An old Schlage. Not too much trouble. He placed his pack on the ground, pulled out a bunch of paperwork and brochures designed to support his cover if he was caught, and peeled back an inner lining, exposing his lock-pick kit. Besides the slave device for the fiber-optic cable, he carried no other special equipment. If caught, he felt it would be a hell of a lot harder explaining a bunch of 007 gee-whiz gear, so he'd opted not to bring any.

Putting the penlight in his mouth, he raked the lock set for about a minute before the pins sheared and the bolt sprang open.

"Decoy, am I clear? This cage is going to make some noise."

"Yeah, you're good."

He pulled the gate open, wincing at the screech it made, the hinges reluctant to break out of their rusty hibernation. He opened it just enough to enter, then slid through. He spent a couple of seconds relocking it from the inside, then made his way to the roof.

Crouched on the shale tile, he began to scuttle the length of the roof, keeping the apex between him and the people on the lawn out front. He reached the far side without any trouble, seeing his target building below him. Then his predicament sank in.

"Ahh . . . Decoy, is there a ladder on the far side?"

From the pause, he knew Decoy was feeling like just as big of a dumbass as he was.

"I'm looking."

Knuckles waited, wondering how many cases of beer this was going to cost him.

"There appears to be a drainpipe fifty feet behind you. In the crook where the building tees."

Knuckles spat out, "Drainpipe."

"Yeah. Looks like you get to be Koko after all."

He didn't bother to respond to the inside joke, simply

inched along the edge of the roof until he reached the T of the building. He saw the pipe, grateful that it was an ancient cast iron one instead of some flimsy aluminum gutter.

He lay flat on the roof, leaned over, and wrapped his hands around the top of the pipe, taking note of the location of the first anchor point into the wall.

"Get ready for some adventure. This thing breaks and we're in a world of hurt."

Brett came on. "What do you mean 'we'?"

3

Knuckles slipped over the side, clamping his hands in the opening at the top like a vise grip. He hung in the air for a split second, then did a chin-up until his face was level with the roof. He placed his legs on either side of the pipe and slid down until his feet made contact with the anchor.

He slid his hands on the outside of the pipe and began a slow descent, grateful for the gloves he'd worn, initially to prevent any fingerprints but now saving the skin on his palms.

He shimmied down until he was at the first-floor level. He looked beneath him, then simply dropped, hitting the ground harder than he wanted, rolling with the impact into the pool of light from an outside lamp. He scuttled back into the shadows, his target door fifty feet away.

"I'm down. Am I clear?"

"Stand by. Let me sweep."

Knuckles used the time to break out the lock-pick kit.

"Okay, the four out front are still gabbing, but you're shielded by the secretariat building. Nothing else moving."

He sprinted through the light and slid into the alcove,

the plan now back on its original track. He pulled the picks that had proven successful earlier on a mock-up and went to work on the lock, a grin sneaking out when it popped in seconds. *Nothing like rehearsals.*

He slipped into the darkened hallway and jogged by memory alone. The National Museum office was four doors to the right. The server room was two doors beyond that, down another small hallway.

He reached the turn and was brought up short by Decoy.

"Knuckles, Knuckles, we got a gaggle at your entry point. Don't know what they're doing."

It hit him immediately. *The rope. They found the rope.* It was the one risk he had been willing to take, because he couldn't scale the wall without some mechanical help, and the odds of someone stumbling across it in the dark were astronomical.

Damn Murphy.

He raced to the server room door, aiming his penlight at the keypad. "What're they doing?"

"More people are gathering where you breached the wall. The four out front have gone over, along with some other stragglers. They found something."

He punched in the keystrokes he'd gotten from headquarters and said, "They found my rope."

He yanked the door, but it didn't budge.

Shit.

"Brett, Brett, code isn't working. What was it again?"

"Six-four-eight-two-pound. I say again six-four-eight-two-pound."

He said, "I just did that," as he punched in the numbers again.

The door refused to move.

"Brett, that code isn't right. What else could it be?"

Decoy came on. "Knuckles, abort. They're fanning out. They know someone's inside."

"Brett, I can't get out to Luk Luang. Stage on Phitsanulok."

"Ahh . . . Roger. Moving, but you realize that's in front of the police station?"

"No shit, now what's the damn code?"

Decoy said, "Screw the code. Get out of there. They've started to search and men are coming from the police station to help."

Brett said, "Try the pound sign first."

Knuckles did, and the door opened.

"I'm inside. Give me a trigger when someone enters this building."

"Trigger now. They're inside your building now."

Knuckles snicked the door closed behind him, praying that whoever entered didn't have the combination for the keypad. He quickly analyzed the mass of blinking lights from the server rack and found the main fiber-optic hub. He pulled out the slave device and clamped it to the cable, waiting until it began blinking a steady green.

Keeping his voice low, he said, "Slave in place. I'm coming out."

Brett said, "I'm staged. I'll be coming from north to

south. Heads up—this road is full of pedestrians and vendors. The street market is still hopping."

Which is why it hadn't been chosen as an entry point in the first place. Well, that and the fact that climbing the wall in front of the police station didn't seem that smart. Now it seemed a hell of a lot smarter than going out the way he'd come in.

Knuckles placed his ear against the door and heard two voices speaking in Thai. Someone had turned on the hall light, letting a feeble glow spill underneath his door. From his earlier recce, he knew that this hallway led to a door outside. If he could just get out of the server room, he could play cat-and-mouse to the far wall of the compound, avoiding the search party.

"Decoy, you know where the hallway to the server room exits?"

"Yeah, I got it in sight now."

"Is it clear?"

"Two men moving around to the adjacent building. Give them a second."

Knuckles listened again, hearing the sounds of the voices moving away, back down the main hall.

"Your exit's clear."

Holding his breath, he cracked the door and saw the men had disappeared. He left the server room and sprinted down the hall, pulling up short at the end.

"I'm about to exit."

"Go. You're clear. Move straight across to the overhang of the next building."

He did as directed, running blindly into the night. He reached the alcove and squatted down, thinking, *One hundred meters. Only got one hundred meters.*

He shuffled the length of the alcove and peeked around the corner, seeing a parking lot with shrubbery and trees on the far side. No sign of the wall, but it had to be just beyond.

"Knuckles, pack of guys rounded the corner from the north. They're beating the bushes. Move."

He slid along the wall until he ran out of building, saying, "I'm going to sprint across the parking lot. Can I make it?"

"You'd better be Jesse Owens, but there's nobody to your front."

He took off at a dead sprint, reaching the far side of the parking lot before hearing someone shout behind him. He made it into the foliage and kept going, almost slamming into the compound wall. He immediately turned north, running parallel, trying to find a way over the fifteen-foot barricade.

"What's the posse doing?"

"Looks like they've seen you, but nobody's giving chase. Everyone is just gathering together."

Panting, knowing he sounded like a bull elephant in the brush, he saw nothing to help him over the wall and felt the panic begin to rise. *Calm down. Always a way out. Just find it.*

"Knuckles, they've started to move toward you. Three groups of four, spread out and searching."

He slowed, wanting the stealth to prevent them from zeroing in on his position. He heard them yelling back and forth and saw the flashlights bobbing behind him. A building appeared out of the darkness, angled away from the wall. The farther north he moved, the more he was hemmed in.

What if it joins the wall? He'd be trapped. He looked behind and saw that it was irrelevant. He wasn't slipping through the cordon they had made.

He began to jog in the darkness, the building getting closer and closer. He exited the foliage, hitting pavement, and picked up his pace. He turned to check the pursuit and ran into a metal Dumpster, the clang causing an excited rise in the voices behind him.

He saw the flashlights begin to bounce around crazily and knew they were now closing fast, feeling the kill. He then realized the cause of the noise was his salvation. Three feet from the wall, the Dumpster stood six feet tall. He scrambled on top, heedless of the racket he made. He could clearly make out distinct voices and saw the lights less than seventy feet away. He tight-roped his way along the edge of the Dumpster, reached the side closest to the wall, and launched himself into the air.

He caught the top of the wall and slammed face-first into the masonry. Ignoring the pain, he pulled himself up using adrenaline alone and flipped to the far side, landing in between two street vendors.

Free.

The vendors simply stared, slack-jawed, making no

move to intercept him. He sprinted across the street, ripping off his balaclava.

"Brett, Brett, in position for pickup."

"Moving."

He reached the far side and slowed. He began moving north, blending in to the small stream of pedestrians still out this late. He had walked no longer than four seconds when he heard shouting behind him.

"Brett, I got an issue. What's your location?"

"I see them. I'm just north. Two cops running toward your back. Want me to interdict?"

Knuckles thought about it. Thought about the cameras all around and the fact that introducing the van would complicate matters for the inevitable follow-on investigation. They'd *know* he was the guy if he did something right now. Even if he got away here, they'd now have a description of both him and Brett, along with the van. *That's assuming you can get away.* Not a sure thing considering the Metropolitan Police Bureau was less than one hundred yards to the south.

"No. Let it ride. I've got nothing on me and there's no way they saw me come over the wall. No reason to suspect I did anything. I'll talk my way out. I'm going off team net and putting the cell back into OEM configuration."

He fiddled with his smartphone, leaving the Bluetooth in his ear, now glad he hadn't brought the extra equipment. It would have been hard explaining why he was carrying night observation devices and a Glock, even without anything tying him to the Ministry of Education.

He waited for one more shout before turning around with a confused "You yelling at me?" look on his face, then patiently waited for them to catch up.

Everything was going fine, him answering the questions with his prepared explanation of why he was in the area, the men digging through his bag and finding only brochures and documents that backstopped his story. Fine until one of them pulled out his balaclava, still drenched with sweat.

He saw the cop smile. *Shit. So much for walking away.*

"Why do you need a ski mask in Thailand?"

4

I pulled into the parking lot at 0630, stopping right under the Grolier Recovery Services sign. Usually, the lot was full and I had to park on the other side and walk to my office. Then again, usually I was still sound asleep at this time. I saw Jennifer's car and wondered if she'd been here for two hours, stretching and eating Power-Bars.

I entered and found Jennifer sitting on the floor, stretching her quads. I saw a half-eaten PowerBar on the desk and smiled.

"Aren't we the eager beaver?"

She stood up and bounced on her toes a little bit. "I've been reading about running injuries. Jury's out on stretching, but nobody says it can hurt."

Today was Charleston's Cooper River Bridge Run, and it was Jennifer's first. A few months ago she'd been attacked by a man and had taken up running as a sort of therapy to get over it. I'd encouraged it initially, until she'd gone overboard, running all the damn time like Forrest Gump. Well, that's not true. I still encouraged it. Encouraged anything to help her get over the trauma, since my killing that asshole hadn't been enough.

"You still going to try to beat forty-five minutes?"

She placed her hands against the wall, now stretching her calves. "I'm not going to try, Pike. I'm going to shatter that time. I hope you can keep up."

"Don't worry about me. Worry about yourself. Especially when I'm dragging your ass up the bridge."

Running is a mental game, and Jennifer was a gymnast, not an endurance athlete. She'd run plenty of three- and four-mile jaunts over the past few months, but I knew she'd hit a wall and wouldn't be able to keep a forty-minute pace for the entire six miles. Especially after the long climb to the top of the bridge. Maybe forty-five, but no way forty.

"I ran seven miles three days ago at a little under a seven-minute pace. Back and forth across the bridge. I'm good."

The comment gave me pause. *She's just saying that to scare you.* Except that Jennifer didn't know how to bluff. Didn't believe in mind games. Which scared the shit out of me. *Should've done more running.*

She said, "You ready to go?"

"Yeah, just let me get the Taskforce phone."

She stood by the door as I rummaged through my desk. "What are you bringing that for? We're still on stand-down, right?"

Ostensibly, Grolier Recovery Services specialized in facilitating archeological work around the world. With

Jennifer's anthropology degree and my background in the military, we hired out to various clients who needed specialized consulting in anything dealing with archeological work in a foreign country, from host-nation clearances to security on-site.

In reality, the company was a sophisticated cover for a counterterrorist unit simply called the Taskforce. It allowed penetration of denied areas when other means had failed. Our last mission had been a little bit of a doozy, with the commander of the Taskforce mandating a forced vacation because of the repercussions. As if I needed some downtime from exterminating a roach.

I zipped the phone in a fanny pack, saying, "You never know what could pop up. A little time off is fine, but this is starting to drag."

She frowned but said nothing else, holding the door open for me. Our office was on Shem Creek in Mount Pleasant, and the start of the race was only about a half mile away on Coleman Boulevard, so we'd decided to park here and walk, since the entire stretch of Coleman was going to be a nuthouse of about thirty thousand people.

We reached our corral and I began to notice all of the stares Jennifer was getting. She was wearing nothing but a pair of Lycra stretch pants, which clung to her legs like a coat of paint, and a sports bra, her midriff exposed for all to see. In my rational mind, I knew the attire was simply something she was comfortable running in and nothing different than what a host of other women around us wore, but the goggle eyes were aggravating nonetheless.

Our connection was definitely more than that of simple business partners but still less than a relationship. The trauma she'd been through had stymied that. Having a little experience in personal tragedy, I was content to let it ride. Let her get over it in her own time. That didn't mean I was content for her to be viewed as a piece of meat.

Tightening her ponytail, oblivious to the stares, she said, "What's the frown for?"

I quickly pasted on a smile. "Nothing. It's showtime. Get ready to rumble."

We heard the announcer cheer as the Kenyans were let loose, running faster than a human being should be capable. In short order, we were walking to the start line, then jogging in the massive crowd of people, Jennifer weaving in and out, trying to keep her pace but prevented by the slugs who came to run once a year.

After about a mile of bump-and-go we reached the bottom of the bridge, the long slope to the top a daunting obstacle to the once-a-year runners. They began to walk and the crowd thinned. Jennifer glanced back at me once, then took off like a gazelle, intent on making up lost time, churning up the slope like it didn't exist.

Holy shit.

The rest of the run was a blur as my vision narrowed to the small of her back, my mind ignoring the pain. I felt like I was back at Special Forces selection, willing myself forward, thinking of nothing but driving my body faster than it was prepared to go.

We finished in 41:48. It would have been quicker but Jennifer didn't have free rein with the crowds around. *Thank God*. We crossed the line and continued walking, Jennifer's face all aglow and me trying to keep from vomiting, straining to keep upright to save my dignity. *My own fault for getting lazy on vacation.*

I felt the pain in my knees and wondered how much was laziness and how much was just the march of time. Eight years ago, when I was Jennifer's age, I could have done that pace hungover while carrying a rucksack. Now, at thirty-eight, I could feel the frost creeping in. It was still outside the window of my house, but it was coming.

We wandered around for a little bit, getting some free bananas and water at the post-race stalls, then went down East Bay Street for the after-party. Something I was hoping would make the pain worth it.

Getting to the rooftop deck on top of the Vendue Inn, I fought through the crowd to the bar, checking the Taskforce phone out of reflex. I pulled up short, Jennifer bumping into me, surprised to see a missed call from a blocked number, which could have meant one of two things: Either I'd missed out on the credit card deal of a lifetime, or Kurt Hale, the commander of the Taskforce, had tried to reach me.

I dialed this month's current number, letting it bounce and hum through Lord knows how many different switchboards in an effort to confuse anyone who might have been tracking the call. Eventually, I heard a human voice.

Jennifer started to ask who I was dialing, but I held up a finger, answering her question when she heard me speak a known phrase. Minutes later, I was connected with Kurt, and when I hung up I couldn't decide if I was happy or incredibly pissed off.

Jennifer had patiently waited, using the time to get some more free fruit and a couple of Bloody Marys. She handed me one and said, "So what's up?"

"Knuckles is in trouble. I don't know what sort, but it has something to do with our company."

"*Our* company? Grolier Services? How can that be? He's just a fake employee. They can't use that without us, can they?"

"No. Well, we've never really discussed it with them. We're the first company that was formed from the ground up by operators, independent of the Taskforce. Maybe they consider it part of their stable, like every other cover organization. I won't know until I talk to Kurt. He wants to meet in DC."

"When?"

"Tonight. You don't have to go if you don't want to. No big deal."

She kicked a deck pebble with her foot, debating, then said, "Are you coming back here or going somewhere else?"

"I'll definitely be coming back here, but it might be just to pack."

She held my eyes for a moment, then shook her head and said, "Can I shower first?"

5

Malik Musavi, Persian carpet salesman. The very notion disgusted him. He hated the playacting but knew it was necessary—especially given his organization's amateurish attempts in this country a year and a half ago. So he trudged up Sukhumvit Road, trying to decipher the address of the Oriental rug merchant while simultaneously waving off the insistent Bangkok tuk-tuk drivers, a pathetic smile slathered on his face.

He despised working undercover and hadn't done it in years. In fact, since he was a young recruit in the newly formed Islamic Revolutionary Guard Corps of Iran—otherwise known as the Pasdaran. Because of his language skills, he had been recruited into the Quds Force—the Pasdaran element responsible for spreading the revolution beyond Iran's borders, along with other unsavory tasks. Back then, he had always posed as a student, which was a little easier to pull off. Even in places like Argentina and Venezuela. Now a brigadier general within the Pasdaran Quds, he hadn't been tactically operational in ten years, but he'd been given a blessed opportunity. A mission of the highest priority, and after the debacle a year and a half ago, there was no way he was going to sit in Tehran and read reports like he had for the previous operation. Especially when those reports detailed bombs accidentally going off in Bangkok apartments. Or even worse, the gleeful stories from the Great Satan's press about his men whoring in Pattaya the week before the debacle. *His* men.

Not only had the Quds failed to kill a single Zionist diplomat, one of the men was arrested running away from the misfire, *with his Iranian passport*. Well, arrested after he threw a grenade at the pursuing police, only to have it bounce off a tree and blow his own legs off.

The entire episode still made him seethe a year and a half later. The damn Zionists penetrated Iran with impunity, murdering a plethora of nuclear scientists, and his men couldn't even kill a single Jew-dog in the freewheeling country of Thailand. In fact, they couldn't kill anyone at all, police, Jew, or otherwise. Not counting themselves, that is.

He came out of the reverie when he realized he'd bypassed the Oriental rug store he was searching to find. He backtracked, worked up his smarmy smile, and entered, ready to playact again.

Thirty minutes later he was back on the street, lighter in business cards and acting disappointed in the rejection from the store. It seemed they were comfortable with their artificial rugs from China, not that he really cared. It was the effort that mattered.

He flagged a tuk-tuk and gave the man a destination a few miles north on Sukhumvit, the ride forming the first leg of his plan to lose the surveillance currently on him. He hadn't minded someone watching him earlier—in fact he wanted that, since it would simply confirm his cover— but he needed to be clean in order to meet his contact from the Ministry of Intelligence and Security.

The tuk-tuk, nothing more than a motorized pedicab, had the ability to bob and weave through traffic, thereby severing him from anyone following on foot. Of course, he knew the surveillance effort would be prepared for that, and a mounted force would continue, riding mopeds, bicycles, or even another tuk-tuk. This was their city after all. The trick was to force the mounted operatives to get on the ground for a foot-follow, replacing the men he'd left behind. Sooner or later, they'd run out of people.

After ten minutes of the tuk-tuk hacking its way through the congested traffic, the incessant bleating of horns starting to cause a headache, he paid the driver and entered a pharmacy. He bought a packet of over-the-counter medication and exited, back on foot. He continued north, pausing to stop occasionally at the myriad of street-vendor shops, acting like a tourist. Crossing the street and zigzagging through the various shopping areas, he was able to identify two of the surveillance operatives on him by their actions. Both now on foot.

When he figured he'd traveled far enough to separate the second set of operatives from their vehicles, he flagged another tuk-tuk and repeated the procedure, continuing north on Sukhumvit. He had the driver stop suddenly at the Asok Skytrain station and rapidly transferred to the elevated rail system. He took it three stops to the Chit Lom station, sure that this final leg had cleansed him of any surveillance still in play.

He exited the Skytrain and saw his MOIS contact studying a route map on the wall, a folded newspaper in his left hand. He approached, standing behind the man's left shoulder to shield the pass. He pulled the folded newspaper out of the contact's hands and turned away without a word.

He had begun walking to the exit, congratulating himself on the successful mission, pleased to be back in the game after spending so long behind a desk, when he saw a man he recognized. One of the surveillance opera-tives from earlier, staring at him and talking on a cell phone.

He felt a bump in his heart rate but showed nothing outward, continuing to the exit and ignoring the opera-tive. He walked down the stairs at a casual pace, debating. Had the man seen the pass? Did they know the contact worked at the Iranian embassy? Know he worked for the MOIS? If so, they might decide the action was worth stopping him on the street for questioning. A little ex-ploratory search would ensure he was arrested because of what he now held. But he couldn't simply throw it away. He needed the information it contained, and then it needed to be destroyed. He couldn't toss it into a trash can, letting it float about until discovery. Too many other operations had failed because of just such a bet on blind luck.

In this business, he had learned that luck favored the opposition. The Great Satan routinely bulled around, bouncing off of stale rumors, only to find the golden egg in a trash can at the most inopportune time. He was sure it was no different here.

He ran through his options. On the plus side, the fact that he saw the cell phone instead of a radio meant the man was alone. He was using the cell phone as a backup because he was out of radio range with the rest of the team and so he couldn't be vectoring in a plethora of people. It was one-way communication, probably to a central operations center. They'd have this station to work with but nothing else.

Need to eliminate him before others arrive. Before he can give a complete report on what he's seen. He knew it would put him in the crosshairs of suspicion but saw no other choice if he wanted to continue.

He went down the stairs at a casual pace, giving the man plenty of time to follow. Across the four-lane road he saw a section of old apartments, crammed in between the glass and steel of the high-rises. He veered toward them, skipping through the stop-and-go traffic.

Walking through the parking lot parallel to the apartments, he ignored the security booth and guards that serviced the area, knowing his brashness would get him through. Sure enough, they paid him not a second glance, and his head began to swivel for cameras. He saw none. He continued on for about seventy meters until he found an alley sandwiched between the old buildings, the stench from rotting garbage overpowering. He opened the newspaper, removed the envelope inside, and stuffed it into his jacket, then reached into his waist and pulled out a wooden-handled ice pick, his hand trembling slightly from the rush. He flattened against the alley wall and waited.

But not for long.

He heard the man's footsteps, first running, then walking, then nothing. Malik knew the operative was momentarily confused by the loss of his target. And that he would check out the alley.

Soon enough, he heard the man approach. He knew what would happen next: In an effort to keep from burning himself, the operative would casually pass by, as if he had a destination in mind, and simply glance down the alley.

His back pressed to the wall, Malik saw the shadow before the man. As soon as he glimpsed the swing of a leg, he stepped out, grabbed the man's shirt, and whirled him into the passage, slamming him into the bricks with a forearm to the neck. Before the target could react, Malik drove the ice pick into his right eye, all the way through until it hit the skull on the far side, then oscillated the pick in rapid circles, ripping the brain tissue. The man began to twitch as if he were having a seizure, then slid down the wall to the ground. Other than the ocular fluid that had sprayed at the puncture, there was almost no blood.

Pleased, Malik wiped the ice pick on the man's sleeve and dragged him behind a Dumpster. He dug through the clothes, finding a police badge and a truncheon. No gun. Turning to leave, he heard a noise deeper in the alley. He whirled around to find a homeless man staring at him, standing on a grimy mattress. The man held out a cup, speaking in Thai, oblivious to what had just transpired.

Malik couldn't believe his luck. He approached, holding out a wad of baht. He dropped it in the cup and waited for the inevitable Thai thank-you, both hands pressed together in front of the face and head bowed. As soon as the bum looked at his feet, Malik hammered him behind the ear with the truncheon. The man howled and fell to his knees, holding his head. Malik hit him again, knocking him unconscious.

With the man prostrate before him, Malik sagged against the alley wall, catching his breath. When he was in control again, he rolled the bum until he was faceup. He used the truncheon to kill him outright, feeling the bones crunch in the victim's face from the repeated blows. Malik checked for a pulse, and when he found none he placed the ice pick under the bum's arm, then pulled the police officer back into the open. He dropped the truncheon near the cop's outstretched hands and fled.

He conducted a hasty surveillance-detection route, the charge from the killings raging through his body. He forced himself to act naturally, cognizant of the myriad of cameras on the city streets. He casually stopped in various stores and outside stands, meandering farther and farther away, all the while fighting the overpowering urge to run like the wind, the fight-or-flight response overwhelming.

When he was convinced he was clean, he sat on a bus-stop bench and opened the envelope, hoping against hope that the mission was a go and the sacrifices he'd just made wouldn't simply end up with his catching a flight to Tehran.

The report was in Farsi, and within two sentences, he knew he wouldn't see his capital any time soon.

Cailleach Laboratories confirmed researching vaccine outside of normal protocols. Have genetically developed a viral strain for testing purposes. Strain is lethal according to source reporting from inside Cailleach, Singapore. Primary research scientist is confirmed as Dr. Sakchai Nakarat.

He scanned through the rest of the report, looking for the golden egg that would continue the mission. And found it at the bottom.

Scientist's son // Kavi Nakarat // attends the European International Boarding School, Bangkok.

He sat back for a moment, savoring the flush of being operational again and the pride at the enormity of the mission placed upon his shoulders.

The IRGC was responsible for the entire nuclear weapons research infrastructure inside Iran and had been searching for all manner of ways to redirect the West from their laser focus on its development.

Fanning the flames of Syria had proven inadequate, and tit-for-tat reprisals against Israel for the death of Iran's nuclear scientists had ended in embarrassing failure. They needed something bigger. Something that would cause the entire West to focus on its own survival, country by country, starting with the Great Satan. And now maybe they had found it.

Time to get busy.

6

Elina Maskhadov sipped the small cup of coffee and waited, fingering the simple detonator poking out of her sleeve. Not out of nervousness, which would have been understandable, given that the button would shred her along with every other human in a fifty-foot radius, but for reassurance. Even out of reverence for what she was about to achieve.

The café began to pick up with government functionaries, and she waited still. Waited on her targets. She hated anyone associated with the traitorous Chechen regime of Ramzan Kadyrov, but her targets deserved special attention. A blood-feud eye-for-an-eye.

Only twenty-six, her entire existence had been spent under the constant threat of death, living like an animal in the hills outside of Grozny—or Dzhokhar, as the Chechens called it, after Dzhokhar Dudayev, the assassinated first president of separatist Chechnya.

In the old days, she had been too young to understand why the Russian Federation came to put an end to the separatist movement, but she had understood well the toll it had taken. The first battle for Grozny had ended in 1996, and calling it brutal was an understatement, with the Russian military preferring to simply carpet bomb than try to achieve any discrimination between targets. Despite the devastation, the Chechens had prevailed, and the Russians withdrew. Nine years old at the time, she had moved back to the city with her family, only to find a wasteland of rubble.

Three years later, the Russians came again, this time with even less restraint. The war lasted until the new century, when the Russian Federation finally managed to take Grozny again. Or take what was left of it. She couldn't believe the devastation. It was as if a giant had descended with a sledgehammer, then set about methodically destroying every single building. At sixteen, she found it ironic when, in 2003, the United Nations declared Grozny the most destroyed city on earth.

Throughout her life she had only wanted the fighting to stop. She'd had cousins and uncles who had taken up arms, and had even lost her fiancé to an unlucky artillery round when he had gone to get water, but she had never considered joining the cause. Never felt the urge to fight. Until the "peace" came.

Elina glanced across the intersection and saw her partner at another café, also patiently waiting. The Chechens had learned their lessons well, the primary one being to always alter their tactics. Always keep the enemy guessing as to how the next strike would come. In this case, they had deployed in an X ambush, with all four corners of the busy square holding an instrument of death: a female with enough Semtex and ball bearings to butcher anyone near her.

The initial strike would be done autonomously, by whomever achieved the biggest target first. The other three would wait for the reaction. When the response came, they would then trigger, one by one, taking out targets of opportunity along all three approach routes.

Elina looked back into her café and felt the blood begin to pump. Four men belonging to the Kadyrovtsy entered, laughing and joking.

Probably just worked up an appetite beating someone to death.

Initially a part of the presidential security service, the Kadyrovtsy, as they were called, had grown into a militia of their own, answering only to the puppet president installed by the Russian Federation, Ramzan Kadyrov.

Ramzan, a Chechen himself, understood the familial dynamics of the conflict and developed his own counterinsurgency plan. In his words, if you want the insurgents, target the families. And this he began to do, dragging in anyone remotely associated with the separatists. As it would be hard to find anyone in Chechnya who didn't know someone fighting, that left the population wide open.

The Russian Army pulled out and left him to it, and a reign of terror began, with men literally ripped off the streets, never to be seen again. Or to be found later brutally tortured to death.

Elina's surname, Maskhadov, brought special attention, as she shared it with Aslan Maskhadov, the Chechen general who was credited with victory in the first Chechen war and designated the number two wanted man in Russia after the Chechen loss in the second war, when he'd become a guerilla fighter in the hills.

She'd felt the first sting when she'd left her apartment one morning and found her uncle on the front stoop, naked and dead, covered in puckered scars from a blowtorch. There followed one after another, with cousins and brothers found brutally tortured or simply never seen again. She felt an impotent rage.

There was nothing anyone could do. There was no money to travel somewhere else and no way to stop Ramzan's Kadyrovtsy from doing whatever they wanted. In truth, many in Grozny turned a blind eye to the secret war, as Russia liked the results and had let the money flow as a reward, giving Ramzan credit for the rebuilding of the city.

In 2004, she, like everyone else in the world, became entranced by the Beslan school crisis engineered by Chechen separatists. Over a thousand people were held hostage, including hundreds of schoolchildren. Among the other hostage takers, in plain view of the television cameras, were nineteen black-clad women wearing suicide vests, demanding vengeance for the loss of their loved ones at the hands of the security forces. The talking heads nicknamed them the Black Widows.

Ending in tragedy on all sides, the crisis was a dramatic

introduction, but it wouldn't be the last. Elina began to follow the shadow war, and the Black Widows began to show their terrible power. Whenever they struck, they killed twice as many as their male counterparts. And they struck often: in Moscow subways, on commercial aircraft, at government offices. They were everywhere, and death followed them slavishly.

The Black Widows had captivated her in an abstract way, as a sort of fantasy to which she could relate. Six months ago, it had become concrete. On a brisk, clear morning, Elina's father was taken away, this time in front of her. The Kadyrovtsy refused to listen to her pleas and beat her into submission with batons when she wouldn't let go of him. He was found in the woods three days later, the official story stating that he had tried to escape. The scars on his body said otherwise. Burying his body by hand with her mother, Elina decided to fight back.

To become what the enemy feared the most.

In the coffee shop, Elina waited, hoping and praying that the man who had taken her father would appear. She toyed with the idea of saying something to him. Perhaps, right before setting off her explosives, asking him if he still hit women. Letting the realization blister his brain just before the explosives did.

There were now five Kadyrovtsy around the table. A pretty good target. She debated a moment longer, then stood, slipping the detonator into her palm. As she approached the table, two more men entered, and Elina saw her father's murderer.

They went to their own table, and Elina was torn. Kill two, or kill five? Her orders were to cause as much damage as possible, but her overwhelming desire was to kill a single man.

Before she could decide, an enormous explosion rocked the air no more than seventy meters away, throwing her to the ground. She recovered quickly, knowing what the others did not: The attack was on.

She stood, looking for the larger group, pausing when she saw a leg no more than four feet away, a shoe still on its foot, the top shorn at midthigh, the femur stark against the red meat.

A second explosion cracked through the air, this one farther away. She knew she was running out of time. She looked for the murderer and found him with the larger group, all of them animatedly shouting, as if to determine what to do. She suppressed a grim smile.

She began a slow stalk toward them, silently chanting, "*Allahu akbar*," over and over. They decided on a course of action just as she came abreast of them.

She closed her eyes and pressed the trigger.

And nothing happened.

She hit it again and again, and still she remained standing. Still remained of this earth. She was thrown aside as the group of Kadyrovtsy raced into the street, toward the explosions.

No! No, no, no. Don't let him escape.

She watched the group reach the far side of the road, a stinging sense of failure dragging her down. The men swerved and ran along the closest clear path, the one avenue that hadn't been touched. Yet.

When they reached the corner, she saw her partner stand, dressed completely in black. As they ran by her, the Black Widow raised her fist, and a blinding flash erupted. The shock wave knocked Elina down a second time. When she stood again, she saw the castoffs of a charnel house. Bodies torn apart haphazardly and pieces thrown a great distance. Spinning around like a lopsided top was the head of her father's murderer.

7

I kept my eye on the front door, watching for Kurt Hale, while Jennifer scanned the menu. We'd managed to catch a nonstop flight to Reagan National Airport at noon, and I'd convinced him to meet us for lunch instead of dinner. As owner of Grolier Recovery Services, I couldn't go to Taskforce headquarters without a threat of burning the cover, since the headquarters staff ran around telling everyone they were working at Blaisdell Consulting. Going inside "Blaisdell" headquarters might have raised a question as to what "Grolier Recovery Services" was doing, so we picked a third location. Actually, I picked it because I didn't want to go to something like Starbucks, which would have been Jennifer's choice. We went to a nice little watering hole right near Georgetown, so the clientele would be an eclectic mix of students and businesspeople.

Jennifer put the menu down, glanced along the length of the bar to the door, and said, "Why is it that every time you pick a place, it's some saloon?"

"Marshall's isn't a saloon. It's an institution. And it

was the first place I could think of that would allow us to talk without being bothered. I knew it would be deserted right now, and the floor plan gives us a clear visual of anyone who enters. No surprises."

"Please. Spare me the tradecraft BS. I caught the beer specials on the way up the stairs."

The door opened, and I saw Kurt silhouetted by the light from outside. He was dressed in khakis and a blue button-down, looking like eight thousand other businessmen and lobbyists in Washington. Well, that is, until you saw him up close. He was larger than most men, and his nose was slightly bent, like he'd been punched a few times too many. Nobody was going to confuse him with an environmental lobbyist.

He sat down across from Jennifer, ignoring the seat that would put his back to the door. He shook our hands, saying to Jennifer, "How come every time I meet Pike it's at some local pub? Whatever happened to a coffee shop?"

Jennifer smiled and looked at me, waiting on an answer.

"Hey, sir, take a look at the layout and you'll know why. Besides, L Street is hell and gone from Arlington, and you said get away from Taskforce headquarters."

He waved his arm as if shooing off a fly. "Whatever. I read the chalkboard outside."

He said nothing else as the waitress took our order, waiting until she was out of earshot. I let him take the lead.

"Knuckles has been arrested on suspicion of breaking

into an official government building. I need you to go to Thailand as the owner of Grolier Recovery Services to see if you can get him out. At the very least, just to act like an owner concerned about his employee, to strengthen his cover."

"Why? What the hell was he doing using *our* cover?"

"We're tracking a facilitator in Bangkok and found out the Thai police were on him as well. We needed to know what they knew to help complete the picture and to find out if they were going to arrest him. If they were, we needed to know how much time we had to play with. If the Thais get him, he'll just sit in jail. We wanted to beat them to the punch. Drain his brain for a potential follow-on hit in Manila."

"That doesn't answer my question."

He laid it out for me, the whole Ministry of Education connection and Grolier Recovery Services, ending with the details of the mission.

"Brett, Retro, Buckshot, and Decoy are still in country, still covered by Grolier. They've done what they could, but the Thais have moved Knuckles to a holding prison in Chiang Mai. They don't have anything concrete, and Knuckles left no traces of the B and E in the ministry, so it's become a bit of a standoff. They smell something but don't know what it is. I need you to get over there and engage the State Department. Get them on board with his case."

Speaking of stink, the last statement definitely had an odor. "I don't get it. The secretary of state is a member of the Oversight Council. Can't he pull some strings? What am I going to do that he can't do ten times over?"

The Oversight Council was the approval authority for all Taskforce operations. Since it operated outside of traditional statutes embodied in US code—a nice way of saying "illegally"—it had its own chain of command, so to speak. Comprised of thirteen individuals, including the president, it had final say on anything the Taskforce did. The secretary of state was a voting member and could get Knuckles out in short order.

"The council has decided not to intervene on any official level." He saw me start to bristle and held up a hand. "The consensus is that such interference will only provide proof that Knuckles was doing something illegal on behalf of the United States government. It'll just make matters worse. They want to handle this as if he truly *was* an employee of Grolier, which is why you, as a concerned employer, will now rush over to Thailand and begin raising a ruckus to get him out."

"Sir, I've been to Thailand a ton of times when I was in Special Forces. They can hold his ass for as long as they like without charges. He could stay in jail for years without US government help."

"I know. We won't let that happen. If we need to pull the trigger on the big guns, we will."

I'd known plenty of commanders who would tell me what they thought I wanted to hear, but Kurt wasn't like that. He had never lied to me before, and I knew he wouldn't now.

I said, "Are they afraid they'll make matters worse for Knuckles or for themselves? Is this about getting him out or about protecting their own sorry asses from Taskforce discovery?"

He said nothing, but his face betrayed the truth.

"That's just great. They know Knuckles will rot in jail forever before he'd say anything, so they're just going to let that happen to protect themselves."

"Pike, I won't let it get that far."

"What about a breakout? You have almost two whole teams over there."

"Pike, come on. Get real. You think the Oversight Council is going to sanction a jailbreak? Anyway, we pulled the other team. That entire operation is on hold until we get this sorted out."

Jennifer spoke for the first time. "How are we getting there?"

I turned to her, surprised. "You want to go?"

"Of course. I'm not going to let Knuckles rot, and all you'll do is make everyone mad. I'm fifty percent owner too."

Glad for the change of subject, Kurt said, "I've got the Rock Star bird fueled up and ready to go. It's still leased to Grolier, and it's what I used to get Knuckles over there in the first place."

"Is it loaded with a package?" I asked.

"Yes. It is."

Hmmm . . . no question about why I asked.

The Rock Star bird was a Gulfstream IV, just like the

rock stars used. The primary difference was that instead of guitars and hot tubs, it had a package of weapons and a technical kit hidden in special compartments. Its lease and origins covered under about forty-two different layers, it had ended up on our company ledger sheet from an operation a couple of years ago.

Kurt stood, throwing some bills on the table to cover his meal. "Look, I've got to get back. I know how you feel. I feel the same way. It's why I'm giving you the Rock Star bird. Just get over there and get Knuckles out."

I had about four hundred other questions but remained mute. I shook his hand, and we began our fifteen-minute wait, giving Kurt time to clear the area and break any connection to us. Jennifer said, "You didn't ask him why they used our company in the first place without consulting you or me."

"There'll be time for that later. It wouldn't have mattered here anyway."

"Are we going straight to Dulles?"

"You are. Get the plane ready to go; file a flight plan for Charleston, then Chiang Mai. Wait for me at the FBO."

"What are you going to do?"

"A little mission prep."

8

Malik spoke over his shoulder as he peeked out of the blinds.

"Has anyone paid you more scrutiny than normal?"

"No, sir. Actually, they've quit looking at us. We've been attending class for over a month."

Malik turned, speaking to the group. "Don't get careless. They are on me night and day now, and it was almost impossible to get clean for this meeting."

He didn't tell them why that was the case. Since the discovery of the dead police officer he'd been questioned twice. Both overtly pleasant affairs, nothing more than poking his story to see if they could find a hole, but a sinister cloud hung behind the smiles of the Thai officials. Luckily, he'd made progress on the Persian-carpet front, with orders from three separate stores to back up his cover. The backstopping for the business itself was as strong as that of any company on earth; his company was fully owned and managed by the Pasdaran, blended into the myriad of textile industries the Revolutionary Guards Corps dabbled in.

The men eagerly nodded their heads, wanting to prove they were better than the idiots who had screwed up the mission against the Zionist diplomat a year and a half ago. Malik kept his stern visage but was inwardly pleased. He'd handpicked each of them, fighting with their respective Quds commanders to get them released for this mission. Since he had the ear of the ayatollah himself, it wasn't much of a battle.

The men were all young, were all here on student visas, and had all been living their cover for a little over two months. They were clean-shaven, and if you didn't look at their passports, they could have been from Italy instead of Iran. Each had a specialty, giving the team expertise in everything from computers to explosives. All were extremely well trained but had been picked for another critical reason: their fervent belief in exporting the revolution. They hadn't even been born when Iran became a theocracy bathed in blood, but they had been steeped in its mystique from the moment they could walk. There would be no Pattaya whores with this group.

"Okay. Good," Malik said. "What do we know about the son?"

Roshan, the engineer, spoke first. "We've located him, but taking him will be difficult. He attends a boarding school way north of the city center. The school is located on the grounds of a gated community, primarily full of European expatriates. He's not allowed to leave during the week but is free to come and go on the weekends."

Not good. "We don't have time to waste guessing

where he will be on the weekend. What about his mother? Where's his true home?"

Roshan said, "His mother is dead. He's an only child, which is why his father put him in the boarding school while he works in Singapore."

Malik considered. They'd have to mount a surveillance effort against the boy just to determine likely ambush spots, and they'd be able to do it only on the weekends. He was looking at three weeks or more to get the mission done, and he wasn't sure he had that kind of time.

"Have you looked at the school? How hard would it be to get him there?"

"Not hard to take him, but they'd know he was missing within eight hours when he missed bed check. There would be a full-on search, starting with alerting the father."

Maybe. It would be risky, but he didn't see much of a choice. If they could get the boy, then move immediately to the Iranian embassy, they could hold him indefinitely. It would mean bringing the ambassador and a host of other people into the mission, along with alerting the mullahs about what he was doing. Possibly causing them to balk at the diplomatic explosion the mission might engender. But they'd risked greater things. Two years ago they'd tried to kill the diplomat from the Kingdom of Saudi Arabia right inside the home of the Great Satan. This would be nothing compared to that action.

His pacing and reflection were interrupted by Sanjar, the computer expert.

"Sir? I don't think we will need to guess about where he will be on the weekend."

"Why?"

"I hacked his Facebook page, and he uses Foursquare. Uses it relentlessly. I have a pattern from the last two months of weekends, and he usually goes to the same places."

Sanjar might as well have been speaking in Thai to the older general. "What are you talking about? Explain."

"Foursquare is a social media program that lets you announce where you are at any given time, allowing your friends to track you and possibly meet. Every time Kavi enters a location, he plugs it into Foursquare, which then posts the location on his Facebook page in real time. In the last two months, he's mainly gone to the nightclubs on Royal City Avenue and to a large mall called Terminal Twenty-one."

Malik couldn't believe someone would tell the world what they were doing every minute of the day. "What do you mean 'in real time'? You mean it appears when he sends it, or does it upload later, as a history?"

"It's instant. I'm currently building a database of his habitual patterns, focusing on the venues where he's a mayor."

"Mayor?"

"Yes, sir. With Foursquare, the person who logs in the most at a given venue is awarded the honorary title of mayor until someone else logs in more than him. Kavi is mayor of two different places, which means he frequents them a lot, and it also encourages him to keep going back. He won't want to lose the title."

The idiocy boggled Malik's mind. But he was more than prepared to use it.

"Are you sure you're clean? Nobody is on you?"

"Yes. We've done everything as instructed."

"Okay. Use this week to conduct reconnaissance on the possible locations. Plan an attack at the most likely ones. Insha'Allah, we'll have the key to the virus this weekend."

9

It wasn't until they had checked into their hotel in Bang-kok, after the visit to the prison in Chiang Mai, that Jennifer found the passport. A brand-new one, blue, with an entry stamp into Thailand and a picture of Knuckles inside. She flipped it closed and tapped her palm with it, a little disgusted at her naïveté.

In truth, she should have known something was up when Pike went to visit Knuckles in a suit, claiming to be from the State Department. He'd told her it was simply to keep the prison from giving them the runaround and that she'd be the one to represent the company. When he presented a black passport at the prison, she knew he'd been planning it all along.

After passing through the entry control point and moving into the visitation center, she asked, "Where'd you get a diplomatic passport?"

"Before we left. While you were getting the plane set up at Dulles."

"Isn't that doing exactly what Kurt wanted to avoid?

Highlighting State Department interest? What if they contact the embassy? What'll we say then?"

Pike flicked his eyes at her, a little annoyance coming through. "I've spent a lot of time over here. Trust me, they won't contact the embassy. They've got a bunch of foreigners in this jail, mostly for drug running, and they get visits all the time from representatives of other countries. Did you see all the people sitting around in the entry control point? They're waiting to visit someone. Probably be waiting for days. We just skipped all that."

Before she could reply, the door opened on the other side of the wire-mesh wall, and Knuckles was shown in by a scowling, chubby Thai guard with deep-set eyes. She was shocked at his appearance. He was gaunt and pale and looked like he had lost twenty pounds.

He shuffled forward, both his arms and legs shackled, barefoot, wearing a cheap peasant top and what looked like pajama bottoms. He was shoved onto the stool across from them, and the cuts and bruises on his face became visible. He smiled, and she saw he was missing two teeth, the smile becoming a grotesque sneer.

Pike said, "What the hell happened to you?"

Before he could answer, Pike stood up and waved to the guard. "What did you guys do to him? What's going on here?"

To Jennifer's astonishment, Pike switched to Thai, chattering in a singsong, his voice rising, conveying what he was saying by emotion alone.

Knuckles ignored the conversation, saying, "Hello,

Jennifer. I'm glad to see Grolier Services cares so much about their employees that they'd fly halfway around the world to check on them."

"My God, Knuckles, what have they done to you?"

He flicked his head at the conversation going on with Pike. "Let him get done with Piggy. I don't want to tell the story twice."

"Can I get you anything? Medicine or food?"

"Don't bother. Piggy'll just take it to spite me."

She saw Pike wave off the guard. Knuckles waited until he sat back down next to her.

Pike asked, "Is what he says true? You killed an inmate?"

"Yeah. That's true all right, but it was because they were beating the shit out of me."

"So you *killed* one of them? Jesus, Knuckles, what am I supposed to tell the State Department now?"

Knuckles's expression became feral. "It was kill or be killed, damn it. That sadistic son of a bitch over there—the guy I call Piggy—runs his block like a little kingdom, granting favors for payment. He tried to take my watch, and I brought him down."

When he didn't continue, Pike said, "And? You obviously didn't kill *him*."

"And he moved me to a cell with some sort of mafia group to teach me a lesson. They waited until nightfall and I had to take on seven of them. I didn't mean to kill one, but he left me no choice."

Knuckles saw Pike's disbelief and smacked the wire

mesh with his fist. "I didn't ask for this. He's the one that's responsible." He leaned back and said, "In the end the whole thing didn't matter. Piggy's got my Rolex anyway."

Pike said, "So you're not in general population now? You're in solitary?"

"Yes. A new section of the jail. Individual cells with no windows. Run by Piggy himself. See that PDA on his belt? It's a high-tech detention system, and he controls my life with it. Water, light, the cell doors, everything. He likes to keep me in the dark."

Pike swore. "This is going to make getting you out a damn sight harder. They had nothing on you before."

Knuckles's demeanor cracked for the first time. "Pike, you gotta do something. He's a sadistic son of a bitch and he's going to kill me. I swear to God this place is just like *The Deer Hunter*. I'm waiting on him to give me a pistol with one bullet and start a betting pool."

Pike slowly nodded, his eyes unfocused, thinking. Jennifer said, "We're going to the embassy right after this. We'll find someone to help. They can't keep you locked up forever. You're an American citizen."

Knuckles said, "Tell that to the other Americans in here. Thailand has the death penalty for running drugs. I'm pretty sure killing someone probably warrants torture before death."

"But it was self-defense! They were beating you. The embassy won't take that sitting down." She turned to Pike. "Will they?"

He ignored her. "Knuckles, hang in there. I'll get you out. I promise. Piggy should back off a little bit now that we've been here and seen you."

As if on cue, Piggy walked over to them and cut in. "Time's up. Back to cell."

Jennifer said, "You'd better not hurt him anymore. I'm going to the embassy right after this."

Piggy's face split into a leer. "Go to your embassy. I don't care. If you really want to help him, you and I could work something out."

He laughed at the shocked look on her face, then jerked Knuckles to his feet. Jennifer said nothing as Knuckles was half dragged out of the room.

After the door closed, she said, "Pike, we need to do something soon. Regardless of Piggy hurting him, if he catches a disease in here it'll probably *be* a death penalty."

"I know. Come on. Let's get to Bangkok."

"To the embassy?"

"Yeah. Sort of."

FROM CHIANG MAI they flew straight to Bangkok, the Gulfstream jet making the trip infinitely shorter because of the ease of private aircraft facilities outside of the other commercial air traffic. Landing at the older Don Muang Airport to the north of the city center, they paid for a private car, with Pike giving directions in Thai.

Jennifer sat in silence, watching the traffic begin to build up after they'd exited the toll road. Eventually, she turned and said, "Where did you learn to speak Thai? You never told me you could do that."

He smiled. "You never asked. Anyway, it sort of became a moot point after 9/11. After I joined the Task-force. Like speaking Latin. I wish I'd learned Arabic or Farsi."

"Where?"

"In the Army. Everyone in Special Forces has to learn a language, depending on your group's focus. Before I joined the Taskforce, I was in a group that focused on the Pacific Rim and Asia, so they sent me to learn Thai."

"Well, I think it's a little amazing."

He laughed. "That's because you can't understand it. Trust me, I'm saying things like 'We demand a donkey ride to Bangkok.' I'm so rusty that Piggy back there probably understood two sentences out of all that shouting."

After forty minutes they began traveling south down Wireless Road, Jennifer no longer asking questions, distracted by the massive ebb and flow of the world that was Bangkok.

She caught a glimpse of an American flag and focused on the building near it. The taxi kept going past, and she said, "Pike! That's the embassy right there. Tell the cab driver to stop."

"We're not going to the embassy."

"What? You want to go to the hotel first?"

"No. We're going to JUSMAGTHAI."

"What in the world is that?"

"Joint US Military Advisory Group, Thailand. I want

to talk to a friend first, get a feel for the embassy before we go there."

"Who?"

"A retired SF guy. He works at JUSMAG, doing exercise facilitation for units coming in here. He's been in Thailand forever and deals directly with the embassy all the time."

They crossed under Rama IV Road and did a U-turn, and the driver pulled to a stop adjacent to a walled compound with men in uniform in a guard shack, the Thai flag floating in the breeze.

"This isn't American," Jennifer said.

Pike said, "It's a Thai military compound, but JUSMAG is inside."

A man appeared outside of the gate and waved them into the drive. Pike exited, and Jennifer saw them hug. Momentarily, the gate opened, and Pike entered the car again. The vehicle pulled into a small courtyard, the man who'd waved them in waiting patiently on the curb.

Pike said, "Stay here. I won't be long."

"You mean I'm not coming?"

The door half open, he said, "Uhh . . . no. My buddy got the car in, but I'm not sure where they'll check IDs. They don't let civilians in here."

"But you're a damn civilian!"

He exited, saying, "Not today I'm not."

Muttering under her breath, she watched him walk away.

An hour later and they were in their high-rise hotel on

the Chao Phraya River; Pike had refused to talk about what he'd found out and exasperated Jennifer when he bypassed the embassy yet again.

When she pushed, all he had said was, "Look, I'm going to help Knuckles. Actually, *we* are. In fact, I've got to meet a man in an hour who might help us more than the embassy can. My buddy did the introductions. Let me talk to him first. If it pans out, I'll tell you what we're going to do. If it doesn't, I'll head to the embassy like Kurt instructed."

She'd exploded at that, saying, "Bullshit! Tell me now. You're treating me like a child. Like when we first met. How is this guy going to help when the embassy can't?"

Pike said nothing for a moment, deciding. "He's got infrastructure here. Things that'll help us with Knuckles."

"You mean he has some pull with the embassy?"

Cryptically, he'd said, "Yeah, something like that."

Now, HOLDING THE passport for Knuckles, her patience with the subterfuge had run out. She waited for Pike to finish putting his toilet articles in his bathroom. When he came out, he pointed at the connecting door to her room and said, "You going to unpack, or what?"

She held out the passport like she was holding a bag of dope. "What is *this*? Where did it come from?"

Pike took a deep breath and let it out, looking a little sheepish. "It's for Knuckles. I got it the same time I got my dip passport."

"Why?"

He began fiddling with his luggage again. He said, "In case."

"In case of what, Pike?"

He said nothing, ripping through his bag like he'd lost something, flinging underwear and T-shirts onto the bed, a pathetic attempt to get her to drop the discussion. She repeated the question.

"In case of what?"

He halfheartedly stuffed a T-shirt back in, then zipped the bag closed. He dropped it and looked into her eyes.

"In case he doesn't have a passport when we break him out, all right?"

10

Soi Cowboy hadn't changed a whole helluva lot since I'd been there last. A ribbon of dirty bars and strip clubs near the intersection of Sukhumvit and Ratchadaphisek Roads, it was famous the world over for its sex shows. At night it was full of colorful neon and was actually sort of attractive—especially after a few beers. In the daylight it looked worn down and sad, a tattered world the sunlight dared to expose.

Strangely, it reminded me of Christmas from my youth. Driving through our poor neighborhood at night, I would be amazed at how regal the houses looked with their icicle lights blinking and twinkling, knowing the poverty was hiding in the shadows, waiting for daylight to render the harsh truth behind the glitter.

It was still way too early for anything to be open, and the urchins sweeping up the garbage from the night before barely gave me a glance. It was all Thai right now, with men eating lunch from street vendors and women preparing the bars for the night ahead, waiting on the influx of fat Westerners. Desperate middle-aged men and dangerous ones lower on the age scale, all willing to pay to have someone tell them they were worth the gift of life that God gave them. Like the telling would make it so.

Clearly, I wasn't looking for a small boy to take home, so they let me be. I stopped, studying the hand-drawn map my friend at JUSMAG had given me.

When I'd mentioned the prison breakout to Kurt in DC, it seemed to be the perfect solution. He'd balked but then had given me a fully equipped Taskforce aircraft. I was fairly sure he knew what I would do with it. I'd still have to get his permission, but I thought I could. Especially given Knuckles's current predicament.

I'd tried to keep what I was planning a secret from Jennifer because I knew she wouldn't see it my way. At the end of the day, she believed in the nobility of the world and felt sure that the State Department would come through. Even with all she had experienced, she still didn't understand that good was just a word and evil could—in fact mostly did—triumph no matter how virtuous the cause. I knew differently: Just because you were on the right side of things didn't mean you would win. Sometimes you needed to be a little bad to ensure the good.

I was looking for a specific bar owned by an American known only as "Izzy." Well, I'm sure he had a real name, but that's all my buddy had given me. I hoped the name didn't foretell who I'd find, some guy looking like the Situation or, given his age, a weathered Fonzie wearing a leather jacket in the Thai heat and covered in gold chains.

Izzy had flown for Air America, the thinly disguised CIA front used during the Vietnam War for covert operations in Laos and Cambodia. After the war, he'd stopped in Thailand for a visit and had never gone home. He'd married a Thai, had a few kids there, and, from what my buddy said, had been involved in all sorts of shady shit, both officially for the United States and unofficially for pure profit.

I had almost reached the end of the ribbon of asphalt when I saw the sign on the second floor, above a bar made to look like a speakeasy from the 1920s, the felt drapes hanging in the window showing their stains in the light of day, the bar stools outside upended on the tables.

I tried the door and saw it was unlocked. I entered, the darkness closing in when the door shut. A man stacking racks of glasses shouted in Thai that they were closed. I answered him in Thai, stating my business. Maybe it was the name, or maybe it was that I spoke the language, but his eyes widened and he left, scurrying up a stairwell on the right side of the bar.

Soon enough, I was met by a Thai man taller than most, about twenty or twenty-five years old, with a hint of half-breed in him. A Eurasian with one foot in Thailand and one somewhere else. I gave the bona fides I'd been provided, and we went up the stairs. I was shown into an area that looked like a living room, with old velour couches and overstuffed leather chairs. On one was a Caucasian man of about seventy, wearing eyeglasses and dressed in a suit. He was sitting with his legs crossed, relaxed, reading a spy novel.

He put the book down, saying, "A guilty pleasure. These novels are always so full of shit, but I can't help myself. If only it were so easy."

He stood and shook my hand. His grip was firm and up close his eyes seemed to penetrate through my head, as if he were intent on reading my mind.

"Please, have a seat. I'm Izzy."

I sat and waited for the formality of tea being brought out, the tall Thai behind me over my left shoulder. A warning.

Izzy began with pleasantries designed to ensure I was who I said I was, although he never once asked me who I was working for, sticking solely to my background with my friend at JUSMAG. He'd been in the game for so long he wasn't even curious and understood such knowledge could be dangerous.

I did the same thing, never saying anything related to my business, sticking with the workings of the bar downstairs. Eventually, the pleasantries trickled out, and I knew it was time when he asked the Thai man to leave the room.

I laid out my requirements, starting with the vehicle, then moved on to more valuable things, hoping he wouldn't get skittish when I stated I needed two indigenous men along with the vehicle, both prepared to enter a prison. The request didn't seem to bother him at all. I didn't give him any operational parameters, but he was shrewd enough to see exactly where I was going.

"They won't let whoever you're after simply walk out of prison, even with an official vehicle. He needs a release from the bureau of prisons. And that is something I cannot do."

"Let me worry about that."

"I apologize, but I can't. My men will be on the inside, possibly to remain when your charade is found out. I need more reassurance."

I paused, wondering how to word this in such a way as to give him what he wanted without compromising Taskforce abilities.

"Let's just say the man went to prison because he was facilitating a penetration for an organization. He got caught, but the penetration didn't. I can get this done."

He studied me for a moment, the wheels in his head turning, now beginning to wonder who I really was. He slowly nodded.

"Okay. You will have your men and the vehicle. Anything else?"

"No. I can handle the rest."

"Then there's the matter of payment. Your friend told you I'm not cheap, I assume."

"Yes. I'll have to redirect some funds, but I can put them wherever you would like. Just tell me where and how much."

"I'm afraid it won't be money."

"What, then? I don't have much else to offer."

"I have a child. My youngest. I would like him to go to a school here. A private one that is very, very well regarded. The money is no object, but I'm afraid they frown on my business. They've denied him admission because of my past."

The statement confused me. "What the hell can I do about that? You want me to rough up the headmaster or something? I'm sorry, but that sort of thing is off the table."

He smiled warmly. "No, no. Nothing like that. Nothing violent, but surely a man who can get an official release transmitted to a Thai prison can bring pressure to bear in other ways."

11

Crossing the Key Bridge, Chip Dekkard couldn't believe what he was hearing. He said, "Hang on, hang on. I gotta close up."

He pressed the button that raised the glass shield between him and the driver up front. Once it was secure, he went back to the phone.

"What the hell do you mean a lab tech died? You guys assured me you could get this done in accordance with all applicable regulations."

He listened a little bit more, the traffic in downtown Washington, DC, a low hum in the background. The mention of a date caused his blood pressure to rocket.

"Wait, wait. This happened three days ago? And I'm just now finding out? Jesus Christ! Shut it down. Shut it all down."

The person on the other end started to protest, and Chip cut him off. "Shut it down, now. No more protocols. No testing, nothing. Destroy the virus and shut it down. And in the future, tell your boss that if he wants to keep his job he needs to understand a fundamental truth: Bad news doesn't get better with age."

Chip hung up the phone without another word, wondering how he could have been so stupid as to allow the project to start in the first place. The CEO of a major US conglomerate, he oversaw multiple companies producing everything from textiles to pharmaceuticals. Seven months ago, one of the firms in the portfolio, Cailleach Laboratories, had come up with an idea: a vaccine for the H5N1 avian flu virus. But not for the one that currently existed. A vaccine for a mutated virus.

The major health bodies, such as the World Health Organization and the US Centers for Disease Control and Prevention, were all petrified of H5N1, as it had upwards of a seventy percent mortality rate when contracted by humans. The good news was that while it could spread like wildfire in birds, killing them in the hundreds of thousands, it didn't transmit human-to-human very easily. In fact it was nearly impossible. So far, almost all of the deaths related to bird flu were the result of someone working with infected poultry or other avian species.

The bad news was that viruses mutated continuously. All health organizations felt it was only a matter of time before this occurred with H5N1, creating a virus now transmittable human-to-human, bringing on a pandemic that would dwarf the 1918 Spanish flu due to the interconnected reality of the modern world and its proven lethality.

Cailleach Laboratories had proposed forcing a genetic mutation, in effect creating the killer, then developing a vaccine to combat it. It had already been done once for simple research purposes, raising a hue and cry from the US National Science Advisory Board for Biosecurity. They demanded censorship of the details to preclude someone with nefarious purposes from re-creating the study. The controversy had provided the genesis of the idea.

Cailleach had no intention of keeping the time bomb intact for potential abuse. Once the vaccine was created, they would destroy the virus and bide their time, waiting on the natural mutation. When it occurred, they'd make a proverbial killing, as it took upwards of six to nine months to create a new vaccine. While their vaccine would most assuredly not be perfect, as there was no telling how the virus would mutate, Cailleach would be head and shoulders above everyone else, getting a vaccine out much earlier and making an enormous profit in the panic from the onslaught of the pandemic.

The downside to this, of course, was the virus itself. They were playing with fire, and they knew it. They'd decided to set up shop in Singapore because of the stringent US requirements for inspections and licensing. Not to mention the litigious nature of American society. Vaccine production in the United States had dropped from twenty-seven producers in the 1970s to three today, simply because the cost wasn't worth the risk. At the end of the day, you could prevent the disease, then find yourself on the short end of a thousand different lawsuits claiming everything from flat feet to deafness due to the vaccine.

Chip had been told Cailleach could handle the production safely, inside the Biopolis campus in Singapore, a biomedical complex that was fast becoming the world leader in such research. That statement had just been proven wrong. Instead of becoming the world's savior at the onset of an outbreak, they had come close to causing it. He shuddered to think of the potential liability. The exposure.

He was brought out of his thoughts by the limousine's stopping. He exited outside the southwest gate to the White House, wondering how he was going to maintain focus for the Oversight Council update, given what he'd just heard.

After clearing security, he went through the gate and entered the Old Executive Office Building, adjacent to the West Wing. He walked up to the conference room a little early and found Kurt Hale at the podium, ready to brief.

Being one of only two civilians on the council, he always felt out of place at these meetings and rarely said a word. But he'd played a significant role in President Warren's reelection and remained a valued adviser, so he'd agreed to a seat on the council, only voicing his opinion when he felt he had something to offer.

In short order, the room became crowded with the other members of the council, a low murmur spreading as the officials talked among themselves, waiting on the president. He entered at the stroke of the clock, saying, "Let's get this rodeo going, Kurt. I don't have a lot of time."

Kurt began with an overview of Knuckles's status and the risk of Taskforce exposure. The discussion brought Chip back to his own near miss, and he let the voices drone on, thinking instead of what cleanup still remained in Singapore.

He returned to the conversation when he heard the secretary of state, Jonathan Billings, raise his voice.

"What do you mean, 'exploring options'? Pike was supposed to go to the embassy as the president of Grolier Recovery Services. According to the ambassador, he hasn't shown up yet and he's been there for a couple of days."

Kurt said, "I know, I know, but they've got Knuckles for a homicide now. It's become more serious than Pike just solving the problem by walking into the embassy and waving some business cards. Maybe it's time for official intervention."

Billings didn't respond, looking to the president, who said, "What's coming out officially on that? Anything?"

Billings said, "No. Nobody has notified the embassy at all. As far as they know, Knuckles is still just another arrested American. Nothing on the death in the prison."

President Warren said, "Okay, then we continue as planned. We can't amp it up until they do."

"But Knuckles is in trouble," Kurt said. "From what Pike said, he's in real danger. We wait, and it may be just to process a body back home."

The president held up his hand, indicating the conversation was over. "We wait. This is the closest we've ever come to exposure of the Taskforce. You know that. Knuckles can take care of himself for a few more days." President Warren looked at his watch, then said, "What else have you got?"

When Kurt didn't respond, he said, "Look, have Pike keep an eye on him. I won't let him get killed. We'll pull out the stops if we have to. Just give it some time. I don't feel we need to man the battle stations just yet."

Kurt took a breath, then switched gears, putting on the screen the picture of a swarthy fiftysomething man with a jet-black mustache, looking vaguely like Saddam Hussein before he was jerked out of a spider hole with a Prophet Moses beard.

"The penetration of the metropolitan police bureau worked, although not like we thought. It turns out they've been following a Persian-carpet salesman from Iran, not our suspected Hezbollah facilitator. They've kept track of him because of the Iranian bombing there last year, only they don't know what they've got. This man is Brigadier General Malik Musavi of the Islamic Revolutionary Guard's Quds Force."

He let that sink in, then continued. "Malik is a very, very big fish. He's been on the US screen for a long time, conducting all sorts of external operations, including the attempted assassination of the Saudi diplomat here two years ago. He hasn't been operational on the ground in years. His job is simply supervising external missions from inside Iran."

President Warren said, "How sure are you?"

Kurt smiled. "Positive. We have his photo from years ago, and he's traveling under his true name, just with a different occupation. Don't know why he would do that, but it's him. No doubt."

The secretary of defense asked, "What's he doing? What's this mean?"

"That's the million-dollar question. We have no idea."

"And you want Omega for him? Is that it?"

"Well . . . that's not my call. Just bringing it to the council's attention."

Hearing the discussion, Chip finally spoke up. "But he's a state entity. An official Iranian general, not some substate whack job with a bomb. It's outside of the Taskforce mandate." He turned to President Warren. "Isn't it?"

Warren took a breath and let it out. "What about that, Kurt? Chip's right. Expansion of the mandate, isn't it? You're not allowed to mess with any official state activities. That's CIA all the way."

Kurt said, "Well, it's not as black and white as taking out a Russian would be. It's a hell of a lot more gray. The Treasury Department has already labeled the Quds Force as a specially designated terrorist group and frozen any assets they could find, and Iran is on the official US list of state sponsors of terrorism."

Billings said, "That doesn't make them a foreign terrorist organization. Your mandate exists within the State Department's official FTO list, and they're not on it."

Kurt said, "Yet. You and I both know there's a bill in

Congress right now to force the State Department to call the Quds Force a foreign terrorist organization, making them on par with al-Qaeda."

The secretary of defense spoke up. "Enough of the bullshit about lists. You don't even have a mission. A reason to go after this guy."

"That's true, but I do know the guy's a killer. Responsible for American deaths all over the place, from Iraq to Afghanistan. I don't know what he's up to, you're right, but I do know how to find out."

"How?"

"Give me Omega, and I'll ask him."

12

Malik fidgeted outside the pastry shop, feeling exposed by all of the CCTV cameras around the mall, waiting on the target to arrive. Thinking again that this plan was borderline idiotic. Wondering if he wasn't about to be part of the second set of Iranians that did some buffoonery on Thai soil.

Their initial attempt had been Friday night—last night—when they'd tried to take him at the nightclubs off of Royal City Avenue but had failed due to the crowds around. The perfect opportunity just hadn't presented itself, even as the Foursquare intelligence had proven very accurate.

Missing the objective on Friday had caused Malik considerable concern. He didn't want to wait another week for the boarding school to release the son again. Sanjar, the computer expert, had recommended using a downtown mall called Terminal 21 the following day, Saturday.

Malik said, "A daylight kidnapping? In a mall? No. If it comes down to that, we wait a week."

"But I've studied the mall. Kavi always checks in to a

place that sells desserts and coffee on the fourth level. Like clockwork."

Malik told him to bring up Terminal 21 on his computer and saw the thing was a monstrosity, with every floor named after a different section of the world, from the Caribbean to London. What was worse, it was connected directly to the Asok Skytrain stop, which would be the way Kavi entered and left.

Malik said, "And how do you propose to get him from the fourth level to the street? Perhaps I could come in with a large Persian carpet, try to sell it, and when that fails, you could knock him out. I'll simply roll him up in it, in full view of everyone. Then we'll carry him out right to the Skytrain. Is that what you're thinking?" Malik turned away, saying, "We wait until next Friday and try again."

"Sir!" Sanjar said. "Please listen. The dessert bar is right next to a hallway leading to a stairwell. That stairwell connects to a parking garage on the third level. This will work."

"You cannot attack him in the café!" Malik snapped. "I don't care how close the stairs are! Three feet is too far."

Roshan, the engineer, spoke up. "Sir, I don't think we'll need to attack him. Kavi is completely ignorant of personal safety. I think we could engage him in conversation and have him follow us to our car."

Eventually, Malik had broken down and agreed to try, which left him sitting nervously across the way at another café, wanting to bolt from the overt risk he had been talked into taking.

He saw the target enter and begin talking to other Thai teenagers. He watched the doctor's son fiddle with his phone and knew he was logging in his location. Malik shook his head, still befuddled by the social networking site. The time slipped by and he thought about aborting.

Abruptly, the other Thais left, taking him by surprise, and Malik called his men forward. Roshan and Sanjar entered the café and ordered something, but he couldn't tell what.

He watched Sanjar sit near Kavi and begin working his own smartphone. Logging in his Foursquare location and letting Kavi watch. Shortly, the two were engaged in conversation, with Roshan joining.

Malik had given them twenty minutes and no more. If Kavi wasn't leaving with them by then, they were to abort.

Twenty-five minutes in, Malik got angry. He texted Sanjar, punching the keys on his phone.

Get OUT.

Sanjar glanced his way, then began working his thumbs over the phone. Malik felt his cell vibrate; it read *2 min*.

He was about to respond when the group stood up. Laughing, with his arm around Sanjar's shoulders, Kavi walked out of the café and entered the hallway. Never suspecting the danger he was in. Never realizing that there were different types of predators in the world.

They went down the hallway and turned into a stairwell. Malik followed discreetly behind, watching them act like the best of friends. Malik took note of the cameras in the hallway and knew they had taken a great risk. If he couldn't convince the father to call the school and prevent a search, it wouldn't take much to have their faces all over the country.

They went down one flight, Malik hanging back until he heard the door to the parking deck open, then rushing forward. He entered the garage in time to see Roshan open the back door to their car, then Sanjar wrap his arms around the doctor's son, causing a look of bewilderment on Kavi's face.

A look that changed to fear when Roshan brought out the hood.

1 3

Sitting across Highway 107 in Chiang Mai, I felt the first trickle of adrenaline when I caught sight of Jennifer walking out of the prison entrance with Piggy holding her arm. I watched her say something to him, then walk briskly to her car, retrieving her purse from the front seat. I knew why. She couldn't very well have taken that into the prison, because I'd given her a little hush puppy for protection. A Ruger Mark III .22 with an XCaliber Genesis suppressor.

Designed mainly for removing guard dogs, it would do the job up close on a man. And if Jennifer had to use it on Piggy, it would definitely be up close.

She walked back to him and followed to an old Toyota, getting in the front seat. I waited until they'd cleared the parking lot, headed north on Highway 107, before I triggered.

"Koko's on the move. Target's with her."

Decoy said, "Roger."

All I could do now was wait for phase two of the mission, either getting married up with the cloned PDA or getting a Prairie Fire alert from Jennifer requesting backup. I prayed mightily that it would be the former.

It had been forty-eight hours since my meeting with Izzy, and we'd used every bit of that time conducting reconnaissance, from developing a pattern of life on Piggy to finding out the procedures for vehicle transfers of prisoners. I'd visited Knuckles twice during that span, ostensibly to make sure he was well, but in reality to glean as much information as I could. On the last visit, I'd seen someone had played drums with his face again and was convinced I was doing the right thing. Unfortunately, the prison didn't agree with my assessment. Getting him out had turned into a long string of dominoes, with every one a potential single point of failure.

The prison was fairly new, in the northern section of Chiang Mai outside the city proper. Built to relieve over-crowding at the old prison downtown, it was now over-crowded as well, housing both people serving time and people awaiting sentencing and subsequent transfer to a permanent facility. That was the only good thing, as pris-oners were moved out daily, thus making it routine.

My stroke of genius was to use this routine and con-vince them that Knuckles was being transferred to Bang-kok, the theory being that Chiang Mai would forget him once he was out the doors, and Bangkok wouldn't check on him until prodded by the State Department—which would never happen. With the bureaucratic chaos that was Thailand, he wouldn't be missed for weeks—if not years.

Unfortunately, because of Knuckles's little fight, Piggy

had moved him into the newest section under his personal command. This made his transfer no longer routine, as Piggy himself had to approve the release, and we'd never pull off this charade against anyone with a reason to stop it. A single phone call would be the domino that fell flat.

I had to get Piggy out of the prison, and I was using Jennifer to do so. Remembering his comment on our first visit, I knew he'd run at the chance to hop in the sack with her. All she had to do was pretend like she was reluctantly doing it for a quid pro quo for Knuckles. The naïve American about to learn a hard lesson in life.

When I'd given her the mission she'd balked, saying, "Why do I always have to play some sort of floozy? Surely there's something else I can do to get him out."

I'd said, "Jennifer, we need him out of the prison for an hour. A coffee break won't cut it. Given the drive time to his house and back, that means only thirty minutes of stalling. Thirty minutes and you can flee the house like you misunderstood."

"Come on. Did you see that guy? You're putting me in a house by myself with someone who wants to attack me."

Like an ass, Decoy had blurted, "Yeah, but you're good at that shit. I remember what you looked like in Prague dressed like a hooker."

I saw her eyes water, and she left the room. Too late, I realized she was reliving the attack on her just months ago, and now, callously, I was throwing her directly into what she feared the most.

Decoy said, "What did I do? What was that about?"

"Nothing. Don't worry about it."

Besides Jennifer, there were just two people on earth who knew what had happened to her: me and the guy who'd done it. Since I'd slaughtered him with my bare hands, that left only me, and Jennifer wanted to keep it that way. Nobody else on the team had a clue, and now they were potentially about to misjudge Jennifer's reaction as her not being able to handle the stress of mission profiles because I'd been blind to her specific fear. I couldn't let that happen. Couldn't have them questioning her capabilities for the wrong reasons, because it might prove catastrophic under fire.

I stood and said, "Wait here a second."

Before I could leave, Jennifer reentered, eyes clear and voice firm.

"Okay. I'll do it. Who's my backup?"

Decoy, looking a little ashamed, said, "I'm your backup. I got your back."

He always pretended to be a chauvinistic man-whore, hooking up with anyone willing in any town he entered, but in Prague I'd seen what he was really like underneath the bravado. No way was Jennifer going to be in any danger with him on the prowl.

Now, watching her drive away with that sadistic pig, I hoped she didn't lose it on her own. Hoped she could keep it together long enough to play the part.

14

Jennifer, her purse clutched tightly in her lap, said, "You said maybe we could come to an accommodation about my employee. Maybe we could get some coffee, discuss how exactly I can help you."

Continuing north on Highway 107, Piggy put his hand on her thigh. "Yes, that's just what I want to do. But why pay for coffee? I have free coffee, tea, beer, whatever you want at my house. It's only a short drive."

She brushed his hand away, saying nervously, "Where is your house? Where are we going?"

She ignored his answer, because she knew the entire route already. Instead, she focused on the Symbol handheld computer he'd thrown into the backseat. One more string in the domino chain, as Pike had told her.

Originally, her mission had simply been to keep him occupied, but after the team's repeated attempts at cracking the Wi-Fi network in the prison, they'd given her another mission.

The hackers had failed, which meant they needed to access Piggy's actual PDA. The encryption in the prison was simply too strong, even with the fifty-pound tech help from Taskforce geeks in DC, leaving them unable to open Knuckles's special cell door. They'd decided on a shortcut, which had been thrown into her rucksack to carry after she'd agreed to become the diversion.

Piggy placed his hand on her thigh again and said, "You can help your friend out very much. Food, medicine, maybe even release. It depends on how much you care for him. How long are you planning on staying in Chiang Mai?"

She gave a tepid smile and left the hand on her thigh, feeling sick to her stomach, knowing what he was asking. Knowing he was intimating that there'd be more than one "meeting." She gave him the truth.

"Hopefully, I'm flying back to Bangkok today."

This brought a scowl, making him look like a petulant child. "Then we should make the most of this, shouldn't we?"

She didn't answer, seeing the intersection for the road leading to the Mae Ping River a hundred meters ahead. And the pickup truck idling next to it. She felt time begin to slow.

Piggy said something else, turning the wheel and exiting the highway. Looking out the window, Jennifer saw Brett sitting impassively in the cab of a beat-up Nissan truck, the front end aimed toward them. Waiting.

Just as her door passed, she saw the pickup jump, and she braced for impact, shouting for effect. The vehicle hit them solidly in the right rear quarter panel, causing Piggy's car to skip lightly. The impact was hard, but not as bad as she expected. They came to a stop after a few feet, the Toyota skewed sideways, with Piggy yelling in Thai.

He cursed and shut off the car. As soon as he exited, she grabbed the Symbol PDA and ripped a clone device out of her purse. Nothing more than a thumb drive with a cable attached, it had the necessary software to duplicate his PDA in a couple of minutes. She plugged it into the mini-USB port and watched the Symbol screen go blank. Now all she could do was wait until it came back on. Supposedly in two minutes.

She glanced to the rear and saw Brett waving his hands in the air, with Piggy pointing a finger in his face. She went back to the PDA and did a double take, returning to the window. Sitting on the dingy outside patio of a homemade roadside café was Decoy, a small grin on his face, his eyes hidden by sunglasses, watching her work.

A minute and forty seconds gone, and the PDA was still blank. Two minutes, and she began to sweat, looking to the rear again. Brett was holding his hands out, still talking. Piggy had calmed down.

Running out of time.

Three minutes. Blank screen. She saw Brett putting his wallet back in his pocket and knew only seconds remained.

She stared at the screen, willing something to appear. *Come on. Come on!*

To her surprise, it flickered, then scrolled Thai letters. *Yes.*

THE WIDOW'S STRIKE 89

She ripped out the clone device, tossed the PDA into the back, and threw the thumb drive out the passenger window, then whirled around when she heard the driver's-side door open, praying Piggy hadn't seen.

He sat down, saying, "All you Americans think you can buy your way out of anything." Smirking, he placed his hand on her knee again. "Luckily for both of you that's true in my case."

Relief flooded through her, the hand a small price to pay for success. She gazed out the window as they pulled away, seeing Decoy mount a beat-up Honda motorcycle.

I COULDN'T HELP but smile when the call came in, both because it meant phase one had succeeded and because I knew it irked Brett.

"Pike, this is Blood. Inbound with clone."

Brett was new on the team, having been there barely a year. He'd come over from the Special Activities Division at the CIA and, as such, didn't come with a call sign attached. On our last mission—his first with me—he'd made an absolutely asinine comment about the old mother's remedy Mercurochrome, calling it Monkey's Blood. I had anointed him with the call sign Blood at the start of this mission.

Being an African-American, he'd immediately bitched, saying there was no way he was going with that call sign, moaning about stereotypes, Crips and Bloods, gang members and everything else. Unfortunately for him, you don't get to pick your call sign. If you did, every commando in the Taskforce would be called Thundercock. The call sign picks you, like it had here.

In the end, he'd gone with it. After all, the only ones who would hear it would be the team. He knew we were color-blind and that we understood where it had come from. Even still, like Jennifer with her call sign of Koko, it irked him. And made the rest of the team laugh.

I alerted Retro, who was waiting in the prison transfer van, bringing him forward. Before it arrived, Blood pulled up in his mangled Nissan.

"Any issues?"

He handed me the thumb drive. "Not getting that, but Piggy's an asshole."

"Let's hope this clone worked, or we're dead in the water. Clock's ticking now."

All I was asking from Jennifer was thirty minutes. She'd be out whether we were done or not.

He said, "Free to go?"

"Yeah. Give me a shout when you link up with Buckshot. I'd like the warm fuzzy that we have an exfil vehicle in case we're coming out hot."

A van with no windows in the back pulled up, official Thai emblems on the side. In the driver's seat was a Thai man in a police uniform. Izzy's guy, and the one who'd be going in with me. He was the same one who'd shown me into Izzy's bar, standing behind me while we talked. He was called Nung, "number one" in Thai, because he didn't want to give out his real name.

I went to the rear of the van and opened it, seeing another Thai man in uniform in the back, called, imaginatively enough, Song—or "number two." Sitting across from him was Retro, now dressed in prison garb and "shackled" to the floor.

I passed Retro the thumb drive and he immediately began working our own PDA. It wasn't a Motorola Symbol, but Retro was convinced it would suffice. He'd said all he needed was a processor, Wi-Fi, and VOIP capability, and that the specific model didn't matter. He was a little bit of a computer geek, so if he said it would work, I went with it. After all, I didn't have a whole lot of choices.

While he finished the download, I gave final instructions. "Okay, Nung, you're leading the way. Remember we have three posts to get through. You handle the Thai, only turning to me if we get any push-back. I'll play the State Department mean guy. You got the cell phone jammer?"

Nung, looking completely calm, simply nodded his head, making me wonder what the hell he'd done in the past.

How can you not be nervous with this weak-ass plan?

The tactical side of the house was a microcosm of the operational plan—namely that we were going to convince one post in the prison that the other one had said it was okay to proceed, hoping that neither found out.

"Song, you have any questions about your script?"

He shook his head no.

"Remember, you're the critical piece. They *must* think you're Piggy."

He said, "No problem, no problem," in that singsong Thai way.

I said, "How we looking, Retro?"

He punched a couple of buttons, read off something on the screen, then grinned.

"We're golden. Knuckles's cell door is no object."

15

Jennifer fought to control her emotions. No sooner had the adrenaline subsided from the clone mission than she felt it begin to build back up as they drew closer and closer to Piggy's house, each passing mile reverberating in her like the clank of a roller coaster heading inexorably to the top of the hill.

Driving down a tidy lane with space for only one vehicle, she counted the houses, knowing his was the tenth one from the intersection. Too soon, it was upon them. When Piggy turned off the car, she clicked the timing feature of her watch, seeing it begin to count down from thirty minutes, each second seemingly longer than the last.

Piggy gave his lizardlike smile and said, "Shall we?"

She simply nodded and opened her door.

Inside, the house was surprisingly clean, with teak furniture and a large flat-screen TV mounted on the wall, a faint fragrance of citrus in the air. Piggy went into the kitchen, bringing back two bottles of Singha beer.

Jennifer waved him off, saying, "Really, I just want to discuss how I can help my friend. Can we do that?"

Going to the couch in front of the television, he said, "Certainly."

She sat on a teak chair across from him, dropping her purse next to it. He said, "No, no. Sit here. Next to me."

She felt clammy. Nauseous. She didn't think she had the strength to do this. She focused on Knuckles, remembering why she was here. Remembering Decoy outside, just a press of the button on her phone from breaking down the door. And hesitantly moved to the couch.

As soon as she sat down, he scooted next to her and began rubbing her thigh, causing every muscle in her body to become rigid.

She said, "Stop it. You said we'd talk first."

He leaned over her, and she could smell the spice on his breath. "Talk later. Payment up front."

Enough.

She pushed him away and jumped to her feet, glancing at her watch. With dismay, she saw only ten minutes had elapsed. She began to tremble.

Piggy stood up, now clearly angry. "Don't pretend you have no idea why you're here. Pay up or instead of helping your friend, I'll have him hurt."

She saw her purse across the room. She needed to stall. To get to it. *How? What will he believe?* She sagged her

shoulders and said, "Okay, okay, but let me get something out of my purse. A condom."

She moved to it, hearing, "No condom. I'm not sick."

She picked it up and reached inside, feeling the heft of
the Mark III. She said, "Yes. You *must* wear a condom.
I've heard of all the diseases here."

She turned around to find him right on top of her,
grabbing for her purse and shouting, "No condom!"

She jerked the purse out of his hands, and he swung a
wild right cross at her head.

MARCHING UP TO the entry control point in what I hoped
was a prissy, State Department way, I presented my black
passport and said, "I'm here to witness the transfer of
American prisoner alpha twelve twenty-eight."

The guard said something in Thai too fast for me to
catch, and I turned to Nung, letting him take over. They
bantered for a little bit, most of which I missed, but it was
something about an odd time of day, or not the usual
time, or some other bullshit.

Eventually, Nung got him to at least check his computer, and I felt the pucker factor get very, very tight. If
the Taskforce failed on this one, I was headed out the
door and flying straight home to punch some hacker in
the mouth.

After I had finished up my meeting with Izzy, I'd figured I had about an eighty percent solution, so I'd called

Kurt, laying it all out. He was on his way to an Oversight Council meeting, which were never good, and had very little time to talk. He'd given me permission to coordinate with the hacking cell and "explore options," but he'd told me in no uncertain terms that all I was to do was develop the situation. No execution. Which is why I'd ignored the last two blocked calls that had come in. I didn't want to hear about some Oversight Council handwringing. If Kurt could have seen how Knuckles was deteriorating, he'd have executed the mission himself.

Using the cyber-penetration of the police bureau from the Ministry of Education—the very reason Knuckles was in prison to begin with—the hacking cell had been able to duplicate a prison release form and inject it into the official system. Well, at least that's what they'd said. Now I would find out if it was true.

The man hunted for a bit, then turned back around, shaking his head. This time I caught every word. "No such request in the system."

Damn it. Useless fifty-pound heads.

I said, "Check again please. Maybe it went into the wrong inbox."

"There is no inbox. It's a special system."

I raised my voice. "Check it again. Now. I'm not leaving without him."

Inside, I was getting ready to do just that.

He banged on the keys a few more times, searching various pages, then paused. He leaned into the screen, and I began to have hope.

He turned around, his face suspicious. "I've found it, but it's on an outdated form. It went straight to the archives as something old. Why isn't it on the correct form?"

JENNIFER HAD NO conscious thought, her body moving instantly, like a cat dodging the lumbering strike of a Saint Bernard. Holding the purse, she collapsed her right arm against her head and blocked Piggy's wild punch with her left, ducking under the arm and getting behind him. She snaked a hand back inside the bag and closed it on the butt of the pistol, seeing Piggy whirl around, his face contorted in rage, his fists balled at his sides, embarrassed that he hadn't landed the swing. Not realizing that it wasn't blind luck.

"I say no condom, I mean no condom!"

Her mind flashed to Lucas Kane. She felt his attack against her, the cord cutting into her wrists as she fought to escape. The stench of his body.

Standing just outside of her reach was another man with the same predilections. Wanting the same thing from her. Willing to take it by force. The thought struck a primeval fear, the terror as strong as a person trapped in a room on fire. She began to pant, the panic rising. *Get out. Get out now. Before he gets his hands on you . . .*

And then she felt the rage.

Piggy shouted something unintelligible in Thai.

She said nothing, letting the blackness grow.

Piggy switched to English. "Drop the purse!"

She let go of the pistol and did as he asked.

Piggy smirked. "Yes, that's right. If you want the help, you have to pay for it. This doesn't have to be hard."

She caught a trace of her fear-soaked sweat rising from the gap in her shirt, wondering if Piggy could also sense the destruction about to come. She raised her hands in a fighting stance and looked him in the eye.

Confused, Piggy said, "What are you doing? You want to go to prison with your friend?"

She savored the anger flowing through her, a river of violence splashing inside of her looking for a way out. Drawing strength from it, she smiled and said, "Bring it on, you little toad."

He gave a guttural scream and charged, swinging both arms in a windmill of ineffective blows. She ducked under and out, grabbing his wrist as he went by and locking up his elbow. Using it like a pry bar, she levered him face-down onto the floor.

He screamed again, threatening her with all manner of vile things.

She said, "Turn your head. Look at me."

He rolled until he could see her, his left ear still on the floor.

She said, "I wanted you to watch this." And lashed out with her foot, catching his elbow against the joint and shattering it, like she was breaking a stick for firewood.

This time the wail was short, as he passed out from the pain. The front door exploded inward, and she whirled against the new threat, seeing Decoy coming through instead.

He took in the scene and said, "Jesus Christ! Why didn't you alert me?"

She said, "No need. He was no threat."

Decoy stared at her for a moment, then picked up her purse and handed it to her.

"Told you that you were good at this shit."

16

The Thai corrections officer repeated the question. "Why is the prisoner release request on a form from two years ago?"

Outwardly, I showed nothing, but my mind was ricocheting around like a bullet, trying to find an answer that would preclude a phone call. Which, if what I was doing was for real, would have been exactly what I would want. *I have no idea. Why don't you call the assholes that made it and let's get this cleared up?*

The officer muttered something in Thai. I didn't catch it all, but it sounded like bitching about idiots at headquarters, and I felt an edge. Nung heard it too and walked right into the role, surprising me again.

"Don't complain about the bureau headquarters. You people out here always give us trouble. What difference does the form make? I've just driven for hours and it's still an official request."

"Trouble? You idiots transfer prisoners every single day, and you can't ever get it right. *You* set the protocol and then never follow it."

Nung acted like he was biting back a response, then said, "Just get the prisoner. I'll talk with the people who made the mistake."

The one thing we had going for us was that the form was in *his* official system. It wasn't like we'd brought it with us, some forged piece of paper he could question, and that seemed to turn the tide. That, and the fact that a prisoner breakout this elaborate was outside the scope of his imagination. He printed out the requisition, then pressed a button, getting us through gate one.

"Follow me to control block four. But this prisoner is special and will need local release, regardless of your official requisition."

Piggy.

I acted like he'd just given me a birthday present, smiling and moving into the prison. We went through the visitation area and entered the cell blocks proper, the stench hitting me immediately. A cloying odor of unwashed bodies and fetid water, it caught in the back of my throat like sour milk.

The prison was a two-story U-shaped building with a courtyard in the middle. The open end of the U held a single building not connected to the other cell blocks and was the newly constructed maximum-security facility holding Knuckles. We had to pass through the courtyard to get to it, and had to get permission to do even that— our next hurdle.

We reached control block four, which was nothing more than a cage housing a corrections officer who controlled the doorway access to the cells in this block, as well as the courtyard. The first officer told the man in the cage why we were there, handed him the release form, then turned and walked away. The man took one look at the name and brought out his cell phone, saying, "I'm sorry, but I have to get permission from the maximum-security area prior to letting you enter the courtyard."

I glanced at Nung, and he slid his hand into his pocket, turning on the cell jammer. I'd given it to him on the off chance they'd make me wait at the front entrance, only letting him proceed forward as an "official" prison representative. The jail was supposed to routinely leverage the encrypted Wi-Fi system for VOIP phone calls through the Symbol PDAs, but on our reconnaissance, we had found they didn't really use it, preferring to simply dial a cell number. I needed to force this guy onto the backup of the VOIP.

The guard turned away, the phone to his ear. He stood with his back to us for a few seconds, then pulled the phone away and stared at the screen. He muttered something, then opened a cabinet and pulled out a duplicate of the PDA Piggy carried.

Here we go.

I dearly wanted to call Retro using my covert radio, but camouflaging it with my cell phone would be a little weird, given that nobody else's cell phone seemed to be working for some strange reason, and I couldn't very well wander around simply talking to the air.

I glanced at Nung and found him as impassive as ever. Even a little bored. Either he was a cold-blooded bastard, or he didn't have the intelligence to realize the risks involved.

The guard was now talking into the PDA, speaking in a whisper and glancing at us. I saw his eyes widen, and he hung up. He punched a button and said, "Follow the yellow line until you reach the next control, directly across the courtyard. The man who will release your prisoner will meet you there."

Perfect. On to gate three.

We exited into the courtyard, the sun blinding but the heat mild compared to the humid air of Bangkok. Following the yellow ribbon of paint, I saw the segregation cells of the maximum-security facility. Brand-new, with the paint still fresh, it looked like a benign hospital wing.

We marched up like we owned the place, playing the shell game again, with Piggy now "not here" but "understanding" our importance, with us saying we'd talked to him at control four and he'd open the door for us once we checked in. I prayed the new guard didn't call control four, because the switcheroo was getting ridiculous.

Two minutes of tension—or, in Nung's world, two minutes of absolute boredom—as we went through the cell-denial/PDA dance again. Within minutes, Knuckles was brought to us, looking forty years older, with scabs dotting his body like a leper. The only indication he wasn't an AIDS victim was the look in his eyes. They were bright blue and dancing. He rolled right into the charade, acting like he'd been waiting for the State guys since day one.

We began following the yellow line back out, with me actually having to help Knuckles walk, the shackles on his legs scraping the concrete.

Embarrassed, he said, "Sorry, man. Other than seeing you, I've been crammed in that hole the entire time."

I patted his back, saying, "Cut the apologies, you pussy. Give it to the Taskforce when I tell them how I had to carry you out of here."

He grinned and said, "Glad the Taskforce lives up to what they say."

The smile was grotesque, his missing teeth making him look like a meth addict, and I felt a spike of anger at how he'd been treated. Along with the Oversight Council's bullshit tap dance on his fate.

We entered the courtyard and shuffled as fast as Knuckles could manage, given his chains and health. As we walked on the little yellow ribbon the Thai prisoners in the courtyard only gave us a courtesy look, and I was beginning to pat myself on the back for my incredible knack for operations when Knuckles brought me back to reality.

"Pike, that crew to the left works for Piggy. They're the ones I fought. They're looking hard at us for a reason."

I kept walking and saw four prisoners break from the group and start keeping pace with us. The gate to the main prison building was still seventy meters away.

"What's their story?" I said. "Do we need to worry?"

"Oh yeah. That old guy with the tats is the leader. He's working with Piggy. He'll know this is bullshit without Piggy being here. Best case, he wants a last shot at me. He won't give a shit about a fight. He's had people beating my ass every night, and he's going to want a final beat-down."

The group of four changed direction and began moving toward us.

I said, "Keep cool. I'm a State Department guy. A US official. They won't do anything here."

Knuckles said, "You think they know that because you're wearing a suit? They've probably never even heard of the State Department. Either way, they don't give a rat's ass. I killed their boy, and they're in prison. All that asshole wants is a final shot. You can't hurt him."

I kept walking, seeing the gate getting closer.

"What about the guards? What will they do?"

"Nothing until the fight is over. Happens all the time. Pike, you've got to hammer them quick. Trust me, I know. You want some help from the guards, you have to show some strength."

I watched them advance, running through the options and finding nothing but land mines.

"Damn it, we can't do this. You don't know what it took to get in here. If we raise a stink, we're done."

Chains clanking, shuffling forward like something out of a Tolkien novel, he stated the obvious.

"The stink's already here. Get ready to fight."

17

I saw the four break from a tight-knit walking group and spread into a fighting formation. I didn't want to believe it, but I knew Knuckles was right.

"Nung, I should've asked, but can you fight?"

He kept walking forward, as if he hadn't heard. Bored out of his mind because he had snuck into a Thai prison to break out a *farang* and was now about to get his ass beat by a gang of Thai mafia. *Probably going to infiltrate Iran as a male prostitute after this.* I was beginning to wonder if he was crazy. Literally crazy, not crazy in a cool, badass way.

"Nung?"

For the first time, a grin slipped out, and he showed some emotion. "Yes, I can fight. Is that what you'd like? Remove them?"

The men were about ten meters away, baring their teeth. For a split second, I thought about flinging out an ID, claiming State Department immunity or some other shit. Anything to stop the contest about to occur. Seeing their snarling visages, I knew it would be a waste of effort.

"Oh yeah, that's what I would like. You get the two on your left. I'll take the two on the right. You sure you can do this? I don't want someone jumping on my back."

The men closed within eight feet, and he skipped a little bit, a small Muay Thai dance, raising his fists head-high, saying, "Yes, I can do this. I was beginning to wonder why my father said this would be fun."

Father?

With that, he hammered the first guy in the upper thigh with a kick, snapping his shin forward like a whip and bringing the prisoner to his knees like he'd cracked him with a tire iron. The man barely had time to wonder why he'd lost control of his leg when Nung wrapped his left hand into his hair and punched him straight above his nose, dropping him flat-out.

I missed the rest as I focused on my own targets, both circling around to keep me off balance. I decided the State Department route wasn't a bad idea, keeping Knuckles behind me in his chains.

"Stop this! I work for the United States. Let us pass."

The men grinned, raising their fists. I flicked my eyes toward the wall, and sure enough, the guards ignored everything, simply looking on in interest like a gaggle of pedestrians watching a street fight in New York.

I played the pussy card one more time. "Please, don't hit me! Leave us alone!" I gave what I hoped was an expression of absolute fear, then waited for the strike, cowering.

It came quickly, and the return was just as fast. The

first guy, convinced he could get through me without issue and on to Knuckles, simply hooked a leg behind me and pushed, attempting to put me on the deck. Instead, I wrapped up his leg with my own, planted my feet for stability, and looped my arm around his neck, then gave him four straight punches to his face. He was combat ineffective after two.

The tattooed leader clocked me on the side of the head with a wild punch, then leapt onto my back, his arms around my neck, starting to choke me. I jerked upright, preparing to jump straight back and land on him with my body weight, when the arms left my neck, then the body. I whirled around and found him sitting down, legs straight out, Knuckles behind him, twisting his head around like he was Linda Blair in *The Exorcist*, the man screaming in a high-pitched wail.

I shouted, "Don't!"

Knuckles looked at me, a ragged bloodlust in his eyes.

"Damn it! Don't do it!"

He kept the head twisted for a moment longer, his jaw clenched. He squinted at me, begging to kill the guy. My eyes bored back into him, an unspoken command to stop. We played the stare game for a second, me feeling the pressure of time and him feeling the need for revenge, then he switched positions, looping his arm around the leader's neck and cutting off the blood-flow to his brain. A second or two of flailing, and the leader was out cold. I whirled to find Nung and saw him standing over two prostrate bodies. Now back into bored mode. He glanced

my way, then glanced at the guards, an unspoken command telling me to get this show moving.

They were finally starting to move our way, some jogging, most walking. We began shuffling as fast as we
could on the thin yellow line, me shouting about the
weak response from the guards, waving my black diplomatic passport in the air like I hoped a State Department
guy would do. The guards acted confused, first attempting to stop us, then coalescing on the prostrate bodies.

Nung began shouting something about going to the
infirmary, and they let us pass, but I knew we were now
on the clock, with a lockdown coming.

We made it through control block four and into the
prison, with me snarling at every guard I could see, whip-
ping them verbally into letting us through. We shuffled
past anyone giving us a question and reached the gate to
exit the prison. Then the alarm went off.

Here we go.

Immediately, the initial guard we'd met when we'd
entered the prison went into battle-drill mode, shutting
down all activities except for slapping on riot gear, a Pav-
lovian response that potentially could keep us inside forever. I could see our prison van outside, a mere forty feet
away. Behind steel bars.

I said, "Open the gate. We're leaving now."

He ignored me. I glanced back down the hallway and
saw official bodies pouring out, like an anthill had been
kicked over.

"Open the damn gate!"

He shouted something, pointing toward a row of chairs, obviously wanting us to wait. Nung stepped forward and spoke softly in Thai. The guard asked him to repeat it, and Nung waved him over. When he reached the edge of the cage, Nung snapped his hand through the small window like a snake, clamping the man's neck.

Nung spoke slowly enough that I could understand. "This prison is run like a child's school. We have appointments to meet. Justice to bring to the *farang* we've picked up. Open the gate."

The man's eyes bulged, and he slapped the desk, desperately trying to hit the switch behind him. He found it, and we were out, moving straight to the prison van and Retro.

18

We made it out of the parking lot without any trouble, the officials focused on the inside of the prison. Thirty minutes later, we met our own vehicles for transfer to our aircraft. I saw Jennifer sitting in the passenger seat and winked at her.

"Glad to see you made it out without having to use the hush puppy. Good job with the clone."

She smiled weakly but said nothing. I knew that look. She was embarrassed about something. "What happened? Did you have to trigger Decoy? I got my thirty minutes, so you can't be worried about that."

Decoy turned from helping Knuckles. "Hell no, she didn't trigger me. Didn't call at all. And yeah, you got your thirty minutes. Could have had twenty-four hours. Shit, a decade after what Jennifer did to him."

I started to ask for the story, then said, "Okay, later, at the hotwash. Right now, let's get gone."

The transfer complete, I pulled Nung aside.

"Hey, I don't know what you do for a living, but I

might be able to use you in the future. You've got some serious skills. Can I call you?"

He smiled and said, "Yes. I can work again, if the price is right."

He wrote his number down on a scrap of paper, and out of curiosity, because I wasn't paying him a damn thing for his help, I said, "How much did you make for this gig?"

He said, "No money at all. I got my brother into school. A chance for a better life than I have."

He handed me the number, then turned without another word, got back into the prison van, and drove away.

THE PILOT SAID we were on final for Bangkok, and I waited until the wheels touched down before hitting the connect button for my "company" VPN on my laptop. I wanted to delay the SITREP to Kurt as long as possible.

I had four different missed calls from him, each one purposely ignored, and I knew he was going to be hot. Especially if the calls were to give me a direct order to back off of Knuckles.

I heard the computer going through its plethora of switches, getting rerouted about fifteen times before some algorithm decided it was safe for the computer on Kurt's desk to start ringing. Anyone looking would think I was calling Charleston, South Carolina, instead of Washington, DC. I glanced back into the plane and saw everyone staring at me, wondering what was going to happen when Kurt found out what we'd been up to.

He came on immediately, and, as expected, he was a little ticked off, but not nearly as much as I'd imagined. In fact, it almost seemed like he was putting on an act.

"Pike, what's the protocol for situation reports with deployed teams?"

"Sir, I know. I should have called back, but I was busy. Sorry. I mean, it's not like I'm on a mission profile."

"No, that's right. Because you wouldn't answer your damn phone."

The statement got my attention. "You have a mission for me? Seriously?"

He leaned back in his chair, suddenly suspicious at the eagerness in my voice. "Why haven't you mentioned Knuckles?"

"Uhh . . . well . . . would you like to talk to him?"

All I got was silence.

"Sir, they were going to kill him. I had a solid plan, and I executed. It went just like I briefed you before."

He said nothing for a moment, then let out a breath. "I suppose I knew that was coming. So you got him out. What's the damage?"

I succinctly gave him the CliffsNotes version of the mission, leaving out Izzy and my buddy at JUSMAG, simply alluding to in-country assets like I had when I got permission to talk to the hacking cell. He listened, then interrupted my story.

"Cut to the chase. What's the risk to compromise? Do I need to go into damage control with the Oversight Council?"

"There was a little drama, but we got out clean. There's only one guy who really cares about investigating, but he'll be in the hospital for the next few days. On top of that we found some incriminating information on him. The indig helping me is going to pay him a visit."

Song, the man who'd portrayed Piggy with Retro, had found a ton of bad stuff on Piggy's cloned PDA, which explained why he took it home with him every day instead of leaving it at the jail. It had an absolute treasure trove of illegal shenanigans that would have put him in prison pajamas overnight. I'd called Nung before leaving Chiang Mai and given him some instructions to give Piggy a little visit in the hospital. He'd either let Knuckles ride or start practicing how to shower with his back to the wall.

"Will that be enough?"

"Yeah. No way is he going to want to admit to getting his ass beat by a woman he was blackmailing for sex. Especially when he sees the evidence we have about his other activities."

"What about the local help? What do they know?"

"Nothing. Let's just say they're used to working without information."

"How'd you get them? What's the cost?"

I said, "That's the beauty of it. It didn't cost any money." I told him about the school admissions problem. As I recounted the story, I saw his demeanor shift. *Guess he's not seeing the beauty of it. . . .* I finally saw some real anger.

"Damn it, Pike, you want me to go to the Oversight Council and have someone interject into a foreign boarding school's admission process?"

I became a little indignant as well. "Yeah. I do. Get the SECSTATE to make a call. Hell, it's because he wouldn't interject on Knuckles's behalf in the first place that we're in this situation. I'm sure he knows someone who knows someone who can help."

Kurt said nothing for a moment, then shifted gears. "How's Knuckles?"

"He's pretty beat-up, but mostly just bumps and bruises. We'll get him a checkup in Germany, but my bet is he'll be running fine in a couple of days. What he really needs is a dentist."

"And the team?"

"Good to go. Jennifer and I are the only ones who have done anything overtly operational. Everyone else is still clean. What's the story?"

I knew he wasn't asking to be polite. He wanted to know if we could go operational after the prison bust.

"Knuckles's bug turned up some interesting information, and we got clearance to investigate. I need you to get eyes on. Nothing more until I can relieve you with the original team we pulled out. You're just there to get a handle until we can reinsert the team. Then you come home."

In fifteen minutes, he gave me a rundown for an Iranian Quds Force general currently in Thailand, and the mission to track him—which immediately raised some flags.

"You want me to hunt a foreign intelligence asset? The council gave Omega authority for a state-sponsored target?"

The Taskforce called each phase of an operation a different Greek letter. Omega, the last letter, meant we had authority for a takedown, but we'd never targeted anyone from a sovereign government. We dealt strictly with substate terrorists.

"No, no. Don't get eager beaver. We're nowhere near Omega. We just want to get eyes on this guy, that's all. See if we can find out what he's up to."

"Good enough. You got an anchor we can start with?"

"Yeah. I'll send you a complete package, but you need to play this by the numbers. I understand getting Knuckles out. Shit, I practically dared you to do it. I'm glad you executed, but this target is too sensitive for any freelancing."

"Because he's an Iranian general?"

"Because he's very, very good. And he's more than likely doing something very, very bad."

19

Having arrived forty minutes early for his meeting with the scientist, Malik began to feel the Singapore humidity sink into his clothes.

He'd caught the first flight out after the capture of the son and had spent the majority of yesterday afternoon getting familiar with the area. The Biopolis complex had been little trouble to find, and even less trouble to get to, as it sat right down the road from the Buona Vista LRT metro stop. That hadn't made him any more confident, because he knew the trouble would be located within the complex.

A campus of over a dozen buildings, all named with a biological tint such as "Helios" and "Genome," it was festooned with cameras and security. It seemed every single building had an entrance guarded by uniformed men, along with a phalanx of biometric badges and scanners. This would have been bad enough on a normal day but was made much worse on a Sunday. The place was mostly deserted, making him feel like every guard was eyeballing him.

He wandered around a little bit, then took a seat at an outdoor café that served Peranakan cuisine. It was located behind the Chronos building, underneath a laboratory for tropical diseases—with the usual guard force at the main entrance.

Not liking the menu a single bit, he'd ordered a cup of tea and surveyed the area. The food selection notwithstanding, he did like the multiple escape routes the café afforded, so he'd decided to stay to use it as the initial contact location. He dialed his cell, letting the scientist know where to find him.

This meeting, he knew, had the greatest level of risk. He hadn't had time to personally show the scientist the danger he posed. No chance to reinforce the fear necessary for total compliance. If the scientist had taken his initial phone call from Thailand and immediately called the police, he would be caught like a fish on a line. He hoped the man hearing his son begging on the phone would be enough.

Although that mission in and of itself had been fraught with risk.

Malik couldn't help but smile at the memory. Kavi's eyes bugging out of his face in confusion just before the hood descended.

Kavi would have spotted a Thai scam four miles away. Would have instinctively known when to turn away from an alley with Thai danger. But like a mouse sniffing the nose of a foreign snake, he'd had no sense of the peril.

Until they pulled the hood over his head.

His men had operated perfectly, even considering their disobeying of his orders to leave the dessert café. Actually, that, in itself, showed an ability to assess. To analyze and succeed.

Malik had rented a villa near Soi 3, a few blocks off of Sukhumvit Road, as the safe house to store Kavi, and when the team had finally relaxed after the takedown, they'd begun patting themselves on the back and praising Allah, the fervor of their mission intertwined with the revolution. With the need to identify and associate their life with something greater than themselves.

Malik had joined in, of course, but he had long since lost the sheen of the revolution. He no longer ran about chanting everything that spouted from the ayatollah's mouth and rarely even prayed, using the proclamations from Muhammad himself about the exertions of the jihad allowing him forgiveness from this task. He knew he was stretching his job as an excuse, but he'd seen beyond the curtain and understood how the world really worked.

As he'd grown up in the IRGC, he'd learned a hard truth: Allah didn't help those in need. They helped themselves, or they perished. Praying made no difference whatsoever. He'd seen that up close in the brutal fighting with Saddam Hussein. Thousands of mere boys thrown into the breach and slaughtered, their skulls used to create a shrine to Saddam Hussein. Even as his faith faded away, his loyalty to the state had become entrenched.

He despised the West for what they did to his country. The sanctions and other punishments. For nothing. Iran hadn't done anything the West hadn't perfected first. In fact, they'd learned from the West how the game was played. Israel's killing of Iran's nuclear scientists. The United States' drone attacks in Pakistan and elsewhere. It was the same in effect. The difference was the hypocrisy.

Why was it okay for the United States and Israel to have nuclear weapons, but not okay for Iran? When did Allah proclaim that to be the way of the world? They were just afraid of his country becoming a power. Becoming a threat, where they no longer had the monopoly on violence. A goal he was willing to die for. Which he might, depending on this meeting.

The mullahs had sanctioned the mission but had stated that the repercussions of failure would be profound. In their obtuse way, they had sent him a veiled threat: If the Great Satan connected who was behind the attack, he would be forfeited.

Because they are afraid to fight.

They would rather have shouted "Death to America" from their knees while allowing the West to cripple them. Too afraid to strike back. As an original Islamic revolutionary who had overthrown the shah and shown the Great Satan's impotence when he'd helped capture the US embassy and its personnel, holding them hostage for over a year, he found it ironic. How could you brag about the revolution, then fear retaliation in the same breath? Where had the audacity gone?

He snapped out of his reverie when a man rounded the corner. A short Asian, deeply tanned, with a flat face that barely held the glasses on his nose. The man glanced around nervously, scanning the restaurant and skipping forward in stuttered movements. Like the same mouse sniffing for the snake. Only this one recognized the danger.

Malik stood and said, "Dr. Sakchai Nakarat? Please have a seat. We have much to discuss."

20

As the scientist took a chair, Malik scanned around, looking for the net closing on him. Seeing nothing, he glanced at his cell for an alert. He had brought both Roshan and Sanjar with him, leaving the other two team members at the safe house with the son, and was using them on both ends of Biopolis Way. If any police vehicles closed on the Chronos building, they would have to pass by his team.

The phone was clear, and he sat down.

Dr. Nakarat remained mute. Malik saw a slight tremor in his hands and relaxed, believing the initial phone call had worked. Even so, he started with the threats.

"I assume you did not alert anyone about our conversation?"

"No, no. I have told no one. Please. I've followed all of your instructions. What do you want? I have no money. I think you've made a mistake. Please, let my son go and I promise I won't tell anyone about this."

"You *do* have something I value, but before we get to that, I want to make sure you understand what will happen to your son should anyone suspect anything. Make no mistake—he will be killed in a most painful manner. Of course you will not speak to anyone, but you must also watch your mannerisms. Your day-to-day interactions. No one must suspect a thing or Kavi will pay the price. You understand?"

"Yes! Dear God, yes. What do you want?"

"It's simple. You have been working on a vaccine for an H5N1 virus modified for airborne transmission in humans. I want five samples of that virus, along with the recipe for the vaccine."

He saw the doctor blanch, the blood draining from his face. He thought it was the enormity of the request until the doctor recovered enough to speak.

"I . . . we . . . yes, we were working on a vaccine, but we were ordered to stop. The virus has been destroyed. I don't have five samples."

Malik heard the words but had trouble assimilating them. Before he could speak, Dr. Nakarat began babbling.

"A man died during the research. We couldn't continue. The vaccine didn't work anyway. It failed completely in males and rendered females as asymptomatic carriers. They carried the virus without getting sick. You see? I don't have five samples. I'm telling you the truth. Please, let my son go. I'll give you anything else I have. Anything I can find."

Malik understood now why he had gone white. He believed he was killing his son because he couldn't help.

"Can you re-create the virus?"

Dr. Nakarat squeezed his fists together. "No! Not by myself. I'd have to use the entire team."

Malik scowled, and the scientist became shrill. "Please. There may be one sample. I heard management talking about saving a copy of the virus. I didn't see it, but maybe you should ask them. I can contact them right now. Bring them here."

He pulled out his phone and Malik raised his hand. "Stop."

Clearly, the scientist was cracking. He couldn't even see how stupid his statement was.

Dr. Nakarat waited, his hands trembling hard enough to rap the phone against the table in a drumbeat.

Malik said, "You will get this sample. You have access to it."

"No! I don't. I swear."

"Think, doctor. You were shut down because of the risk involved, yes?"

When he nodded, Malik continued. "There is no way they took such a dangerous thing out of the lab. They can't simply lock it up in the glove box of their car. Where would it be in the lab? In a controlled environment?"

Dr. Nakarat's eyes darted left and right as he began cataloging his workspace in his mind. After a few seconds, they settled back on Malik, now with some hope.

"The patent reefer. That's where it will be. We have a double security zone there, not because the material in it is dangerous, but because it's proprietary. They don't want anyone stealing the formulas through industrial espionage."

Malik smiled. "Good. Very good. Can you access it?"

"I suppose so. I have in the past, but only with other scientists. I have never gone in there by myself. And the company will know every move I make. I'm telling you, they're serious about espionage. I'll have to log out the sample, and they'll know."

"No, doctor. You're still thinking with the company. You need to be thinking with your son. I ask again, can you do it without alerting the lab?"

At the mention of Kavi, Dr. Nakarat began to tremble anew, a thin sheen of sweat appearing on his upper lip.

"I'll have to create a reason to go in. Something tomorrow. I won't be able to access it until Tuesday at the earliest."

"Tuesday? I want it right now."

"That's impossible! It's Sunday. The lab is closed! No way can I do that. I couldn't even get into the patent reefer today if I wanted. It's locked down and alarmed. I need at least a day to create an excuse, or they'll know."

Malik fought the logic in his mind but eventually relented. "Okay. Tuesday it is. I need you to call your son's boarding school and tell them he is with you. Tell them you had a family emergency or something else that will keep them from attempting to find him." He watched the scientist's shoulders droop and said, "I'm not stupid, doctor. Please believe that I'll know before you what treachery you plan."

While the doctor called, Malik considered what he knew. *One sample*. Not the original plan. He'd only be able to create one cluster instead of five spread throughout the United States. One cluster that might be contained if the American health-care system was fast enough. He needed to come up with something to defeat that. Then he remembered what the scientist had said about the vaccine.

It didn't work anyway. Didn't that make the entire mission moot? He had planned on Iranian scientists genetically reproducing the vaccine, getting enough doses to protect as many people in Iran as possible, starting immediately, before the virus was released. Of course, they'd leave out all the dissidents who continually attempted to protest against the regime. Kill two birds with one stone, as it were.

Now they had nothing. They'd simply end up with 50 percent of the population running around like rats carrying the black plague.

Rats carrying the plague. Malik's fertile mind turned the thought over, and an idea began to form. When the doctor ended his conversation with the school, he said, "All's well?"

"Yes. They believe he's visiting me here."

"Good. Tell me about this vaccine. Does it really protect females?"

"Yes. Well, it keeps them from showing any flu symptoms but doesn't destroy the virus. It's worthless. I thought we might have found the genetic flaw from that generation of the vaccine, but we never got to test the final one we produced. We were shut down before then."

"Can they pass on the disease, or do they just carry it?"

"They're contagious, but not airborne. We ran a test on the virus after we developed it but before we began the vaccine protocol. If we put a ferret in one isolator box and let him breathe into a tube, forcing the exhalations into the other isolator box with a healthy ferret, we succeeded in killing both ferrets. That's how we knew it was airborne. We ran that test again with the vaccinated females but didn't get the same results. If we manually transmitted bodily fluids to other ferrets, though, they became infected."

Dr. Nakarat held his hands up. "I see where you're going with this. Trust me, the vaccine failed. Once the secondary ferret became infected, he was as pathogenic as any of them, airborne or otherwise. Lethal."

You have no idea where I'm going with this. "I want that vaccine as well. Not the final untested one. The generation before it, that you tested."

"Why?"

"Not your concern." He passed across a cell phone. "Call me when you have the virus. There's only one number in the contact list. Mine. I will know if the phone contacts anyone else." Before the scientist could pick it up, he said, "Give me your cell phone in return."

"Why?"

"Because I don't want you leaving here and thinking up something stupid or inadvertently giving away what you're doing when someone calls. Just tell everyone it died."

Next, Malik slid across a hotel key-card. "That's to a suite in the Marina Bay Sands hotel. From here on out, don't go home. Sleep there."

Now becoming numb at the loss of control, the doctor stammered, "W-what about clothes? Toiletries? I need to go get them."

"There's a mall in the hotel. Buy what you need and charge it to the room. Do not go back home. Eat, sleep, and shop at the Marina Bay Sands. Until this is done, that is your entire universe. Understood?"

When the scientist picked up the key, Malik clamped a hand down on his arm and squeezed. "Do not, in any way, attempt to cross me."

Dr. Nakarat nodded his head over and over again. When Malik released his arm, the doctor scampered away without even looking back, the mouse escaping the snake.

Malik realized that the doctor hadn't even had the presence of mind to demand the most rudimentary requirement of a hostage negotiation: proof of life. He'd spoken to his son on the initial phone call, and that was it. The doctor hadn't even asked about transfer procedures. Now it didn't matter what Malik did with the son, as the next meeting would be the final one. It would be too late to demand anything, as he could simply take what the doctor brought.

He found Sanjar and Roshan outside the Buona Vista LRT station. "Have the team dispose of the boy. He's now become superfluous. Make sure they do it in a planned way. Nothing sloppy. Make sure that he won't be found. Nobody will be looking from this end, so the only mistake will be our own. There's no urgency to the situation. Whatever you do, don't kill him in the house. My name is on the lease."

When Sanjar nodded, Malik turned to Roshan. "You worked on the Chechnya cell before this mission?"

"Yes."

"Get me a contact. Someone who can provide a *shahid*."

"Why them? We can do that ourselves, through Hezbollah."

"Trust me, Hezbollah has nothing as deadly as what they can provide."

21

"It wasn't your fault," Doku said. "The circuitry had a short in it."

Elina said, "I told you that. Did you not believe me?"

Doku smiled. "I never questioned your commitment, but others would have. It's good you came back with the vest."

Elina simply nodded, but inside she relaxed. After the strike against her father's murderers she had fled the square, returning to live like a wolf in the forest, debating what she should do. She'd stayed for two days, considering her options. She knew the insurgency leadership would be questioning her commitment. Wondering if she was now the enemy—and she'd seen what punishment they meted out to traitors. It would be much, much worse than what she had attempted on the Kadyrovtsy. A slow, painful demise. The only way to prove she was still a Black Widow was to return, but the visit would be fraught with risk. Doku's statement gave her hope that she'd made the right choice.

He continued. "The attack was spectacular, right in

the heart of the beast. Early counts are upwards of fifty people killed, many more injured. Very few civilians."

"I saw my father's murderer. That's all I cared about."

He said nothing for a moment, considering her words. "So you are done?"

"No," she said, "Kariina did my duty for me. I still owe for others of my family."

Doku turned to the window. Speaking over his shoulder, he said, "I'm very glad to hear that. You are different than the other female *shuhada* I have trained. As dangerous as they were, you're smarter. More cunning. More driven."

He turned back and said, "Tell me, could you be a *shahid* against someone other than the Kadyrovtsy? Someone that is unrelated to the tragedy that befell your family?"

"Why?"

"Because I have a mission for you. A very special mission."

22

"Pike, you'd better get up here."

I stared at the handheld radio for a split second as if it were a snake, then snatched it up and scrambled to the ladder, Jennifer and Decoy hot on my heels. I knew that little sentence would be nothing but trouble.

We'd rented the upper floor of an apartment complex just off Sukhumvit Road, getting both apartments along with roof access. It was the closest place we could find to the anchor we'd been given that would still allow us to maintain anonymity.

Reaching the ladder, I said, "What's up? The general finally show?"

I knew that wasn't it, because that wouldn't have required my presence. Only a jot in the logbook.

The anchor from Kurt had turned out to be a house, recently rented, with the general's name on the lease. That's all we had as a starting point, and so far, it had been a bust. We'd maintained eyes on it for close to two days with little to show for it, which would be embarrassing when we were relieved by the inbound team. There had been a couple of men who came and went, and they did look Arabic, but that didn't mean a whole lot, given the house's location.

It was situated about a block off of what was known as "Little Arabia," just off Soi 3 in downtown Bangkok, which, considering the general's nationality, had seemed to make sense.

Little Arabia was just that: a slice of the Middle East right smack in downtown Bangkok, complete with women wearing full-length abayas and niqab face veils, men in traditional gulf attire—which we charitably called a man-dress—and signs in Arabic. It had made any close-in re-connaissance hard, because we would have stuck out as bad as if it had been Fallujah.

I exited the roof access and found Knuckles staring at our Wasp screen, while Retro fiddled with a computer. We'd decided to use the UAV first, before getting more aggressive, which is why access to the roof had been key.

Knuckles said, "Take a look. The two tenants are emptying the place, taking out all the Persian rugs."

I studied the screen, seeing an open trunk of a car in the walled courtyard, the two men coming and going from the house, loading what looked to me like cinder blocks.

"What do you make of it? Are they leaving?"

Which would suck, because we had no other anchor.

Retro said, "That's not what's interesting. Look at this. I've been running a feed. I've got it on tape. The first carpet they brought out was big. And it was moving."

"Moving?"

He hit play, and I saw both men come out of the house, one on each end of a large rug. When the first man hit the bottom step to the courtyard, the rug began to writhe up and down, left and right, until it popped out of his hands. He immediately jumped on it, while the second man began beating the top part of the carpet with something I couldn't identify. After three or four blows, the rug became still, and the men loaded it into the backseat of the car.

What the hell? Who do they have?

Retro said, "We kept eyes on afterward, and the rug doesn't move again. Whoever is in it is either dead or out cold."

Shit. This really causes a dilemma.

My mission was simply to get a handle on the general, then pass off everything I knew to the inbound team— the clean team—for them to exploit in accordance with whatever the Oversight Council deemed necessary. In no way was I to do anything that might invite compromise of my team or the mission. Interdict this escapade, and the Iranians would *know* they were being watched. Don't interdict, and whoever was bound up in the rug was more than likely dead.

Which really made life difficult when you were supposed to be the white knight. A choice that had no good ending. I had seen this exact same thing play out in Iraq. Watching a nobody who was going to lead us to a somebody, only to have the nobody begin to do something evil right in front of us, like shoving some poor Iraqi into the trunk of a car.

The choice then had been horrific, stretching my sense of right and wrong to the breaking point and leading to a moral equivocation. If I saved the Iraqi, the terrorist would know his contact was blown, forcing us to start at ground zero as he moved operations and remade his cellular infrastructure, burning anyone who might lead to him. But if I didn't, I was culpable for a death, because I had the power to stop it.

It was much more than a simple equation of immediate right versus wrong, because saving the one guy in the trunk most definitely would ensure that others would die later on. The terrorist would remain operational while we climbed up the tree again, and every day lost in the hunt was another day for him to kill.

It had been a hard decision, but I made it with the overarching mission in mind.

Knuckles said, "They're locking up the house. They're finished. What do you want to do?"

I felt the time disappearing like water down a drain, knowing there was only so much before it no longer mattered and the sink was empty. I considered the same choices as before, along with the repercussions. The general, according to Kurt, was up to some very destructive actions. Much worse than the killing of a single guy. Hell, I didn't even know if the man in the rug wasn't bad as well, somebody who had been facilitating Iranian operations and was now no longer of any use.

On the other hand, I didn't know if he *was* either.

"They're in the car, lights just came on."

Screw it. Anyone bitches, I'll say we did the same thing in Iraq.

"You got a pinecone on the Wasp?"

Knuckles grinned. "Yeah."

"Deploy it and vector me in. Jennifer, stay here and help with the airborne surveillance. Get Kurt on the VPN and let him know what we've got. Everyone else, kit up."

Back in Iraq, on my call, we'd saved the man in the trunk in a vehicle interdiction, and he'd ended up being nothing but a farmer with some bad luck. I'd gotten a ration of shit about it until we'd killed the terrorist two nights later in blind luck. Or maybe it had been karma. The farmer became a staunch supporter of all Coalition operations, along with his entire extended family—which, although it wasn't why I had executed, had helped the overarching mission.

I figured Spock could kiss my ass again. Sometimes the needs of the one outweighed the needs of the many.

While the rest of the team raced back down the ladder, Knuckles's grin faded to a sour look. I said, "Hey, you're still too beat-up. Somebody's got to man the beacon, and we might need your insider knowledge of the prison in about six hours."

Jennifer smiled at that, saying, "I'll make sure he stays on the roof."

As I turned to go, the weight of the decision sinking in, she grabbed my sleeve. "This is the right thing, no matter how it turns out. Don't second-guess once you're on the road."

The comment brought a measure of calm, reminding me of why I had joined the Taskforce in the first place, an organization designed to prevent death and destruction by preemptive actions. She was always a good sounding board, which was the very reason I had asked her to join as well. Her moral compass had no equivocation. It was black and white, right and wrong. Nobody else could puncture my sense of superiority like Jennifer. And nobody else could poke her back in the eye like I could.

I said, "Yeah, yeah. Don't worry. I'm doing it for the guy in the carpet. I wouldn't execute just because I want to go kick some ass. I'm not like Knuckles."

She gave me her disapproving-teacher look, and I said, "Just get that beacon emplaced, or it's a dead issue. That thing isn't the best we've ever used."

Which was an understatement. I, personally, thought the pinecone was the dumbest idea ever conceived. Something that sounds great on paper but ends up being a waste of tax dollars. It had been thrown in as a benny when we'd modified the Wasp UAV, but as far as I knew, it had never been used operationally because of its shortcomings in emplacement.

Basically, it was a normal beacon that operated off of the cell network, about the size of a fifty-cent piece and twice as thick. The unique thing was how it was emplaced. It was secured onto the bottom of the Wasp with electronic magnets and had a single wing sticking out of its side that also served as its antenna. When the power was cut to the magnet, it fell free and floated down, spinning like a seed from a pinecone on its single wing, autorotating until it made contact with the target, where another magnet held it in place. As a beacon it worked pretty well, with a battery life of over twelve hours. The problem was getting it on the target.

The big idea had come because of the Wasp's limited range. It couldn't track a car like the Predator or Reaper. Its range was just too shallow, and it flew too slowly to be able to match the speed of a car. The great idea had been to equip the Wasp with the pinecone, the theory being that when you saw you were going to lose the car, you'd beacon it for further tracking. Unfortunately, the very things that made the Wasp unsuitable for tracking on its own made it unsuitable for emplacing the beacon. It had proven impossible to drop the pinecone with any hope of it hitting a moving car. Great idea in theory, sorry in execution.

Until now. The Bangkok traffic would limit the speed these guys could move, and with its stop-and-go nature, we actually might succeed. Especially since there was no way the target was going to be breaking any traffic laws with a body in the back.

For once, I hoped I'd eat my words about how stupid the idea had been.

23

Retro tossed me a small duffel when I reached the bottom of the stairs, saying, "Usual kit. I didn't put in anything unique, so speak up if you think we want something."

I unzipped it while we moved through the apartment, seeing a Glock 30 and an H&K UMP, both suppressed and both chambered for the .45, along with night-observation goggles and other pieces of kit.

I said, "Grab the spare Wasp," then pulled out an innocuous Bluetooth earpiece and put it in, saying, "Commo check. Knuckles, you got me?"

"Yeah. Loud and clear."

We hit the parking lot, and I slapped the spare Wasp's pinecone onto our own car, asking, "Got the track?"

Jennifer came on this time. "Yeah. Got your track. Vehicle's on Sukhumvit, about out of range. Knuckles is lining up for a dive-bomb now."

I tossed the keys to Blood, getting into the passenger seat. "Tell him if he screws this up, he'll spend the next ten years staring at a screen instead of going on hits."

We maneuvered down the alleys until we reached the intersection with Sukhumvit, waiting to be told which way to go. After a full minute, I began to fear the dive-bomb mission had failed. It shouldn't have taken more than thirty seconds.

"Koko, what's the story?"

Jennifer, hating her call sign as much as Brett despised his, came back a little short. "Stand by. I'll alert when we're in motion."

I grinned and muted the connection, saying, "She sounds a little pissed."

Decoy said, "I sort of like that call sign. I could have called her Curious George."

Decoy had knighted Jennifer with the call sign "Koko" on our last mission together, after the gorilla that used sign language, and she'd tried mightily ever since to get us to forget it. It worked a little bit. We used it only on the radio. I'd learned early that she wouldn't respond to it in person, but in the middle of the mission she had no choice.

Brett said, "I'll trade with her. *Blood* is ridiculous."

We all started to chuckle, and I was glad to see everyone relaxed and calm. It meant we were clicking, something we would need in the coming moments. Decisions would be made in the blink of an eye, and undue stress tends to short-circuit logical thought, causing catastrophic mistakes.

Retro, in the back working a tablet, said, "Got the beacon, but it isn't moving."

Which could have meant one of two things: The dive-bomb had missed and the beacon was sitting in the middle of Sukhumvit Road, or the car was stopped in traffic. At least it would tell me left or right.

"Which way?"

"North. They went north on Sukhumvit."

Blood pulled into the traffic, and we slowly marched forward.

Jennifer came on. "Pinecone is in place. Knuckles is still overhead with the Wasp, and it looks like a clean hit, dead center of the roof."

All right.

"Good work. Keep the Wasp up as long as possible. Any word on Kurt?"

"They're tracking him down. I'll let you know as soon as I make contact."

I wondered if that was true. Would she call me if Kurt told us to stand down or let it go to rescue whoever was in the rug?

Retro said, "About a half mile in front of us, moving now."

Which might as well have been on the other side of the world given the traffic. Eventually, we left Sukhumvit and entered the expressway, still heading north. We lost the Wasp and were on our own. The traffic opened up, and we closed the distance.

"What's ahead of us, Retro? Where's he going?"

"The only thing big is Don Muang, right off of 31."

"How far?"

"About ten klicks."

If they were headed to Don Muang Airport, we'd need to stop them before they got there. Once they were inside, there'd be way too much security to attempt any sort of a takedown. But a vehicle interdiction on the freeway was a nonstarter. No way could we do that clean.

Why would they be going to the airport? They certainly can't put the rug through an X-ray machine. Unless they've already made arrangements.

"They're off 31," Retro said. "Now headed west on 304."

"Distance?"

"Exit two klicks up."

Soon enough we were behind them again, now running into traffic, but not as much as on Sukhumvit.

"What's ahead of us here?"

"The only thing out west is the Chao Phraya River, about eight klicks away."

We kept going, keeping about one kilometer back, me wondering if we were going to follow them to Burma. The beacon had just crossed the river, with us just behind, when Retro said, "Exit, exit, exit. One klick ahead."

Endgame.

"Okay, listen up. I think they're going to another safe house. Someplace out of the city. We'll let them settle, then pick up surveillance again. We see any indication that they're going to smoke the guy in the rug, we intervene. Otherwise, we jump-TOC to here."

I got the okay from my group of shooters and said,

"Koko, Knuckles, you copy? Go ahead and break down the TOC. You know the beacon track. Do some research on the area; see where we can stage out here. Hotels, apartments, the usual."

I got a roger and settled back to wait. Eventually, we were off the 304 and onto surface streets. After traveling a few more kilometers, we entered dirt roads, with little traffic, and still the target continued, now headed back east. The buildings faded away until there were only sporadic houses, then expanses of woodland.

Where the hell is he going? Farther east and he's going to run into the river.

Which is exactly what he did.

Retro said, "Vehicle stopped. Right on the Chao Phraya."

"Next to a house?"

"Not that I can tell from this map. Looks like the road just dead-ends into the river. He's about five hundred meters up."

"Blood, find a side road and pull over. Decoy, break out the Wasp."

Within five minutes we had the UAV constructed and launched. It homed in on the target beacon and began circling, all of us crowded around the screen as Decoy maneuvered its flight.

Retro was right. There wasn't a house around, but there was a dock, with three long-tailed Thai boats tied to it. Really nothing more than large canoes. We could see the two men struggling with the rug between them, loading it into the farthest boat, precariously wavering as they crossed from one boat to the other.

They then began going back and forth, loading the same square shapes I had seen earlier. Blocks of some type. Maybe radios or boxes of equipment.

Blood said, "What the hell are those things? Looks like cinder blocks for a building."

And it clicked. *They're going to dump him in the river.*

24

I spun away from the video screen, scrambling for the car door, saying, "Load up! They're going to kill him on the river, unless we can stop them from leaving."

Within seconds, we were throwing dirt on the road. Blood forced the vehicle as fast as he could down the track, weaving through the potholes, the bumps rattling our teeth.

"Watch where the hell you're going!" Decoy shouted. "I can't control the Wasp."

Blood ignored him.

I asked, "What're they doing?"

Decoy struggled to hold the screen still, the grainy image a blur. "They're off the dock, but I don't see a wake yet."

Blood rounded a corner and immediately fishtailed around a tree that was inexplicably growing in the middle of the road, slamming us all into the right side of the car and causing Decoy to lose the video relay.

He swore, got it back in his hands, and spent precious

time reorienting the Wasp. When he found the dock, he swore again.

"Boat's on the move, and hauling ass."

Seconds later we no longer needed the Wasp, as the dock appeared out of the gloom. Blood slammed on the brakes before we ended up launching into the Chao Phraya River, and we exited on the run.

I said, "Which way?"

"South. The boat went south."

Straining, I could faintly make out the white foam of its wake. I threw on my night-vision goggles and could see it clearly enough to make out the two men inside, the NODs turning the boat into an eerie green apparition racing steadily out of reach.

Great. Now we're going to chase them in a long-tail. This is turning into a comedy.

I thought about letting them go and recocking on the house. That, after all, was the mission. Sooner or later, they'd be back. I then thought about Jennifer's words.

Shit. No way can I face her without even trying. Damn do-gooder.

"Load up. Decoy, you got the helm. Everyone else, get ready to assault."

Decoy said, "Me? Why me? I don't know a damn thing about these boats."

We crossed the first boat and went into the second, both dangerously rocking. I said, "Because you're in the Navy, damn it. It's a boat. Surely you've been on one."

"I'm a SEAL, not a paint chipper. And it's not a boat. It's a canoe with an engine."

I knew he was right, but we settled into position anyway. Basically, a long-tail was a narrow sampan with a giant car engine on the back, built out of whatever the Thai owner could scrounge. The driveshaft of the engine extended out from the stern for about five or six feet before entering the water, giving the boats the nickname *long-tail*. They had become something of a Thai tradition, grafting big-block Chevys or Fords to sampans in order to churn around the river with a power plant that anyone could fix rather than using some special marine technology. Of course, it inevitably led to the usual macho "my boat can beat your boat" contests. Just like teenagers drag racing in the Deep South, but on a river with a boat that could barely float. In the end, the world was no different in Thailand than it was in rural Georgia.

While we untied the bow, Decoy pushed the shaft left and right, getting a feel for it, then fired up the engine. The propeller immediately churned the water, and the boat launched forward, throwing me onto my back.

I sat up as we weaved left and right, heading the wrong way. I saw Decoy fighting the engine and looking for a rudder.

I shouted over the engine noise, "The tail with the propeller is the rudder. Thrust vectoring. Push it left to go right and right to go left."

He did so and we whipped around, now heading

south. He shouted, "You know so much about this Thai shit, why aren't you back here?"

I grinned. "Because I'm on the assault. An Army guy."

I left him scowling, turning to the rest of the team. "We close on them and disable the boat. No lethal force unless they initiate. No shooting below the gunwales. That's where the precious cargo is. Blood, you and I will focus on the engine in back. Retro, Buckshot, you cover the threats. Anything hostile, take them down."

I looked forward and saw we were closing the distance to the other long-tail, now about seventy meters ahead. The riverbanks were dark, sporadically illuminated by small houses. From the middle of the river we had about a hundred meters on each side, so I wasn't too concerned about anyone witnessing our actions. Without NODs they'd see nothing except the wake of our boat in the moonlight, and with our suppressed weapons, all they'd hear would be the engine of the long-tail. It might spike a bit of curiosity, since it was so late at night, but probably not much.

Decoy said, "I'm taking them down the left side."

He gunned the engine, and the bow rose out of the water, the gap between the boats shrinking in seconds. We hunkered down, placing the barrels of our UMPs on the gunwale, trained on the other boat. We sliced forward like some twisted version of an eighteenth-century naval battle, pulling abreast of the target.

No command was given, and none was needed. Blood and I began spitting out rounds, the only noise the clanking of our bolts cycling and the dings of the bullets tearing into the engine block. At least for a second.

A crack from an unsuppressed weapon split the air, then another as both terrorists began firing wildly in our direction, hitting our boat but little else. Decoy jammed the throttle, and we skipped out of the kill zone, the four of us returning fire. A hundred meters away, Decoy cut the engine; the action had happened so quickly I didn't even get a rise in heart rate.

"Well, I guess that answers the lethal-force question."

I looked back and saw the boat remaining where it was. No wake, so we'd put the engine out of commission. "Anybody score a hit?"

Retro said, "One is down for sure. I couldn't hit anything else once Decoy started running."

Decoy bristled, about to say something, when I cut him off. "Don't worry about it. No reason to sit trading rounds from five feet away once we disabled the boat. We can take our time now."

I scanned the far shoreline to see if there was any activity, then noticed water around my ankles.

Blood said, "Pike, we got an issue. They hit some bolt up front, and it tore out a hole."

"Plug it."

"Can't. It's about three inches across. We're sinking."

Decoy gunned the engine, and the water sluiced to the back, the bow now out of the water, along with the hole.

Jesus. So much for taking our time.

Decoy kept us headed upriver while the four of us

bailed out the water. Once it was fairly empty, Decoy swung the boat back around, losing speed and dipping the hole in the water again.

He picked up just enough speed to keep the hole out, shouting, "What do you want to do?"

As I bailed, I asked, "You guys think you can hit the final man on the run?"

Both Retro and Blood grinned. "Piece of cake."

I said, "Don't shoot below the gunwale." I turned to Decoy. "Take 'em on the right side."

We closed the distance in a blur, racing through the water. Through my NODs I could see the lone terrorist shifting back and forth, wondering what we were up to. I knew he could only hear the engine at this stage, our boat a dark blob closing the distance.

Just before we pulled abreast, Decoy swerved, closing the gap between the boats, now bringing to mind a medieval jousting tournament. Only this asshole with a gun could cause damage with blind luck.

Man, I'd rather stick with the naval battle. With some damn cannons at a distance.

We drew parallel, and as if on cue all four of us began tracking, our night vision, weapons, and skill giving us an unbeatable edge. The terrorist got off one round, shooting blindly into the night, the recoil from the handgun throwing his aim off as his body was punctured multiple times. I saw his head snap back from a round that wasn't mine, then drop with the peculiar rag-doll effect of the dead I'd seen many times before. I knew he was no longer a threat.

In a flash, we were beyond him and racing away. Retro and Blood did a fist bump, not so much because of the killing, I knew, but because they'd lived through the threat. They'd made a choice few others on earth would have made, one that had absolute consequences, and they'd succeeded.

That, and because this one had been easy. Although you never knew when death would call, easy or not. No action's success was a given, and we'd all danced on the razor one more time. Definitely worth a fist bump.

Decoy turned the boat around, bringing in another load of water. I started bailing again.

Decoy gunned the engine again and said, "What now? We can't pull up next to it without sinking."

I thought for a moment, then said, "Who wants to get wet? We're going to have to boat-cast."

Retro pointed at Blood. "He's the Marine. Make him go."

I smiled and handed Retro the can I was using to bail. "Then you get to keep this afloat. Decoy, left side this time."

He went as slow as he could while still keeping the hole out of the water, which was still pretty damn fast. The engine screamed, the jury-rigged propeller churning water and leaving a wake behind like he intended to start pulling an inner tube full of kids. A homemade speedboat not designed for the work we had placed upon it.

We closed the gap with Retro pulling cover, the boat leaning dangerously as Blood and I lay on the edge of the gunwale, upsetting its balance. When I saw the bow of the target appear I pointed at Blood, who crossed his arms and rolled off the side, hitting the water on his back.

I followed immediately, the speed greater than I anticipated. I skipped for a second, then sank in the fetid river. I began to swim to the boat, one hand above the surface holding my Glock.

Blood reached the stern, treading water, his own weapon out. I went to the bow. I signaled *one, two, three,* and we both rose up, pulling ourselves above the gunwale and putting our barrels inside the boat.

It was clear, both terrorists visible and leaking blood from multiple holes. The only thing moving was the carpet.

So he's alive.

25

Chip Dekkard heard the name of the company and felt the blood drain from his face. He prayed nobody noticed, glad to see the rest of the members of the Oversight Council focused on Kurt Hale.

"We dug pretty hard, and we can't find any reason why the IRGC would be interested in Cailleach Laboratories. Most all of their research is for benign things, like acne. There's nothing dangerous that we could find, but there's no other reason for kidnapping the boy. Once we got him evacuated and stable, he said he had no idea why he'd been taken. The family had no money to speak of, but they made him call his father and set up a meeting. It has to be something at Cailleach."

Jesus. They're after the virus.

He heard President Warren say, "What about the father? The scientist? What's his story?"

Kurt said, "He does have a pretty extensive résumé working with infectious diseases, most notably H5N1 for the government of Thailand, but since he's gone into the private sector he's mainly worked on over-the-counter remedies for the common cold. A waste of talent, but that's what he does."

I need to tell them. Let them know what the Iranians are after. And yet he waited, not wanting to cross that Rubicon. As the conversation continued, he began to rationalize why he shouldn't.

They haven't made the connection to my conglomerate. It's too deeply buried, and the virus has been destroyed. The Iranian will get nothing, and no good will come out of laying myself bare. There are stockholders to consider. Ordinary people who will lose if I bring this up to the president of the United States. I have a greater responsibility.

He heard his name a second time, as if from a dream, and realized it was the president.

"Chip? You with us here?"

"Sorry, sir. What was the question?"

"You know anything about this Cailleach Laboratories? It's in your neck of the woods."

He paused, giving the impression he was cataloging what he knew. In reality, he was fighting a war inside his soul. The battle raged, and one side eventually won.

"No, sir. It's not one I'm familiar with, but there are literally thousands of international pharmaceutical companies."

The secretary of defense said, "Why don't we just call the guy? Set it up without Taskforce fingerprints and find out what's going on? If his son was kidnapped, finding out he's safe should get the doctor to immediately quit whatever he's doing. No more leverage."

Kurt said, "Of course, that was our first priority, but the doctor doesn't answer his phone. It goes straight to voice mail, and it was the only number the boy knew. We have the numbers for Cailleach, but I didn't want to unilaterally call without talking to the council first. I do agree with the thought, though. My recommendation is to simply alert the authorities in Singapore. Have them go get the doctor, let him know his son is safe, and give him protection until we can sort this out."

Jonathan Billings, the secretary of state, said, "You mean including the Iranian connection? How are we going to do that without getting into a huge diplomatic row? The Thais will eat us alive. It'll expose Taskforce operations."

Kurt said, "No, no, definitely leave out the Iranians. We can craft a simple kidnapping story. Something criminal. The boy doesn't know they're Iranian. He doesn't have any idea why this all happened. We can keep a break between what transpired in Thailand and what we tell Singapore."

The director of the CIA spoke up, enthused. "We've got a very good relationship with our Singapore liaison service, and they're pretty damn good on counterterrorism. They'll play ball and won't ask too many questions.

The SECDEF said, "Speaking of what transpired in Thailand, what did the team do with the two dead terrorists?"

Kurt said, "Rolled them up in the carpet and dumped them in the river. Pike said the Iranians had put a little thought into disposing of the boy, and the team simply used their method. Pike's convinced they'll rot before anyone finds them. Maybe a finger bone a few years from now, but nothing will surface any time soon."

Chip Dekkard winced at his straightforward delivery, a subtle reminder of the stakes involved.

"What about the other Iranians?" the SECDEF asked. "The general?"

"Well, what we know from the boy is that three are unaccounted for. We have no evidence that Malik left Thailand, but I'm convinced he's in Singapore with the two other unknowns, traveling under a different passport."

President Warren said, "Okay, let's get on the Singapore authorities. Get that in motion now. Run it through official channels. State and CIA have the lead. Work it through the ambassador and the station."

Chip thought, *Need to get word out fast. Make sure the traces of the research are completely cleaned up before the authorities get involved.*

President Warren said, "What about the team?"

Kurt said, "We need to get them out of Thailand immediately, along with the boy. He needs to be isolated until we can figure out how to mitigate any damage. I can do that with internal Taskforce assets if you give the word."

"You mean bring them home?"

"Well, yes for the boy. Get him in a comfortable hotel, treat him like a king, have him talk to his father once we get things sorted out."

"And the team?"

"Sir, we still have a Quds Force general running around trying to do something bad. We don't know what that is. We might find out from the doctor once the Singaporeans have him safe, but we should pursue this from both ends."

"Which means what?"

"Send Pike to Singapore. Let him do what he was already doing. I've got the follow-on team prepped for Thailand, so it'll be two or three days until we can integrate a long-term cover for operations in Singapore, but there's little threat from Pike poking around for a few days to prep the battlefield."

Secretary Billings snorted. "'Prep the battlefield' is right. Every time that guy gets involved people start dying."

Kurt locked eyes with him. "*Terrorists* start dying, and you'd do well to remember the difference. There really *are* monsters in the world no matter how hard we try to pretend there aren't. Pike doesn't make them up, but he *does* hunt them down. And yes, he kills them if he's forced to. Right now there's a boy in Thailand who's damn glad of it, even if you aren't."

26

Dr. Nakarat felt the sweat beading under his arms and knew he looked guilty as sin. Knew the man behind the counter was going to arrest him, but it was too late to turn back now. He'd already badged in through the anteroom door, then signed a hard-copy roster with his name and reason for entering.

He'd spent all day on Monday brewing up a bunch of false cocktails, trying mightily to create a problem that only something from the patent reefer might fix. Eventually, he'd found an excuse, but it was so weak anyone with any scientific background at all would question its validity. Nakarat prayed the man behind the counter had no such skill.

The guard barely glanced at the reason given, instead focusing all of his attention on Dr. Nakarat's badges, ensuring they were not forgeries. After scanning a hologram through a black light, he instructed Nakarat to place both thumbs on a blank screen to his front. The image came back positive, and the guard was satisfied.

"Fifteen minutes. No more."

The guard punched a button, and the reefer door opened, exposing a large vault maybe thirty feet deep, with row after row of small drawers, each with a complex scientific label.

Dr. Nakarat entered, not sure what he was looking for. He'd been inside the reefer only a few times, and it was always as a tag-along, following someone else. Someone who knew where he was going. He stared at the nearest row of drawers, feeling again like a grad student trying to decipher a test question he hadn't studied for. He turned and saw the guard staring at him, a question on his face.

He hurried deeper into the vault, acting like he had a destination in mind. He began running his fingers down a row as if he were searching a library shelf and noticed the drawers were color coded. He recognized many of the labels and realized he was in the dermatology section.

Where would they hide it? Where would I put it if I were going to hide it? Would I use the sections to camouflage it, or would I use the space, regardless of what section it was in?

He decided it would be a little bit of both. They'd want it out of sight from casual discovery, but also in a section that had little habitual traffic. Which meant something old. Something no longer hot in the research hierarchy.

Having a healthy knowledge of the goings-on of the lab, he knew that Cailleach's current focus was dermatology, or, more precisely, acne, so he immediately dismissed that entire section.

He scooted to the back and began searching each section on the lower level, near the floor. He recognized every label as legitimate and wondered if he should just begin opening drawers to see what was inside. He glanced at his watch and felt the panic rise.

He was killing his son. His hands began to tremble at the futility of it all. There were over five hundred drawers, and he didn't even know if there *was* a sample to begin with.

He reached a section with labels marking a failed attempt at a new form of eyedrop. Dr. Nakarat remembered it well because they'd dumped an enormous amount of money into the research but just couldn't get rid of some nasty side effects. In the end, they'd chalked it up as a loss and kept the patent samples just in case something in the future would bring them value.

The drawers were all low to the floor, and the section was definitely not one that would be accessed any time soon. He began running his fingers down each one, looking for something that didn't fit. Praying for a miracle. He found it in the second drawer from the bottom. A label that held the number 33 and *As*. The chemical symbol for arsenic.

Poison.

He pulled open the drawer and found a small Pelican box with a biohazard symbol. Now trembling from fear of what was in front of him, he fought to remain calm. He glanced back at the door and saw the guard had lost interest in him.

He opened the box, seeing a single vial inside, stoppered in rubber and padded with foam. No labels on it at all. He reverently slid it out of its foam cocoon, holding it gently in both hands.

He looked at his watch and saw his fifteen minutes were up. Carefully, gently, he placed the vial in the small of his back, trapped by the elastic of his underwear. He waddled to the front of the vault, moving stiffly to prevent the vial from shifting.

He passed the guard and thanked him for his time, shuffling to the door, feeling the sweat rolling down his sides.

The guard said, "Hang on."

Nakarat turned, his heart racing, knowing he was caught.

"You have to sign out the sample. You can't just take it."

What sample? Can he see the vial in my underwear?

Then it hit home: He'd forgotten to take out the sample for his concocted experiment. The excuse that gave him the reason to enter in the first place.

He felt light-headed and faint. He wiped his brow and said, "I decided to try something else. While I was looking, a thought came to me about another solution. You just never know when inspiration will strike."

The guard said, "Yeah, well, you need to sign to that effect. Every time the reefer is opened, I have to account for the actions that occurred. They'll marry up the time of opening with the log. Something's gotta go down in it."

Nakarat walked back to the desk and slowly bent over, dreading that he would feel the vial sliding down his haunch, then down his leg, only to break on the floor.

He made his statement, then placed his hand on the small of his back as he stood upright, grimacing as if he was in pain. He felt nothing. No lump. No vial.

Satisfied, the guard bade him good day. Nakarat stood for a moment, afraid to move. The vial had slipped from the elastic in the small of his back, which meant it was now somewhere in his underwear. Hopefully snagged in the crotch, but possibly about to slide down his leg.

The guard gave him a strange look, and Nakarat came close to blurting out the problem. He caught himself and turned away stiffly, feeling the vial for the first time. Against his rump. He took a small step forward and sensed it shift lower. Another step, and he felt it caress the back of his thigh, held precariously by the fabric of his pants. The door was a mere three steps away.

Three paces. Three paces of slippage. This is insane.

He stared at the portal of freedom for an eternity, his conscious mind unwilling to cause his muscles to trigger potential disaster. From somewhere far away, he heard the guard ask if he was all right. He needed to move. He forced his legs to function, walking like a marionette. One. Two. Three.

He turned the corner and clamped his hands on his calf, trapping the vial before it could travel farther. He slid it down, cupped it in his hands, and walked as fast as he dared back to his office. He closed the door and gingerly set the vial down. He created his own padded case using a box of gauze and locked the makeshift ensemble in his lower desk drawer, next to the two samples of the vaccine he'd already taken from his laboratory. Then he collapsed into his chair.

He was breathing in a rapid pant, his eyes closed, wiping the clammy sweat from his neck, when his intercom buzzed.

"Dr. Nakarat? Could you come downstairs to the front office? There are a couple of policemen who need a word with you."

MALIK SCOOTED HIS chair back into the shade of the canopy, pushing away the plate of "Persian" food. The restaurant claimed to be authentic, but the Indian doing the cooking could have used a few hometown lessons.

All in all, he was pleased with the progression of the mission. He'd put Sanjar and Roshan on the doctor his first day back at work following the meeting. When he'd left the lab and traveled in a beeline to the Marina Bay Sands, Malik was convinced he was in the pocket and would do nothing stupid.

Thailand was coming to closure as well. After getting briefed on the plan for the disposal of the boy from the team, he'd given the go-ahead, and one more loose end was done, he was sure. The body wouldn't be found for weeks, if not months, and there would be no way to tie it to his team. He was looking forward to getting a complete report later today, at the prearranged contact time.

The only glitch in the entire operation was from his own hierarchy. The IRGC had demanded the vaccine before he could proceed, something he obviously couldn't provide. He'd assured them it was on the way and had set things in motion anyway.

He held no illusions about what he was doing but knew that his choice was the right path. If you wanted to take on the superpowers, you needed to be willing to risk it all. He was now convinced the mullahs were defeatist sheep, afraid to step into the arena. Afraid to risk what was necessary. He knew the West would be brought to its knees long before the virus struck Iran. By then, they'd be able to use the Great Satan's own research to overcome any pandemic in Iran. He didn't have a vaccine now, but he would before it was needed.

Let it destroy America first. By the time she is a smoldering ember, she will have figured out how to stop the onslaught. And give us the solution for free, as a gesture of humanity.

The IRGC, of course, didn't see it that way. He'd had to think about how to keep them at bay until the mission was done.

The groundwork in place and with nothing else to do, he was burnishing his cover on the off chance he would need it as an alibi. Exploring Little India, he'd found an Arabic section, with the streets named after Middle East capitals, like Baghdad and Muscat. Sprinkled throughout were various Persian-carpet stores, along with shops selling other textiles he could plausibly claim, such as scarves, drapes, and raw fabric.

He plied them all and had even managed to get further contacts for two who had shown interest in his "business." Something that would go a long way to backing up his story, should he ever be pushed.

He'd eventually tired of the charade and had stopped for lunch within view of the great Sultan Mosque, toying with the idea of attending midday prayers. When the call came through the loudspeakers of the mosque, he pushed his plate away, waving at the waiter to bring his bill.

He'd decided that consideration of prayer was good enough, but the guilt forced him to leave. He couldn't listen to the rhythmic chanting while sitting in a restaurant drinking tea. He paid his bill and began walking back the way he'd come, away from the mosque and toward the Bugis MRT stop.

Moving south on North Bridge Road, he rounded the corner to a large hospital and felt his phone vibrate. He snatched it out of his pocket, saw it was the doctor's number, and smiled. The mission was going as smoothly as he could have wanted.

"Hello, Dr. Nakarat. You called quicker than I thought you would. I guess getting my material wasn't as hard as you predicted."

What he heard next came out in a jumble, and he was sure he'd misunderstood.

"I don't have it! The police showed up at the lab. They were looking for me. I didn't call them, I swear! I don't know what they wanted."

"Slow down. What happened?"

"I don't know. I went to the patent reefer and found

the virus. When I got back to my office the secretary on the first floor told me some police were there to see me. I swear to God I didn't call anyone!"

All Malik heard was that he'd found the virus. The fact that the doctor was calling meant he wasn't in police custody. Malik wasn't even upset at the lack of operational security on the phone.

"So you have the material now? What did the police say when you met them? How did you get away?"

"I didn't meet them! I went down a back stairwell and fled!"

"With the material?"

"No, it's in my office. I swear I didn't call anyone. Please don't hurt my son."

"In your office? With the police?"

"I don't know. . . . I ran out of there. . . . I'm not sure what they wanted. Maybe there was an alarm on the virus case or something."

"An alarm that triggered someone to come from the outside in? Instead of the internal security already in place? No. That's not it. It's a coincidence. You need to return to your office and obtain the virus. Do you understand?"

"I can't! They'll just capture me! Please! I tried. . . . I tried. . . ."

Malik heard the doctor break down, with nothing but sobbing coming from the phone.

He said, "Doctor, listen," and waited for the weeping to fade. When it did, he continued. "Wait until late tonight; then go back to your office. Get the material and call me."

His voice hitching, Nakarat said, "But I'll have to go through a security gate. The guard will stop me."

"Maybe he will and maybe he won't. We won't know until you try. Let me clear things up for you, because it's really quite simple. One, you do nothing, in which case your son dies. Two, you attempt to get the material and get arrested, in which case your son dies. Three, you get the material and call me. In this case your son lives. This is the only option favorable to you. Understand?"

After a moment of breathing hitches, Malik heard, "Yes, yes. I understand."

27

"I could climb to it. Get in from underneath the Sky-Park. Then I could just access his floor from the service stairwell."

Looking at the map of the Marina Bay Sands hotel, that was possibly the dumbest idea anyone could have ever come up with. Not to mention I was completely surprised at who had broached it.

"Jennifer, please. It's almost sixty stories in the air. You'll have to work your way under the SkyPark platform. It's not like a straight rappel. I know you don't want to give up the lead you found, but let's not do something stupid."

Before we'd left Thailand, we'd done a pretty thorough dig into the general, trying to get a handle, and had initially come up empty. Everything we had on him under the name Malik died in Thailand. No credit card usage, passport, or anything else in Singapore. We'd used digital reach-back with the analysts in the rear to build a thorough targeting matrix and had come up blank. He'd cleaned his tracks completely, and we were having no luck with any historical patterns.

Jennifer had asked the hackers to forward his room bill from the hotel in Bangkok. They'd initially refused, saying it was scrubbed and clean. No information we didn't already have. I'd ordered it anyway, even though I thought they were right.

While the rest of the team went back to the targeting matrix, trying to find some angle we had missed, Jennifer stared at the bill. She knew all we needed was one little bit of digital fingerprint to work with, and I'll be damned if she didn't find it.

"Have you cracked the hotel itself, looked at the initial reservation?"

Via our "company VPN" the analyst said, "No. We got that from the credit card statement. Takes too long to get into the hotel and find his reservation. Too risky, and there won't be anything we don't already have."

I could tell he was miffed at someone questioning his job but I also knew nobody was perfect. I let it run.

Jennifer said, "Even with the confirmation code? It's on this bill. Should be easy. I want to see the initial reservation."

The analyst started to protest, and I said, "Just do it. Can't hurt."

Thirty minutes later, while the rest of us were spinning our wheels, Jennifer turned away from the reservation on her screen and said, "Run this number through."

The analyst, interrupted from talking to the team, said, "Why? What now? You're slowing down progress."

"It's some sort of frequent flyer/hotel bonus points number. See where else it's been used."

It turned out to be registered to some bogus Iranian carpet manufacturer and was now tied to a different reservation, under a different name. At the Marina Bay Sands hotel in Singapore. I couldn't help but feel a little smug for no reason whatsoever. After all, it was Jennifer who had found it, and yet she was part of *my* team.

I was also astounded at the utter stupidity of the slip, but that's the way with this type of work. It was a stark reminder of how easy it was to be compromised. You never knew what was going to get you. How many digital scraps were tied to the Taskforce? From Thailand? From other missions? Something to worry about later. For now, we had a mission to accomplish, and the Iranians had given us the means to do so.

Lucky for us, the IRGC likes collecting bonus points on their secret missions.

Getting the deployment order from the Oversight Council, we'd immediately packed our bags and headed to Singapore, leaving Buckshot to play escort for Kavi Nakarat, getting him out of Thailand via other Taskforce assets. The police in Singapore had not been able to locate the father, Dr. Sakchai Nakarat, so we were still in play. The intent of our mission was the same as before: Get a handle on the Iranian general and pass off his pattern of life to the inbound team.

In my mind, the easiest way to do that was to get a block of rooms at the Marina Bay Sands. Unfortunately, it was way, *way* over our authorized per diem. I knew Taskforce finance would bust a gasket when they got the bill, but hey, sometimes you sleep in a swamp, sometimes you get a five-star resort.

The Sands was a technological marvel that encompassed a high-end mall, casino, and convention center. The hotel was three separate fifty-five-story towers capped with what looked like a cruise ship on top, called the Sky-Park. The tower construction was what was causing our current dilemma.

We were in tower one, and our target room was in tower three. Ordinarily, this would have been no issue whatsoever, but there was also some rock star celebrity delegation in tower three, and its elevators were now manned with uniformed security to keep out the paparazzi. You had to have a key that registered in that tower to go up, as the three towers weren't connected horizontally. Only on the top and bottom.

We'd learned quickly that, due to the size of the hotel, establishing a base of surveillance to catch the general leaving was impossible. There were simply too many exits. We needed early warning, a trigger that he was on the move and a direction. Which meant we needed access to his room.

Initially, we were just going to forge a key-card for access to the elevator, using a special device that would spoof the door locks—which was how we would access his room—but the guards ran the key-card through a wireless reader. Connected to the reception desk, the reader showed who you were, when you checked in, your room number, and when you were scheduled to check out.

The forged key only tricked the door. It couldn't access the database. Basically, we'd have to spoof quite a few different systems to trick the guards, and we didn't have time to test all of the intricacies. Too many single points of failure, which led us to our current predicament and Jennifer's idea of climbing from the top of the building down.

Decoy said, "Pike's right. There's no way you're going to free-climb underneath forty meters of outcropping hanging two hundred meters above the ground. This isn't Yellowstone, with a bunch of pitons already seated."

Jennifer said, "Wait. I'm not talking about going underneath the observation deck. Look at the blueprint. I can rappel right over the side near tower three and only have to go under about ten meters, on a curve. From there, I can get into the service stairwell through the window-cleaning balcony."

I said, "Still the same problem. What are you going to do, rappel down, and then start swinging until you collide underneath with the pylon on top of the tower? No way."

"Kurt said he gave us a complete package, didn't he?"

I didn't like where this was going, knowing she was way ahead on something. "Yeah, so what?"

"Well, it has climbing gear. Right?"

I relaxed. "Yeah, but that still doesn't alter the problem. I'm not dropping you over the side with a rope and harness. Swinging like Tarzan isn't the answer."

"What about the Hollywood rig? And using the PVAC? I could drag myself down."

She said it like "Peevac," an acronym for Personal Vacuum Assisted Climber, a device invented by a bunch of college students on an Air Force challenge. Basically, it was two vacuum-assisted hand attachments connected to a suction generator held on the back. Theirs sounded like a jet engine and had giant hoses going from the back to the hand devices, looking like something out of a bad science fiction movie. We'd laughed about it when one of our R and D guys said we should take a look. We quit laughing when we saw an engineering student go up a ninety-foot wall unassisted. A brick wall, with a rough surface.

We'd taken the design and refined it. The hoses were a third of the size, and it only sounded like a large blender now. As good as it was, it wasn't designed for something two hundred meters in the air.

"Jennifer, you have to test the PVAC on the chosen surface before you use it. It's not designed for unknown construction. We don't even know if it'll hold your weight here."

Blood was looking thoughtful. He tapped the map and said, "Yeah, but if she has the Hollywood rig, we'll be holding the weight. She'll just use the PVAC to pull herself under. It should work for that."

I glared at him, not wanting anyone to encourage the debate. He looked sheepish and said nothing more.

Knuckles, turning from the map, said, "She can get over from the hot-tub area. It's on the opposite side of the infinity pool and built for privacy. We could stage left and right, ensure it's clear, then let her over. One controls the belay, everyone else provides early warning. Pike, this'll work."

Jennifer gave him a look of gratitude while everyone else eyed me to see what I would say. I thought the idea was idiotic, but I was torn because the other members of the team were siding with Jennifer. Treating her like an equal, which was something I wanted. If I said no, they'd always wonder if I was protecting her because I didn't trust her abilities. Meaning they shouldn't either.

She can *climb like a monkey. And we don't have any other way.*

"All right. We have about six hours until nightfall. Jennifer, hit the mall and get a couple of bathing suits for cover. I'll be the belay at the hot tub. Retro, get the guys in DC to give us a readout on his door lock. Get all activity, tied with the time of entry. I want to know when they opened along with how long before they opened again. Marry that up with the maid service so we can exclude false entries. Blood and Decoy, head to the airport and download the kit. You know what we need. Knuckles, you and I will recce the deck to see if this circus stunt has a chance of working. You focus on cameras and foot-traffic avenues of approach. I'll find the launch point."

Jennifer smiled and said, "This will be easy. Trust me."

I shook my head. "'Trust me' is usually what I say when I'm sure something's going to shit."

28

After an hour, Jennifer felt a little bit like a lobster in a pot. The key-card track to the general's room had showed the door had been opened, but nothing since, which meant someone had opened the door and exited, or someone was still inside. They had to assume it was the latter, given the previous entries.

She was beginning to second-guess her great idea of rappelling over the wall. Not only could they not guarantee the room was empty, but the rock star in tower three had chosen tonight to take over the observation deck. Not more than fifty meters away and one level lower, there was an enormous party going on. Five minutes couldn't elapse without some drunk couple passing by to get another fill at the bar or gaze at the infinity pool.

She hadn't thought about it before, ignoring the glam of the Marina Bay Sands hotel, but the infinity pool had turned out to be a magnetic attraction. Just across from the hot tub, through the screen of lounges and foliage, it was an Olympic-sized pool that appeared to fade into the skyline of Singapore two hundred meters in the air. A unique marvel that caused all the invited party guests to come see and take pictures.

It didn't help that she was seated next to two obese gentlemen from Greece. One kept sliding closer to her in an attempt to make accidental contact with her thigh. The man would have disgusted her on an ordinary day, but tonight it was infinitely worse. She couldn't allow any contact whatsoever, because he'd feel the harness attached around her waist.

She waded into the center of the hot tub and turned around to face Pike, sliding her hands over his knees. Showing the slobs that she was taken.

She felt Pike stiffen and inwardly smiled.

She said, "You about ready to go back to the room?"

Meaning, *How long should we wait?*

He slid his hands over hers, raising them off of his knees.

"I'm enjoying this. You mind staying for a little bit longer?"

She pulled up to her waist, leaving the harness in the darkness, resting her elbows on his knees, relishing the discomfort she was giving him. She leaned in.

"I'm enjoying this too. More than you are."

She watched his face contort, trying to read his emotions and seeing only confusion. She broke into a grin, the exhilaration of what she was about to do flowing through her. Along with enjoyment of her ability to twist him up.

It wasn't fair, but she did enjoy it. Enjoyed the safety

of his company. She could act like a woman without any fear of repercussions. And not just from something as minute as rejection. He was her small corral of protection. The one man she could flirt with who would demand nothing in return. The one man she knew would never hurt her. Ever. Her own little fishbowl, partitioning her from the dangers of the real world like a goldfish was from the ocean. Dangers that had found her more than once and left her broken.

She said, "I heard Decoy go into the wall. You didn't have to do that."

He glanced away, embarrassed. "Well, he didn't have to say that. Sorry you heard."

She'd come back from getting him a set of board shorts and a one-piece for herself and had moved toward the bathroom to see how it fit with the harness. When she'd drawn abreast of the door, she'd heard Decoy in the other room of the suite say to someone she couldn't see, "I don't really give a shit if we get in at all. I just want to see that body in a bikini."

She'd bristled, about to burst in and give him a piece of her mind when she'd heard a thump against the wall, then Pike saying, "She's about to risk her life, you fuck. I've lived with the jokes before, but I won't hear them again."

Her hand over the doorknob, she'd waited. She heard some strangled breathing, then a voice she recognized as Blood's say, "Pike. Enough. You're going to choke him out." Having seen Pike work, she knew the scene without needing to enter.

She'd moved back to the bathroom of the suite, but not before hearing Pike say, "No more jokes. Ever."

Afterward Decoy was exceedingly courteous. Along with everyone else on the team. She valued it, even though she knew what Decoy had said was exactly that: a joke. He didn't mean any harm and thought it was funny. It just wasn't funny to her.

She patted Pike's knee and backed up. "Don't be sorry. I know where I stand, and I appreciate it."

The words made him more uncomfortable, if that was possible. "Look, I didn't do that because I think you need help. . . . I . . . he just pissed me off. . . . You do just fine by yourself."

She smiled again, liking the fact that he was embarrassed about stepping in. Liking that he thought she would be angry at him for defending her.

She came forward again and squeezed his hands. "You have your moments, but that wasn't one of them."

He gave her an awkward smile, clearly afraid to open his mouth.

The obese Greeks stood up, crawling out of the hot tub like a couple of crabs and leaving them alone.

He waited until they were out of earshot, then said, "You ready to do this? It's a long way down."

She said, "Yeah. Way to change the subject. He's still in his room, so no chance of leaving any time soon."

His face clouded over. "Come on. You're about to launch out two hundred meters in the air. Sorry about the mission focus."

She smiled again. "Your buttons are *so* easy to push. I was teasing. Yeah, I'm ready. This'll be easy, although I'm glad you're on belay. I didn't want to say it in the room, but I wouldn't do this otherwise."

He said, "I know. Trust me, I know. Might be your mistake. Knuckles has a lot more experience in the Hollywood rig than I do. The Taskforce started using it after I left the first time."

"How hard could it be? I mean, it's just a cable and a descender. If it can hold Arnold Schwarzenegger for a stunt, it'll hold me. All you have to do is give me slack."

He turned and flicked the descender they'd emplaced earlier, the running end of the thin steel cable coiled next to the bushes around the hot tub. It was barely noticeable in the darkness. A small piece of gear that could have been mistaken for window-cleaning equipment.

"This shit is made to be hidden from showing up on-screen. It's not made for operations. Something that allows an actor to hang from a ledge without danger. Not something that allows an operator to perform. I don't like it."

She said, "I trust it. That cable can hold a car. The only thing that will make it fail is if you let it run free. And I know you won't do that. Not if you want to sit in a hot tub with me when I'm not wearing a harness."

She saw the emotions flit across his face and realized

too late the double entendre that had unintentionally escaped. His mouth opened and closed, saying nothing. Before the silence could grow uncomfortable, they were saved by their earpieces chirping.

"Exit from the room. I say again, exit from the room."

She felt the adrenaline rise and said the word he always did, trying for his usual confidence.

"Showtime."

29

Jennifer glanced left and right while Pike prepared the descender.

He said, "Security, give me a readout. We clear?"

"West clear."

"North clear."

"East red. I say again, east red."

Which meant the side with the observation deck and the party. The south side of the SkyPark, where Jennifer was going to descend, faced the South China Sea, so there was little chance anyone would witness her actions from the ground.

Recognizing the voice, Pike said, "Whatcha got, Knuckles?"

"Nothing big. Man and woman doing some heavy petting in the shadows. I can't tell if they're just looking for privacy or going to continue up to the infinity pool."

"We got a couple of seconds?"

"Yeah. Looks that way. Just don't let them see you controlling the descent if they decide to move."

Jennifer was clipping the shoulder harnesses in place

and seating the central plate when Pike said, "You willing to pull a Dar? I don't think I'll have the time to walk you all the way down."

Jennifer knew Pike was referring to Dar Robinson, the stuntman who'd perfected what they called the "Hollywood rig," using it for high-level falls in order to allow a top camera to film the shot without worrying about an airbag being in the scene from the ground. The difference was he would free-fall for upwards of a thousand feet before being slowed, whereas she had planned on a gentle slide down the side of the building. "Pulling a Dar" meant she'd simply jump, falling unassisted to the top edge of the tower, then get braked to a halt. Hopefully.

Pike said, "Or we can wait until Knuckles says it's clear. I'm just afraid of losing our window. The general might return soon. With a Dar we cut our time in half."

She snapped the harness closed and cinched the barrel nut on the carabiner holding the chest plate. *It can't be more than forty feet. Not that far.*

She said, "Yeah. I can do that. Just don't let me go beyond the curve. There's no way I can climb up this cable."

"I won't. I set it for thirty feet. It'll be like a bungee jump."

He helped her out of the hot tub, laughing at the Vibram FiveFingers shoes on her feet.

"What? You want me to do this barefooted?"

He clipped in the cable, ensuring it was seated to the

plate at her front. "No, no. If you're going to pull a circus stunt, might as well look like a clown."

She punched him in the arm for the comment. He ignored her, now all business. He tested the lead of the cable a third time, then proceeded to go over her harness from head to waist, just like a jumpmaster prior to a parachute operation. Satisfied, he glanced over the side and keyed his Bluetooth. "We're ready to execute. Status?"

"West still good."

"North the same."

"Still got the cupid couple in the east, but you're good. They definitely aren't going to focus on anything but body parts."

Jennifer climbed over the railing and stared down into the black night, the ships in the harbor blinking like stars far away. Pike held up the PVAC straps, and she slid her arms through, cinching yet another harness around her shoulders and groin. Last, after seating her hands into the suction devices and checking to ensure the hoses wouldn't snag, she strapped on a large butt pack, swiveling it to her front.

She turned and faced Pike, trying to project confidence but feeling a nagging fear eroding into her like a river into sand. Pike checked the descender one more time, ensuring the cable would feed without snagging and the length was set correctly, then stood up.

He held out his fist for a bump, surprising her. He'd never done that before. She wasn't sure if it was a good sign or an indicator of how little faith he had in this mission. She rapped his knuckles and he said, "I spent so much time on the method of infil I forgot to ask, you have any questions about the Third Eye?"

"Nope. That's the easiest part of this thing."

He leaned over once more, then said, "Well, you're wasting time then."

She nodded, closed her eyes, and rocked forward, then backward, holding the railing and chanting in her mind.

One . . . two . . . three!

She pushed off and immediately felt the sickening drop in her stomach. She accelerated, first feeling still air, then a hurricane force ripping at her ponytail, reminding her of high dives in her youth, the fluttering of the cable sounding like a whip in front of her face. She waited for an eternity, past one high dive in her mind, then two, then three, and knew with sickening certainty the system had failed.

An involuntary scream tried to escape as her eyes snapped open. She allowed a low-pitched growl and snapped her hands on the cable in a desperate attempt to alter her fate. Then she felt a jerk in her groin, and she slowed quickly to zero.

She got her bearings and realized she was staring into the South China Sea; her back was to the wall, and she was swinging toward it.

She rotated around but got only two-thirds of the way before colliding into the wall with her shoulder. She bounced and settled. She did nothing for a second or two, simply hanging and taking deep breaths.

She heard, "Jennifer, you okay? Cable's stopped."

She smiled. He hadn't said *Koko*, which meant he was truly worried.

"Yeah, I'm fine. But I'm *never* doing that again. Rotating now."

She grabbed the cable and pulled herself sideways, using the friction of the Vibram shoes against the wall and swiveling the chest plate until she was head-down, her right leg snaked around the cable.

She heard, "Good to go. Getting back in the hot tub. Call if you need something."

Smartass.

She fired up the PVAC, the blenderlike sound screaming to her in the night. She attached the suction devices to the wall and said, "Slack."

She suddenly dropped three feet, breaking the seal of the PVAC and swinging out away from the wall. Luckily, she was still above the curve. If that happened after the slope began to the tower, she wouldn't be able to reach to use the PVAC.

"Too far. Go about half of that."

"Roger."

She reattached the PVAC and said again, "Slack."

This time she glided gently down the wall, reaching the curve. She began to walk the PVAC down the slope, seeing the tower to her front, repeating the slack call every few seconds.

She reached the railing and pulled herself over. She lay next to the service stairwell for a moment to catch her breath, then released the PVAC harness. She shrugged out of it, followed by the Hollywood rig, attaching both back to the cable.

"I'm in. You can hoist the kit back up."

"Roger all. Good job, Koko."

The call brought another smile. *Need to get him a call sign that sucks.*

She waited until the PVAC and descender harness disappeared from view, then tried the stairwell, finding it locked. Nothing she hadn't expected. She used the forged key-card they'd made earlier, and the door opened. Within minutes, she was outside the general's suite on the fifty-third floor. Just another guest in a bathing suit coming back to the room. She wished she'd remembered to pack a towel to complete the disguise, but so far nobody had appeared in the hallway.

She pulled out a radarscope from her butt pack and placed it on the door. Designed to determine if any threats extended beyond, it picked up minute movements through upwards of twelve inches of masonry, including something as small as the rise and fall of a chest.

The radarscope showed the room empty. Even so, she called Retro before using the key.

"Retro, Koko. About to enter. Any activity?"

"You're clear. Nothing since he left earlier."

She armed herself with a Glock, keeping it close to her chest, and popped the door. She let it swing open, waiting for any reaction. When none came, she swiftly cleared the suite, putting the barrel of the Glock in every crevice.

Satisfied it was truly empty, she reached into the butt pack and retrieved a squeeze bottle not unlike those used in restaurants for ketchup.

She pulled down all four towels from the bathroom and spread them on the bed. Putting on a pair of elbow-length dish gloves, she liberally sprayed each towel with the squeeze bottle, first one side, then the other.

Called the Third Eye by the R and D team, the bottle contained a radioactive isotope that could be tracked once on the skin of the target. The constant with any beacon was that it had to be concealed, using something to mask its location. A shoe, a belt, a hat. Something. This was fine if the target knew he was wearing the beacon. The problem with an unwitting target was that he might not wear the concealment device, instead deciding to put on a different pair of shoes.

The Taskforce had researched forever trying to develop what they called the "Naked Man Tag," a mythical beacon that could be emplaced on a naked man without his knowing, but the closest they'd come was the Third Eye, which was really nothing more than a throwback to the spy dust used by the East German Stasi during the Cold War.

All it did was send an alarm to a device that recognized the isotope, letting someone know the target was in the area. Since they all knew what the general looked like, it would be enough information to position themselves on his line of march for the start of the surveillance.

The difference between the Taskforce isotope and the old Stasi one was theirs would wash off easily, meaning that a shower would render it useless, which was why she was placing it on the towels. Well, that and the Taskforce isotope wouldn't cause cancer like the one the Stasi used. At least that's what the R and D folks said. Pike had told her it wasn't called the Third Eye because of its surveillance applications, but because the target's kids would be born with an eye in the middle of their foreheads after use.

She hoped he was kidding.

She folded the towels, placing them exactly as she'd found them, then turned to leave. Getting to the door, something tickled her brain, and she surveyed the room again.

She didn't know what it was. The room looked like any hotel room. Any expensive five-star room, that is. Bed made with chocolate on the pillow, flowers set up, everything in its place. Then it hit her.

There's no luggage. No clothes, computers, or anything else.

She went to the bathroom and found a toothbrush, used; some shaving gear; and a tube of toothpaste. That was it.

She left swiftly, closing the door and zipping up her butt pack. She called Pike.

"Mission complete. I'm setting the wireless receptors where we discussed, then coming home."

"Any issues?"

"Not with the mission, but something's not right. There was nothing in the room. No signs of life besides a wet toothbrush. No luggage or anything else."

"Maybe he travels light."

She thought about the frequent-flyer number she had found, the convenience now rattling her.

She said, "Maybe he's ahead of us on this thing."

30

D r. Nakarat finished drying off and dressed in the clothes he had purchased the night before. Much fancier garments than he was used to wearing, but the mall attached to the Marina Bay Sands had no thrift shopping.

The store had been right next to a wireless carrier, and he'd toyed with the idea of buying a new phone, using his credit card. In the end, he didn't have the courage. Someone could be watching his credit card usage, and he'd been told to only charge to the room. It wasn't worth the life of his son.

He sat on the bed, watching the time drip by. He thought about getting breakfast, but he had no appetite. In truth, he felt nauseous.

On the counter next to the wide-screen television was a box of gauze. Inside was death. Something he wished he'd never created, but he had, and now it would haunt him forever.

Although he'd been frightened to the point of incapacity, he'd managed to get into his office and back out again with little trouble. The guard manning the front entrance had said nothing at all, clearly unaware of the police visit earlier.

He'd grabbed the virus and vaccine samples and come straight back to the Marina Bay Sands, only to spend the rest of the night staring at the ceiling of his darkened room.

He knew the man planned nothing good with the virus. This wasn't industrial espionage. It was something more, and that fact tore at him. Made him question his choices. His oath.

First, do no harm.

At four in the morning, he'd come close to calling the authorities. Telling them everything and, he knew, killing his son. The pressure had been incredible. He'd sat in the darkness and wept, all alone with his thoughts.

In the end, he'd left the phone on the hook. He'd lost his wife to cancer a year and a half ago, the wound still open and as raw as if it had been raked with a wire brush. He couldn't lose his son, especially at his own hand.

He opened the instructions he'd been given, making sure he had memorized everything exactly. He felt certain he'd be watched and didn't want to give any indication he was doing anything other than what he'd been told. A simple mistake could be catastrophic if the man thought he was trying to trick him. For this reason he'd discarded the idea of passing a vial of water. He was sure the kidnapper would have some method of testing what he brought. Would be able to see through any ruse.

His watch alarm chirped, sending a shock down his spine. It was time.

He slowly stood. Moving robotically, he placed the box of gauze in a small shopping bag. He put the untested vaccine sample in his shirt pocket, then wrapped the tested, failed vaccine into a rag and placed it in the shopping bag. The man had said he didn't want the untested vaccine, but he was bringing it just in case. He'd have given the man his vital organs if he so asked.

He took one last look around the room and exited.

My "IPOD" VIBRATED and I looked at the screen: Receptor one had been triggered, meaning the target had left the room.

I made sure everyone had received the alert and that their equipment was functioning, then simply waited on a direction, staring at the screen for the next trigger.

The false iPod was nothing more than a wireless device that received the signal from the receptors Jennifer had placed on all available exits, telling us where to focus our efforts. It looked like a fifth-generation Nano and would even play music—albeit just enough to "prove" what it was.

The receptors were the key. Basically minuscule Geiger counters, they received the gamma projection from the isotope the general had toweled on his body, then sent a signal, alerting us that he had passed. In addition to the ones Jennifer had placed about the hotel, we each had a larger one with more functionality that also showed signal strength. It wasn't perfect, but it would give us a little edge on how far or close the target was—which would only be necessary in a large crowd, since we could all ID the general by sight.

We were staged in a cloverleaf and not positioned to cover any specific exit, but instead were able to react to multiple points. The formation did little to start initial surveillance, since we were spread way too thin, but did allow us to collapse together once we knew which way he was headed. We'd have been dead in the water without the Third Eye tag, and I didn't like trusting it. Technology had let me down too many times.

I felt the iPod vibrate again and saw that receptor five had been triggered.

He's coming through the lobby. Which wasn't much help. All that did was eliminate the street exits from tower three. The lobby was huge, and from there, he could travel to the mall, casino, or any of the other street exits.

I checked my smartphone's moving map and saw Knuckles's position. "Knuckles, Pike."

"Yeah, I got it. I'm on him. Moving now."

"All others, collapse. Knuckles has the lead. Let him trigger, then someone pick up the eye."

It might have sounded strange asking "someone" to identify and start the surveillance, but surveillance operations were fluid. The worst thing a surveillance chief could do was try to order everyone around like soldiers on a map. I needed them to be thinking and executing on their own, not waiting on my call. I would never have the correct situational awareness and had seen plenty of surveillance operations go to hell because the SC thought he knew better.

The first signs of trouble came quickly.

"Pike, Knuckles. I've got a major signal but no rabbit."

"You mean he got by you before you could PID?"

"No, I mean he's standing within fifteen feet of me. The iPod is going crazy, but he's not here."

What? I ran through the possibilities and came up with the only one that made sense.

"Look for an Arab. We have two other unknowns here from Thailand. That'll be the key."

"Signal's now fading. I lost him."

Shit.

Decoy came on. "I got a weak signal. He's on the escalator headed down."

Down meant the promenade underneath the hotel. A moving mass of people all headed to the casino, mall, or metro. A surveillance nightmare. We needed to get a handle quickly, or we'd lose it completely. I checked the map on my phone.

"Koko and Retro, take the tunnel leading up to the mall. Blood and Knuckles, get down to the metro. See if you can pick him up. I'm right behind you. Decoy, start fishing; see if you can get a stronger signal. Everyone ignore the casino. I doubt that's a destination."

I started moving fast, getting to the escalator headed down underneath the street. I reached the promenade and was met by a mass of people all swirling around with different destinations.

He's gone. We'll never get him in here.

Decoy said, "Got a signal. It's weak as shit."

"Where? What direction?"

"Metro. It's past the mall tunnel."

I started jogging, hoping to jump ahead of the target. "Koko and Retro, collapse on the metro."

Knuckles came on. "I got a signal now too. I'm in the hallway leading to the Bayfront metro stop."

"What do you see? Have you identified?"

"No way. There are hundreds of people here."

"Everyone get to the Bayfront stop. Get an ID. Send any pictures of possibles; I don't care how tenuous."

The Bayfront was on the yellow line, which meant a north-and-south route. North took him to the green line, South to the red.

Either way, we were about to be split.

31

Dr. Nakarat boarded the train and took a seat, glancing nervously at the people around him. All he saw were Asians. Packed around him like sardines, which did nothing but make him more suspicious.

One stop later, he exited and moved to the red line headed north. He nervously paced in a three-foot circle. When the train arrived, he watched everyone getting off, convinced some magical technology had allowed the man to meet him here.

When no one approached, he boarded and found one of the last seats available. He rode through the Raffles Place and City Hall stops, staring at everyone who entered. Nobody paid him the least bit of attention. His heart started to race when the train moved again.

The next stop was his.

JENNIFER CALLED AFTER the City Hall stop and said she still had a signal but no identity. Which, given the number of people inside the train, wasn't that big of a problem. I was two cars back, and they were so full I was beginning to wonder if Singapore had a load limit. It reminded me of an old Army saying: How many Rangers can you get on a deuce and a half? Answer: One more.

We'd lost Decoy and Blood to the northbound line, but they would be only one train behind. I had Knuckles with me, and Retro was with Jennifer in the car with the signal, so we should have been able to sort it out once we were out of the crowds. The only thing that was concerning me now was that nobody had spotted anyone remotely Arabic. Well, Decoy had sent a picture of an Arab woman, but that was it.

I started second-guessing the entire operation. Maybe the frequent-flyer number was confused, or the hotel room was nothing but a false plant, or the whole thing was a setup to get us going the wrong way. You name it, they were all running through my mind. But at the end of the day there were too many things that lined up.

It was an Iranian carpet company. With the same number as in Thailand. Keep pulling the thread. Something's here.

I looked at the metro map and took a breath. The next stop, Dhoby Ghaut, was a transfer for three different lines. Disaster.

"Everyone listen up. I think he's getting off at Dhoby. We'll have about fifteen seconds to identify where he's going or we'll lose him forever. Forget the ID. Focus on the signal. Keep it in play."

I got a roger, and the train pulled into the station.

*   *   *

Dr. Nakarat exited the train at a slow pace, unconsciously not wanting to begin the final walk to the meeting. He was jostled harshly by the torrent of people moving through the station, all intent on getting on or getting off. He got his bearings and headed to the Penang Road exit, feeling like he was walking to his doom. He broke into the sunlight and saw the signs for the park across the street, just as it had been described.

He crossed Penang and walked up a stairwell that zigzagged back and forth, traversing the hill. He didn't notice the young man sitting on the bench staring at him intently.

He reached the top of the stairs, momentarily confused. There were more roads than he'd expected, along with a hotel to his right he hadn't been told about. He saw a sign for the museum and followed it, walking steadily uphill, the heat sparking the first beads of sweat.

I waited on the call from Retro or Jennifer, pissing everyone off in the car because I didn't exit when the door opened. I stood like a statue, just inside the entrance, letting the mass of people flow around me.

If they don't call, it's not this stop. Everyone else on this train can kiss my ass.

"Dropped signal. I say again, dropped signal. He's off."

I immediately exited, now in a rush that confused the people around me. Knuckles followed, grinning his meth-addict smile and scaring the hell out of the smaller Asians exiting.

I said, "Koko, Retro, head to the connector lines. Knuckles and I will take street level."

We started moving at a slight jog, and my receptor pinged for the first time. I glanced at Knuckles, and he nodded. He was getting it too.

We kept the pace, and the signal got stronger and stronger. We broke out into the sunlight and I paused, trying to figure out which direction the target was going.

Knuckles immediately went left and I went right, paralleling Penang Road. My iPod display continued to get weaker and weaker.

"Knuckles, it's not this way. What do you have?"

"I've lost signal. He didn't come this direction."

Which meant he'd crossed the street.

I saw the last pedestrians jogging toward the station from across Penang, men in suits and women skipping, ungainly in heels, and knew I'd miss the light. I sprinted anyway, meeting Knuckles just as the cars started moving, blocking our way.

"Damn it! We're going to lose him here."

Without being told, Knuckles alerted the rest of the team. "Everyone, target entered Fort Canning Park off of the Dhoby Ghaut stop. Lost contact. I say again, lost contact."

Which would cause a rehearsed battle drill to be performed, with all teams starting a search pattern to pick up the signal again, focused on the park.

I pulled up a map of Fort Canning on my phone, the time slipping away. It was fairly large, crisscrossed with multiple roads that could be used for pickup, along with a hotel and some bunker from the loss of Singapore to the Japanese in World War II, now a museum.

I was formulating a plan of attack when Knuckles elbowed me.

"Pike. Take a look directly across the street. There's an Arabic-looking guy on a bench, and he's swiveling his head around like crazy. Looking for something."

I focused on him and saw Knuckles was right. He was all by himself at the base of a set of stairs, and he wasn't acting relaxed at all, like someone who'd decided to take a seat for a break. He was twitching around like he was on crack.

I ran through the possibilities, spinning what I knew around in my mind, looking for connections. Like staring at the spot on a 3D poster, the truth sprang out of the mishmash.

"Jesus. He's one of the Iranians, and he's pulling countersurveillance. Contact the Taskforce. Get a picture of Dr. Sakchai Nakarat. We're following the wrong guy."

32

Inside the bunker at Fort Canning Park, once the final British holdout in the fight for Singapore and now known as the Battle Box museum, Malik wandered about, looking at the various exhibits. It reminded him of the bunkers he had fought in during the Iran-Iraq War. He couldn't help but be intrigued by the displays, a soldier again, and like all soldiers, he was interested in a way that others would never understand.

The rooms were frozen in time, with some walls even bearing the Morse code marks of the Japanese from after they had assumed control. He entered a chamber full of mannequins, incredibly lifelike in the gloom, peering at maps in an effort to stave off the inevitable defeat. He found it prophetic. No amount of military might would halt what he was about to unleash. Just like the British depicted in this room, the West would not be able to stop the onslaught.

He glanced at his watch and saw the next tour was a mere five minutes away. The tour with the doctor in tow.

He meandered through the maze of various displays,

having seen them all before on his reconnaissance. Eventually, he reached a hallway that was not illuminated, with the arrows painted on the floor directing him to continue on past. He did not.

He walked down the length of the hallway until it dead-ended into a ladder. It was the escape corridor for the bunker. Created in World War II to allow the command to flee if the enemy breached the entrance, it would serve the same purpose here.

Not a part of the tour, and having nothing to see besides a rusty iron ladder at the end of a musty hallway, it would allow the final layer of security for the meeting. If the doctor had somehow planned a trap to ambush him, if his men alerted him in any way, he would climb the ladder from deep underground and escape—away from the known entrances and exits of the museum out front.

Prudent always, he would have taken the same precautions no matter what, but now it seemed especially vital. The original police contact with Dr. Nakarat would have been bad enough, but it was compounded by the fact that he couldn't reach his team in Thailand.

He wasn't overly concerned yet, since this very thing had happened a few times in the past, but it did cause him to raise his caution level. At the least, he would have liked concrete knowledge about the fate of the doctor's son. Not knowing left a gap that didn't sit well. Intelligence that could be used against him in the coming meeting.

He looked above him to the hatch leading outside,

making sure he could still see daylight around the rim, meaning someone hadn't replaced the lock he'd cut.

Satisfied, he was turning back into the museum when he got the call from Sanjar saying the doctor had exited the metro and was now heading into the park.

As Knuckles and I were speed-walking across the street, both of us studiously ignoring the man on the bench, Decoy called.

"We're in the park. West side near the reservoir. Need a lock-on."

We reached the far side of the street and went east down the sidewalk, away from the man on the bench. I'd already given the team an update on what I thought was happening, along with a photo of the suspected counter-surveillance. Now we waited on the photo of the rabbit.

I said, "He entered from the north, right off of Pen-ang. He's not too far ahead of us. Close on the Fort Canning Hotel."

Continuing east, we reached a tunnel that looked like it led into the park, underneath another road. I relayed the location to Koko and Retro, who were seconds be-hind us, and started sorting out the search to prevent duplication of effort.

"We'll take the buildings to the east of the museum. Looks like some sort of shopping area. Decoy's got the hotel. You guys check out the tourist shop at the apex of the traffic circle."

Moving steadily uphill, I began to sweat profusely in the heat and wondered if just that alone would wash the isotope off our target. The R and D guys said ordinary perspiration would have no effect, but I wasn't sure if they'd tested it in the humidity that was Singapore. Ordinary perspiration here was like a shower.

We reached a sign cut from stone that read FORT CANNING CENTRE and saw a long, two-story building full of shops and restaurants fronted by a tree-lined stone promenade full of Western tourists. Some type of photo shoot was occurring, with multiple women dressed in various historical costumes roaming the grounds, followed by guys with lights and cameras.

We had begun slowly walking through the complex trolling for a signal, just two more tourists out on a stroll, when Jennifer called.

"Pike, I've got a hit."

DR. NAKARAT CONTINUED up the path and reached a roundabout. Ahead of him was a small one-story building, an arrow pointing the way to the ticket counter for the museum. His instructions were not to enter alone, but to wait for the tour that left every thirty minutes. He bought a ticket and joined a group he presumed was also taking the tour, a mix of Asians and Westerners. Within minutes, a guide rounded them up and they were walking down a tree-lined path to the entrance of the bunker.

He felt light-headed, clutching his shopping bag with both hands as he stumbled along, last in line.

They passed through the entrance, and the guide began talking. Dr. Nakarat heard not a word, focusing on when he was supposed to break from the group.

They went through exhibit after exhibit, all full of startlingly lifelike mannequins dressed as World War II British soldiers. He counted the rooms as they left, waiting on number eight. Eventually, he lost track of where he was, the bunker a maze under the ground.

When they reentered the conference room depicting the surrender, he began to worry. Was he supposed to count this as a room again, or was it just a pass-through?

He felt claustrophobic, panting in the dank air, the glaring bulbs hanging overhead leaving sinister shadows everywhere. A lady next to him asked if he was okay. He took a deep breath, remembering the words about his interactions with others. Remembering what was at stake if he failed. He told her he was fine and gave what he hoped was a sincere smile.

The tour guide pointed down a dark hallway and described the escape way, snapping him out of his funk.

That's the meeting location. But the tour guide isn't supposed to take anyone down there.

He began to panic, believing he would be blamed. He backed up, preparing to follow the arrows on the floor to the exit. Preparing to run.

The tour guide waved them forward, and the mass began walking toward an area with multiple televisions replaying history on an endless loop, away from the escape corridor.

He waited until the entire group was in the television room and out of sight, then began walking down the hallway with trepidation. He couldn't see in the gloom and placed one hand on the wall as he slid along. Toward the end, a dim light appeared from above. Sunlight, from some sort of opening, creating a halo around a shadow. He stopped and peered intently.

A voice came forward from the darkness.

"Hello, Dr. Nakarat. I presume you're alone?"

33

Hearing Jennifer's call, I pulled up short, finding a little nook in the building where I could talk freely and waving at Knuckles to keep searching.

"Koko, say again?"

"I've got a signal here. It's weak, but it's beating."

"What's your location?"

"Right outside the souvenir shop, around the corner from the ticket office."

I could see the entrance to the bunker just down the path, but the ticket office was too far away. All I saw was a small group of tourists heading toward the Battle Box.

Jennifer said, "I'm losing signal. He's moving away. If you don't have a hit in a minute or two, he's got to be going to the sculpture garden on top. Break, break, Decoy—he might be headed toward you."

Decoy came on. "No signal yet. Blood and I will troll east and west."

I thought for a minute, then said, "Okay, Blood and Decoy, continue with the lost contact. Jennifer and Retro, hold up. Knuckles and I have the east; you guys have the north. He can't get out without running into one of us. I'm afraid of him slipping through while we search. Let's make him come to us."

After twenty minutes of waiting, me on one end of the shopping promenade and Knuckles on the other, without any alerts from the team, I was beginning to second-guess my decision.

Maybe he's already slipped through.

I was about to break down our box and launch into a full-on grid search when my phone buzzed. I opened the message and saw a picture of an Asian man with glasses, peering at a test tube.

The doctor.

He looked vaguely familiar, as if I'd seen him before, but I knew that might just have been my overactive Western prejudice. I was in Singapore, after all. Everyone was Asian. And they all looked alike.

"All elements, take a look at the photo. Anyone seen him before?"

Jennifer came on. "Pike, Pike, he was just here! He bought a ticket to the Battle Box. He's in that tour group."

I looked at the time, then the map. Twenty minutes.

He's still in there.

"Decoy, Blood, lock down the exit to the bunker. It comes out on your side."

I saw Jennifer and Retro jogging up the walkway. Over the Bluetooth I heard, "We got tickets. What do you want us to do?"

"Get inside. Locate him."

They stopped running and veered toward the entrance, handing their tickets to the custodian manning the door. To my right I caught hurried movement and saw a man who'd been hidden before by the shrubbery, now leaning over the railing to the coffee shop he was in and holding a cell phone to his ear. An Arabic man.

Or Persian. Holy shit! The general's in there. That's the meeting site.

I started running immediately, hoping to knock him down before the cell signal connected and the alert went out, shouting into my Bluetooth, "All elements, all elements, the general is inside the bunker. I say again, the general is inside the bunker. Watch yourself. Knuckles, on me. I've got the other Iranian."

I approached from the man's blind side, seeing he was intently focused on the bunker entrance and wasn't talking. *No cell connection yet.*

I got within five feet before my movement alerted him. He whirled and I charged, hitting him full in the chest and punching the hand that held the cell phone, sending it skittering away. We fell forward and he began shouting a single word over and over in a language I didn't understand.

We landed in a jumble sideways on the ground and I started to battle for dominance. I managed to wrap up one elbow to force him face-first into the ground and made the mistake of assuming he couldn't fight. He immediately rotated completely around onto his back, relieving the pressure on his elbow and opening me up. He kicked my shoulder, breaking free, and began scrambling for the cell just as Knuckles rounded the corner.

I shouted, "Get the phone!"

He had his hand on it when Knuckles kicked him full in the face, just like he was trying for a forty-yard field goal. The man's head snapped back, and he went limp. Knuckles picked up the cell.

He shook his head and stabbed the "end" button.

34

M alik could almost smell the fear coming off of the doctor. He pointed at the shopping bag.

"I assume that's the material?"

"Yes, yes. The virus and the first vaccine. I also have the second, untested vaccine. I know you said you didn't want it, but you can have it as well. Just let my son go."

"Don't worry about your son. Once I'm sure you haven't tried to trick me, he'll be fine. Hand me the bag and catch up with the tour. Continue on, then return to the hotel. I'll contact you there."

The doctor hesitated, trying to show bravado but failing miserably. "No! I want to speak to my son. Call him now, from here."

Leaching false charm, Malik said, "I'll do no such thing. I've been very reasonable. You must do the same. Don't cause trouble in here. Don't create a scene, or your son will surely die."

Malik watched the confidence erode and waited. The doctor's shoulders slumped in defeat, and he handed across the shopping bag. Malik was reaching to take it when his cell phone vibrated. He put it to his ear but couldn't make out what was being said, the call sounding like an accidental dial, with muffled words and noises. Then he heard a single word, shouted from a distance.

Snatching the bag from the doctor's hands, he pulled out a suppressed pistol and snarled, "So you brought some friends?"

Dr. Nakarat appeared completely confused. "What? No, no! I've done exactly what you said! There's been a mistake! Nobody is with me! I didn't do anything! Don't hurt my son!"

Malik snarled, "Your son is already dead. And so are you."

He raised the pistol, expecting the scientist to cower. Instead, the doctor wailed and attacked, a futile whirling of arms straight into Malik.

Malik got off one shot, into the wall, then hammered the doctor above the ear, sending him to the ground. He heard footsteps and whirled to the ladder, shoving the pistol in his belt and taking the rungs as fast as he could. He slammed open the hatch and clambered out onto an expansive green, groups of people staring at him curiously. He began sprinting.

I FINISHED TYING up the Iranian, using the thick foliage to cover his body, and began running through options.

Things were breaking fast and we needed to stay ahead of the curve. Stay ahead of the flex that was coming.

Decoy called first. "I got the doctor. He came running right out of the exit. He's a crying mess, but no question he was at the Marina Bay Sands. My iPod is about to vibrate apart."

"Where's the general?"

"I don't know. I've got to get the doc under cover before we draw a crowd. Koko and Retro are inside."

Jennifer came on. "Pike, this place is clear, but there's an open hatch in the back. He's on the surface and running."

Damn it.

"Blood, get moving. Up top. Run him down, but watch for weapons."

He said, "You want a unilateral takedown? Without Omega?"

I had no authority for a capture and in fact had been explicitly given my left and right limits, but the Iranian countersurveillance had forced my hand. This was turning into a mess.

I said, "We're already halfway through Omega right now. I've got an Iranian on the deck, and we're compromised. Get him. We'll sort it out later."

I heard, "Roger," and knew we stood an even chance of capturing the general. Blood was something of a freak when it came to moving on foot. He could run faster than anyone I had ever seen.

*   *   *

IGNORING THE PEOPLE around him, Malik continued running to the back of the park, pulling up the message system on his phone and hitting a prestaged alert. When he entered the tree line next to the reservoir, he slowed to a jog to get his bearings. It would be better to be right the first time than to get lost and have to backtrack.

He found the path from his map reconnaissance earlier and veered southwest, following it down the hill toward a bus stop on River Valley Road, where Sanjar would be meeting him.

He dialed Roshan's number again and got nothing but voice mail. He slammed the phone shut.

From the high ground, he could see River Valley Road to his front, about two hundred meters away. He picked up his pace, being careful not to fall on the slope. He heard crashing above him, turned toward the sound, and felt his heart in his throat.

A black man was bounding down the hill like a billy goat, trying to intersect him on the path by coming straight down. More leaping than running and covering enormous ground with each hop, the man was hooking his arms around trees as he came on in a controlled fall.

Malik began sprinting again, trying to match the man's speed but seeing he wouldn't make it out by staying on the safety of the path. He needed to intersect River Valley Road much quicker than the dirt track would.

He turned ninety degrees and followed the pursuer's example, leaping down the hill. In seconds, he was going faster than he could ever recover from, fighting now to simply stay on his feet with the use of only one arm, the other clutching the shopping bag in a death grip.

His legs caught something in the underbrush, and he went face-forward through the air. He tucked his arms around his head and began rolling down the slope, the shopping bag slapping him on the back at every rotation. He slammed into the trunk of a tree sideways, miraculously unhurt.

He heard the noise of his pursuer and saw he had closed the gap to less than fifty meters, if anything moving faster than he had before. In a panic, he swiveled about, searching for the shopping bag. He found it four feet away, snatched it up, and sprang out onto the four-lane road, desperately looking left and right for the bus stop, unsure of his exit point in relation to the plan.

He heard the crashing behind him grow and began sprinting north on the sidewalk, ignoring the plan in a desperate attempt to escape. Gasping for oxygen, his lungs burning like hot coals every time he drew a breath, he speed-dialed Sanjar, praying he was in a position to react.

He heard his pursuer's feet slapping sidewalk and knew he had only a few seconds left. The phone connected, and before he could even speak he heard, "I see you! I see you! I'm headed right at you."

And his salvation appeared, swerving toward the sidewalk not more than thirty meters away.

He didn't dare look behind him, didn't dare lose a millisecond of his lead, knowing the man would use it unmercifully. And might still even without the look. He saw Sanjar slam into the curb and the back passenger door fly open. With his last bit of flagging energy, he churned his legs as fast as he could, then threw himself lengthwise in the back, screaming, "Go! Go! Go!"

He felt something thump the roof as they sped away. When he looked back, he saw the black man standing on the sidewalk, his fists clenched.

35

I passed control of the Iranian to Knuckles and said, "Decoy, what's your location?"

"Family restroom on the other side of the souvenir shop. I got it locked down."

I told Knuckles to remain with the man we'd caught, ensuring he went nowhere, then began jogging back down the path to the ticket office/souvenir shop. I was going to have to make some quick decisions, because we were now spread way too thin, with Lord knew how many threads blowing in the wind from our actions. I wasn't even sure what I would do if Blood caught the general.

"Retro, what's the status inside? What's the tour group doing? Are we compromised?"

"No, we're good. They heard something, but Koko stepped in and started asking questions like she owned the place. She's now talking to the tour guide, getting him to start doing some in-depth history. Everyone seems to be enjoying it. Except for the tour guide. I think Jennifer knows more than him."

Jennifer and her history knowledge. Who'd have thought that would come in handy?

"Can you break free?"

"Yeah, but Koko's going to have to stay for cover."

"Do it. Get up top. Help out Blood."

He didn't ask any more questions, knowing I didn't have the answers. The command was simple: Figure it out.

I made it to the bathroom and knocked. When Decoy let me in, I saw the doctor sitting on the toilet with the lid down, staring at the floor, catatonic.

Before I could ask a question, Blood came on.

"He's gone. A car pulled up outside the park and he jumped in it."

Damn it. The other countersurveillance guy from the front of the park.

I said, "What the hell? You're telling me a fifty-year-old Iranian outran you?"

I heard consternation. "Hey, I had to find him first. I was right on his ass. He was mine, and he knew it. He had an escape plan in place. That car didn't appear by magic."

"Okay, okay," I said. "Knuckles, get with Blood and Retro and figure out an exfil plan with the package we caught. Let me know what it is. I want to be out of here in fifteen minutes or less."

Knuckles said, "Uhhh . . . you know we all took the metro, right?"

I said, "Figure it out."

I turned to the doctor. He gazed up at me, tears

streaming down his face. He said, "You killed my son. You killed my son. . . ."

"Dr. Nakarat, your son is alive. We rescued him two days ago. The police here have been trying to find you to tell you that."

He said nothing for a minute, his lips trembling. I expected him to leap up and hug me out of sheer joy.

Instead, he slid off the toilet in a ball and began weeping uncontrollably.

36

M alik sagged against the seat, getting his ragged breathing under control.

Sanjar said, "What happened? Where is Roshan?"

"I don't know. Let me think for a minute."

The one thing he was sure of was that Dr. Nakarat had brought the police. That was the only thing that could explain the events that had transpired. Malik was surprised at the doctor's courage, given the fate that would befall his son and the absolute lack of any indication of such nerve.

And yet he had. He'd somehow met the police beforehand and had explained the entire contact plan. They had known about the virus before Malik had even entered the bunker. Before he'd staged his countersurveillance team, which is how they'd found Roshan. They had been one step ahead the entire time due to the doctor's treachery. Which meant they would never have allowed the doctor to bring him live virus samples. What Nakarat had passed him had to be fake. A trick to entrap him.

The mission is done.

The thought brought a wave of shame. He had failed. Again. Not only that, but he'd lost one of his men in the process. He wanted to scream at the injustice.

He turned over in his mind what he could salvage. Anything to make the sacrifices worth it. And thought of the doctor's expression in the bunker. The demand to speak to his son, and the look of absolute surprise at the mention of the police. As if he didn't really know they were there.

The more he considered it, the more it seemed true. Why, if the doctor had gone to the police, would they send him alone into the meeting? With a dummy virus and vaccine samples? They would have known the whole plan for the meeting, including the tour group instructions. Why not build the tour group with nothing but special-tactics police? Have the doctor embed with them, then simply arrest him—eight or nine against one? Why go through the charade of sending in the doctor as a singleton?

Why indeed? Since it had allowed Malik to escape? If they really knew about the meeting, would they have left the escape hatch open? Wouldn't they have done a complete reconnaissance and blocked all exits? This was their country, after all, and that's what he would have done.

No, Roshan had alerted to something that happened outside, which indicated that the police were *reacting* to what they'd seen, not executing a plan.

Then he remembered the visit earlier at the lab and the doctor's escape.

They weren't after you. They were after him.

Which meant the virus was real.

The notion brought a sense of victory at first, then a terrifying dread: *What if your fall broke the container?*

He vividly remembered the bag flailing in the wind as he went down the slope, hitting his back repeatedly as he rolled. Afraid to touch the box of gauze, he first unwrapped the vaccine from the rag, relaxing a small bit when he saw the tube was intact. Wrapped around the tube appeared to be instructions for administration to a host, from the doctor. Doing what he could to save his son, and evidence that Malik's thought process wasn't off base.

He then gingerly opened the gauze box, trying to peek between the cracks, looking for liquid in the gauze, as if that would save him from the invisible death floating inside the car. He breathed a sigh of relief. The glass of the vial was unbroken, and the rubber stopper was in place.

He closed the box and thought about the mission. They had the doctor now, which meant they would know about the virus soon enough. He needed to get out of Singapore immediately, before they could collate their information and try to react.

He began cataloging what the doctor knew, what information they could glean that would prevent his own escape. Outside of a description, he could come up with nothing. The room at the Marina Bay Sands went to an Iranian account, yes, but the credit card trail would end there, under a wholly different name than what he was using. The same for the cell phones he'd bought. It wasn't like Iran was going to help them in their search.

The thought of the cell phone purchase caused a bolt of adrenaline. *The doctor still has the phone you gave him. With your number in it.*

He picked up his own phone and stared at it, wondering if it was being tracked right this minute.

He said, "Sanjar, drop me off at the next corner. I'm going to catch a cab to our embassy to coordinate transport of the virus. I'll meet you back at the hotel in less than thirty minutes."

"Yes, sir. What about Roshan?"

Another risk. Another gap in the mission, but a small one. Roshan, he knew, would say nothing. He was well trained and had nothing incriminating on him. If he stuck to his training, he'd be released in a matter of hours from the Singaporean police.

"Roshan is gone, but hopefully only for a short time. We must ensure his sacrifice is worth it. If we get caught, it will all be a waste. Have everything packed when I arrive. We're leaving Singapore immediately."

"Where? Where are we going?"

Malik picked up the vaccine, wondering if it really worked as the doctor stated.

"To meet a woman. A very special woman. Our *shahid*."

37

Elina slowly walked down the aisle of the aircraft, trying to keep from bumping her carry-on into the man in front of her, the anxiety rising with each step. She reached the exit door, seeing the pilot smiling and wishing her well. She nodded, plastering on a fake smile of her own, and exited the aircraft into a world that frightened her to her core.

Moving with everyone else, she left the aircraft gate and entered the hallway of the Hong Kong International Airport, jostled by the waves of people all anxious to get to immigration and customs. She stood confused for a moment, wondering where she should go.

She had never traveled outside of the Russian Federation, and apart from one trip to Moscow, she had never been more than fifty miles from Grozny. In truth, she had never been on an airplane, a fact that she had lied about to her friends because it had brought a secret shame. Now it brought nothing but fear.

When she'd visited Moscow she had felt bewildered but at least could speak the language. Here, she was completely out of her element. Almost everyone was Asian, and they all appeared to be staring at her. Apprehension bubbled up inside her. A xenophobic feeling that was almost overwhelming, making her want to return home to what she knew. Return to where her mission made sense.

Straining to read the English on the airport signs, she began following the crowd, believing that they knew more than she. She couldn't help but notice the Asians wearing surgical masks, just like the ones she had been instructed to purchase. The sight confused her. Made her question her purpose.

Surely I'm not going to martyr myself here. Why? What has Hong Kong done to Chechnya?

After the praise Doku had given her, she had agreed to the new mission. He'd said she might not understand the target she would attack, but that others did. Others who held the fate of her country close to their heart. He had admonished her not to question, but to simply execute. He'd ended by saying she would be the most valuable Black Widow in history. The one who would turn the tide against the hated Kadyrovtsy.

When she'd asked how an attack outside of Chechnya could do that, he'd initially told her that they required support for the fight, and this attack would cause others to provide help for their cause. That didn't sit well with her. She may have been a simple peasant, but she wasn't stupid. Something Doku was well aware of.

In a little bit of a pique, she'd said, "So I'm to sacrifice my life to ensure that we will be given arms? Is that it?

You do them a favor, and they return the favor? Using me? Who will I attack?"

Doku had paused at that. Then he'd said, "No, no. You're not something for simple barter. There are others who support the Russian Federation. Others who keep them in power and, by extension, keep the Kadyrovtsy operational. Your attack will cause them to cease the support."

Still not convinced, she'd said, "Who? What others?"

"You'll be told that when the time comes. Remember your operational security. Remember your training. And trust that we know what we're doing."

Now, standing on a moving sidewalk, a bit of technology that almost caused her to fall over, surrounded by Asians who would have had trouble finding Chechnya on a map, she wondered, *Am I simply a pawn? Something to trade, like the saddle for a horse?*

She banished the thought immediately. Doku was an honorable man. Someone who had fought and bled for their country. He had always treated her with respect and had never lied. She would trust in what he said. At the very least, she would meet the contact and let him tell her the mission.

She stumbled off of the moving sidewalk, almost run over by the scrum of passengers speed-walking behind her. She let them pass and chose to continue in the center of the terminal, without the mechanical help.

She continued on, seemingly walking for miles. She became more and more anxious, feeling a tightness in her chest that left her unable to catch her breath. She believed she was heading the wrong way and had no one to turn to for help. She was petrified to ask directions. Convinced they'd see through her subterfuge. Convinced someone was going to stop her, question her, and then arrest her. She had done nothing wrong, but the fact that she held a forged passport from the country of Latvia did nothing but increase her fear.

She saw the sign for immigration ahead and let out a mental sigh. *Just get to the hotel. One step at a time. Get to the hotel.*

She was chanting the mantra in her head when a shorter Asian woman, wearing a surgical mask, stepped into her path.

In accented English, she said, "Please remove your head scarf."

Elina felt faint. She barely understood the woman and wanted to turn away, to flee back to her plane and demand it return her home.

"What? Remove my head scarf?"

The woman nodded.

Elina began to panic, believing there was some magical piece of technology that could spot an imposter. She stuttered, stalling for time, when the woman pointed to a desk behind her.

The counter was curved and modern, with a plethora of computer displays behind it, all manned by other Asians in masks. It had a placard on the front that read

TEMPERATURE CHECK in English, along with Chinese symbols that she assumed said the same thing.

The woman said, "We check passengers for sickness. Your scarf blocks the sensors."

For the first time, Elina noticed the myriad of cameras around her, all screening the flow of people into the immigration area.

She removed her scarf, feeling sick to her stomach. The woman nodded and smiled. A man behind the desk waved her on, and she entered immigration, confused by the whole process.

She stood in line behind an affable man with an English accent. He attempted to strike up a conversation.

"They're serious about the flu, aren't they?"

She nodded weakly, afraid to open her mouth.

"I come here all the time, and I always wonder, if I had a cold, would they keep me out? How can they tell the difference between bird flu and the common cold with just a temperature check?"

She nodded again, the conversation hammering home how little she knew of the world.

Bird flu? What on earth is that?

38

Kurt Hale fiddled with the Proxima projector, mindlessly adjusting the focus yet again. It didn't help him make a decision, but it did kill a little more time.

Ten minutes until the council update. Or what may forever be known as the first spontaneous combustion of the president of the United States.

The video-teleconference with Pike in Singapore had been over for more than two hours, and he still couldn't decide what catastrophe he should broach to the Oversight Council first: the fact that Pike's team had ignored orders and unilaterally attempted an Omega operation against an agent of a sovereign country—and failed—or the fact that that same agent was now running loose with a lethal and highly pathogenic genetically engineered bioweapon.

Maybe lead off with the one Iranian we did manage to catch, along with the fact that we have no support assets in country to exfiltrate him.

The thought made his head hurt. *Jesus. What a goat rope.*

He remembered his last conversation with the secretary of state, Jonathan Billings, and knew he was going to get roasted—although at the end of the day, he stood behind Pike's actions. The only thing Pike could have done differently was alert the police when he realized he was following the doctor. Instead, he'd attempted an interdiction with his team, and Kurt understood the decision.

Given Pike's status in the country, he couldn't call the police himself without an avalanche of repercussions and questions to answer. He would have had to call back to the Taskforce, then have them inject the doctor's location into the CIA network, followed by the station alerting their liaison. In other words, lose the doctor yet again.

No, Pike had made the right call. If he'd stood on the sidelines, the doctor would have been killed, and they'd have no idea what they were up against.

At the end of the day, hunting humans was an imperfect science. The target was usually someone who had lived on the run for a while, honing his survival instincts and wanting to live to fight another day. You just couldn't predict every outcome. The unexpected happened, and you either rolled with the punch or ceased to exist. Operations weren't video games with checkpoints that you could attempt over and over until you found the perfect solution, although he'd have a hard time selling that to this crew. Most of the Oversight Council had no idea what the Taskforce did to accomplish missions and lived in a zero-tolerance world.

A world that doesn't exist.

The door opened and the members of the council all began to file in, right on time. Last was the president, who said, "Hey, Kurt. These emergency meetings are getting to be standard procedure. From the message you sent out, this sounds like the Cuban Missile Crisis. Tell me that was just your way of ensuring we all showed up."

As everyone took their seats, over the scuff of the chairs, he said, "Sir, you know that saying 'I've got good news and bad news'?"

"Yeah."

The room now quiet, Kurt said, "Well, I've got bad news and worse news."

For the next forty-five minutes the council said not a word as Kurt laid out what he knew, some members' mouths actually dropping open as the briefing continued. Kurt finished and waited for the bloodletting.

It began—and ended—with Billings. "I told you we should have never let Pike's team go to Singapore. He's nothing more than a hammer that sees everything as a nail. What the hell are we going to do with a captured Iranian asset?"

President Warren, in a tone that reminded everyone in the room of his position, said, "Seriously? That's what you care about? Cut the bickering. Forget the operation. That's the least of our worries. This has the potential to make the Cuban Missile Crisis look like a bad day on the golf course."

Billings turned red but said nothing. Ignoring his discomfort, President Warren continued. "Let's take it from the top, starting with the virus." He turned to Chip Dekkard. "You work in pharmaceuticals. What's your assessment of the danger if it gets out? How bad can it be if we know it's coming? If we prepare?"

To Kurt, Chip looked pale and slightly green, like he was about to be sick. Even a little dazed. He took a moment, then responded. "Sir, if what Kurt says is true, it's going to be catastrophic if released. We simply don't have the production capability to ramp up enough antiviral medication to slow the onslaught. The demand will be huge. And there is no vaccine. We won't be able to even begin production until we isolate the virus, which means someone has to get sick first."

"So someone gets sick. Then we get the vaccine. How long before that's accomplished?"

"Six or eight months."

The room broke into a low buzz, and Kurt heard various members talking about what they could do in the meantime. How they could prevent a panic and stabilize for six months. Chip cut them off.

"People, you're not listening to me. This isn't going to be a particularly bad flu season. It's going to be a catastrophic wipeout that the world has never seen. H5N1 has a seventy percent mortality rate. The only thing it didn't have was the mutation to get around the human species. If this virus has that ability—and I'm not trying to be over-the-top—we're looking at the deaths of hundreds of millions of people. The entire collapse of our health-care system followed by our economy, then quite possibly our country."

The secretary of defense snorted, "Come on. We had the flu epidemic in 1918—while we were in the middle of World War One. That didn't cause any country to fall apart, and that was with hundred-year-old medical practices."

Chip said, "I'm glad you mentioned 1918. You talk about modern medicine, but there's a flip side to being modern. They also didn't have modern automobiles and certainly didn't have air travel. It was much harder for that flu to get around then, and yet it did. In two years that pandemic killed more Americans than all the foreign wars we have ever fought combined. It killed upwards of five percent of the entire global population. And its mortality rate was between ten and twenty percent."

When nobody responded, his voice became shrill. "Do you hear what I'm saying? One or two out of every ten that got it died. This virus is going to kill seven. And it's going to spread faster than we can contain it. If it gets out, it will make 1918 look like an outbreak of the common cold."

He leaned back in his chair again, saying, "In fact, the only good thing we have going for us is that H5N1 is so deadly, it might kill the host before it has a chance to spread."

Nobody said a word, struggling to cope with the magnitude. The director of the CIA broke the silence.

"If that's true, why on earth would the Iranians even

use it? If there is no vaccine, it'll eventually reach Iran and wipe them out as well."

Someone muttered, "Because they're crazy."

"No, they're not," the director snapped. "They're definitely operating on a different agenda, but they aren't crazy. They protect the regime at all costs, using logical cost-benefit calculations. Hell, their quest to become nuclear is for that exact reason."

Kurt said, "Maybe they don't know what they've got. Or maybe Malik doesn't understand the damage it could cause. He's not a doctor or anything. The bottom line is that they have the virus. The only questions left are whether they'll use it and whether we can do anything about it."

Billings said, "I'm inclined to agree with the CIA on this. They won't use it if they realize the cost. I think it's just a deterrent, a cheap nuke. We should take this slow and easy, not push them into something we'll regret."

The SECDEF exploded, "Have you lost your mind? No way am I letting that bunch of loonies hold the key to Armageddon."

Chip surprised Kurt by shouting a follow-up. "I agree! We need to kill this general and get the virus back. Ensure it's destroyed."

The only thing that guy has ever said at a council meeting was questioning whether we should go after an Iranian. Now he's bloodthirsty?

President Warren held up his hands for silence. "We don't know their intentions, but we do know they have it. I'm inclined to let the Taskforce continue to track, but not for a blanket Omega operation. Let's sort it out. Get more information, then come back and reassess. Kurt, do you even have anything to go on?"

"Very little. We tracked the general's phone immediately, but it ended up being under the seat of a cab. The driver couldn't remember who had left it. We found the hotel of the Iranian we'd caught, and doing some linkage work by hacking the registration computer of the hotel, we think we know the names the other two are using. They both took a flight that left Singapore directly to Hong Kong. It's not a sure thing by any stretch of the imagination, but it's all we have at this point."

"What about that other Iranian? What are we doing about him?"

"I'd like to exfiltrate both him and the doctor back here. Get some debrief and interrogation going. Apparently the doctor was working on a vaccine, and he might be able to jump-start any research that becomes necessary. I'm just thinking worst case. I can do it, but I'll need some help from the CIA station. There's a US Navy base at Sembawang, in the north of Singapore. We have some assets I can use in Malaysia for a waterborne pickup, but I'll need help getting the package on the base and through the indigenous guard force security."

President Warren glanced at the DCI, and he nodded, saying, "I can get that done."

President Warren said, "Okay, make it happen. Bill-ings, I want you to put Cailleach Laboratories under a microscope. Who owns it, who runs it, and who made the call to create the virus. Somebody at State had to clear its credentials for work in Singapore. I want to know who it was and why."

Chip Dekkard cut in. "Sir, I can do that if you want. It doesn't sound like these guys followed procedure anyway, so the State Department will probably have less luck than me, given my connections in the private sector."

Billings said, "Sir, he's right. I guarantee that all of the credentialing is on the up-and-up."

President Warren said, "All right. Chip, you got that ball. Thanks. I appreciate the help without the government paycheck. Final thing: I want the CDC read onto the potential threat. Don't give out any specifics. Just get them on war footing. On the lookout for an outbreak so we can mitigate the damage, using the minimum information you need to justify it. Whatever you do, don't go overboard on the threat. Just give them enough to get them prepared for what's coming."

He paused until he had everyone's full attention and then said, "People, the biggest threat right now is panic. Maybe the Iranians intend to use the virus and maybe they don't. Either way, the word gets out and we'll have an epidemic of fear that'll match the actual release of the virus. Nobody, and I mean *nobody*, is to breathe a word of the true facts until absolutely necessary. If I hear anyone on this council is out stocking up on Tamiflu, you'll regret ever working for the government. Understood?"

He went from face to face, getting a somber nod from each member.

He then looked at Kurt. "Get to Hong Kong. Give me some good news for a change. I'd like the highlight of our next meeting to be something better than our only hope is that the virus kills so quickly it'll mitigate its own spread."

39

Malik entered the dingy elevator, jostling between two middle-aged Indian men and an Australian backpacker with a braided beard. Assaulted by the stale odor of cigarettes, he felt his feet sticking to the floor like it was coated in flypaper.

A small price to pay.

Unaware of the depth of the penetration or knowledge the enemy now held, he'd had Sanjar locate a cheap hostel that took cash. One that wasn't a stickler for recording passports.

Sanjar had found exactly that inside an indoor flea market, a maze that wound around not unlike the souks of his home. Just off Nathan Road on the Kowloon side of the harbor, it was actually six or seven different hostels, each one taking up a floor. All housed what he would charitably call frugal travelers, from touring college students to men such as the Indians in the elevator with him. Malik decided they'd stay here until he could obtain new identification, which was what he was doing now.

Leaving the elevator, he slipped through the flow of

people in the narrow hallway of the market, hearing at least four different languages and passing stalls that sold everything from T-shirts to Internet time.

He turned north on Nathan Road, and the world became much more homogenous, a river of people, all Asian. He walked up a few blocks, keeping pace with the foot traffic around him. He passed a subway station spilling people onto the street, a seemingly endless stream adding to the current of the human river. Had he not been preoccupied with the upcoming meeting, he might have studied the people flowing south on the opposite side of the street. Might have cataloged them as a precaution. Might have saved himself some trouble later.

RETRO AND I exited the subway station and took a moment to get our bearings. Hong Kong was about as crowded a city as I had ever been in, but luckily it was fairly compact, unlike the urban sprawl you see in the United States.

Retro saw a sign pointing the way to the ferries at the harbor only a few blocks away, and we began walking south, toward our target.

We'd gotten the go-ahead to transition to Hong Kong and had squeezed the only lead we had: the two names we believed were associated with the Iranian we had caught. Unfortunately, neither had panned out. Once they left the aircraft, they simply disappeared, like I figured would happen. There was no known registration at any hotel we could find. We'd flown anyway, waiting on the forensics of the cell phone we'd captured with the Iranian.

By the time we had arrived, the forensics had been completed, and the phone had little to offer, having only spoken with three other handsets: the doctor's, the general's phone we found in the cab, and an unknown number, presumably belonging to the countersurveillance that had saved the general at the park. We tried to track it, but it was off the grid, more than likely thrown away because of the compromise.

Digging further, building the spiderweb, we had scrubbed the connections from the unknown phone and hit a potential lead.

Outside of cab companies and the other phones we already knew, it had called a number of low-grade hostels on the Kowloon peninsula, with five located in one building and two in another on the eastern edge of the peninsula. It wasn't much, but it was all we had.

The two on the eastern edge were a tick above slum land and had databases we could hack. Our target names weren't registered, which meant little in the greater scheme of things, but I decided to concentrate on the other five. They appeared to be cash-and-carry-type affairs, with nothing on the Web.

I could have split up the team, focusing on both targets, but that would have left me without the ability to react immediately to what we found. On the other hand, while focusing on one would allow me to start immediate surveillance, it would get me nothing if we were on the wrong target.

Ordinarily, this type of mission would have been old hat, and we would have had the luxury of a slow, deliberate process. Here, I felt the press of time—and the threat of a global pandemic. At times like this I wondered if I wouldn't have made a good shoe salesman.

Jennifer and Decoy had conducted a reconnaissance and found that the five hostels were serviced by the same elevator; each hostel was on a separate floor deep inside a claustrophobic market catering to foreigners. Retro and I were going to emplace a wireless covert camera in view of the doors, then we were going to pull old-fashioned stakeout work, keeping eyes on the door 24/7 in the hopes of spotting our quarry.

MALIK SAW A sign for Kowloon Park and crossed the street, still headed north. He passed two men speaking Urdu and wearing *taqiyah* skullcaps and knew he was close. He crossed Haiphong Road and saw his destination: the Kowloon Mosque and Islamic Centre. He studied it as he approached, looking for anything that didn't seem to fit. He saw nothing alarming.

He passed through the wrought-iron gate and marched up the stairs as if he had been there a hundred times before, not wanting to encourage anyone to be helpful because he appeared to be new. Not wanting anyone but his contact to remember him at all.

Using his memorized instructions, he moved through the building until he reached a small sitting room in the back. Pushing through the curtain, he recognized the man inside. A cleric who worked for the mullahs themselves. And he didn't look particularly happy.

"General. Come in. Sit down."

Malik did as he asked, saying, "I'm surprised to see you. I hope my request in Singapore wasn't mistaken as something needing the attentions of someone as important as yourself."

"From what you told us, it was no mistake."

"The plan is proceeding perfectly. I couldn't very well fly the vials in my carry-on bag."

"Perfectly? Do you know what happened to Roshan?"

"Yes. He was arrested. Don't worry, he won't talk. Even if he does, he has no knowledge of the overall plan."

"He wasn't arrested. He disappeared. Just like your men in Thailand. Someone is tracking you."

Malik absorbed the information, slowly nodding his head. He had begun to suspect the same thing. At least as far as the Thailand team was concerned. "If what you say is true, we need to counterattack. I'm due to meet my *shahid* tomorrow. I can send her immediately, but I would like to set a trap for those who took Roshan. They will surely follow me here."

"There are others who think we shouldn't execute at all. That there are too many fingerprints pointing to the republic as it is. Rumor has it you're using a Chechen. Is this true?"

Irritated that his Chechen contacts had leaked the information, Malik said, "Yes. Why is that an issue?"

"The Russian Federation is our ally. A relationship we don't want to upset. Using one of her citizens could prove problematic."

"Problematic for the Chechens, yes. Not for Russia. Think about it: The *shahid* will give them free rein to do whatever they want in Chechnya. The world will be appalled at the carnage, all done at the hands of a Black Widow. We're handing them a gift."

The man considered for a moment, then reached underneath his chair and retrieved a satchel, passing it over.

"Your new documents are there, along with a cell phone."

"Thank you, but I have Sanjar getting phones as we speak."

"That is well and good, but this phone will remain with you always. So we can contact you should we need to. Be sure and answer it."

So, tightening the noose, are we?

Malik opened the satchel and saw the small dry-ice box containing both the virus and the vaccine. He said, "Of course. I am always at the ayatollah's mercy."

"There is also the matter of the vaccine. Where is it?"

Malik feigned surprise. "It's here. Right here. You were only supposed to leave me three doses for my team, then take the rest for development."

"What? Those weren't the instructions given at the

embassy in Singapore. You gave them the vials, telling them they both held the virus."

Which was absolutely true, but Malik had known this question was coming and had decided to play stupid, giving them the faulty vaccine to provide breathing space for the mission. They would never let him continue if they knew a successful vaccine didn't exist. All he needed was one dose for the Black Widow.

Malik said, "There is some mistake. Those were not my instructions. Look, I can't open the vaccine here, and I need it for the mission. I will bring it to my contact in the United States after setting loose the Widow."

The cleric regarded him with a scowl, Malik knowing the entire operation now hung in the balance.

Eventually, he said, "Okay. Because of your past service and judgment, I'm going to let you continue, but keep that phone on you at all times. Malik, I believe in you, unlike others. Don't prove me wrong."

"What about the men searching for me?"

"I'll get another Quds Force here. Come up with a plan."

Malik nodded and said, "Thank you. Insha'Allah, this strike will cause the Great Satan unimaginable pain."

The cleric stood to leave, his parting words sending a chill through Malik.

"There will be pain, no doubt. If you fail, if the West learns the source of the attack, the pain will be yours to bear."

40

Sitting in a booth, Jennifer scanned the menu of bar food and said, "You really have a knack for finding Western bars. It's starting to amaze me."

We needed a place that had free Wi-Fi, and as fate would have it, there was a pub called Murphy's on Nathan Road just blocks from our cameras. An Irish oasis in a world full of foreign cafés serving fried grasshoppers. We'd gone inside, and I'd found it just my kind of place. The only downside was I had to drink iced tea with lunch.

The signal strength booming on my tablet, I dialed in the IP address of the cameras and said, "It's the other way around. They find me."

She closed the menu. "Just once, could we get something besides hamburgers? We go to the most exotic places, and you refuse to eat any of the food."

"But this place has the Wi-Fi we need."

"No, we don't. We're on our lunch break."

I said, "Surveillance chief doesn't get a break."

She gave me her disapproving-teacher look and motioned over the waitress. I hid the tablet page and was in the middle of ordering when my earpiece chirped.

"Pike, Pike, you seeing what I'm seeing?"

Son of a bitch.

Jennifer stiffened slightly but showed no other outward sign she'd heard. I keyed my headset and continued to order, letting them know I was engaged. I heard, "Got it. Glad to see someone's eating. Ernie just left the building."

We had a picture of the countersurveillance operative from Singapore, and Decoy had remarked on how much he looked like the Muppet Ernie from *Sesame Street*; thus, that's what he was now called.

I ignored the earpiece, keeping my attention on the waitress and waiting on Jennifer. She interrupted my order by looking at her watch and exclaiming, "Whoa! Pike, we lost track of time. We gotta go!"

I snapped my watch up and pretended surprise. "Shit! You're right. Sorry about this."

I threw some bills on the table, and we exited to Nathan Road.

"We're out. Which way did he go?"

"Our way. Setting up trigger now. Stand by."

I'd split the team into pairs on both sides of the market, which gave us the ability to pick up a follow no matter which way he exited and allowed the flexibility to rotate the teams in for chow and bathroom breaks. I really hadn't expected anything to happen this quickly, but I was happy it had. Ernie wasn't the general, but he would lead us to him. Of that I was sure.

"Pike, this is Decoy. I got eyes on. He's headed north, paralleling Nathan Road."

About a block away.

I motioned to Jennifer and we began moving north on Nathan, closing the distance.

"Decoy, who's your backup?"

"Pike, Knuckles here. I got eyes on Decoy. I can relieve him."

"Roger that. Retro, Blood, jump ahead to the north. Get in front of him."

"Already moving."

I was trying to build a bubble around Ernie so that no matter which way he went, he'd bump into someone. Given the manpower, I'd done about as much as I could.

We continued through the mass of people, not moving fast enough to spike anyone, when I heard, "He just went left. West. He's headed to Nathan Road. I'm off."

Perfect. Coming right to me.

Jennifer and I began scanning the crowds, knowing he was within seconds of running into us. It was the hardest part of surveillance: acting like you had a destination while trying to find your target. You always had to keep in mind the third man—the cameras and people around you who would trigger law enforcement if you did anything awkward.

Retro said, "I've got him. He's moving to the subway. He just went down."

The subway station we'd used to get here was right in

front of us, and we went down as well, letting Retro handle the eye.

We reached the platform, and I said, "Which train? We're here."

"North. He's headed north."

Jennifer tapped my elbow and said, "I see Retro."

Which was good enough. We got on the same subway as Retro, a car behind him.

Ernie got off three stops north, at Mong Kok, and went east on Argyle Street before entering a shopping mall. Retro pulled off, and Blood took the lead.

I called Retro. "What is this place? Get a data dump."

He came back in minutes. "It's called Sin Tat Plaza. It's an electronics mall known for selling gray hardware."

"What's that mean? 'Gray hardware'?"

"Counterfeit or resold electronics. Mostly mobile phones. Stuff that isn't strictly black market but also isn't authorized by the manufacturer."

Shit. He's buying untraceable phones.

"Blood, give me a lock-on. Jennifer and I are coming in."

He directed us to the second floor, and I got eyes on Ernie. I waved Blood off and took the eye, window-shopping with Jennifer.

Ernie wandered around for a little bit, then went back outside, traveling north on Tung Choi Street, continuing his shopping. Eventually he reached a small four-story office complex with a number of shops on the ground floor linked together in a little indoor cul-de-sac. In the center was a guard desk housing a single man, who was apparently bored beyond belief, not even stopping anyone from reaching the elevators.

Ernie looked at a piece of paper in his hands, then glanced around the circle of stores, finally settling on one. He entered, and I held back. It was small enough that I didn't want to go in with him for fear of getting burned. He exited about eight minutes later carrying a bag.

"Blood, I'm still on him. Go in the store and buy a phone. See what the procedure is."

We needed to find out the numbers he had purchased, and I wasn't sure how we would do that, since we were now in the land of Communist China and calling in a liaison favor was out of the question.

Ernie went straight back to the subway, riding it underneath Victoria Harbor to Hong Kong Island. He passed through the admiralty station and exited at Central, now walking north and entering the International Finance Centre mall, a high-end shopping plaza as different from Sin Tat as a filet mignon was from a hot dog.

What's he getting here?

It didn't make any sense. Knuckles now had the eye, with Retro as backup. I said, "Get ready, people. Something's about to happen. Remember, he was pulling countersurveillance in Singapore, so look sharp. Keep him in sight no matter what, but don't let him burn you."

I positioned in a café with view of the entrance he had used and waited, the tension mounting, my subconscious telling me to get in the hunt. Get eyes on. I ignored the urge and played the tourist with Jennifer.

I waited for the call that he was meeting the general or conducting reconnaissance for a strike or something equally nefarious, but all I got was simple shopping updates. He went into the two-story flagship Apple store and bought a couple of iPads, then found a SmarTone booth and purchased a plethora of stored-value SIM cards. Nothing more. It was almost like he was truly a tourist from the Middle East using his time in Hong Kong to outfit himself with the latest electronics.

He didn't conduct anything remotely like a surveillance detection route and didn't seem to care if he was being followed. I began to wonder if he was a decoy. If his mission was precisely to pull us out and away from the real action. I was considering breaking off when I got the call that he was headed back my way, and I waited to pick up the eye.

Jennifer saw him first, and we let him pass. He reached the door, and we got our initial sign that he wasn't a tourist. He sat on a bench at the exit and did a half-assed job of acting like he was reading the iPad box, flicking his eyes all around and studying everyone who passed him.

Unfortunately for him, he'd made the amateur mistake of starting his detection while he was already in a box. He'd walked into us, so we were now out of suspicion. After all, how could *we* be following *him* if we were already here when he arrived? Not only that, but his actions gave me plenty of time to leapfrog people in front of him again. Clearly not that well trained.

I made the call to the team and formed a loose bubble around him outside, going so far as to position a team inside the subway station, letting them know his awareness level was now up.

Continuing his amateurish actions, he waited until the lobby was relatively clear, then leapt up and began speed-walking out the door. Right into my first position.

Eventually, after continuing his junior-varsity surveillance detection, including jumping on then off the subway, he ended up at the Island Shangri-La hotel, a five-star resort adjacent to Hong Kong Park.

Amateurish as it was, his antics forced us to really hang back, and we lost him inside the hotel, but the location, coupled with his actions, told me all I needed to know.

Something special is inside this place.

41

Elina awoke early, feeling more tired than she should have given the opulence of her room. The anxiety inside her had only increased after meeting her contact the day before, keeping the needed sleep at bay.

A young man with a thin mustache, he had given no information on her mission. Not the location, the purpose, or the target. And she'd tried hard to find out. Instead, he'd provided her with an Apple iPad, a cell phone, and several prepaid SIM cards. He'd then given her instructions for the meeting today, admonishing her to be alert for anything suspicious, which did nothing but increase her unease.

She hadn't left her room since checking in, the masses of foreign people swarming around the city making her feel light-headed and lost. The thought of someone hiding inside the crowds, looking for her, made her want to forget the mission. To flee back to the comfort of Chechnya, where the beast was easy to see. Easy to fight.

She banished the fears through willpower alone, remembering who she was and why she had been chosen.

Bringing forth the iron forged by the enemy she now fought. She collected her new phone and left the room.

Exiting from the south, she moved through Hong Kong Park, stopping to survey the pond in the center, as she had been told.

A group of old men and woman were executing a delicate ballet of tai chi, and she paused a moment longer, watching the symmetry and enjoying the peacefulness.

She prayed again that she wouldn't be asked to attack people such as this, wherever she was directed. Prayed for a target worthy of her sacrifice.

She had begun again on her instructed path when a placard set into stone caught her eye. She moved close enough to read it, curious about the history of the park.

Underneath the Chinese Hanzi, in English, was nothing more than an admonishment to avoid contact with all birds in the park and to immediately wash your hands if contact was made. *On a brass plaque set in stone?*

Elina couldn't make sense of it, then remembered the temperature check in the airport, designed to prevent "bird flu" from entering the country. Clearly, it was already here and was dangerous enough to warrant permanent warning markers.

She reached the Peak Tram station a hundred yards farther, a funicular railroad leading to the highest point on Hong Kong Island. She opened the door to the ticket counter, seeing a sign declaring that the handles were disinfected every hour.

She purchased a ticket and loitered at the end of the

station platform, taking note of any Caucasians as instructed, but seeing only obese Westerners with rowdy kids. She tried to focus on them, to spot if someone was paying her any particular attention, but was drawn to the locals sprinkled on the platform. About half were wearing surgical masks.

Apparently, the people here lived in daily fear of this bird flu. She began to suspect the very air she was breathing, her xenophobia spiking again. How had she not heard of this before? Was this why she had been instructed to buy the same masks? Should she have been wearing one now?

The tram arrived and she took a seat in the back, keeping everyone in front of her and in sight. It chugged up the slope, grinding along like it had for over a hundred years, the spectacular view being recorded by a plethora of tourist cameras. Elina ignored it all, concentrating on maintaining calm.

Eventually, it ground to a halt at the top of Victoria Peak, with the tourists spilling out and entering the viewing platforms. She ignored them and continued with her instructions, crossing over the shopping area to the Pok Fu Lam Country Park, a huge expanse of woodlands that ran from the peak all the way to the ocean below, covering the back half of the island. She entered the walking path, getting passed by joggers and hikers on their way to the summit.

As she became lost in the forest, the path reminded her of home and brought some measure of peace. She found herself alone and picked up her pace down the slope. She counted picnic shelters, and when she passed the third one, she slowed, looking for her sign that the meeting was on.

A few feet past the shelter, scribbled in chalk on the path, was a marker stating MILE THREE, ostensibly for someone jogging, but in reality the signal for her. She felt the tension return. She rounded a corner and saw a man sitting on a bench. As she got closer, she recognized the contact from yesterday. He studiously ignored her, focusing on the path to her rear, and she continued on.

She reached the fourth picnic shelter and took the path that led to it, walking beyond the tables and continuing into the tree line. The path ended on a knoll buttressed by a brick wall. A set of stairs led to a picnic table hidden by the wall. Sitting on it was a swarthy man with a full mustache.

He smiled and said, "Hello, Black Widow. Come, have a seat."

She did so, and waited on him to continue.

"What's your name?"

"Elina."

"Elina, you may call me Malik, and first let me tell you how pleased I am to meet you. You will strike a great blow against your enemies and will be remembered long after you have become a martyr."

"Who? What enemies do you speak of? Nobody will tell me anything. It's always something I will learn later."

He appeared surprised at her response, but not angry.

"The supreme enemy against Islam in the world. The Great Satan itself."

He smiled as if she should feel honored. Instead she felt disappointment, her fears confirmed.

"Why do I care about America? They've done nothing to me. To my people."

Taken aback, Malik seemed to consider his next words carefully. "Your people are persecuted by a power that is propped up through the West, much like all the other infidel Muslim regimes around the world. The Arab Spring has caused many to fall, forcing the United States to pretend it supports the change, but they cannot hide their backing for despots, including your Russian Federation. The West allows Russia to call you terrorists, and the Russians in turn use the United States' own attacks as proof that they are no different. The Great Satan kills innocents with Predator drones under the guise of counterterrorism, and Russia assassinates your people using the same mantle."

She considered his words, seeing the truth they held. She knew of the Predator strikes, of course, precisely because she had heard the Russian president use them as an excuse to conduct brutal purges in Chechnya. She had assumed the statements to be simply more lies, but maybe they weren't.

One thing her short trip to Hong Kong had taught her was precisely that she knew nothing of people beyond the borders of Chechnya. Neither did the chain of command of the Chechen insurgency—especially the Islamists who came and fought for religion under the guise of nationalism. They preached a rhetoric that sounded stale even to her naïve ears. Unlike the man sitting in front of her. Maybe she should learn about the world before deciding.

"What would you have me do? What can a single Black Widow do in the United States that isn't just a pinprick?"

"You will become a weapon unlike any other the earth has ever seen."

He pulled out a syringe, causing her eyes to widen.

"This is a vaccine. You will take it once you are back in your hotel room. After twenty-four hours, I will give you a virus. The vaccine does not kill the virus, it only makes it dormant. The virus will live inside of you without hurting you. The only way you can spread it is through your bodily fluids. When the time is right, you will martyr yourself in such a manner that your bodily fluids are spread over a great area."

At first, his words made no sense. She wrestled with them in her mind, and then it became clear: She would do exactly what she had attempted in Chechnya, only instead of ball bearings, the death would be in her blood. The thought made her queasy.

"But when I trained as a *shahid*, it was against a specific target. The killing started and ended with the explosion. This will be the same way? This virus will only kill those who contact my . . . who touch the . . . who clean up what remains? That's who it will kill?"

"No. Once outside of your vaccinated body, the virus

will kill everyone who contracts it in a wave of infection greater than any seen by modern man. It will overwhelm the United States' medical systems and cause a wholesale collapse of their economy. It will destroy the Great Satan. All you have to do is unleash it."

Destroy the Great Satan. By killing innocents.

"But we aren't at war with civilians. I don't want to kill women and children. That's what the Russians do. I want to attack the enemy."

He grasped her hands in a kind gesture that was soothing. His words were calm and seemed born from some truth she had yet to experience. "There are no innocents. Trust me. Do you think the United States feels that way when it bombs women and children in Afghanistan? You mention Russian tactics. Did Russia take such precautions when it destroyed Grozny? They call it collateral damage to hide their culpability. Unlike them, I call it what it is: war. They chose the method of combat. We only return the favor. I was told you were the strongest Black Widow ever seen. Remember the fire that led you down this path."

She took the syringe, conflicted. He patted her shoulder. "Don't worry about killing infidels, no matter their age or gender. They may not all carry a gun, but they want to destroy Islam, be it in Chechnya or Iran. Their hearts are black. Given the chance, they would kill you for nothing more than your religion."

She said nothing. He continued. "Did you set up an e-mail account as instructed?"

"Yes." She gave him the account and password, then asked for his e-mail.

"Don't worry about sending something over the Internet. We'll use the drafts folder of your account to pass any messages. Otherwise, I'll use the cell phone you were given. If you switch out the SIM card, put the new number in a message."

"When will I get the virus?"

"The vaccine takes twenty-four hours to become effective. I'll contact you for a further meeting."

"Where will I go once I'm infected? Where is the target?"

He smiled and patted her hand. "All in good time. This is the point where you hear 'I'll tell you that at a later date.' You have no need to know that now, but trust me, the target has been specially selected. Before you reach it, you must be extra cautious in everything you do. You can't easily spread the virus through the air, but according to the doctor who gave it to me, you *can* spread it. And that's something we don't want prematurely."

"What do you mean, cautious?"

"Wear the surgical masks you were instructed to buy. Use a hand disinfectant regularly. Only drink from bottled water, and dispose of the bottle in a manner so that someone else will never retrieve it. Don't eat in restaurants with silverware. That sort of thing. A premature infection would give the United States time to work on mitigation. We need multiple points of infection simultaneously to overwhelm the system. One point won't work."

"But I'm only a single person. Are there other Black Widows out there?"

He looked her in the eye. "No. You are the only one. The target itself will facilitate the spread. Once you are infected, you are our single hope. Remember that, and the reason you were chosen."

42

Looking through the plate-glass doors from across the street, I saw two security guards sitting at the desk in the middle of the office complex. Two. Not one.

I passed the monocular to Blood and said, "Take a look. What the hell are we going to do now?"

His eye to the scope, he said, "We just need to get them both out of the way. A little harder."

"*Little* harder? A lot harder. We need an additional man, and everyone's committed."

After identifying the Island Shangri-La hotel as an area of interest, we'd wasted a good six hours trying to figure out why, only to come up completely empty. Nobody remotely in the ballpark of our targets was registered, with just two other men of Arabic descent in the entire hotel. Both came up clean as having flown in from Saudi Arabia a week earlier. Knuckles wanted to squeeze them dry, but we had little time available, and in my mind there was only a small chance an IRGC general from Shiite Iran would be doing anything with businessmen from Sunni Saudi Arabia. Except trying to kill them.

I decided to forget the hotel and focus on the cell phones Ernie had purchased. Initially, I only wanted the numbers associated with each, but that had gone out the window when Ernie purchased preloaded SIM cards. Since he'd bought at least ten, we had no idea which SIM we should track, as he could simply switch them out at any given moment. The SIM, or subscriber identity module, was what contained the "brains" of the cell phone and was where the phone number, call logs, contact list, and everything else about the phone were stored.

Well, almost everything.

Every cell phone also has what's known as an International Mobile Equipment Identity, or IMEI. Basically, it's nothing more than a large, unique number that identifies the handset every time the phone talks to a tower. It's the same regardless of the cell service provider or SIM card used and was what brought us back to the original store Ernie had used to purchase the phones. If we obtained those numbers, we could track him and anyone else he provided the phones to.

"Koko, this is Pike. You moving yet?"

"Yes. I'm walking to my start point now. What's up?"

"I have an additional mission. There are now two guards in the office complex. Decoy will take care of one, but I need you to get the other one out of the building."

"What on earth are you talking about? I'm dressed like Catwoman. All I've got as camouflage is a cheesy cotton cover-up. On top of that, I'm supposed to be on the roof before you enter."

"I know, but I can't enter with the guard there, and Decoy is the only other guy on the ground. He's going to trigger the first guard to move. I can't have him do both. You'll just look like a crazy homeless person. Go in and ask him to show you where the subway is located. Get him on the street and pointing the way."

"What about Blood?"

"It's a two-man climb through the air-conditioning duct. I can't do it myself. And he's the only one who's been inside the store."

After abandoning the hotel as a start point, we'd turned the formidable research capabilities of the Taskforce onto the office complex and the little shopping promenade located on the ground floor. Luckily, the building had been constructed before Hong Kong was turned over to the Chinese in 1997, so they were able to find some British floor plans, which showed us how to get in.

While the stores were locked tight with roll-up steel doors, the crawl space in the roof above was wide open. All we needed to do was get to that, and we could simply drop into the store without worrying about penetrating the door. It never ceased to amaze me how people could spend a fortune on the obvious access routes such as doors and windows and yet ignore everything else.

After gleaning everything we could from the Taskforce, we'd conducted on-the-ground reconnaissance, starting in daylight to identify cameras and alarm leads, then at night, when we were going to conduct the break-in, for atmospherics. Yesterday morning, at two A.M., there had been only one guard.

Decoy came on. "Pike, I can trip the camera, then head your way. I can be in and out before the first guard returns."

The guards were stationed at a desk in the center of the cul-de-sac, in front of the elevators, with the shops ringed around them. Their primary focus was two monitors on the desk with feeds from the cameras throughout the building. Decoy was simply going to short out one camera located outside the western exit, which would send a signal the guard would have to explore. As soon as he did, we were going to slip inside and head straight to the men's room adjacent to the elevator shaft and then access the ceiling. That, of course, was back when there had been only one guard in the plan.

"Too much risk. You might still be inside when the first guard gets back. Besides, I need you on-site in case we have to ramp it up. If the first guard doesn't bite on the camera, I might need you to trip the door alarm."

Both side exits were armed with a silent alarm, but, as the office complex had twenty-four-hour access, the front door was wide open.

Jennifer cut in. "I'm here and ready. On the corner to your south. But don't blame me if your exit isn't set. That's a four-story climb and will take me some effort."

"Good to go. We can burn the time inside. All stations, give me an up."

"This is Retro. System is running. Standing by for the camera feed."

"This is Knuckles. Exfil route is open. Just waiting on the word to shoot."

"This is Decoy. You want me to trip?"

I took a deep breath and glanced at Blood, his ebony skin hidden in the shadows, contrasted starkly by the teeth of his smile.

I said, "Execute. Koko, stand by until I trigger you."

It would have been more fun if something sexy had happened at the word *execute*, like a door breach going off or gunfire. Instead, all I got was, "Camera's shorted. Standing by."

Both guards fiddled in their seats, obviously bored. Then one leaned in and pointed at a screen. The other one said something and stood up. Seconds later he was out of sight, headed down the hallway to the side exit.

"Koko, go."

She must have inched up as I got the final check, because she was at the door immediately, and she was right. She looked ridiculous. Black skintight shirt and leggings, wearing Vibram FiveFingers shoes, all covered by a shapeless orange smock. She fit the bill of a crazy homeless person. An attractive crazy homeless person, maybe, but crazy nonetheless.

We watched her talk to the guard, then begin waving her arms around, pointing this way and that. I knew what the problem was instantly.

That bastard doesn't speak English.

He picked up a phone and called someone, then led her out of the building. We waited until they separated from the entrance and then scurried through the front door, running straight into the bathroom.

43

Blood set his pack on the floor and went into a stall while I placed an acoustic device against the door. I listened for a second, then turned to him and nodded.

Standing on the water tank, he maneuvered one of the ceiling tiles aside, then scampered into the hole like a squirrel. I removed the device from the door, grabbed my pack and passed it through the hole, then clambered up.

I moved down the steel I-beam, giving him room to reposition the tile, and we sat in the darkness for a second, letting our eyes get used to the gloom, the lights from below faintly illuminating the space. Saying it was claustrophobic was an understatement, with barely two feet between us and the floor above. Stinking from mildew, the beam covered in something I hoped wasn't rat dung, I seated a headlamp with a red-lens light.

Blood did the same, the feeble glow barely penetrating the darkness, but doing enough to show us the beams we would need to traverse to the store.

Would be pretty embarrassing to fall through the tiles onto the guard desk.

I keyed my headset and said, "We're in," and we began to crawl toward our first objective. We passed a large aluminum air duct, and Blood whispered, "Exfil."

We were going out through the roof, but the only way between floors, outside of using the stairs or elevators, was through the ductwork in the building. And the only way into that was from the outlet in the store. In effect, we either succeeded or learned to live like the rats who'd shit everywhere until the rest of the team could figure out how to exfiltrate us.

I heard Chinese spoken below us, and we paused. The tone sounded conversational, without alarm, so we continued on, moving like a couple of sloths. We reached what should have been objective number one and Blood paused, scanning left and right with his faint light until he found a CAT 5 digital cable snaking its way up an I-beam.

I swung my pack around and pulled out a hijacking device that was the size of a large beeper with two spring-loaded claw feet on the side. Praying the video feed wasn't encrypted, I clamped it to the cable, the claws biting through the plastic covering to the wires beneath. I switched it on and got a green signal.

"Retro, switch is active. You got a feed?"

Retro, located next door in a hotel room that was rented by the hour, said, "Stand by."

We sat, breathing through our mouths in shallow pants while the guards continued to talk. A bead of sweat built up on my nose, then dripped onto the ceiling tile beneath me. I wiped my eyes, feeling the seconds tick by.

"Pike, Retro. I got it. Feed's active. I can see both guards. They're sitting down chatting."

"Roger. Moving."

We reached the far wall and Blood began scooting east until he reached a junction of two I-beams. He leaned into my ear.

"This is where the motion detector is."

I nodded and slid my pack around again, pulling out a clear plastic water bottle with the lid cut off and a length of string taped to the bottom. Blood gingerly pulled open a tile. Sitting directly below him, mounted on the wall, was the motion detector. Blood had surreptitiously taken a picture of it earlier, while "shopping" for phones, and the Taskforce had identified it as an old model. One that was easy to trick.

It didn't really detect motion but rather the infrared energy projected by the human body, much like those annoying garage lights that flip on when you walk by them. The sensor constantly evaluated the amount of infrared coming its way and was calibrated to detect the heat put off by human skin. Unfortunately for it, while light passes just fine through windows or other transparent things, infrared energy does not. Thus, the thing could be stymied with something as simple as a clear water bottle. The trick was getting it on.

The sensor was angled down, where the threat was supposed to be located, so as long as I wore insulated gloves and kept my hands high, I would be good.

That's what the Taskforce had said, anyway.

I got comfortable on the beam, lying lengthwise. I put on the gloves and slowly lowered the bottle, getting its lip beneath the sensor. I inched it up and over, then sealed it down with a very light strip of Scotch tape.

"Retro, Pike. Guards moving?"

"Nope. Still just sitting around."

I nodded at Blood and dropped the twine affixed to the bottom of the bottle through the open tile. Blood slid over until he was hanging, then lightly fell the short distance to the ground. I passed him my pack and followed suit.

The store was only about thirty feet by thirty feet, most of the space taken up with row upon row of cell phones.

I whispered, "Where to now? Where do they keep the receipts?"

Blood pointed to a small filing cabinet beneath the cash register. It was secured with an incredibly complex original equipment lock that took all of five seconds to break. I wasn't sure why they even bothered to use it, since it could have been picked by a five-year-old with a plastic spoon. We split up the receipts and began going through them.

Every cell purchased by a foreigner had to record the passport information of the person who bought it, which was a two-for-one in this case. All we had to do was find the receipts for anyone from Iran and we'd know the IMEI and the name the person was using. If we found more than one, I was going to kick a wall.

Two minutes later Blood tapped my arm. He was holding a Xeroxed copy of Ernie's passport, along with a receipt for the purchase of four different Samsung Galaxy phones. Including the IMEI numbers.

I grinned, laid out the receipt and passport photocopy, and scanned them both with my Taskforce smartphone, sending the PDF file to Retro.

We packed everything up just like we'd found it. Then, while Blood opened the air conditioner intake, I repositioned the ceiling tiles back in place.

I took the string attached to the water bottle and wriggled into the duct, letting it play out. Blood followed, bringing up the intake grillwork. When he nodded, I ripped off the bottle and pulled it inside. As soon as it was clear, Blood reattached the grille. We inched backward until we hit a ninety-degree upright bend and I squatted down, allowing him to climb over me and onto my shoulders, his feet on my hands. When he was ready, I stood up and then pressed upward as far as I could, like a demented cheerleader at a football game. I was struggling to maintain the weight and about to let him slide back down when his feet left me.

I looked up to see them snaking inside the next floor's duct. I waited until he had accessed the office above, knowing he couldn't turn around inside the duct. Eventually, his head poked back out, and he lowered a line with a loop on the bottom. I placed my foot in it and waited until he was back out again.

I heard, "Pike, Blood. I'm set."

"Coming."

I placed both hands on either side of the duct and began inching up, the rope sling stabilizing me while Blood hoisted. Eventually, I reached the open duct and snaked my way inside. I spilled into the office and found Blood was sweating profusely.

"Man, you need to go on a diet. I got the short end of the stick on that one."

I outweighed him by about fifty pounds, so I guess he had a point.

"Sorry. Let's get the hell out of here."

We exited the office, now on the second floor, and jogged to the stairwell, right where the blueprints said it would be. Blood had his hand on the door before I saw the problem. I slapped it away.

"This thing has an alarm lead."

The plan was to exfil through the roof, monkey-crawling across a rope and into the hotel room adjacent to the building. We figured the roof access would be alarmed but didn't mind that, because we'd be out and across before anyone reached it to explore. When they found nothing, they'd assume it was simply a malfunction. Now we'd be giving them a hell of a head start, because they'd get alerted while we were still running up the stairs.

"Koko, Pike. You set?"

I got nothing.

"Koko, Koko, this is Pike. You set?"

"Pike, this is Knuckles. She never called for the shot."

Shit. Knuckles was in the same room as Retro and was going to use a ResQmax line thrower to shoot her the rope once she was on the roof. It looked somewhat like a handheld leaf blower with a folding stock attached and worked off of compressed air, so it was fairly quiet and could reach distances upwards of one hundred meters. We, of course, had modified it to make it much smaller and almost silent. The downside was that it couldn't toss a heavy rope like its bigger brother, so we'd have to shoot a thin line to the rooftop, then tie that to the real rope, pulling it across as our escape bridge.

Which should have already happened.

"Koko, Koko, you there?"

I heard nothing, then someone panting. "Yes. I'm here if you'd give me half a second to anchor myself to talk."

"What's your status?"

"I've got two floors to go. And before you start complaining, the damn guard didn't speak English, but he knew someone who did. A policeman who was kind enough to personally put me on the subway. I've been up and down the peninsula."

I saw Blood laughing and couldn't help but grin myself. "Okay, okay, no rush, but there's an alarm lead here, so when we start coming, we're going to be moving fast."

She spat out, "Fine. That's just fine. Now let me climb."

I grinned again at Blood, both of us acting like school-boys, when Retro came on.

"Pike, you might have to rush after all. One guard just moved to the elevator."

44

The grins vanished. Blood began walking down the hallway, checking doors. I said, "Why? What's he doing?"

"I guess just making the rounds. Find a place to hide."

Blood came jogging back. "All the doors have keypads. We can't even get back into the office we used."

My mind began to spin, looking for options but only returning to the thought of us running from floor to floor trying to outwit the guards, with them closing the noose every time we tripped a stairwell alarm. Until they flooded the place with police.

"Retro, can we get into an elevator? Can we hide there if we don't push any keys?"

"No. What do you think I'm watching him on? The elevators have cameras."

Damn it.

"He's stopped on the second floor. Now unsighted."

Because these hallways don't have cameras.

I raced to the nearest office door, pulled out my phone, and took a picture of the keypad.

"Retro, I need the factory code for this keypad. It's got the word *Onlense* on the handle."

All keypads come with a factory code that's imbedded into them, and the code is usually standard across the lines of that company. You're supposed to alter the factory code once you have it installed, but nobody ever does, including banks and even nuclear facilities. It's a little locksmithing secret that had saved me before.

Retro said, "Stand by, I'm working it."

Knuckles came on with some encouragement. "This is exactly what got me into trouble in Thailand. I'll bet the prisons here are better, though."

Given the size of the building, and depending on which way the guard left from the elevators, we had a couple of minutes to work with. If I saw a light coming down the hall, we'd have no choice but to run into the stairwell.

"Blood, head down the hallway and peek around the bend. Tell me if he's coming."

"And if he is?"

"We run into the stairwell, out the ground floor, and onto the street."

"But I'll be down the end of the hall. About a mile from the stairwell."

"Yeah, and you're faster than me. Go."

He turned and said, "That happens, it's every man for himself. I'm pretty sure I can outrun the cops, leaving them to chase only you."

Retro came on. "Okay, it's a Chinese company called Guangzhou Onlense Science and Technology."

"I don't give a shit who makes it. What's the code?"

"I'm working it. Stand by."

I gauged the distance to the stairwell door. "Blood, what do you have?"

"I got a flashlight, but I can't tell if it's coming or going."

"Damn it, Retro, we need that code."

"Pike, this is Blood, it's coming this way. Not moving fast."

"Close back on me. Get back to the door."

He shuffled toward me, moving at a slow jog, saying, "We got maybe thirty seconds."

I looked down the darkened hallway, illuminated only by emergency lighting, and caught the faint bounce of the flashlight.

Better to be through the stairwell door before he turns the corner.

"Retro, never mind. We're getting out now. Decoy, you still on the street?"

"Stop, stop! It's pound six six six star."

Great. Sign of the devil. That's gotta mean something.

The light flashed brighter and I jabbed the keypad, now committed to getting inside the office or getting seen. The light turned the corner and the keypad flashed green. I ripped open the door and we fell inside. Brett whirled and grabbed the door handle, preventing it from slamming shut on its automatic arm. After he snicked it closed, I called for an update.

"Retro, it worked, but it was close. What's the guard at the desk doing? Anything alerting?"

"No. I think you're good."

"Okay. Tell me when he's back in the elevator. Koko, how's it coming?"

"Got the line. I'm anchoring now."

"Good to hear. Remember, we're going to be moving fast, so no time to adjust anything once we crack the door down here."

"Roger."

We waited for maybe five minutes, catching our breath, then Retro said, "He's in the elevator. Headed up."

I looked at Blood and he nodded.

"Koko, here we come."

I cracked the door and snuck a glance out. Seeing nothing, I led the way to the stairwell, not even pausing when I reached it. I broke the seal and knew the clock was now ticking.

We raced upward, taking the steps two and three at a time, Blood slowly but surely leaving me behind.

Retro said, "Guard on the ground floor just stood up. He's going to the elevator."

We crossed the third floor, then the fourth, continuing on to the roof. Blood cranked open the door, then held it for me. I slid out into the gravel and pivoted to the left, running to the opposite side where the anchor rope was located.

I reached it but didn't see Jennifer. I whirled around and she rose from behind a heating unit.

I said, "Go, go."

Without a word, she leaned out over the edge and grasped the rope, hand-walking until she was hanging over the four-story drop before locking her legs around it. She began to monkey-crawl at astonishing speed, seeming to slide like ice on a countertop across the chasm.

"Blood, get on it. I'm setting the cutter for three minutes."

Jennifer had rigged the anchor point with a pair of self-cutting flex ties that were designed for releasing prisoners remotely, such as when you captured a bad guy having dinner with his family. They incorporated a time-release cutter that could be set for whatever duration was needed and were pretty handy when you didn't want to leave the family tied up—possibly for days—but also didn't want them to go shouting to the police until you were far enough away. Handy for other things as well, like now.

Blood clambered out, and I hit the timer, only to hear Retro say, "First guard in the elevator didn't go down. He went up to you. Just left the fourth floor at a run."

Which meant he'd be here in seconds. Before I was across.

Going to have to take him down. Can't let him see the rope.

Best case, when he woke up they'd have nothing but one big ol' mystery on their hands. Nothing stolen, only some sort of magic vanishing act after being attacked by a wraith.

I raced back to the stairwell door, turning the corner just as it opened. I darted left, letting the door block me from view. I waited until the guard stepped forward, shining his light left and right. When the door swung closed, I pounced, wrapping his neck in a guillotine choke. He flailed around as I buried my shoulder into the back of his head, cinching shut the blood flow into his carotid arteries. In seconds, he was out.

I lowered him to the ground and took off at a sprint back to my escape bridge. I could see Blood climbing through the window, Jennifer and Knuckles inside. I grabbed the rope and hung out over the gap. I brought my legs up and began scrambling upside down, moving as fast as I could, wishing for Jennifer's speed.

I was halfway across when I remembered the cutter, and the time I'd lost taking out the guard. Just as it sliced through the flex ties of the anchor.

I felt a sickening moment of weightlessness, then began swinging, moving faster and faster. I cinched my hands as tight as I could and tucked my head, spinning my legs to get my back to the wall. I just about made it, colliding on my side with the rough brick hard enough to almost dislodge me from the rope.

I slid down about five feet, feeling the heat build up through the leather in my gloves, and before I could clear my head, I felt my body being hoisted against the brick. I wrapped my hands into the rope and planted my feet against the wall, walking up as the team pulled.

I made it to the window ledge and was unceremoniously pulled inside. Blood ripped in the remainder of the rope while Jennifer slammed the window shut and jerked the drapes. I just lay on the floor gasping for air.

Knuckles said, "I'll bet following those Arabs from Saudi Arabia would have been a hell of a lot easier."

45

The small sitting room at the back of the Kowloon Mosque and Islamic Centre was now Malik's to use as he saw fit, the contact from Iran having enough clout to ensure that Malik wasn't disturbed by any of the other patrons. He had no idea what they'd been told and really didn't care.

He'd transformed the place into a tiny surveillance center, getting the feeds from the cameras located on the four corners of the building and the front entrance. The view wasn't the best, just a narrow slice of vision from each one, but if Sanjar did his job correctly, a narrow slice would be enough to spring the trap.

After being told his new team was on the way, he'd set the hook last night, providing an irresistible lure for whoever was tracking him. Now he was letting the enemy spin into overdrive trying to track his bait. Other men in the Quds Force would have tried to create an ironclad trap, something heavy-handed that they felt would guarantee a reaction, but they underestimated the enemy.

As much as he hated the Great Satan, he also understood them. Understood that they were not the buffoons the Arab street portrayed, blundering around blindly. Yes, they had a penchant for stomping around with all of the grace of a hippo, but hidden among the idiots were men as deadly as any in the world. Cunning vipers who lived among the shadows much like him. Men who understood his world well enough to take out his chosen team. They would see through all but the lightest of touches.

Unfortunately, he feared the team sent to replace them did not have this same depth of understanding. When he'd briefed them last night they had seemed antsy for a fight, convinced either Allah or their own skill would guarantee success. He had no intention of using any of them overtly. They would be bit players in the upcoming drama.

He glanced at his watch, then used a landline to dial a hotel number, not wanting the hotel to have a record of one of his new cell phones. When the front desk answered, he gave a room number, and Sanjar came on after a single ring. He said, "Turn it on and place one call to whomever you wish in town. Leave it in place for one hour, then begin your walk."

Sanjar said, "Do we know the devils are here?"

"No, there is no way to prove it without giving up the trap. Trust me, though, they're here. I'm sure of it."

Malik didn't hear the same confidence come back through the phone. Sanjar asked, "The men are set?"

"Yes. You had no trouble finding the DVDs?"

"None at all."

"Insha'Allah, we will be rid of these hunters in an hour."

DECOY SHOUTED FROM the bedroom of the suite we were using as a tactical operations center, "Pike, phone just went active. Same location."

Which did nothing to clarify what was going on. We'd returned to our hotel after the near-disaster, happy to have a thread to pull, only to find a lead waiting on us. Apparently, the third phone we had been trying to track—the one that had called the cheap Hong Kong hostels in the first place—had placed a call to the general's phone while we were playing cat burglar. The Task-force had geo-located its position at the Conrad Hotel on Hong Kong Island. Which made no sense whatsoever. Through a process of elimination, we had figured it was Ernie's phone and that he'd ditched it before leaving Singapore. Now it was active, and not at the hostel Ernie was using.

Knuckles pulled up the grid on our "company" laptop, using a hidden partition in the hard drive. He was looking a hell of a lot better, and I was glad to have him back in shape. I'd purposely kept him out of any sharp action, which had done nothing but aggravate him, but he had more to offer than simply brawn.

"What do you think?" I asked. "What's up with the call?"

He stared at the screen for a moment, then said, "I

don't know. Why on earth would *that* phone try to contact the general on his captured cell? Whoever owns it had to know it was no good."

"So you think it's a goose chase? A coincidence?"

"In my heart, it stinks, but rationally it's something we have to focus on. It only rang twice, then disconnected, so it was probably just a knee-jerk dial before moving on to the real phone. A mistake that we can capitalize on."

"But it might just be a glitch in the network. It's happened to us before."

"Too many coincidences here to ignore." He turned the computer toward me. "For one, the Conrad is right next to the Shangri-La hotel, where we lost Ernie. Maybe this was where he was going all along. Maybe that's why we found nothing at the Shangri-La. We lost him at that point, so it's possible."

I thought about our next actions. We had the IMEIs for the other four phones, but so far they hadn't become active. This cell was the only lead we had right now, as flaky as it was. Ignoring it could cause us to lose the virus.

We can always redirect later.

"All right. We're going to stage at the new hotel and track whoever has that phone. I need someone to stay here and monitor it and the other four handsets. I want you to do that."

Knuckles bristled, saying, "Pike, I'm sick of getting treated like a leper. Let someone else do it. I want in the fight. Retro's better at this shit than I am."

I glanced behind me to make sure nobody was listening, then said, "Knuckles, I've got a bad feeling about this. I need some judgment here, not simply a phone track. I need a 2IC that's not engaged. You're taking this the wrong way. I'd love to have you on the ground, but I don't need another gun. What I need is some solid advice I trust. Please."

A small piece of hurt flitted across his face, but only for an instant. "Yeah. I can do it. Shit, anyone could. Get out of here."

I kept my eyes on him for a second, about to say something else, when Jennifer interrupted. Which only made him feel worse, I'm sure. He had become a believer in her capabilities, but it had to hurt knowing I was more willing to take her into a potential gunfight than him. He misunderstood how much I needed his brain, becoming fixated on the idea that I felt he wasn't ready.

She said, "If we're going to start tracking that phone, we need to get set. It's across the harbor."

"I know. Get them moving. Box the hotel. You're the surveillance chief. Figure out how you want to skin it."

Her mouth parted, taken aback at the responsibility. She glanced at Knuckles, then said, "Okay . . . maybe we should talk about that."

"Talk about what? Get the team moving. I'll take over when I get there."

She squinted at me, seeing through the fact that I was using this to make her better and not liking the test. She turned around and began giving orders. When she said she was the SC until I arrived on site, Decoy looked like he'd been slapped. He snapped his head to me, and I bored into him with my eyes, not saying a word. He clenched his teeth and began packing kit.

Knuckles said, "Wow. Not the call I would have made. What with a pandemic on the way. But I guess you'd be better off with me sitting up here."

He had a slight grin on his face, and I knew he was kidding. He understood what I was doing because I'd done the same thing with him on a number of occasions.

I said, "I'll be there before they even get set. I want to get her used to being on equal footing with the team. No better way to do that than putting her in charge. Now scoot over, I need to send Kurt an update."

He passed me the laptop and said, "Well, good luck with that."

I began typing my SITREP, saying, "I don't need luck. I need you watching my back."

46

Sanjar exited the elevator and moved to a coffee stand inside the marble lobby of the Conrad Hotel, purposely giving whatever team was around time to locate him. He had no idea how they would do that, but the general had told him not to worry. There were technical devices that the enemy would use to track his phone. His job wasn't to identify the surveillance. He was the bait, and he would lead them on a trail where others would do so.

He paid for the coffee and shouldered the knapsack Malik had given him, an ordinary backpack no different than the ones used by students on college campuses all over the world, currently stuffed with over fifty counterfeit DVDs of the latest Hollywood movies.

Instead of exiting out the front door, he went back up a level and entered the Pacific Place mall, his first choke point. He meandered through it, stopping at a bakery for a bagel, then continuing on.

Malik had instructed him to walk with a purpose, as if he had a destination in mind, but not go so fast that he would force the surveillance effort to stretch out.

He wasn't to lose them but had to convince them he was doing exactly what he appeared to be doing. In no way did he want them to suspect that he was leading them through a series of gates to sift out their surveillance box.

ANSWERING HER PHONE, Jennifer said, "Where the hell are you? It's Ernie, and he's already on the move. We've tracked him for about thirty minutes."

She listened for a second, then interrupted, saying, "Pike, he's getting on a ferry. Stay on the Kowloon side. We're coming to you."

She heard his answer, wanting to fling the phone out into the water. She hung up and clicked over to the team's internal radio.

"All elements, this is Koko. Pike's still out of radio range on the Kowloon side. He just got on a ferry, which means he's going to pass us as we head across."

Which means I'm still in charge. She didn't add that last little bit, not liking it any more than the knuckle-draggers on the team.

Decoy came on, his words surprising her. "No worries. We're doing fine. Everyone, remember your heat state and pass it if you think you're getting burned. Koko can't read your mind."

A tacit approval of her actions so far, and a reminder to the team that she was still in charge. From Decoy, of all people. The comment gave her a boost of self-confidence. *Which is probably what he intended. I'm never going to figure out what makes these guys tick.*

She said, "Who's on him now?"

"This is Blood. I got him. Lower deck, toward the stern. I'm three rows back."

"He still has the pack?"

"Yeah, he's got it between his legs, and he's not meeting anyone here. Not yet anyway."

She said, "I see Retro. Anyone else up here with me?"

The ferry had two separate decks, and she'd chosen the upper one to stay out of the mix until needed. She was sure others had loaded after her, but she made no attempt to locate them, not wanting to associate at all with the rest of the team and possibly burn the surveillance effort.

Decoy said, "No. I'm on the lower deck, aft."

"Okay, when we exit, Decoy, pick up the eye until we merge on the gangway. Retro, take it from there. Acknowledge."

Retro and Decoy both said they understood, and she settled back, trying to think four steps ahead of what she might be asked to do once the ferry docked, knowing it would be at least forty-five minutes until Pike could catch up. With the mantle of leadership fully on her, she began to think through more than just the mechanics of the surveillance. She began to think about the implications, and they weren't making any sense.

* * *

MALIK HEARD HIS laptop ping with an e-mail and opened the latest batch of pictures from his countersurveillance effort. He'd had Sanjar walk through multiple choke points strategically positioned on his route to the ferry, with prepositioned countersurveillance taking pictures at each one. He intended to analyze them, matching up anyone who was in each batch. The odds of someone walking the exact same route as Sanjar were beyond remote, so if he got a match, it would mean the plan was in motion.

So far, he'd identified a nondescript man wearing clothes that were about ten years out of date and another, taller man. Both had been in two separate sets of photos, but not at the same choke points. He was hoping either one would pop up in this batch, confirming the surveillance. He didn't need to identify the entire team. He only needed to confirm there *was* a team before setting the plan in motion.

He scanned the photos and froze, zooming in on one. *The cleric was right.*

Staring at the lens of the camera was the black man who had chased him in Singapore.

He inserted a SIM card into one of the Galaxy phones from Sin Tat and called Sanjar, now not wanting the Islamic center landline tied to the cell phone they were using as bait.

He said, "They're on you right now. Don't worry about following the route anymore. When you get off the ferry, head straight to the park, but still come around the

Islamic center. Get them to walk by the cameras. Remember, you need to make the fight convincing."

He hung up and dialed another number. "Sanjar is coming now. Don't lose them once they pick up the pack."

The man on the other end said, "What do you want me to do if they don't pick it up? You want me to take them out?"

"No! Don't do that. They'll pick up the pack. When that happens, alert me and follow them until I can bring in the police."

"But I'll be in a position to attack. We'll miss our opportunity. It's why my team was flown here."

Remembering the debacle in Thailand the year before, when the immature men had prematurely exploded an improvised device in their safe house, Malik let some steel into his voice. "Do not attempt anything against the Americans. Understand? I want this handled quietly. Let the police do their job."

He hung up the phone and dialed one more number, this to a contact who would alert the Hong Kong police force.

He had toyed with many different ideas of how to prevent the team from interfering with his plan, ranging from an outright ambush like the one espoused by the new team leader to some sort of poison or accident. He'd realized he was looking at the problem too narrowly. He only needed to remove them, not necessarily kill or maim any of the members. He'd hit upon his idea when talking with Sanjar about Sin Tat Plaza.

China was a free-for-all of copycat articles, from Adidas shoes to Apple computers. The Chinese routinely counterfeited anything they could get their hands on, much to the chagrin of the United States. While the Great Satan screamed about copyright infringements, China did little to stem the black market of goods. Even so, the pressure was there, so he'd decided to use that as leverage. What better way to show China was serious about stopping counterfeit goods than to arrest some Americans who were trafficking in them?

Using his IRGC contacts, he'd let it be known to the authorities that Americans involved in the transport of black-market DVDs were in Hong Kong, and he had set up a sting, with only the time and place unknown. He knew that the Americans would assume the DVDs held important IRGC information and would take them with them for exploitation. All he had to do was locate where they went, then send in the police. With any luck, they'd come upon the entire team watching a grainy copy of the movie *Argo*. It wouldn't matter that there was nothing but smoke in his whole artifice, with no other evidence than the bag of goods. China would want to crow about it anyway and wasn't very concerned with the rights of the accused.

The thought made him smile.

47

Walking up Kowloon Park Drive, Jennifer heard, "He's still on Ashley, headed north. It's tight in here. My heat state is getting bad."

She said, "Pull off. Blood, can you intersect?"

He said, "Looking at the map, Ashley dead-ends into an apartment complex. If he's continuing north, he'll have to cut over to Hankow Road. I'm on that now. Decoy, can you stay on him until he passes the last cut-through? If he keeps going, we know his destination is close and I can take the eye from there."

Decoy said, "Yeah. I can stop here and see that. Stand by."

Jennifer initiated the map on her phone, seeing the large expanse of Kowloon Park just beyond the apartment complex he mentioned, across Haiphong Road. A building at the corner of the park caught her eye. An Islamic center.

She said, "Retro, what's your status?"

"Parallel on Nathan."

"You see the park on your map?"

"Yes."

"Look at the southeast corner. It's the Kowloon Mosque and Islamic Centre. I want you to move to that location. I think he might be headed there."

"You got it."

Decoy said, "He just cut over. He's unsighted."

A minute went by with nothing, putting a knot in Jennifer's stomach. *Should have diverted Retro to Decoy. Shouldn't have let him get out of sight.*

Then her radio came to life. "This is Blood. I've got the eye. Now headed north on Hankow."

Toward the center.

A second later her phone buzzed, a call from Knuckles.

"One of the IMEI phones just went active. It's at the Islamic center next to Kowloon Park."

Which confirmed her thoughts. And also triggered a little bit of an alarm.

MALIK KNEW SANJAR was only blocks away and began scanning his camera feeds. He didn't have real-time radio contact, only the cell phone, and didn't want to miss him.

Watching the screen, he realized that catching Sanjar passing by was going to be problematic. The view was so narrow that he would have only a split second, the cameras obviously designed for looking at tape after the fact instead of continuous monitoring for any preventive purposes. He'd made sure that no such recording was happening now.

Focused on the mass of people flowing up and down Nathan Road, a solitary figure caught his attention, precisely because he wasn't moving. It was the man with the out-of-date clothes. Part of the surveillance effort. Part of the devil's team.

JENNIFER REACHED THE entrance to Kowloon Park and magnified it on her map. A large expanse of terrain smack in the heart of Hong Kong, it housed everything from a sculpture garden to a fitness trail, with the entire area landscaped much like a zoo. The only thing missing was the animals.

The Islamic center was to her right, but she decided to ignore it, heading into the park. She walked for about a hundred meters, winding around the trails until she found a park bench on the north end of a sculpture garden, a lily pond off to her right. She sat, pretending to read her tour guide and waiting on the call that the target had entered the Islamic center, something she was convinced would happen.

The time dripped by and she returned to Knuckles's information about the IMEI cell phone, wondering yet again about the circumstances of the entire mission. None of it fit.

Why would Ernie live in that slovenly hostel if he had a room at the Conrad Hotel? Especially since the name they had from the flight manifest in Singapore, and had now confirmed with the passport photocopy from the Sin

Tat mission, hadn't shown up in the Conrad registry? It wasn't because he was afraid of being found. The room wasn't tied to him. And why would he be using a phone from Singapore after he'd just purchased four new handsets? With one of those new handsets now talking to him on the old, compromised phone?

It was almost like he wanted to be found.

She dialed Pike to relay her fears. Wanting someone else to make the call about ending the effort.

"You back across yet?"

"Yeah, just landed. Where are you?"

"Kowloon Park. I think he's going to the Islamic center on the southeast corner. He gets in there, and all bets are off."

"Any sign you've spiked?"

"Not that we can tell. He's still out in the open, not pulling anything stupid."

"Just keep on him. You're doing great. Sorry for the mess-up with the ferry, but you got us this far. I'll be there in fifteen minutes."

"Pike, I don't like this. I think it's a setup."

"Why?"

"Just the whole set of circumstances. It doesn't make any sense. The general is pretty damn smart, and after Thailand and Singapore, I think he's trying to regain the offensive. We should pull off. Let him think he's won and focus on the other phones."

"Well, do what you believe is right. I'll be there as soon as I can. If you call it, you call it."

She said nothing for a moment, prompting Pike. "You still there?"

"Yeah, I'm here. Pike, I can't call it. I'm not the team leader."

"Jennifer, I'm not there. I wish I hadn't put you in this position, but that's water under the bridge. I can't call what I don't know. You're on the ground. You see something that doesn't fit, then make a decision. Otherwise, he's the biggest lead we have. Nobody is going to second-guess."

Bullshit. Everybody *is going to second-guess.*

All she said was, "Okay. Get your ass up here. I'm ready to turn over the radio."

48

Malik kept his eye on the man with retro clothing, waiting on him to do something alerting. He checked the view of the northern camera, making sure he could see into the small courtyard adjacent to the mosque. A stair-step down from the park, it was a little grotto used for some Chinese ceremony or celebration he couldn't fathom. Forty feet long and twenty wide, it was layered in concrete, with stone benches lining the walls on both sides and small concrete tables interspersed at regular intervals, with the ash of candles or incense burned into the surfaces of the slabs next to the benches. It had never been occupied in the reconnaissance he had done before and was the perfect place for his little drama to play out. He could control the outcome along with the follow-on surveillance effort, as there were only two exits.

He returned to the stationary man and saw him back up. Within seconds, Sanjar entered the screen. A brief blip of recognition, then gone. Right behind him was the black man from Singapore. They disappeared from view, and he felt the adrenaline begin to flow. Even here, where he would have no ability to alter the outcome. He chewed his lip, praying the new men did what they had been asked to do.

Everything up until this point had been easy, something he could have done with a few children from his neighborhood. It would all be irrelevant if they didn't manage to follow the target long enough to give the Hong Kong police a location, be it on the street or in a hotel.

He turned to the grotto camera and saw Sanjar enter. His protégé stood for a moment, then pulled out a map from his pocket and made a show of bringing it to his face. An ostentatious demonstration that he was signaling someone. More fodder for the surveillance to see. More evidence that what was about to occur required their attention.

He saw the team leader enter from the camera's upper reaches. Malik had no sound but knew what was about to occur. He hoped it looked real. He needn't have worried. The team leader whispered into Sanjar's ear, then smacked him on the back of the head. Sanjar looked shocked, as he probably was, and pushed the man. They began shouting, then Sanjar, apparently truly furious, punched the team leader in the mouth and knocked him to the ground. He stood over him with a snarl on his face, only to be attacked from the left, by the man who was supposed to pick up the surveillance to follow.

Idiot!

Malik's great plan was breaking down over nothing

more than childish emotion. He couldn't believe it. How were they supposed to compete in the world of the vipers when he was given men such as this?

He stood up, fists clenched, wanting to run into the grotto but knowing it was worthless. He saw Sanjar fall, roll to his left, and get up on his knees, holding his hands up, as if begging for mercy. He dropped the backpack and stood. Then he lashed out with a foot, catching the team leader in the testicles and felling him like a tree.

Sanjar screamed something at the other man and took off running, the man in hot pursuit.

Malik let out a breath. The wrong man was now chasing Sanjar, but the entire team knew the plan. As long as they stuck to the script, the trap was set.

Except for the idiot in the grotto now cupping his balls. No way would the Americans enter for the bag as long as he lay there rolling around.

He willed the team leader to rise. To vacate the small concrete space and allow the American devil to retrieve the bag. On-screen the man was breathing in ragged gasps, a thin stream of spittle on his lips, curled into a ball. If he waited too long, the trap would fail.

Get up!

He saw the team leader rise, the grainy image doing nothing to mask the pure rage on his face. A rage that would want an outlet. Perhaps he would give him Sanjar when this was over. After all, the script hadn't called for a kick to the groin. The man limped off to the south, around the corner of the building away from Nathan Road. Out of sight.

Malik waited, both the man with the bad clothes and the black operative still out of view of the camera. The clock ticked, and still nothing occurred. He unconsciously held his breath.

And then the black man cautiously advanced, looking left and right. He paused, surveying the scene, then approached rapidly, snatching up the bag. He ran four feet before stopping abruptly. Malik saw him talking to the air, then dropping the bag.

What is he doing?

JENNIFER HEARD THE situation reports from Blood and began to believe she had been mistaken in her misgivings, silently thanking the gods that she hadn't called off the surveillance and missed the golden egg that had just been laid into their lap. Whatever was occurring had nothing to do with them. The fight was clearly real, an internal dispute between factions.

It had happened faster than she or the rest of the team could collate, and now Ernie was on the run without the pack. Only a single man standing between them and retrieval. The virus could very well be inside that ruck, and for whatever reason the men at the meeting had chosen to fight instead of pass.

She maintained her position in the sculpture garden,

listening to the updates on the radio. Blood said he'd lost sight of Ernie; then Retro said the final man had left the area. She heard Blood commit to the grotto, moving toward the bag. Then she caught sight of Ernie running to her front.

He was followed by another man, and as they reached the edge of the sculpture garden, both slowed. Ernie stopped completely and was met by his chaser. The man slapped his shoulder hard, and Ernie pushed back. But there was no longer any fear in either of them.

What in the world?

She stood up, moving to the grotto at a rapid pace, studying them both. When she reached the far side of the garden, right next to the entrance of the grotto, she saw Ernie put his arm around the other man's shoulder.

A trap. It's a trap.

"Blood, Blood, this is Koko. Let the bag go. I say again, let the bag go."

"What are you talking about? I have it now with no issue. I screened it. No explosives or anything. It's full of DVDs. No threat."

"Drop it. Drop it now. I don't know why it's bad, but get rid of it and get out."

Decoy cut in, his voice patronizing. "Koko, he's got the bag without a problem. Let's reassess back at the hotel. We're exfiling now. Get off the radio and meet us in the TOC."

Two hours before, she would have acquiesced, but Pike had squarely placed the mantle of leadership on her.

On *her*. Letting Decoy override her decision was the easy path. The one she should have chosen. He would be to blame if the decision was wrong. But now she couldn't, because she *knew* it was wrong.

She keyed the radio, her voice steel. "Drop that fucking bag right now. Acknowledge."

She waited, then heard Blood say, "Okay, bag at my feet and the guy who got his nuts kicked doesn't like it. He's blocking the exit."

49

I reached the outside range of our little covert radios in time to hear the last exchange, and it sent a spike of rage through me. Yeah, I should have been on-site, but I wasn't, and Jennifer was the designated team leader. It would have been nothing but a little give-and-take, but it looked like she had been right, and the seconds wasted were now turning out to be the difference between life and death.

I keyed my mike, letting my anger out while assessing the situation. "This is Pike. I'm on-site. All elements shut the fuck up. Blood, don't push the issue. Back off. Retro and Decoy, provide backup to Blood. Koko, give me a SITREP. What's the reason for your call?"

Before she could answer, Blood said, "The guy has a weapon. I can see it underneath his shirt. We're going into a fight. Do I have clearance for lethal force?"

Jesus.

"No. No, you *don't.* Don't get into a gunfight unless he shows a weapon. Decoy, Retro, where are you?"

I was running full out now, inside the park and trying

to get to the location with the skimpy directions I had heard over the radio. Retro said, "I'm on him. I got the grotto covered. Blood, exit to the south."

It was going to happen more quickly than I could control. I reached the sculpture garden Jennifer had described and heard gunfire. The masses in the park all jerked to life, most stiffening and looking left and right, some hitting the deck. Ahead of me two men began running toward the sound of the weapons. I recognized Ernie.

"Blood, Blood, you got two inbound. Coming right at you. Decoy, Retro, enemy coming from the west."

I heard nothing but more sporadic pops, as if they were trading shots hidden behind cover. Which was the worst thing we could have. We needed to hit them with overwhelming force and disappear.

Retro came on. "Blood's hit. I can't get to him, but he's okay and under cover. The asshole's hiding in the pillars and taking potshots. All I can do is suppress."

I saw Ernie and his pal running to the end of the garden, both with weapons out, a good seventy meters away. Too far for a shot with the civilians scrambling around.

"Decoy, where are you?"

"I'm coming, I'm coming."

Ernie reached the entrance to the grotto, leaping over a woman screaming uncontrollably on the ground. His first foot hit the ground, and she grabbed the leg still over her body. She rose, twisting him in midair and driving him into the concrete.

Jennifer.

His buddy whirled and raised his weapon. I screamed to stop the shot and saw his head explode. Out of the bushes, Decoy burst onto the deck and hammered Ernie in the face with his weapon. He jerked Jennifer to her feet and both raced down the stairs into the grotto.

I ran as fast as I could, closing the distance in seconds. I heard a firecracking of rounds, then nothing. I slammed into the grotto, leaping straight down from the top of the stairs, and found the team split between a dead Arab and Blood getting first aid.

Jennifer was wrapping a compress around Blood's upper arm with Decoy helping. He saw my anger and raised his hands as if I was going to knock him out, which, actually, I was considering.

He said, "Don't even start. I got it, I got it. I screwed up. She's good at this shit."

I heard sirens coming, and then my phone rang, with Knuckles on the caller ID.

We have to get out of here.

I answered and said, "Knuckles, I don't have time. We've got a mess here. I'll call you in a few minutes."

He said, "Make the time. The other IMEI phone just went active. It's located at the Shangri-La hotel."

50

Malik saw the new team leader enter the grotto, a murderous glint in his eye, and knew the mission was about to implode. There was no way the American would take the bag once that idiot confronted him. He grimaced, a small part of him hoping the man would push the issue far enough to get his ass kicked, but consciously knowing that was the worst thing that could happen. Then they'd both be involved with the police.

He accessed the Widow's e-mail account and rapidly typed a message, keeping one eye on the drama, the lack of sound making it seem as if it were miles away instead of just outside the building he was in.

He'd ordered the Widow to check the account every ten minutes and now wished he'd made it every five. He wanted to get her moving immediately out of Hong Kong as a precaution. As soon as he was done, hitting save and causing the e-mail account to register an unsent draft, he picked up the Galaxy phone Sanjar had purchased and dialed the bait phone's number but got no response.

He heard muffled gunfire and jerked his head to the screen, his mouth falling open. *Shooting? The idiot escalated to using his weapon?*

He'd believed that if the plan failed it would be because the Americans refused to take the bait, the end result being their leaving the bag, forcing him to come up with some other method of interdicting the team. As he watched the scene unfold in the narrow frame of the camera, he knew he'd now have to worry about the mission, period.

In grainy black and white, he saw the black man aiming a pistol at something out of range of the camera. The man spun to the ground from an unseen force and scrambled out of view, followed by a flurry of activity, the cheap camera making it hard to discern what was going on. He saw the team leader—the idiot who had started the fight—step into view and begin firing wildly at something out of sight. The man spun a half step as if he'd been punched in the shoulder, his two-handed grip broken. He held his ground, the pistol in one fist, continuing to fire, his other arm hanging limply at his side. He got off two rounds before his body was whipsawed by invisible rounds. He fell face-first into the concrete. Malik watched for a sign of life. Instead, a dark pool spread underneath the body on the black and white screen.

Malik began calculating the damage and realized the new Quds team was forfeit. Forget the authorities simply arresting the Americans. At the very least, they'd have the dead team leader and a passport from Iran. Minimal investigative work would lead to the rest of the new team.

Sanjar was the only one with a clean break. Hopefully he'd had the sense to flee.

He thought about his own escape and realized he was in as safe a place as possible. No way would the police come storming into a mosque. At least not until they'd cleared such a search with the proper authorities. Eventually they would, though, if only to ask for the nonexistent tapes for the cameras outside.

He took stock of his vulnerabilities, staring at the phone he had used. The only connection between him and everything that had occurred. He'd called both the team and Sanjar on it. He ripped out the SIM card and the battery, putting both in his pocket. He then stomped on the phone, smashing it, more out of frustration than because it was necessary.

He sagged in the chair and rubbed his face, still incredulous at the debacle. He heard running feet outside his door, men chattering in Arabic. He knew it was only a matter of time before they barged in on him, blathering about the fight that had occurred. He would need to be ready. Able to pretend he was as astounded as they were to keep them from alerting the authorities about the strange man in the back room.

A chirp from his computer jarred him out of his dismal thoughts. He brought the computer out of sleep and saw a new draft message from the Widow. With the SIM card she was using.

He inserted a new SIM card into the other phone Sanjar had purchased, activated it, and dialed. When the

Black Widow answered, he began giving instructions in a low voice, ensuring she repeated everything he said.

I HEARD THE sirens getting louder and said, "Knuckles, hang on. I got a situation here."

Luckily, the grotto had an exit right next to the mosque, which spilled out onto Nathan Road. Nobody had been inside when the fight went down. All they knew was there had been gunfire. We had maybe ten seconds before people got up the courage to explore, but that should be enough.

"How's Blood doing?"

Moving to the exit, Decoy said, "Just a ding on the biceps. He's okay."

Jennifer finished wrapping it and said, "The problem is the blood everywhere. He's going to stand out."

"Retro, give him your jacket. Everybody else get ready to exfil. Meet back at the hotel. Arm the alert on your phones. I want to know your location to the meter. You get picked up, hit the alarm. We'll figure something out."

Retro said, "My jacket? Why *my* jacket?"

Jennifer said, "Because it looks like you got it from Goodwill in 1988."

Decoy poked his head around the wall and said, "Clear here. Crowd's gathering outside. We can blend if we leave now."

Blood pulled off his shirt, the left side soaked red. Retro stripped the jacket off and handed it over.

I said, "Go. Get out. Decoy and Jennifer first. Retro five seconds after. Blood, you come with me."

By the time Blood had the god-awful Members Only jacket zipped, the others had disappeared. We flowed into the crowd, pretending to gawk along with everyone else. Police were running on foot from a substation up the street and I could see flashing lights coming down Nathan Road.

I didn't want to walk in front of the Islamic center but also didn't want to move toward the police. I opted to jog across the road, between the cars, not moving fast enough to draw any attention. Easy to do with everyone focused on the park.

I dialed my phone. "Knuckles, we had a gunfight. The bastards were hunting us. They set a trap."

He said, "I know. I'm outside the main entrance to the park right now. Here's the status of our IMEI track: New phone just went active inside the Islamic center. Old phone is offline. Also, as I said before, new phone is active at the Shangri-La hotel. What do you need me to do?"

Huh? "Hang on—you're where?"

"Outside the park. I heard the status on the radio. The repeater's in my room."

What the hell?

We reached an alley, and Blood took it with me following. "So you came down here? I told you to monitor the phone net."

His voice came back a little miffed. "You told me to use my damn judgment. And I did. Did you think I was going to sit up there while the team was getting ambushed?"

I knew it was a losing battle. "Never mind. Where's the phone at the Shangri-La headed?"

"That's why I left. We can't get any granular resolution on its movements. Taskforce is petrified about messing with the Chinese cell network. They refused to do it. They'll ping it every ten minutes but won't risk a full-on trace in real time. The pings will come to our phones."

"Why is that? We need the resolution. Did you talk to Kurt?"

"Yeah. Well, I tried. The president himself said no go. They're afraid of China seeing the activity. Apparently, China's on cyber red alert because we've accused them of hacking our networks. National Command Authority won't risk it. A full-on trace leaves too many fingerprints that can be tracked back to the United States."

"So we've got one phone inside the Islamic center and one at the Shangri-La?"

"Yeah. I say forget the center and focus on the hotel. Too much activity here."

He was right. "Okay, listen, since you're so fired up about getting into the mix, get inside the park before it's blanketed with police. We dropped Ernie and another guy at the eastern entrance to the grotto. We didn't get a chance to search them. See if you can get there before the cops. Find their phones and passports."

He said, "That's going to be tough. I'm moving inside now, and the police are already here."

"But they don't know where to look. They'll contain first. I'm sure all they know is that there was a shootout in the park, and this thing is huge."

"Roger all. I'll contact you later."

I hung up and switched to the radio net.

"Koko, Retro, Decoy, you still up?"

I got a roger and gave them a situation update on the Shangri-La lead. "I'm headed back to the hotel with Blood. We won't know if the phone's moved for another ten minutes. Decoy and Koko, get across the harbor. Try to interdict it the best you can. Retro, stay on this side in case the next ping shows it in the middle of the harbor, on a ferry headed your way."

51

Sanjar lay on his stomach, his brain refusing to focus. The world was in a fog, people screaming all around him, sirens blaring closer and closer. He felt like he was underwater, with time operating on a different plane, everything happening around him faster than he could assimilate. He wanted to move but couldn't get his body to perform. He saw the weapon in his hand. He threw it into the bushes in reflex, then tried to stand. Something was on his legs. A heavy weight. He tried to focus. Tried to get his body to cooperate but couldn't.

His head throbbed with incredible pain. He touched his brow and his hand came back red. Dripping red.

I'm hit. I'm hurt. General, I'm hurt. Help me.

He wasn't sure if he said it out loud or simply thought it. Convinced he had been paralyzed by an assassin's bullet, he began to crawl away, using his hands to pull himself along the ground, ignoring the screams around him. He scraped along on the concrete, bloodying the tips of his fingers as he clawed for the cover of the foliage just meters away. The weight on his legs was too much, and the ground offered too little for his hands to grasp.

He rolled onto his back and embraced that he was going to die. He felt the weight against his legs shift when he moved. His head clearing more every second, his mind working to escape, he realized he shouldn't have been able to feel anything if he was paralyzed.

He sat up and looked at his legs for the first time, seeing the body of his comrade lying over him. The head split open, the man's brains layering his thighs, his tongue lolling from the mouth, the eyes open and staring at nothing.

Sanjar's moment of revulsion was short-circuited by his survival instinct. He kicked the man off and stood, still woozy, still feeling the blow to his head.

A woman pointed at him, shouting something in Chinese. He raised his hand to shoot her and realized he was just pointing a finger. He staggered into the bushes to get away, running parallel to Nathan Road. He reached a public bathroom and went inside, sitting down on a toilet and pressing a hand to his head wound, trying to think.

He needed help. He dialed the general's agreed contact number, but the call went immediately to voice mail. He stared at the phone in disbelief, then heard the police cars stop nearby. He staggered outside and began running to the west, putting distance between himself and imminent arrest. People began shouting and pointing. Pointing at him.

He jogged around the lily pond and dove into the bushes, ripping out a scrap of paper with the number to the general's issued IRGC cell phone. He dialed it, then realized he was using the bait phone. No way could he link that with the general's phone given by the cleric. He hung up before it connected, then realized the phone itself held enough incriminating information to damn him forever. He'd contacted three of the men on the new Quds team, including the dead man he'd just kicked off of himself.

He threw the phone into the bushes and activated the final cell he'd purchased near Sin Tat Plaza. Before he had a chance to dial, he saw an old man and woman waving at someone and pointing his way.

He broke out of the bushes, stumbling in a ragged jog. He saw police across the pond, near the grotto, and whirled around, heading toward the main entrance of the park, with everyone pointing his way and shouting. He rounded a corner on the path and saw a phalanx of police rushing toward him.

He sagged to his knees.

ELINA HUNG UP the phone and sat in silence, reflecting on her instructions. Leave again. Go somewhere else. The thought brought a sense of dread that was becoming all too familiar. She didn't want to leave her hotel and go find another one. She'd not left this one since she'd met the contact yesterday and had grown used to the isolation. She'd lived on room service, the small "do not disturb" sign outside of her door a blanket of comfort.

She'd done her own cleaning, keeping her mind busy with daily chores as if she were still at home. Making the bed, washing the dishes in the sink before placing them back outside the door, folding the soiled towels ready for the exchange with the maid. An exchange that took no more than thirty seconds.

Now she would have to leave again, entering the claustrophobic mass of foreign humanity that was crammed on the island. She longed for the woods of her homeland. Longed to at least talk with someone whose primary language wasn't Chinese.

She began packing, banishing the thoughts, a little ashamed at her weakness.

At least the mission is progressing. With any luck, she would be leaving this alien place for good in a day or two.

As instructed, she packed everything into a single carry-on bag, as that was all the ferry would allow. She left the few other belongings behind, hoping the maid would take them for her own use.

Downstairs, she had the concierge hail a taxi and give the cabby instructions. After a short drive, he stopped and pointed at the meter. She handed him more money than was necessary and said, "Ferry terminal? This is the ferry terminal?"

He nodded vigorously and made no move to help her with her bag. She stood on the street as he drove away, seeing that the terminal was very large.

What if I get on the wrong one?

She moved inside, and, after reading the confusing English on all the signs, she approached a counter and bought a ticket. She attempted to confirm it was the right ferry, but the man pointed toward a gangway and turned to the next customer. Realizing he was done with her, she walked toward the gangway. The farther she went into the terminal, the less it appeared anyone spoke English.

She saw the ferry was actually a double-decker hydrofoil, unlike the ones that simply crossed the harbor. The sight caused her nervous stomach to calm.

It has to be the right one.

She walked up the gangway into the lower deck, a large area with seating much like that of the coach section of an airplane, already full of people. She showed a man in uniform her ticket, written entirely in Chinese. He snatched the bag out of her hand and pointed toward a stairwell behind him. She said, "My seat is up there?"

He simply pointed again.

She said, "My bag?"

Irritated, he jabbed his hand toward the stairs, then piled her suitcase on top of a stack of others.

She walked up a short staircase and found that she'd been tricked into buying a first-class ticket. The room was laid out exactly like the one below, the only difference being the size and spacing of the seats. She grinned at how human nature was the same all over the world. She didn't care about the cost, since it wasn't her money.

She showed a second man her ticket, and he led her to

a window seat. She settled in, staring out the glass to kill the forty-five minutes before the ferry departed.

The cabin filled up around her, with only one other Westerner on her level. A female with dirty-blond hair sitting across the aisle and two seats up. Elina studied her, trying to guess where she was from.

Five minutes later, she felt a subtle shift. She glanced out the window and saw the pier sliding by, causing a spasm of fear. She looked at her watch. They were leaving twenty minutes early.

I'm on the wrong ferry.

She had seen a sign for Shanghai, but that had pointed to the other pier. She stood, walking to the front holding her ticket. The uniformed man pointed back to her seat. She said, "Macau? Ferry to Macau?"

The man became agitated, pointing again at her seat, but she'd had enough of the "inscrutable" Chinese.

"No, I'm not sitting down. Where is this ferry going?"

She felt someone pull on her shirt and turned to find the Western woman trying to get her attention.

"This is the ferry to Macau. Is that where you're going?"

American.

"Yes. I am. Thank you. It's very hard to get anybody to understand you here."

The woman smiled, a sincere, warm gesture, and said, "Boy, you aren't kidding. It's worse being a single female. They treat you like you don't exist."

Elina felt an instant connection and a compelling need

to continue the conversation. Then she remembered why she was here. Where she was going.

Don't get involved in questions you don't want to answer.

She thanked the woman and sat back down, her heart stopping its rapid stutter, the fear now replaced with an emptiness that gnawed.

An hour later she'd docked in Macau and exited quickly, wanting to get away from the American lest she ask to pair up. The terminal in Macau was much poorer, showing the wear of time, which made her feel more at ease for some reason. She found a taxi in the swirling mass of people and managed to convey her destination. Shortly, she was in her new hotel room. Another Conrad Hotel. The room was exquisite, making her wonder if the Arab contact thought she could be bought. She dismissed the idea. In her limited engagement he had shown no indication that money would ever induce him to do anything. So there was no way he would believe such a thing about her.

Maybe just a little reward. He had to put me somewhere.

She sat on the bed and turned on her cell, unsure how long she was supposed to wait. She received four text messages, startling her.

They were all from casinos welcoming her to the island. One after the other begging her to show up and win big.

Casinos? Is this the target?

She opened a hotel book and was surprised to see that

Macau had become the number one gambling destination in the world, eclipsing even Las Vegas. She'd had no idea. She parted the shades of her window and saw a skyline in motion, with building after building under construction. Directly across the road was a monstrosity called the Venetian. An enormous building fronted by a man-made lake.

She booted up her tablet, got online, and Googled it, killing time.

Two hours later, after a dinner of room service, the standard "do not disturb" sign on the door, she gave up on meeting anyone that night. She stepped into the shower, exhausted by the day's events.

She toyed with the massage head and leaned against the wall, letting the blast of water pummel her body, amazed at the technology. She bathed herself, then tried every setting, wondering if any of her friends had ever experienced such luxury.

Wearing a towel on her head and one around her body, she sauntered across the room, captivated by the view of the skyline in the setting sun. She leaned against the glass, watching the lights tinkle in the distance. A flash on the window caught her eye, and she realized it was her phone.

Picking it up, she saw a missed call. Immediately, she was brought back to earth. Back to the reality of why she was staying in such opulence. Deflated, she hit redial.

The man she knew as Malik answered and gave her instructions. She took notes and hung up. She had five hours. Five short hours before she entered the mission and left the opulence behind. She wondered again about her chosen path and how this would help her people. She was going to give all she had—her very life—and was unsure about Malik's agenda. He seemed pure, but maybe *he* was being led down a path and using her as a result.

Nothing to do about it now but continue. What else could she do? Going home would garner her punishment, which she knew, given the pressure she'd felt to accept the mission, would mean her death. She held no illusions about the justice of the Islamists in Chechnya.

She dressed slowly, savoring every minute she had left in the room.

52

Kurt was doing all he could to keep from outright yelling at me through the computer screen, clearly on the verge of exploding about the actions at Kowloon Park.

I said, "Sir, it wasn't our fault! They laid a trap, and we came close to triggering it. If it hadn't been for Jennifer, we'd be in the custody of the Hong Kong police."

"Jesus, Pike, I sent you there to develop the situation. Not get in a gunfight. Especially not get in a gunfight on Chinese soil. The council's losing their mind right now. No telling what they'll do when they hear this."

The comment gave me pause. "What's that mean?"

He backpedaled. "Nothing. It's just that this virus threat is really scaring the shit out of everyone, and people are starting to wonder if the Taskforce is the correct tool. They want to go on war footing over it, to include punishing Iran preemptively."

"What the hell are you talking about? They've been building a nuclear weapon for the last ten years and we've done nothing but blow a lot of hot air. Now we think they have a bioweapon and we're going to nuke them? Who the hell is running the show back there? Jesus, give me some space to do what you pay me for. To figure this thing out."

His next words sent a chill down my spine. "Are you alone?"

I turned and saw Decoy out of camera range. I motioned him out of the room and said, "Yeah, I am now."

"Look, the president isn't involved right now. He's read on the vice president, and he's running the show. Which means nobody is."

I was amazed that the political world still had the ability to astound me with its stupidity. "Why is that? If this is so dangerous, the president should be front and center."

Kurt said, "Well . . . believe it or not, the president has come down with the flu. A very bad case of the flu. They don't want anyone to know, but he's doing nothing but the public stuff that was already on the calendar. If it's a private meeting, it's postponed, which means he's waved off on all Taskforce activities. He's apparently getting briefed, but the doctor has ordered rest for at least two days. He's put Vice President Hannister in charge."

Phillip Hannister had been put on the ticket for domestic reasons in the last election. A genius at economics, he'd spent his entire career working with the Federal Reserve and the International Monetary Fund. He was a wizard at domestic debates on the deficit and reducing the debt, but he was an idiot on foreign policy. Which was why he'd never been read on to Taskforce activities. He had no need to know.

And now he was in charge.

I said, "What's that mean to us? I mean right now?"

"Nothing currently. I haven't had a chance to brief them on your escapades. But it would help if you could give me some good news before he makes a decision we'll all regret."

"Well, I don't really have any. I'm trying to track some phones to get some intel and I'm told you guys won't play ball. I have Jennifer on a goose chase to Macau and have everyone else coming back here. These damn ten-minute phone pings aren't working."

I'd pulled in Retro and Decoy but let Jennifer run out her hunch, even thought it meant she'd be on her own in Macau. I was pretty sure getting on the ferry was stupid, but she seemed to think that nothing else explained the last cell ping.

I knew I had been right when she called after docking and said there were no males of Arabic descent anywhere on the boat. In fact, nothing of any suspicion whatsoever.

The final ping we'd received was in the general vicinity of the Hong Kong piers, and because we couldn't get any drill-down, we'd had to use a little deductive reasoning. Jennifer had boarded the boat to Macau, and Decoy had boarded the next ferry across the harbor. Neither had panned out. The next ping had been dead, with no location.

Kurt said, "I hear you, but we aren't going to start a

war with China over this. We can't dig into their network."

I said, "Can't, or won't? I mean, you talk about how scared everyone is; then, when I ask for a lock, I'm told that we're afraid of someone over here *suspecting* we're hacking their network. Who gives a shit about that? So they say we did it. If we stop a damn pandemic, they'll give us flowers."

Kurt looked down, then back at the camera. "It's a little more complicated than that."

And I realized exactly what was going on. It wasn't about someone *suspecting* a hack and a little bad press. It was because we *were* hacking them, and the additional scrutiny could flush that out. They were worried that my actions would blow some other top-secret covert operation.

I said nothing for a second, turning the implications over in my mind. I understood how hard such activities were, and the reluctance to risk the effort, but also that at the end of the day you needed to measure what was gained by acting versus what was lost by inaction.

"Sir, I hear everything you're saying loud and clear. And I realize that's not a Taskforce call. Not our operation. But someone needs to get a handle on the damn ten-meter target. This guy has a weapon that could potentially wipe out a third of the human race. Stack that against the intel we're getting from whatever mission is going on."

"I know. Give me something to work with."

"I did! The damn phones, but we lost them."

"Both? What about the other one at the Islamic center?"

"It ended up on the ferry piers as well, on the Kowloon side. By the time we staged, it was dead as well. I think they met up and no longer needed the phones. Other than that, Knuckles got Ernie's phone. He saw him get arrested, but the cops missed the phone he tossed in the bushes. It's the same one we were already tracking. We'll check it for forensics, but I'm sure it's clean. That's what they were using to bait us."

Decoy entered the room. "Pike, I hate to interrupt, but Jennifer's calling. She wants to know how many telecom companies are in Macau. She thinks maybe we're using the wrong one for the pings."

I turned from the computer and said, "This isn't the United States, with a hundred different networks. Tell her to get back here. We're going to need everyone to figure out a direction to go."

Kurt said, "What was that about?"

"Jennifer. She wants to start pinging other networks on a fishing expedition." As I said it, a horrible truth dawned. "Sir, does Macau have a different network than Hong Kong? Did your guys check that?"

I'd assumed that it would be the same telecom architecture, since the islands were so close together and it was Communist China terrain now. But it hadn't always been that way. Macau had been turned over to the Chinese *after* Hong Kong, and long after an independent network would have been established.

I could tell he'd clicked on the same screw-up I had. "I don't know. Stand by."

I hollered out the door, "Start packing your things. Blood, check on the next ferry to Macau. Retro, get down there and recce the customs and transfer procedures. I want to know if they search bags or put anything through an X-ray. Decoy, call Jennifer back and tell her to stand by. Tell her to get us some hotel rooms in Macau."

Decoy came through the door, dialing a phone. "What's up?"

"I don't think the phones are turned off. I think they just shifted to another network, and we were too stupid to ask the Taskforce to do the same."

Kurt came on. "You get the tracks? They're still active."

My phone vibrated, showing one phone on the island of Macau and the other in the South China Sea.

On a ferry.

53

Staring out her window on the fourteenth floor, eating her final bit of room service, Elina studied the purple neon monstrosity near her hotel, called, of all things, the Hard Rock Hotel. She had no idea why someone would give a hotel such a moniker. She had seen young Chechen men wearing T-shirts with the same logo and wondered if they had come from here. Maybe she'd find out, since her meeting was in a bar off the lobby. In fifteen minutes.

She studied the street in front of the hotel, looking for landmarks. Adjacent to the Hard Rock, she saw another large neon sign proclaiming CITY OF DREAMS. She Googled it on her iPad and found it to be nothing more than a shopping mall. Something that should be easy to ask directions for—and get her to the Hard Rock Hotel.

She placed her plate onto the room service tray and checked her phone for any new messages, halfway hoping there would be one announcing that the meeting was postponed. The phone log was empty. She placed it in her purse and left the room.

Reaching the lobby, she turned away from the main

entrance and walked through a small level of shops, following the signs for the City of Dreams. Reaching the street, she saw the Hard Rock, the neon lights covering its tower flickering a multitude of colors in the night.

She reached the ornate entrance and studied the lobby bar, a sunken, dimly lit den filled with couches and overstuffed chairs. In the back, at a table for two, was Malik.

She paused, wondering if she was supposed to acknowledge him. He half stood and waved, a smile on his face.

He pulled out her chair, as if for chivalry, but she knew it was so that he could keep the chair against the window, allowing him to view the room.

His first words were a mass of information on what to say if she were ever questioned about this meeting. A false story that would provide an innocuous cover and lead away from the truth. He told her to repeat it back, and she did, respecting his attention to detail. Respecting how he had her welfare uppermost in his mind.

He said, "Did you have any trouble coming here?"

"No. Not really, other than the fact that nobody speaks English."

He laughed and said, "So you've seen nothing strange? Nobody who looked like they were following you? Any Western men that you've seen more than once?"

She wondered why he asked. "No, nothing like that. Is there something I should be aware of?"

"Yes. I believe there's a team tracking me, and I want to make sure they never connect us. I can be forfeited, but you must remain in the shadows. Keep your eyes out."

He reached beneath his seat and brought out a small black Pelican box made of hard plastic, the lid snapped shut. He placed it delicately on the table.

"This is the virus. It is very, very deadly. You took the vaccine, yes?"

She nodded, her eyes wide.

"Open this when you are back in your room. It won't harm you but will kill anyone else who has the misfortune of contacting it. Inside is a glass syringe packed in several different plastic bags for protection. Next to the syringe is a rubber-stoppered vial with a cleansing solution. After you have injected yourself, put the needle into the solution and draw it into the syringe, filling it completely up. Let it sit for a few minutes, then spray it down the sink. Use the rest of the solution to thoroughly wash the outside of the syringe."

"Where do I inject myself?"

"Doesn't matter. You only need a drop inside your bloodstream, and there's much more than that in the syringe. Your arm or thigh would probably be easiest."

She placed the box into her shoulder bag, then said, "What about the explosives? And the actual target? When will I get that?"

He smiled and held up his hands. "Wait, wait. We're not through with the virus yet. I'll provide that information when you need it, and I'll provide you with the explosives. Don't worry."

She nodded, waiting on him to continue.

"After you have injected yourself, do not leave your

room for at least twenty-four hours, maybe longer. The doctor indicated that initially you might be virulently contagious, as if you had no vaccine, but he was sure that would pass. The key will be your eyes. They will turn bloodshot. Very, very bloodshot. When that clears up, you can enter the population. Understand?"

"Yes."

"When you do leave, remember what we talked about before. Use a hand sanitizer all the time, drink only bottled water, don't eat anywhere that has silverware and plates to wash. Avoid anything that has the chance of spreading the virus."

He passed across a thin envelope. "This is an open-ended round-trip ticket to the United States. You'll also find a rental car and two hotel reservations. Land, get the rental, and begin driving. The first hotel is midway. The second is your destination. But not your target. You'll have final instructions in the room. Keep your phone and check your e-mail account."

She said, "What about my passport? Won't I need a visa?"

"No. Your passport is from Latvia, correct?"

"Yes. It was the best country because they still have a large population that speaks Russian."

"They're on the United States visa waiver program. You don't need one."

"And money?"

He passed across another envelope. "There are five prepaid credit cards in there with one thousand dollars each. That should be enough."

She felt she should have more questions but couldn't come up with any.

He said, "This will be our last meeting until I see you just prior to the attack. Remember all that I have said. Remember to look around you and to not highlight yourself in any way. You are invisible right now. I want to keep it that way until the time is right." He took her hands. "You are the weapon that will free your people. Remember that when you feel lost."

She started, wondering if he could read her mind. She nodded. "I will. I promise."

He leaned back. "Good. Now go, and good luck. I'll give you twenty minutes before I leave."

She stood and turned without a word, walking back toward the lobby. As instructed, she surveyed the room looking for invisible spies.

She saw a woman in the corner, by herself, and felt a flush of adrenaline.

It was the woman who had helped her on the ferry.

54

Jennifer paid no attention to the meeting occurring at the end of the lounge. She simply sat and sipped her club soda, as if she were waiting on someone to meet her. Which, in truth, she was. Thirty minutes ago, the final ping had placed both phones directly inside the Hard Rock Hotel. She'd called Pike and found that the rest of the team were still minutes from landing at the ferry pier, so she'd gone in alone.

The geolocation of the phones didn't work in three dimensions, so there was really little chance that she'd find anything. The meeting could have been happening at any room on any floor. She simply intended to find a good location with a view of the elevators to gather what she could and await the team's arrival.

She had been astounded when she'd spotted the general in the lounge, then shocked again at who he was meeting. She'd surreptitiously studied the meeting for the last fifteen minutes, praying the team would arrive before it ended.

It didn't work out that way. She saw the woman from the ferry rise and called Pike again.

"Meeting's over. General's still in the lounge, but the unknown is leaving. Pike, it's a woman who was on the ferry with me. A Western woman."

"We're in some rentals and we're about two minutes out. Did he pass anything to her?"

"Yes. A number of things, but they were too far away to identify."

"Take the unknown. We'll take the general."

"How tight do you want the follow? What's my compromise level?"

"Very low. If she's got the virus, we can't lose her. Don't worry about her suspecting something. Just find her bed-down site. If you're compromised hard and she rabbits, take her down however you can."

Great. Just perfect. We'll both go to jail from a catfight.

The woman passed right in front of her and glanced her way, then hurriedly exited the lobby. Jennifer followed, seeing her on the street headed toward the Venetian casino.

She considered her options. She knew she stood out in the mass of Asians and would be easy to spot if the woman had any training whatsoever. She considered simply jogging up to her and engaging her in conversation, just another single female looking for some companionship. She'd sensed the woman wanted that on the ferry. Seeing her caught at the light, she decided to execute that plan.

Casually get next to her at the crosswalk, then express surprise at seeing her.

She quickened her pace so as to be held up at the light as well. The woman sprinted through the traffic to the far side of the road.

Shit.

The woman hadn't glanced back, hadn't acted like she was fleeing, so Jennifer felt fairly confident she was just jaywalking. Having done her homework while waiting on the phone geolocation, the woman's destination was problematic. The Venetian was the largest casino in the world, encompassing a multilevel indoor mall complete with faux indoor canals threaded throughout, along with the enormous casino itself. If the woman entered out of Jennifer's sight, she'd be lost in seconds.

Jennifer waited on a break in traffic, then sprinted across as well, seeing the woman going up and over a bridge that spanned a giant man-made lake.

She lost sight of her entering the building and picked up the pace to close the distance. Pushing through a crowd in the lobby, she jogged around a sculpture, her head swiveling left and right. She saw nothing but Asians. She stopped and did a slow circle, focusing on the stores lining the hallway to the casino. A flash of movement caught her eye, going much faster than the crowds window-shopping, and she saw the woman entering the casino, looking back at her. She waited a beat, then followed.

The room was huge and manned, like all casinos, with massive security, both electronic and physical. If the woman was smart, she'd simply stop and wait Jennifer out. Worst case, she would alert security about someone following her.

Keep going. Please keep going.

And the woman did, speed-walking straight down the middle, bypassing the bar in the center of the hall and continuing to a set of escalators at the back. Jennifer kept her in sight, matching her pace but continually looking for any sign that she was spiking interest.

She reached the escalator with the woman two-thirds of the way up. Knowing it was a huge risk, but also realizing she couldn't allow the woman the head start by waiting until she was out of sight, she stepped on and began climbing. She saw her target's eyes widen, then watched her take off, hopping the steps two at a time.

So much for compromise.

Jennifer did the same.

She reached the top and entered the Venetian mall, a maze of hallways all lined with high-end stores. She saw the woman sprinting down the corridor to the left, looking back every few seconds.

Here we go.

Jennifer considered pulling off and attempting to circle around, to get the woman complacent again, but couldn't risk losing her. There was no chance the woman would outrun her. Not unless she'd spent the last six months exorcising demons through the same roadwork Jennifer had done. She pumped her legs, building up speed, flying by and drawing stares.

The woman reached a large open area and swerved right, Jennifer a few seconds behind. When Jennifer turned the corner, she was faced by a food court peppered with tables and people milling about. The woman was at the far side, now drawing attention because of her sprint. She glanced back once and barreled straight into a table, knocking food and beverages into the air as she fell to the ground.

Jennifer increased her speed, intent on ending the chase here and now, while the target was on the ground.

Scrambling to her feet, an expression of terror on her face, the woman stumbled out of the food court and into another passageway.

Jennifer ignored the people openly gaping at her, making no attempt to justify her actions. *Only a few seconds before security shows up. Need to end this now.*

She raced to the end of the food court, coming up with the rudiments of a plan: Get the purse. Let the woman go, but get the virus.

She had seen the target put everything she had been passed into her shoulder bag, and maybe, just maybe, she could gain control of that before security closed down on them both. A fight was now out of the question, although if it came down to it, both ending up in jail would be preferable to the woman escaping with her deadly prize.

She turned the corner and slowed, seeing a split in the hallway. One corridor was narrow and deserted, an antiseptic beige with no decorations of any type, ending at two double doors. The other led back into the concourse of shops.

She followed the crowds to the concourse, scanning for the target, a full head taller than the people milling around the stores. She saw nothing. She stopped and glanced back to the other hallway, the press of time eating at her. Every second she gave the target led to an exponential advantage, as the possible avenues widened like the ripples in a pond.

She sprinted back to the deserted corridor and raced to the doors at the end. She flung them open and found herself in a large storage room full of cleaning supplies. The target was on her knees at the far end, next to another set of doors. Seeing Jennifer enter, she whipped her head up and snarled.

Jennifer saw a glass syringe in her hands. She screamed, "Don't!"

And the woman stopped.

Jennifer held her hands up in a gesture of surrender. "I'm not going to hurt you. I promise."

The woman pulled off the cap to the needle.

"Don't do it. Please. Put the shot down. I don't know what they told you, but you're holding something that could kill thousands of people."

The woman hesitated.

Jennifer continued. "Don't let them use you. That man you met doesn't care about you. He only cares about harming others. Killing innocent people."

The woman spoke for the first time, her face a neutral

mask. "There are no innocents." And jammed the needle into her thigh.

Jennifer sprang forward, not even consciously sure what she was doing. The woman forced the plunger home, ripped the syringe out, and hurled it at her.

Jennifer snatched a tray off of a shelf and used it as a shield, hearing the syringe thump against it, then shatter on the floor. She held her breath and backpedaled the way she had entered, watching the woman escape through the other double doors.

Every instinct in her body screamed at her to run, a prehistoric fear of the invisible death the syringe held, now out in the atmosphere. But she couldn't leave it for others to find. A time bomb for the end of the world.

Taking shallow breaths, she searched the nearest shelf, finding a bottle of chlorine bleach. She took in a lungful of air and advanced, squinting her eyes out of instinct.

She dumped the entire bottle on the shards of the syringe, coating everything in a pool, the undiluted chlorine vapor causing her to squint for real.

Feeling her lungs demand air, she dropped the bottle and fled, not opening her mouth until she was back in the hallway.

She sagged against the wall and gulped fresh oxygen, feeling nauseous, the thought of the virus inside her making her skin crawl. A lethal, mindless organism replicating in her lungs, starting on its path of destruction.

She wondered if she was now walking dead.

55

Retro and I left the City of Dreams mall and entered the hallway that led to the reception desks of the Hard Rock. We'd dropped off Knuckles in front of the lobby and given Decoy and Blood the northern exit, all of us squeezing out any escape route.

I'd given instructions to maintain a very loose net, wanting to follow the general without spiking him. A tall order since just about everyone around was Asian. We might as well have been on a *Sesame Street* production of "one of these things is not like the others." While not catastrophic, it would have been bad enough except that our target had laid out a pretty good trap recently, and I had to assume that he knew everyone from that day on sight. Since Knuckles hadn't been in the surveillance that led to Kowloon Park, I was betting that he was still an unknown, which is why he got the lobby.

We passed the Hard Rock souvenir shop and I could see the corner of the lobby bar. I put my hand on Retro to slow him right when my radio came to life.

"Pike, Knuckles. Target just stood up. I think I spiked him."

"Did he show recognition?"

"No. Two Aussies went to the bar, and he focused on them. When I entered, he stood. I think he's just antsy."

And well he should be.

"Which direction?"

"Coming your way."

I said, "Retro, get inside the souvenir shop. Get your back to the window, out of sight. I'll trigger when he's past. Blood, Decoy, circle to the City of Dreams. He'll exit that way."

It was a risk, but I'd missed the entire countersurveillance trap the general had executed because of my ferry-ride fiasco, so I was betting I was an unknown as well.

Staring at some ridiculously overpriced watches on display, I caught the general approaching out of the corner of my eye. I turned my head and sauntered away, ostensibly window-shopping. I waited for him to pass. The seconds dragged out into a minute, and I had to move or look stupid.

I turned to enter the souvenir shop, the rotation giving me a glance down the hallway. The general stood in the middle of it, his hands clasped to his front, staring at me.

As I turned, he waved, drawing my attention.

What the hell?

I stopped and he waved again, then motioned for me to come to him.

So much for his not knowing me.

THE WIDOW'S STRIKE   345

He abruptly did an about-face, walking to the table he had occupied before. He sat down and continued to stare at me.

This is certainly a new experience.

I suppose I should have scurried away like a roach, but really, what was the use? I was burned and no good for further surveillance, so I didn't see any real harm in taking up his invitation. I figured I might find out something.

I walked over to him, seeing a bemused expression on his face. He said, "I wasn't sure, but now I am."

I sat, saying, "You're good enough that it didn't matter. You would have been sure the next time you saw me tracking you. I'm burned either way."

"Well, now it appears we have a little situation. I'm assuming you know who I am, and because of it, I'm assuming you wish to take me somewhere unpleasant, which, of course, I can't allow."

I grinned. "You don't really have a say in it. Try to leave and I'll get you, whether you recognize the men about to pound your ass or not."

"Why don't you bring them here? Let them get some refreshments. I've been in their shoes before. I'm sure they'd appreciate it."

"No thanks. I'd just as soon you didn't see how many I have on the ground."

A little dig to get him thinking.

I continued. "Instead, why don't you just give up? Make it easier on all of us."

"For what?" he said. "I'm just a carpet salesman enjoying Macau. I mean you no harm and will be traveling home soon."

A line from Jennifer's favorite movie, *The Princess Bride*, flashed in my head.

I said, "We are men of action. Lies do not become us."

He looked at me like I'd just grown a horn, the stilted prose falling flat.

Oh well.

He pulled out a Samsung Galaxy phone, saying, "I'm assuming this is how you tracked me."

He opened the back and removed the battery and SIM card, then dropped the phone into the water of the flower vase on the table.

He said, "There is only one way you will stop me, and that's right now. I'm going to head over to that security man and ask him to escort me out of here. I will not mention you in any way, unless you alert your team and I feel in jeopardy. Doing so would only cause me issues."

"You make one move to stand and I'm going to knock you out right here."

"Really? And then what? You're going to tell the police that arrive you're a spy for the United States and I'm carrying a deadly virus? What will they think when they don't find a virus on me or in my luggage?"

I said nothing.

"I'll tell you what they will do: They'll arrest us both. We'll be locked down until China can sort it out, and that could take a long, long time. I don't know about you, but I'll be left to rot. I don't mind. My mission is done. Will the US come for you?"

I thought of Knuckles and what had happened in Thailand. The tepid response of the Oversight Council.

I said, "Stopping you crazy bastards from releasing the virus will be worth it. Believe me, it will supersede whatever China does to me or my team."

He said, "Crazy? Not any more crazy than what your country does. Or Israel. You try to destroy our ability to get the very same weapons you and your allies have. You're the only one in history to ever use it, on innocent civilians no less, and I'm the one that's crazy. But I don't wish to debate the state of the world. I told you, I don't have the virus. I'm done and headed home."

So he passed it to the female. I thought about Jennifer tracking her, wondering if she'd found a bed-down site. Praying she had, because I was leaning toward letting him go.

I had to admit, the guy had an enormous set of brass balls and a steel-trap mind. He'd thought through the entire scenario before he'd ever waved. If he hadn't been trying to kill half the world, I would have admired his skill.

I said, "Okay. Go talk to your security guard. We'll be meeting again, I'm sure, on terrain that's much more favorable to me."

He squinted, and I realized I hadn't asked about the virus. About what had happened to it. *Giving away my hand.*

He shifted to stand, and I clamped my hand on his arm in an iron grip. I leaned into him. "But before you go, I have to know where the virus is right this minute. If you don't have it, it means you've set it to be released. Tell me where it is, or I'm going to get us arrested, right here, right now. I get the virus and you go free. Fair deal."

He stared at me for a moment, then said, "It's on its way to Iran. You cannot get it. You don't want us to have nuclear weapons; well, now we have something better. You can have me arrested and beat me for further information, but it won't alter that fact." He stood. "Let your government know that. We have a weapon that is worse than the one they are trying to prevent us from building. Tell them to remember that."

I watched him walk out the front door, talking to the security guard. I saw Knuckles watching as well, then he turned to me with an incredulous look on his face after the general had exited.

My phone rang, and I saw it was Jennifer.

"Tell me you got the bed-down. Give me some good news, because our side of things has been strange to say the least."

What I heard clenched my stomach in a river of fear.

56

So it's inside me.

The thought made her feel queasy, the idea of the virus bubbling away in her bloodstream disgusting. But the mirror didn't lie.

Elina leaned in closer, repulsed at what she saw: Her eyes were bathed in red, as if she had coated them in blood.

I look like a monster.

It had been a day and a half since her escape from the Venetian, and she'd begun to wonder if maybe her contact had been tricked. If the virus wasn't real. She had stayed in her room as instructed and had followed the proscriptions about eating and drinking to the letter—scrubbing the room service plates and silverware with soap and hand-sanitizer before placing them outside her door—but hadn't felt the least bit sick.

She'd used the time wisely, booking a flight to New York and applying for an electronic authorization to enter the United States in accordance with the instructions Malik had passed for the visa waiver program.

He had yet to contact her again, and she wondered if destroying her phone had been a good idea. She'd immediately done so the minute she'd left the Venetian, dropping it over the side of the bridge and into the lake as she crossed back to the Conrad. She knew she wasn't as well trained as Malik, but she did have some history to fall back on. As she had fled from the supply closet, she had wondered how the woman had known where to find her and had remembered the assassination of Chechnya's very first president.

In 1996, Dzhokhar Dudayev was killed by two laser-guided missiles while he used his satellite phone. Everyone knew the Russians had intercepted the call with a piece of magical technology, sending the missiles right to the source. She'd heard the equipment had been provided by the United States and, while running breathlessly across the bridge, had become convinced it was now tracking her.

She'd left a message in the draft folder letting Malik know, but he hadn't responded. It didn't worry her, because he'd said there would be no contact until necessary, and he'd check the e-mail account when he couldn't dial the phone.

In truth, she wanted a response for reassurance. A reminder that what she was doing was just. The woman in the storage room wasn't like the Kadyrovtsy. Bullying, sadistic men who tortured and killed out of sheer pleasure. Instead, the woman had shown kindness on the ferry, her smile something that would have been impossible to fake. It had been genuine, and Elina was convinced she was not the enemy.

And yet, the woman had tried to stop her, which *made* her an enemy. The thoughts were confusing, and Elina wanted to tamp them down. To forget.

She stared into the mirror, her red orbs burning back like the source of all evil.

AFTER A FITFUL night, tossing and turning while her mind wandered in the zone of half-awake/half-asleep, her subconscious running amok with the thought of the virus consuming her whole, she awoke before dawn and immediately went to the mirror. Rubbing the sleep out of her eyes, she leaned in and saw they were clear. A trace of red, but no more than she should have had given the lack of sleep.

She took a deep breath and let it out. She wouldn't need to rebook her flight. She could leave today.

She packed her things, ensuring she had her surgical masks and hand sanitizer, both a large container in her suitcase and a small one she could carry onto the aircraft.

Downstairs, she had the concierge flag her a cab, feeling conspicuous about the mask on her face. She stayed in the lobby, next to a pillar, swiveling her head left and right to spot anyone paying attention to her. Nothing stood out, but that didn't tamp down the trepidation to any great extent.

It followed her all the way to the airport, a brick inside her stomach that made her nauseous, continuing to torture her right up until she boarded her aircraft. It finally left completely when the wheels separated from the ground. Twenty hours later, she landed at New York City's JFK airport. She'd made connections twice in other cities and was physically exhausted, the close confines of the travel forcing her into uncomfortable positions to ensure she didn't have contact with any other human beings. She'd been told that simply touching wouldn't spread the virus, but she was taking no chances.

She exited the aircraft into the gangway, feeling the familiar sense of dread at what she would find outside the door: a homogenous mass of people she couldn't understand. Instead, she was pleasantly surprised. JFK was nothing like the Asian airports.

For one, it was dirty and bordering on decrepit, reminding her of a Moscow subway. Unlike the airport in Hong Kong, with its crisp, almost sterile corridors, JFK was a hodgepodge maze of additions and add-ons, weaving seemingly incoherently.

For another, the airport was anything but homogenous. There were foreign nationals from all walks of life, wearing all manner of native clothing.

The first made her feel at home. The second let her fade into the crowd without a wayward glance. Together, they gave her more self-confidence than she'd felt in weeks.

She passed through customs and immigration without any problems whatsoever. She located her suitcase and took the airport tram to the rental car area at Federal Circle. She saw the Manhattan skyline in the distance, and she wondered what the city was like. The same as Hong Kong? Or Moscow?

What are the people like? The question had more import than simple curiosity. It might help her decide a course of action. An idea began to form.

Stay one night here. Why not? It was her life. She should be able to explore before reaching her target. She wasn't on a timeline . . . as far as she knew.

She reached the rental agencies and obtained her car, being much more friendly than was necessary to the man behind the counter. Despite the mask on her face, he responded to her overtures, and soon enough, she had a hotel in midtown, along with directions. He gave her a free upgrade, and she left the lot driving a late-model Jeep Cherokee.

Her sense of giddiness at her newfound audacity quickly dissipated in the traffic, with drivers honking their horns, cutting her off, and giving her obscene gestures. By the time she reached the hotel on East Forty-Fifth Street, she was in a foul mood.

The valet took her vehicle, and she went immediately to her room, drinking a bottle of water and sitting on the bed. The fear she had experienced in Hong Kong hadn't shown its face here. All she felt was anger at the rude treatment from every stranger she encountered. Most shouting in English that she could barely understand, which told her they weren't from America.

This was a dumb idea. I should have just started my journey. I will find all I need to know on the trip.

She decided to spend the night and leave first thing in

the morning. She definitely needed the rest either way. Her stomach rumbled, and she realized she hadn't eaten for hours. It was seven at night here, but she had no idea what that meant in relation to when she'd left.

She exited the hotel and walked up Forty-Fifth Street. In front of her, just a block away, was a sign for an establishment called the Perfect Pint. It was a three-story pub and restaurant with a European flair. She saw an outdoor deck on the third floor and decided to give it a try.

Inside, she told the hostess she wanted food to go. The woman stared like she was disfigured but directed her to the bar on the second floor. She entered and found a gaggle of men, all sporting shirts and ties, with half wearing a shoulder bag.

Almost to a man, they stared at her as well. She realized they were looking at her face mask. It hadn't stood out in the airport, but was like a neon sign in here.

In a loud voice, one of them said, "You got a disease or something?"

She knew they were drunk. She'd been around men who could hold much, much more liquor than these children and saw the signs even before she had entered.

She also knew the effect her eyes had. Caribbean sea blue, they were always something she could use, as she had in the rental car agency.

She smiled in the mask, knowing it would show above the fabric. And that the man would notice. She said, "No, I'm just paranoid."

He guffawed at the answer and slapped his friend,

smitten by the attention. She walked to the end of the bar and waved at the bartender.

She ordered a bottle of water and a plate to go, and then settled down to wait, watching the group of men. Studying. Should she kill them? If she released right here, would that be the right thing? What had they done, other than getting drunk and annoying her?

She watched and waited, seeing nothing that she wouldn't have witnessed in a pub in Grozny. All the men did was shout and punch one another. She began to feel sick about her choice, knowing there was no return after the Rubicon she had crossed. She could kill herself, but she'd still be contagious. She felt the melancholy return, the same feeling she'd had when she'd learned of the death of her fiancé. A feeling of waste.

The Americans weren't inherently evil. Much like her, they were simply unworldly. These drunks probably couldn't have found Chechnya on a world globe.

A news story about Afghanistan came on the television behind the bar, talking about something called a green-on-blue attack. Apparently, it meant someone from the Afghan forces—working with the United States as an ally—had killed US personnel. The story detailed how a police officer, who'd been training with Americans in an academy in Kandahar, had shown up one morning and gone to the target range. When issued his arms and ammunition, instead of aiming at the targets, he began shooting at the Americans. He killed five before he was cut down by another Afghan policeman.

The story seemed to fire up the drunks, all of them screaming about what should be done. She heard the man who'd asked about her mask say, "Fuck those ragheads. We ought to just nuke the shit out of the whole place."

His partner said something she couldn't hear, and he became more agitated. "Bullshit, man! That whole Islam thing is a fucking cover. They want to take over our way of life. I'm telling you, we ought to kick every one of those Muslims out of here. We don't, and we'll end up getting killed by those sons of bitches."

Another guy next to him said, "You got that right. My brother was in the Army in Iraq, and you can't help those ragheads. He told me stories that are unbelievable. Now we got 'em shooting our own guys. After we've done so much for them. Makes me sick. Kill 'em all and let God sort 'em out."

She heard the words and realized Malik was right. *So it's true. They want to kill my people.*

The man next to him said, "Yeah, maybe in Saudi Arabia, but I got a Muslim that lives next door to me. From Bosnia. He's okay. He doesn't spout all the 'death to America' stuff. He even drinks beer with me."

The man who'd asked about her mask said, "That's bullshit. A trick. I got a buddy in the Army who's been to just about every raghead shit hole there is, and those bastards want a caliphate. They want to take over the world. Shit, they're building mosques all over the damn place."

When his friend showed a look of surprise, he continued. "I'm serious. If someone shows up here and says they're Muslim, I don't care where they're from. They're here to take over our way of life. They don't believe in democracy. We should stop them now, before it's too late."

Elina was shocked to her core. She'd never heard such vehemence against her religion. She had assumed talk like that was just something the Russian Federation used to whip up support. Something that happened in every war. Now she saw the difference. The war was as Malik said. Much larger than her little fight in Chechnya. These men were making no distinction between the conflicts in Afghanistan and elsewhere. No distinction other than the fact that she was Muslim.

The statements enraged her. The man sounded just like the Kadyrovtsy.

If he were in Grozny, he'd be working at the battery factory. Torturing my family.

Her food arrived and she laid her prepaid card on the bar, then sauntered over to the group.

The ignorant man saw her approach and held up his hands. "Whoa, there. I don't want to get sick."

His friends laughed.

She pulled the mask down and said, "I could give you a little virus you'd love tonight."

He put his arm around her waist, looked at his friends, and winked. "Only if it involves oral infection."

The men giggled at the juvenile joke. She leaned in, inches from his face.

"Maybe it will."

She kissed him fully, shocking him, his eyes springing open. A split second later, he was kissing back, shoving his tongue deep into her mouth, proving he was a man while his friends laughed and jeered.

She broke away and said, "You going to be here later?"

His face clouded from the drink, he said, "Oh yeah, I'll be here. All night waiting on you."

She picked up her food, kissed him on the cheek, and said, "I'll come back later and check you for a fever."

"Wait! What's your name?"

"Elina. But my friends call me the Black Widow."

The statement caused the men to stare at her in confusion. One man gave a forced laugh. He was soon joined by others, and the laughter grew until the man slapped her on the butt, now sure he was in on the joke.

She left the bar listening to the band of haters shouting and cheering.

57

I waited for the VPN to connect, not liking that I was going to have to give Kurt Hale the same situation report as yesterday: We'd lost both the general and the carrier and hadn't been able to pick them up again.

We'd spent the last three days pulling out everything we had to get a lead, working around the clock, but had come up empty. We had some possibles that the Taskforce men in the rear were tracking. A tick here and a tick there. Some flight-manifest names they might have been traveling under, but I wasn't holding my breath.

In truth, I'd been going at the problem with only half of my brainpower, worried beyond belief about Jennifer. I'd spent each day mindlessly churning over whatever I could find to keep the team and me busy, and then each night lying wide awake wondering if she was going to die. Feeling the clock ticking inexorably toward an answer I didn't want to hear. It was paralyzing.

Two days ago, I'd had *forever* to convince Jennifer about my worth. To connect. Now I had nothing. I had lost the chance. Something I had taken for granted was gone. *Just like missing my daughter's birthdays.*

The closest I'd come had been after I'd killed the man who had assaulted her. When it was done, I'd tentatively bared my soul, letting her know where I stood, not even sure if I believed it myself. We were both so banged up emotionally, it was hard to separate fantasy from feelings. To separate a world I wished existed from the reality I lived. She'd responded initially but then shut down. It didn't hurt, because I'd understood. I'd waited to give her time to come to grips with her trauma. To realize, like I had, that there may not be gold at the end of the rainbow, but there *was* a rainbow. And now I'd waited too long. When would I learn?

She was locked in a room waiting to get bloodshot eyes, and I was tracking the damn terrorist who had caused it. It made me rethink again what the hell I was doing with my life.

I'd lost my family while I was out fighting in the name of national defense, and now, because I'd brought her into the Taskforce in a misguided attempt to close some loop, I was going to lose the one person on earth who had ever measured up to my wife. I wondered if she was cursing me in heaven.

Jennifer had quarantined herself, providing updates four times a day. Now that it was day three, without any sign of infection, I was feeling a lot better. She didn't have the virus. I was sure of it. After the incident, on a VPN, we'd talked to the doctor who'd concocted the death soup, now ensconced at an undisclosed location, and he had said if she made it to day three, she was good to go.

But somebody else *was* infected, and we didn't know where that carrier had gone.

I saw a shadow on the screen and Kurt sat down in front of the camera. I gave him a succinct rundown, which wasn't a whole lot different from the one I'd given yesterday. He didn't seem particularly upset at the news. More like resigned to the inevitable.

I then found out why. He said, "The council is now split down the middle based on your initial report. Half believes the general just sent it home to Iran. The other half believes there's a carrier running loose."

The idea was ludicrous. "They believe the words of an IRGC general over what Jennifer saw with her own eyes? Jesus, Malik was just trying to get us off the chase! I wish I had never even included the conversation in the SI-TREP."

"People still can't believe that Iran would release the virus when it's not a weapon they can control. It'll hit them as well. They think it makes more sense as a *potential* weapon. Something to use as a last-resort threat, to keep us off of them."

"Sir, Jennifer *saw* the woman inject herself."

"We don't know what was in that syringe. Could have been saline water. Something exactly like what you're saying: misdirection to keep us from trying to interdict the real virus."

"You believe that?"

He leaned back, then rubbed his eyes. "No. No, I don't. I think there's a carrier, and it's coming here."

"What's the president's vote?"

He shook his head. "The president is bedridden. He's gotten worse, and the doctors say it's because he won't get rest. The administration has officially released his condition, and there's overt grumbling from all the pundits about passing command to the VP until he's better. It's a mess."

He seemed a little distracted himself. Not the usual crisp, commanding guy I was used to. He looked tired. Aged.

He said, "They're covering all the bases, however. The carrier is now designated DOA."

Which shocked the hell out of me. DOA stood for *dead or alive* and was a Taskforce designation almost never used. It meant the target was a distinct and urgent threat to national security and could be killed instead of captured. It was very, very sensitive, for obvious reasons, and meant the council truly was frothing at the mouth.

I said, "The vice president authorized that?"

"He did, but just as a mouthpiece. There's a civilian on the council who's been screaming about the threat of the virus. He's some kind of corporate bigwig who owns a plethora of pharmaceutical companies, and he's become something of a subject-matter expert. Everyone's listening to him. Even the ones who think the virus is in Iran."

The answer was disgusting to me. I couldn't believe

there'd be a vote on DOA if *anyone* had a doubt. I would never make that decision unless I was absolutely sure, which is why their doing so scared the hell out of me.

"So someone on the council, who in his heart is sure the virus is in Iran, is willing to kill a civilian he believes is no threat?"

"Pike, nobody knows what the threat is. They think it's everywhere and will mitigate it any way they see fit. How's Jennifer?"

The abrupt shift took me off guard, but I was glad to be on happier news. "She's fine. No indications of infection. I brought the Gulfstream over from Hong Kong. We can fly tomorrow. I'm pretty sure this place is a dry hole anyway. The carrier is either headed to the US or already there. Just give us the word."

He glanced offscreen, then returned. "Yes. Fly home tomorrow. Pike, they want to check out Jennifer. They want to make sure she isn't infected."

His earlier words about not knowing the threat raised a little sniggle of warning. A touch of something rotten. "What? I just told you she wasn't infected."

I could tell he didn't like what he was about to say.

"She took the final vaccine from the doctor when you were in Singapore. The one that he never got to test to see if it worked. They just want to check her out. It's for her own good."

"The whole team took the damn vaccine. So what? She's not sick."

"Pike, we don't know if that vaccine is worth a shit. It

never went through any trials. It could work just like the other ones that *were* tested. If you or the others got the virus, we're pretty sure you'd be dead. Not the same with Jennifer. They're afraid she's become another carrier."

Whoa. No way. "Sir, she'll come up hot on an antibody test because of the vaccine regardless. The doctor said that. They can't prove she's a carrier, and they won't be willing to believe it was the vaccine that caused the positive test. It'll take a week to prove she's not infected. A week we don't have."

He raised his voice, getting angry for the first time. "We can't take that risk, damn it. Just get her here. It'll be okay."

I sat in silence, knowing this conversation was about to go from bad to worse.

He repeated, "It'll be okay, Pike."

"Sir, you were on the call with the doctor, remember? The one thing he said was she would have massive blood-shot eyes twenty-four to forty-eight hours after contact with the virus, vaccine or otherwise. She never had that. She's not infected."

"This isn't a discussion. Get her home."

"Sir, she's the only one who knows what the carrier looks like. If they think she *might* be infected, they have to *know* the carrier is—and Jennifer is currently the only human being on the planet who can spot her."

"Look, Pike, I won't let her get hurt."

I said, "I know you won't. I'm not so sure about everyone else. But even you will get her locked up to prevent her from spreading a disease on the off chance she's contagious. A virus that she *doesn't have*."

He clenched a fist and pounded the table. "I don't like this any more than you do, but we follow orders. Get her ass home or turn over the team to Knuckles and let them do it."

I felt like I'd been punched in the gut. Still staring at the screen, looking Kurt in the eyes, I raised my voice. "Knuckles. Get in here."

Kurt's face showed surprise. Speaking to him, I said, "You people have lost your minds. I'm not bringing her home to a bunch of handwringers who can't even decide what the danger is. People who are willing to kill a civilian even when they don't think she's a threat. You think I'm going to trust them with Jennifer's life?"

The door opened, and Knuckles said, "What's up?"

I stood. "The commander would like to talk to the new team leader."

58

I sat in the anteroom of our makeshift TOC, waiting for the conversation to play out in the bedroom.

Blood was the only other teammate around. He looked at me quizzically but had the presence of mind not to ask any questions. He saw my expression and was content to toy with the bandage on his arm.

I went through the data on the table, absently flipping through the myriad of different leads we had been following. I saw the forensics report off Ernie's phone, the one that Knuckles had retrieved from the bushes after he'd used it to bait us.

The report had taken time to compile and we hadn't been able to focus on it until after my weird meeting with the general. The numbers in it had proven useless. All of them were tied to cell phones we already knew, with the exception of one: Ernie had called a number that hadn't spiked, but he had hung up before it connected. In essence, it was just an entry in his call log, with no corresponding cellular data.

The number was very close to one of the others we'd been tracking. Outside of the country code—which was for Iran—it was only two digits off from another cell phone we already had. After it had come up empty yesterday the analysts had decided that it was a misdial. That Ernie, in his panicked state, had botched the call, then realized it before it connected. But you never knew. Just because it wasn't panning out here didn't mean we needed to throw it away.

I folded up the paper and put it in my pocket just as Knuckles entered the room. He looked like he'd been forced to drink sour milk. He even looked a little green.

He said, "You know what he told me."

"Yeah. And it's not going to happen. That's the only reason I waited here. To tell you that. Let it go. I'm taking Jennifer with me and flying commercial."

"Pike . . . I can't let you do that. Don't make this any worse than it is. Kurt says you can be with her every step of the way."

"I believe Kurt. I truly do, but he's not in charge there. He can say that all he wants, right up until he has to tell me the plan's changed."

"Come on, Pike. Nobody's going to hurt her. You act like we're the damn Iranians. You're talking about the United States government. They aren't going to do anything harmful to her."

I shook my head. "Knuckles, they were going to leave you to rot in Thailand. *You*. The government isn't automatically good. I'm sure every Japanese-American believed the government's words, right up until we threw them into a camp in World War Two."

"Jesus, Pike! What the hell are you talking about? World War Two? You can't compare this to what we did then. The threat was overwhelming. We had Pearl Harbor for God's sake."

I stood up, closing the distance to him. "That's exactly what I'm afraid of. It's not my judgment that's clouded. It's theirs, because the threat *is* overwhelming, and they're too blind to see that Jennifer is the only one who can prevent it from becoming real."

He held up his hands, trying to calm me down. "Pike, we don't get to make our own orders. Let's get back and get her checked out. The president will be up on his feet in a few days. He won't let anything happen, and honestly, they have a point. We can't just wait to see if she makes someone sick."

"She's not going to make anyone sick, damn it!"

Unbidden, his comment sent a thought spearing through my brain like a flashlight in a dark room, illuminating the answer on the wall.

Without a word, I stormed out of the suite. I was four doors away from Jennifer's quarantine room when Knuckles caught up with me.

"What are you doing?"

I reached the door and banged on it, shouting, "Open up."

I heard, "What do you want? You can't come in, Pike."

"Open this door, right now."

She cracked it and said, "Pike, please. Go away."

Knuckles stumbled back when her face appeared, showing me he believed she was a threat.

I said, "You're not sick. You said so today."

She said, "Yeah, but—"

I pushed open the door and closed in on her. "Kiss me."

"What?"

I wrapped my arm around her waist and jerked her to me. She fought, turning her head and screaming, "Pike, no! What the hell are you doing?"

I closed my other hand around the back of her head and prevented her from moving. I kissed her full on the lips, holding it until I was sure, her squirming to get out of my grasp. I let her go and she sprang away like an animal, slamming her fists against me, her face wild.

Knuckles stood outside the door, flabbergasted.

I said, "You want to try to stop me, go ahead, but remember, if Jennifer's a carrier, I'm now fucking highly contagious."

59

Patrick Rathbone awoke with a splitting headache. Not entirely unusual, but the size of the pain was a little out of the ordinary. Called "Bone" by his friends, he spent most nights drinking more than he should.

He staggered to his feet, kicking the clothes from the night before in his small, one-bedroom apartment. He put his hands to his head, attempting to quell the raging hammers pounding his skull.

I really need to stop the boozing. At least on weeknights.

Four years out of college, he was still trying to find his way. With a degree in finance, he liked to tell everyone at home that he worked on Wall Street. Which, technically, he did.

He'd tried to enter the world of money but had failed. Like a hayseed blonde taking a bus to Hollywood, he'd expected to make his way on his charisma alone and found the job market not exactly embracing him. You needed an in from someone already there. Or, lacking that, a skill that few possessed. He had neither, and now he was a special assistant to an equities trader he longed to emulate. But getting coffee and dry cleaning wasn't the way to break through.

He knew that, of course, but like souls everywhere, he toiled away believing that *tomorrow* he'd get started on his life. He'd allowed the bonfire of his earlier ambition to die down to a smattering of embers, along with his circle of friends, who were just as lost as he was. All living in the Big Apple but none tasting the fruit that was promised.

Today, he needed to get his ass to work before he was fired for not showing up with a triple latte.

He staggered to his sliver of a bathroom, his head splitting open in pain. He placed both hands on the counter and stared bleary-eyed into the mirror, shocked at what he saw.

His eyes looked like the sign of the devil. Red orbs staring back, crisscrossed with veins, scaring him.

Jesus Christ. What did I drink last night?

In truth, he hadn't tied one on hard for two days, when that hot Eastern European girl had said she'd give him a blow job. Of course, that bitch had left him hanging.

He took a shower, hoping it would make him feel better. By the time he was done, he felt worse. Like the hangover to end all hangovers. He staggered to his small dresser and began dragging out clothes, losing track of what he was trying to do.

He pulled on his socks, feeling like he was walking dead. He shook his head, focused on getting to work. On saving his job. He took two steps toward his tiny sliding closet and fell to his knees, the pain in his head overpowering. A wave of nausea overcame him. He spewed vomit for a full ten seconds, then began hacking and wheezing. He crawled through the bile, his stomach clenching over and over, a small part of him incongruously embarrassed at the mess.

A larger part spiked in fear. He knew something was wrong. This wasn't the drinking. He crawled to the phone, oblivious to the strings of phlegm trailing from his nose and joining the stream of puke dripping from his mouth. He dialed 911.

By the time they answered, he was unconscious.

60

Malik stood on the corner of East Forty-Fifth Street, ostensibly waiting for the light to change, but in reality assessing everything around the United Nations Plaza, the East River just beyond.

The phalanx of NYPD vehicles up and down the avenue fronting the plaza caused a small bit of concern, but he knew it was just business as usual. The building was constantly barraged with people protesting one event or another, warranting a heavy police presence.

With no Iranian embassy in the United States, Malik needed a secure location to meet his contact, and the UN provided that venue. As much as the two nations hated each other, the United States still allowed a robust delegation from the Persian state to represent Iranian interests inside the United Nations. One such man, embedded in this delegation, was his contact.

Malik crossed the street, acting exactly like the plethora of foreign tourists wandering the plaza. He stopped at a sculpture of a revolver with its barrel twisted in a knot, using the time for a final survey before passing through security. Nothing stood out. Bored patrol officers leaning against vehicles, a Korean family taking pictures of the imposing building fronted by a row of flags, a young European couple reading a plaque.

He had planned on waiting a minute or two longer before going inside, until the Korean turned his camera on the sculpture, with Malik in the frame. He sidestepped the Korean, then walked to the entrance. Passing through the metal detector, he felt sweat break out on his neck from an irrational fear that it would pick up the glass vial inside his pocket.

It did not. Collecting his phone, the guards barely giving him a glance, he wandered into the tourist area, weaving through various displays, giving each the requisite attention before moving on. He burned off another five minutes in this manner, working his way to a stairwell.

He checked his watch, then descended, following the signs to the coffee shop on the lower level. Servicing both UN staffers and the visiting tourists, it was the perfect location to meet.

He passed the gift shop and entered the little snack bar, glancing casually around as he walked to the counter. He did a double take when his scan passed the meeting location. At the corner table was the cleric who had met him in Hong Kong.

Not a good sign.

He purchased a Danish and some tea, using the time to assess. If they were going to pull him back, they would have simply called him on the phone the cleric had passed in Hong Kong and ordered him to come home instead of allowing him to travel to New York.

Feeling somewhat better, he approached, waiting for a pack of children to pass before speaking.

"I'm surprised to see you here, but I'm pleased at the attention."

"Don't be. It's because I allowed you to continue in Hong Kong. I now bear some responsibility for the debacle that's occurred. I don't intend for there to be a second one."

So, he's under fire now. Good. He has a vested interest in success. Malik thought about pointing out that it was the cleric's juvenile team that had caused the problem but knew it would be suicide. No sense in poking the lion in the eye. He decided on groveling—and lying.

"I feel the same way you do. It was not the result I wanted, but it did accomplish its purpose. The team that was following me has lost the trail."

He had no intention of mentioning his encounter in Macau. The Black Widow had escaped and was even now headed to the target, so there was no reason.

The cleric mocked him. "'Not the result'? *'Not the result'?* Do you realize we lost an entire team in Hong Kong?" Waving a hand around the room, the cleric continued. "The Chinese are keeping this bloated organization from doing anything militarily in our country, and now they have a group of our men under arrest. They are already screaming in diplomatic cables. Do you know what will happen if your 'result' causes them to rethink their position on Security Council resolutions?"

Malik said nothing, having not considered the second- and third-order effects of the failed mission inside China.

The cleric continued. "If that happens, both you and I will never see the light of day again."

Malik saw his opening. Saw that the cleric wanted success to quell the failure he'd sanctioned. *Needed* success. He said, "I was willing to forfeit myself for this mission because I believe in it. I'm sorry to include you as well. In the end, the 'debacle,' as you call it, is done. I can't change it, but we can press forward. Stopping now will garner nothing. The Chinese will do what they are going to do regardless. In fact, the mission may be the only thing that tamps down any reaction to the events in Hong Kong. With the ensuing pandemic in the United States and the fear of its spread, the arrests will be forgotten."

"Maybe," the cleric said. "Where do we stand?"

Malik was secretly pleased at the word *we* in his question. "The Black Widow is carrying the virus and is headed to the target."

"When does it leave?"

"Three days. I went to her hotel room yesterday and left her instructions, along with her tickets. She will be there in plenty of time."

"And you're still sure this is the best way? Maybe we should redirect her to a target here, inside the United States."

"No. We need to infect as many people as possible, in

the absence of major hospital support. If she does it like she is instructed, the entire target will empty before anyone realizes they're carriers. They'll fly to a hundred different places and then begin infecting each location. It is the only way."

The cleric nodded. "Okay. Maybe we'll continue. Now, what about the vaccine? I'm under specific orders to bring it back. We need to replicate it immediately."

Malik pulled the vial from his pocket and said, "Here it is. There is enough material left to duplicate, although it will take some time for our scientists to do so."

"Are you sure it works?"

Malik lied, "As sure as I can be. The doctor said it was the final trial and, unlike the other ones, was the first that had worked. Our scientists should be able to prove it."

"I'm wondering if we hold off until that's done. Wait until we can be sure it works. We have no rush."

No, no, no. Malik had wondered what he would say if this most obvious question was asked and now was glad of what had happened in Hong Kong. "If we wait, we run into the Chinese dilemma. It will take them days to formulate a response, but we know it's coming. Those are days we do not have. It could take weeks to extrapolate this material into enough vaccine to inoculate our population. We can build that buffer simply by preventing entry of any Westerner. Let the virus consume them while we work."

Malik watched the cleric consider the statement, hoping he was truly worried about the Chinese repercussions, along with having no knowledge of what it took to develop a vaccine. He pressed ahead, as if the decision was already made.

"The contact here was supposed to pass me the information for our friends in Venezuela. For the explosives. Did you get that word?"

Snapped out of his thoughts, the cleric pushed an envelope across the table. "Yes. It's all in here. Explosives, a boat, and a crew. They don't know where they are going."

"That's fine. They don't need to." Malik placed the original cell phone the cleric had given him on the table. "One other thing: My new passport is from Bahrain, but this phone is tied to a carpet company in Iran. I didn't mind carrying it in the Far East, but inside the United States it's asking for trouble. I didn't want to answer it this morning when my contact called, but I did because you ordered me to. I need another, clean phone. I'll get it myself and send you the number."

"You think the Americans are attempting to track it? That they are locked on to you now?"

Malik held up his hands to assuage him. "No, not yet, but I've learned never to be lazy. While I'm sure I've lost the team completely, they were sent by someone, and those people won't quit. They know someone has the virus. I just want to make sure they're attempting to find the wrong person."

61

Chip Dekkard relished his new role as a referent leader inside the Oversight Council. Up until the current crisis, he could have counted on one hand the number of times he had even opened his mouth. Now he had people like the secretary of state, the director of the CIA, and the secretary of defense hanging on his every word. He originally had signed the nondisclosure agreements for the council simply because the president had asked, in his heart eschewing working for the government and its bloated, inefficient mechanisms. Now he could see how the power was intoxicating, but he still remembered the stakes, which were higher for him than for anyone in the room.

The council was frantic about stopping a pandemic that potentially would wipe out a third of the world's population—as it should have been—but Chip was more worried about the aftereffects. Namely, who would be blamed? Because of this, he had decided to do whatever it took to stop the carrier—or carriers—in their tracks.

Whatever it took.

The president's catching the flu, while ironic, had proven to be the best thing that could have happened for Chip. Since he'd become bedridden, nobody had mentioned a single word about the laboratory or how the research had been approved. Certainly not the vice president, whose sole function at these meetings had been to gain a consensus to protect himself from making a bad decision.

Chip was positive that if he could contain the threat, he could contain the fallout that would come. Especially if he were seen as the man who'd done the most to prevent the tragedy. When it came out, as it inevitably would, he would profess innocence and call in his chips with the administration, including the massive help he had provided getting it in the position it was in.

The irony of that thought was completely lost on him as he waited for Kurt Hale to update the progress on tracking the Iranians and bringing home their own potential carrier.

He'd done his research with his in-house expertise and had become convinced that any indication of infection had to be contained. The virus was simply too virulent to assume *any* risk. This Jennifer Cahill had come too close to the flame and couldn't be allowed to continue walking around. Quarantine was the only solution until the threat had been reduced.

Kurt finished his report, which could pretty much be summed up in his last sentence: "We continue to pursue leads and develop the situation."

Meaning, we've got nothing. Shit. How can the greatest superpower the world has ever seen not be able to stop a single European woman?

The national security adviser, Alexander Palmer, asked the first question. "So what's the next step? Where do we focus our efforts?"

Kurt said, "Sir, in my opinion, this has gotten outside the scope of the Taskforce. We need a full-court press. Get every asset in our arsenal on it. And I mean from every Podunk police department all the way up to the CIA."

Vice President Hannister said, "What will we tell them? How can we do that without a wide-scale panic?"

"Panic is the last thing we want," Kurt said. "Just get out the information on the general. He's here in the US right now, and he's the key."

The secretary of defense asked, "What about the carrier? That's the real threat."

"Honestly, I don't know," Kurt said. "Only one person has even seen her, and we have no names or anything else. Other than she appears to be Western, we have nothing. Malik is the key. Knowing how they operate, the carrier may not know the target. But Malik sure as shit does."

Chip realized Kurt had said nothing about the potential second carrier. "What about Jennifer? When's she getting here?"

With a stone face, Kurt said, "She's here now. Well, she's in New York, but she's not infected."

"What? We gave specific operational orders. How do you know she's here, and why isn't she *here*?"

Chip watched Kurt take a breath, wondering what was going on. Kurt said, "I can track their movements by their phones, and I gave the order for them to continue the mission instead of coming to DC. She's the only one who knows what the carrier looks like. Bringing her here does nothing but slow down the operation."

Chip leaned back, assessing what Kurt had said. It didn't make any sense at all. Since he'd been on the council, Kurt had been the consummate professional soldier, executing exactly as asked. He'd fought decisions, argued points, and even executed in the absence of council orders, but he'd never deliberately disobeyed one. Especially without even mentioning it until asked.

Palmer said, "Kurt, I understand your mission focus, but you aren't the expert on viral contamination. Keeping her in the field could be as bad as the threat itself."

"Sir, she's not infected. She's had none of the symptoms the doctor said she would get, and she didn't infect Pike."

"What's that mean?"

"Pike . . . uhhh . . . drank from her bottle of water accidentally, and he didn't get sick. She's okay."

Before anyone could say another word, the light above the door to the council's secure room flashed twice. Meaning someone wanted in.

Palmer opened it, seeing an aide. They conversed for a minute, then he returned, his face white.

"We've got an outbreak in New York. Five people at Mount Sinai Medical Center in Manhattan."

Chip felt a shift in the room, the fear enveloping the men like a fog seeping out of the vents, a low murmur breaking out.

Questions began flying until Alexander Palmer raised his hand. "Hang on, hang on. Here's all I know: Six people confirmed infected, three dead. They think they know the source. A guy who worked at an equities trading firm, and the first to die. Three others are from his company, one is the doorman to his building, and one is a dishwasher at a diner he frequents."

Chip said, "What are the odds of others coming in?"

"Jesus, Chip, how would I know? You just saw me get the message."

Vice President Hannister said, "How do they know it's avian flu?"

"Because of the president's earlier alert to the CDC. The paramedics who found the victim on his floor had the alert and suspected what they were dealing with. They took appropriate precautions, and the CDC went to work on containment."

Chip looked at Kurt. "When you say Jennifer is in New York, where specifically?"

Kurt said, "What do you mean?"

"I mean where the hell is Jennifer on the surface of the earth, damn it! Is she in Manhattan?"

Kurt was quiet for a moment, clenching his teeth. Then he said, "Yes."

"That's it! Lock her down! Right now! Before she infects the entire East Coast. Thank God we alerted the CDC."

Kurt said, "She just got there yesterday! It can't be her."

He was drowned out by the cacophony, all competing for Vice President Hannister's attention. Kurt raised his voice. "Listen to me. It's the carrier. We take Jennifer out of the fight, and we lose our ability to stop this."

Hannister said, "We can't take that risk. Lock her down. You understand?"

Kurt said, "What the hell are you people talking about? She couldn't have landed here, infected someone, and have them in the hospital in twelve hours."

Palmer, his voice steel, said, "Get her to Walter Reed. Yesterday."

Kurt shifted from foot to foot. Palmer said, "You have an issue with that order?"

The room grew somber, everyone waiting on his response, none liking where the tone of the meeting had gone. Kurt said, "Pike won't let her come in. He won't bring her."

The room erupted again, Chip louder than the rest. "What the hell does that mean? Get her ass here, now."

Kurt searched the table for support, seeing nothing but men scared of an invisible enemy they couldn't fight with American power. Scared into making snap decisions that had no bearing on the outcome. He shouted, "You people are losing your grip! This is exactly what Pike was afraid of. Get control, damn it. Jennifer isn't sick, and she's the only one who can find the real carrier. Don't you see? That person is in New York City right now! The real carrier is here!"

The statement fell on deaf ears, the feeding frenzy in full swing, the men shouting back and forth.

Chip drowned out everyone else. "Get her here on her own volition, or get her here with a team. Just get her here!"

The ongoing racket withered at his outburst, each man unsure of where the statement was leading. Or maybe not wanting to believe it.

Kurt looked him in the eye. "What did you just say?"

Chip matched his stare. "You heard me. She may not think she's a threat, but she is. If she doesn't want to come voluntarily, then we bring her in with Taskforce assets, just like the other carrier."

Kurt said, "The other carrier is designated DOA."

Chip said, "Jesus Christ! We're talking about a worldwide pandemic! Not about semantics. It's *her* call. Not ours."

Kurt looked at the vice president. "Is that the council decision?"

His lower lip quivering, Hannister flicked his head between Chip and Alexander Palmer. Chip nodded at him, trying to give him confidence. Hannister said, "Yes. We need to prove she's no threat, and like Chip said, it's not really our call. If she wants to come in, she's free to do so. We won't hurt her unless . . ."

"Unless what?"

"Unless nothing! We won't hurt her. Just get her to Walter Reed. We've got the best experts waiting on her already."

"Sir, you know how the Asians prevent the spread of bird flu in their domestic flocks?"

"No. What's that got to do with this?"

"Everything. They simply kill every single bird that has a remote chance of contracting the virus. They've killed millions at every outbreak. Is that how you want to solve this problem? Eliminating anyone who *might* be sick? Even the ones who can help?"

Chip saw the vice president begin to waver and cut in. "Don't turn this around, damn it! We're not out to kill her! She's got the opportunity to come in voluntarily! It's not our call. It's hers."

Kurt slowly faced him, the restrained violence causing Chip to lean back in his chair, unconsciously trying to distance himself. Kurt said, "You people sicken me. You want her, do it yourself. I quit."

Nobody said a word, the room silent except for the creaking of the chairs.

Alexander Palmer regained his voice. "Whoa, Kurt. Don't do anything stupid here. We need you on this."

Kurt walked to the door and opened it. "You don't need *me*. You need someone to do your bidding without question. But you're right about one thing: It's not our call. It's Pike's. With or without your interference, he's the best chance of stopping this threat, and he *will not quit.*"

He stared directly at Chip. "You want to try and stop him, go ahead, but get your house in order before you do. You fuck with what he holds dear, and you'd better be willing to go all the way, because he's bringing it to you whether you want it or not."

62

I checked my watch, wondering how long we should sit here waiting on the general to return. It had already been over six hours, and so far nothing. I wasn't too concerned, though, since we'd had to figure out this location on a shoestring. If we actually did find him, it would be a damn miracle.

After hitting the United States in Detroit, I'd asked the Taskforce communications cell for a lock on the one number we had: the cell Ernie had dialed, then disconnected in Hong Kong. The analysts had said it was just a mistake, but it was all I had to pull. Of course, when I told the commo guys to search inside the United States, they'd balked.

The Taskforce was forbidden from interfering with domestic telephony, and because of my current status, I couldn't get anyone to order them to execute. I was just lucky they hadn't heard what had occurred in Macau and still thought I was the team leader.

After some back-and-forth, with me emphatically stating it was an Iranian phone, not one owned by a US citizen, they finally agreed to just check and see if it was active. They reported that it was inside the continental United States, but that was all I was going to get.

So I knew the guy was here, which meant the carrier was more than likely here as well, but I had no locational data. I had one other idea, but it required help from the hacking cell, and that was out of the question, since their activities were very, very sensitive. They wouldn't operate on my say-so, but instead would require authorization from Kurt for any operation.

It was time to get a little devious.

I called our finance section, getting the warrant officer on the phone who dealt with background checks.

Every person who attempted to join the Taskforce went through a battery of psychological, physical, and historical screening. One part of that was a simple credit check, just like a bank ran, to ensure the prospective candidate wasn't at risk of compromise from some foreign agency because he was about to go bankrupt. I hoped to use our access to credit databases to neck down the general.

Donny, the warrant officer, was immediately skeptical when I called, precisely because he never did anything operational. He was in that part of the Taskforce that simply kept the wheels turning—in this case, making sure we all got paid. He was also a friend whom I'd served with in a couple of different units—something I intended to leverage.

He said, "What's this got to do with your pay?"

"Nothing," I said. "I'm checking up on someone else."

"Pike, I can't go mucking around in someone's credit history for personal reasons. Jesus. You trying to sell a car or something? Get 'em to pay cash."

"It's not for personal reasons. It's much, much more than that. All I want you to do is run a rewards number and see if it's tied to an active credit card being used in the United States."

It was very, very tenuous, but I was hoping whoever had created the general's alias credit cards had made the same mistake Jennifer had found in Singapore. Tenuous, but not crazy. More than likely, the same shop was cranking out documents for a whole host of nefarious missions, and cross-pollination would occur. I'd seen similar mistakes in our own intelligence community.

"Why are you asking me? We've got a section that does this for a living."

"Donny, I can't ask them. I don't have time to go into it, but trust me; I'm not doing this for personal reasons. You know me. You know I wouldn't ask if it wasn't critical."

"Pike, you're going to get us both fired!"

No. Just you. I'm already fired.

"Nobody will know. I promise if I get in trouble, I won't bring you into it."

For a second, all I heard was him breathing into the phone. Then he said, "Give me the damn number. I'll call you back."

I'd relayed the phone call to Jennifer, and we'd waited

to see if we were going to buy a ticket home or a ticket to a potential bed-down location. Fifteen minutes later, we had an address to a hotel in Manhattan, and we'd caught the next flight out, feeling the elation of the hunt.

Now I felt nothing but boredom. Stakeouts ranked right up there with a trip to the dentist, especially when they began to drag on with no end in sight, made worse by the size of my measly little force. With only two people, we couldn't do this twenty-four/seven. We certainly couldn't execute follow-on operations, but that was okay.

Once I confirmed the presence of either the carrier or the general, I was going to call Kurt and pass the torch to a viable team, then fade into the background until this mess was all sorted out.

Jennifer and I had split up, with me in a deli a block over and her positioned in a coffee shop across the street from the hotel entrance. Since she was the only one who knew both the carrier and the general on sight, she was getting the brunt of the work. I'd done what I could to alter both her appearance and mine, using techniques the Taskforce had borrowed from Hollywood. I looked like a deranged stockbroker, with a cheap-ass wig, cotton in my cheeks, a three-day growth of beard, brown contact lenses, and a threadbare suit. I couldn't have cared less what the people around me thought, though. The point wasn't to pass myself off as legitimate. It was simply to *not* look like Pike Logan.

Jennifer cut a much better figure after a trip to a beauty salon for a style and color. Now with a short head of brown hair, all it took was a pair of nonprescription glasses and a pantsuit, and she really did blend in. The coffee shop advertised free Wi-Fi, so she'd purchased a cheap laptop to complete the deception.

I ordered lunch and was thinking about bringing Jennifer down the block to do the same when my phone vibrated. It was Jennifer, and I was sure she was going to ask for a break. I was wrong.

Without preamble, she said, "It's the general. He's walking up Forty-Fifth right now."

I forgot my sandwich. "By himself?"

"Yeah. No carrier with him."

But she's close. Has to be close.

My phone vibrated again with another call. I looked at the screen, then said, "Gotta go. Kurt's calling on the other line. Keep eyes on to confirm or deny he goes into the hotel. I'll call back in a second."

I switched over, a little worried about what Kurt would say, but I had known the call was coming sooner or later. "Hey, sir. Listen, I've got eyes on Malik. I need to get a team to my location ASAP."

He said, "In Manhattan?"

"Yeah . . . in Manhattan. You tracked our Taskforce phones?"

In my heart, I knew that was going to happen. In fact, wanted it to happen to leverage a quicker turnaround getting a team or law enforcement on site, but it still was disconcerting.

"I did. Pike—"

I cut him off before he went into some diatribe about following orders and bringing Jennifer in. "Sir, I need a Taskforce team on my trace right now. We can turn it over to FBI or NYPD later, but we've got to keep eyes on this guy. He's the key to the entire mission. We let him go, we lose the carrier."

"Pike, listen, I'm not the only guy tracking you. There's a team headed your way right now. You need to get rid of the Taskforce phone and get out."

What the hell is he talking about? "Give them my number. Tell them to call. I'll leave Jennifer on site and conduct a linkup."

"Their target isn't the general. It's Jennifer. They're locked on right now, probably listening to this call."

Jesus. "Why the hell did you do that? Call 'em off! Redirect them to the general. Come on, this is ridiculous. Jennifer isn't sick."

"I know. Pike, I can't call them off. I resigned as commander."

For a second, I was speechless, the words making absolutely no sense. It was like hearing someone say the earth was flat. Or the United States was responsible for 9/11. The Taskforce *was* Kurt Hale. He'd had the vision for it, fought to create it, and had been its only commander.

I found my voice. "What happened?"

"It's too long to go into, but the Oversight Council needs an oversight council. You guys are the target. You need to get out right now."

"Can't you get George to back off?"

George Wolffe was the deputy commander and a personal friend of Kurt's.

"He quit as well. Blaine is interim commander."

Lieutenant Colonel Blaine Alexander was the officer responsible for Omega operations, meaning he showed up when it was time to execute a mission, after all the prep work had been done. He was a good man, but I knew he would just follow orders. Something of this magnitude was out of his league to question. The one thing he was very, very good at was the endgame. Hunting men.

I said, "Sir, you gotta get back in there. Don't leave me hanging. Quitting is the easy out."

He said, "I'll do what I can. Ditch that phone and call me once you have another one."

I started to respond and saw a Taskforce member walk outside the glass door, looking at something in a backpack. Tracking me.

63

I hung up without another word, then powered down the phone and ripped out its battery, watching the Task-force member like a hawk. He scratched his head and moved on down the street, still staring at whatever tracking device he'd brought.

Someone is on Jennifer as well. I was in a catch-22. I couldn't call her without getting this guy back on me, but if I didn't, she was dead meat. I went to the glass door and glanced out. The tracker had continued down the street. I exited, knowing there were others around and that they knew me on sight. I prayed my improvised disguise would be enough to get me past.

Walking away from the hotel and Jennifer, I turned the corner and stopped a man talking on a cell. "I've got an emergency. I need your phone."

He frowned at me and waved his arm, turning in a circle and still talking. I lightly slapped his head, causing him to pull the phone away and say, "What the hell is your problem?"

I snatched the cell out of his hand and said, "I asked nicely."

He started shouting and I dialed Jennifer's number, then held a finger in his face. He sputtered and began flapping his arms. Jennifer answered.

I said, "Get out. Turn your phone off right now. We're being tracked. Meet me at our linkup. Thirty minutes."

True to form, Jennifer assimilated everything I said and asked not a single question. I heard "Got it." And she clicked off.

I handed the man his phone back, saying, "Thanks."

He snatched it out of my hand and said, "You're lucky I don't kick your ass, MMA style."

I rolled my eyes and tried to walk away. Which apparently gave the guy some confidence. He grabbed my arm and said, "Where you running to?"

I peeled his hand away and rotated it against the joint, bringing him to his knees, my eyes searching the crowd around me for real trouble. Seeing none, I focused back on him.

"Give me the damn phone."

He squeaked and thrust it toward me. I took it, because I might actually need a cell phone in the next twenty minutes, and released his hand.

"I'm walking away now. You stand up, and I'm going to knock you out."

He nodded.

"This thing have Facebook on it?"

He nodded again.

"When I'm done, I'll update your status with its location."

I hailed a cab and gave him directions. "Central Park Zoo, and don't take the long way."

Before we'd started our operation, Jennifer and I had agreed on a last-ditch meeting site should anything go wrong. Nothing different from what I did back in the old days of patrolling the woods. Plan a point to rally if we got hit and anyone was separated. In this case, I wanted a space that was easily located and in a crowded, public area. I'd picked the Central Park Zoo gift shop.

The cabby dropped me off at Fifth Avenue and East Sixty-Fourth, and I entered Central Park on the back side of the zoo. I stripped off the wig and spit out the cotton swelling my cheeks, looking for threats but seeing nothing but families. A map directed me to the "zootique" at the end of a paving stone walkway, just past a building called the Arsenal.

It was small, and I quickly saw that I'd beaten Jennifer. *Or she's been caught.* I went outside and glanced left, toward the direction of the zoo entrance, wondering if I should wait for the thirty minutes we'd agreed upon or get my ass into the fight.

I took four steps, and Jennifer came around the corner, glancing over her shoulder.

Before I could say a word, she said, "Turbo saw me leave the café. His element followed me. They couldn't do anything because I was in the open, but they're right behind me."

Which means they're boxing us in right now. Turbo was a Taskforce team leader with whom Jennifer and I had had a run-in in the past, while Jennifer was attending Taskforce Assessment and Selection. Well, it was a little bit more than that. Jennifer had dislocated the shoulder of Radcliffe, his 2IC, and I'd kicked Turbo's ass after the event was over. It was the worst team we could have chasing us. We weren't going to get a lot of love out of this surveillance.

"Come on. Let's get into the park. They won't do anything inside with all the civilians around. We get them spread out, trying to cover that terrain, and we can lose them."

We began walking through the zoo, headed to the exit leading into the park. I relayed everything I knew, which left Jennifer a little shocked.

"Maybe I should turn myself in. They're wasting time on me. If I'm gone, they'll refocus on the general."

I said, "Screw that. Kurt Hale resigned over this, which means it's something pretty damn bad."

We speed-walked down one of the myriad paths criss-crossing the park, winding around a statue of an Alaskan sled dog, crossing under a bridge, and going uphill into the mall proper.

I saw a squad of police officers coming in from the west side and thought about going right over to them. Getting them involved just to keep the Taskforce team at bay. They would never risk compromise by a domestic operation in front of law enforcement.

We reached an outdoor amphitheater and I saw another squad, this time wearing SWAT gear, talking to two police officers mounted on horses. The sight caused my first trickle of alarm. *They're looking for someone.*

It couldn't be us. It had to be a coincidence. But I hadn't seen a single Taskforce member. They should have been around us in a surveillance box. *Unless they pulled off.*

I stopped at a park bench and took out the phone I'd stolen, telling Jennifer to keep an eye on the cops. I initiated Google Maps and brought up Central Park, orienting myself, now looking for an escape route. Something that allowed taxis. The park was perfect for losing foot surveillance that was more concerned about compromise than stopping us, but it was a trap if somehow the Taskforce had brought the full power of law enforcement to bear.

Straight ahead, past the amphitheater, was Terrace Drive, which connected to Fifth Avenue to the right and Central Park West to the left. Hopefully, we could snag a taxi cutting through. Jennifer pulled my arm.

"Mounted police are eyeing us."

I saw they had separated from the SWAT guys and were meandering south, one looking our way, talking into a radio, the other studying a piece of paper. *A picture.*

"Come on. Walk slow enough to not draw attention."

I was kicking myself for ditching the wig, but hopefully Jennifer's new look would eliminate us as suspects. She appeared nothing like whatever photo they had.

We passed the amphitheater and the SWAT guys started moving our way. One said, "Sir, sir. Hold up please."

I ignored him.

I said, "You think you can outrun these cops?"

Jennifer's eyes widened, but she said, "Yeah, look at the kit they have on."

"Get ready. We go straight ahead full bore, outdistance them, then cut out of the park before they can radio a search pattern. We get separated, we'll meet at Starbucks in Grand Central Terminal. If I don't show in two hours, get out and call Kurt. Get a status from him. Reassess and go from there."

Jennifer reached down and pulled off the sensible office shoes she'd purchased, saying, "Is he on our side?"

"Yeah. I think so."

The SWAT guys started walking toward us in a group, the mounted cops wheeling around. I heard one more shout and figured the game was up. No sense letting them get any closer.

"Go!"

Jennifer broke like a cheetah coming out of the grass, her long legs churning across the ground. Following right behind her, I saw the mounted officers spur their horses into a gallop, closing the distance. *Shit. Can't outrun that.*

I saw Terrace Drive to our front, a set of stairs leading under it. I shouted, "Down! Go down the stairs. Lose the horses!"

An NYPD van screeched to a halt on the bridge, more SWAT officers spilling out, all of them shouting.

Jennifer hit the stairs taking them three at a time, bounding down almost out of control. We reached the bottom and I could see a fountain ahead on a wide-open concrete pad about the size of a football field, a lake on the far side of it. No cover at all. *Bad choice.*

Three beat cops rounded the corner of the tunnel just as Jennifer hit the bottom. One held up his hands, shouting, "Stop!" Jennifer slid low and swiped his legs out from under him, then sprang back to her feet. The two to his right drew their pistols and I threw myself sideways into them in a body block. We tumbled to the ground, and I rolled off and kept running, seeing Jennifer at the end of the short tunnel. She broke into the open, then slammed into the pavement like she'd been poleaxed.

Three SWAT officers closed on her, one holding a Taser and applying juice. Two more appeared from the other side of the tunnel, all of them armed with M4 assault rifles. They heard me coming and all brought their weapons up. One shouted, "Stop right there! Stop, stop, stop!"

I skidded to a halt, not wanting some trigger-happy guy to squeeze, having no idea what they'd been told about whom they were hunting.

I was forced to the ground and both of us were shackled. Getting jerked to our feet, we were led back up to the van. They opened the doors, and on the bench were Radcliffe and two other Taskforce members, all dressed like SWAT officers. He said, "We'll take it from here."

The doors closed and we began moving. Radcliffe pulled out a syringe and said, "Pike, I knew when they said someone had gone bad, it was going to be you."

He plunged it in my thigh, and the world began to swim. The last thing I saw was the fear on Jennifer's face.

64

Elina parked around the back of the hotel, hiding her car as deep in the lot as she could, right next to a Dumpster. She knew it would remain there until removed by the police, long after she was martyred. She locked the doors, then wondered why she'd bothered.

She dragged her little carry-on through the lobby, seeing it filled with children running back and forth, evading haggard parents begging them to sit still. The scene made her smile, reminding her of her nephews, now long since dead.

She told the receptionist her name and stated she had left her key in the room, locking herself out. Ignoring the usual stare at her hospital mask, she presented her passport before the woman asked for a room number she didn't know. As had happened in Raleigh, North Carolina, the night before, the receptionist stated her room number to confirm, to which she simply nodded. Given the key, and now knowing the number, she went to her room.

She knew this was the last hotel. The end of the line,

as it were, but she couldn't for the life of her see why her journey finished here, in Florida. The town was a small little tourist trap, crammed on a spit of land next to the ocean. Somewhat run-down, with shady-looking surf shops and a few neighborhood bar-and-grills, it wasn't the place she would have chosen to unleash Pandora's box. Driving in, the only thing she had seen that might be of interest was the Kennedy Space Center, but surely that would be better attacked by a conventional bomb. *Why use a virus?*

She found her room with a do-not-disturb sign hanging from the knob. Unlocking it, she pulled in her bag and saw an envelope on the bed. She dropped the luggage and stared for a moment, realizing it held her fate. A small sheaf of paper, bone-white, patiently waiting.

She opened it and found tickets for a cruise leaving the next day. Included were instructions for catching a shuttle to the port, the itinerary of the ship, the room number, the reservation number, and restrictions for what she could bring. Everything in it was innocuous, except for a sheet of paper with a date-time group for a meeting during the voyage. A specific place, with a specific agenda.

She dropped the papers on the bed. *So that's it. I'm going to infect a ship full of people.* She thought about the children playing in the lobby and knew they were waiting on the same cruise. Knew they were going to die.

She took a shower, doing monotonous things to take her mind off of the mission and her part in it. Finishing, she lay on the bed watching the Weather Channel, still finding the children encroaching in her conscious thoughts. She left the room and went to the lobby bar.

She ordered a bottle of water, taking her mask off to prevent drawing attention to herself, and watched the lobby. A tall, obese man, wearing a sweatshirt with a Ron Jon Surf Shop logo and flip-flops that were too small for his feet, took a stool next to her, interrupting her thoughts. He didn't seem to care and had clearly had a few drinks before sitting down.

He said, "You taking the cruise tomorrow?"

She nodded, desperately wanting to put on her mask. Afraid to speak.

He said, "They X-ray the baggage now, just so you know. They claim it's because of terrorism, but it's really to find people bringing on booze. They charge an arm and a leg for that shit on the boat." He leaned in and winked at her. "But I've got a way around it. I put my rum in Ziploc bags. Don't show up on X-rays."

He gave a loud guffaw and slapped his knee, then, in a conspiratorial whisper, said, "You bringing on any booze?"

She said, "No, I don't drink alcohol."

His eyes scrunched up like he couldn't assimilate the statement, a tinge of a smile on his face. "Don't drink? What the hell are you going on a cruise for?"

Despite herself, she smiled back. The man was disarming and clearly not a threat.

She said, "Just a vacation."

He said, "You by yourself?"

The question raised a warning. Now wary, wishing she hadn't engaged him at all, she nodded.

He pointed to a table with three other middle-aged men, all dressed like teenagers. "I'm with them, and we're all by ourselves too."

He guffawed at his joke, waiting on her to join in. When she didn't, his laughter petered out, but he remained in the game, not taking her silence as a hint. He said, "If you want to know how to get the best of this cruise, just let me know. I'm a cruising expert!"

She slid off her stool and said, "I really have to get some sleep."

As she walked away he shouted, "I'll see you on board!"

As the elevator doors closed she cursed herself for not shutting the man down immediately. She didn't need some middle-aged Lothario taking an interest in her and potentially interfering with her mission. She wanted to remain invisible, not become a trophy for a pack of middle-aged adolescents to hunt.

THE NEXT MORNING she boarded the shuttle, along with dozens of other families all headed to Port Canaveral. She knew she stood out, being the only single female and wearing a mask that made her look like she was contagious. Which, of course, she was.

She settled into her bus seat next to the window, immune to the stares this late in the game. A foam airplane hit her in the head and she whipped around, finding a boy of about five staring at her. She picked it up off the floor of the bus and handed it to him.

His mother said, "Billy! I'm so sorry. He doesn't usually act this way."

Elina told her not to worry and waved at the boy. He smiled back, a bright gleam that punctured her will like an ice pick. She began to feel lost in the mission again, wondering how killing children would help her people. She consciously brought the men from the bar in New York to her mind. The vile things they had said. She felt the steel of the mission flowing back into her.

After going through a cattle call of departure procedures, standing in a line that snaked around the port building, she eventually reached the platform for admission.

Split off by guides who directed them to the next available customer service representative, she ended up behind the family with the child on the bus. Anxious about the boarding procedures, she watched what happened to them.

The representative asked the family a series of questions, all perfunctory, about whether they'd brought anything on that they shouldn't have, where they were from, and other inane things. She began to relax, until the man asked, "Do any of you have a fever? Feel ill?"

The child said, "Yes. I think I'm sick."

The mother quickly shushed him and said, "He's just trying to get attention."

The man said, "You can't board if he's sick. If he has

a cold or the flu. The boat is like a petri dish. One person sick will get everyone sick."

Elina heard the words and turned away, pulling the mask off of her face.

The father said, "Come on. He's okay. He's faking."

The representative said, "I'm required to hear it from him." He looked the boy in the eye and asked, "Do you have a fever?" The boy looked at his mother, then his father. The man winked and said, "The best answer is 'no.'"

The boy said, "No. I'm not sick."

The representative smiled and waved them on. Elina stepped up and began the same procedure, showing her passport, tickets, and reservation.

When the man asked if she had a fever, she honestly said, "No. I haven't felt sick for months."

65

I woke up to a glaring light. A single bulb hanging on a string, like something out of a bad spy movie. I tried to move and found I was handcuffed to a short, steel-framed cot.

My eyes felt like someone had shined them with sandpaper. I squeezed them shut, then blinked a few times. I lifted my legs and found them free. *So I've got something to work with.*

Although I had no idea how that would help. Maybe I could get the next guy who entered to position himself so I could knock him out with a kick. Of course I'd have to do it in such a manner that it caused the keys to my handcuffs to fly out, landing next to my hands.

I leaned back, remembering the real focus of the abduction: Jennifer. The thought brought a spasm of rage, and I reflexively jerked my arms up, stupidly trying to break the steel. A guttural scream escaped, and I collapsed back onto the bed, breathing heavily.

I heard a door open and craned my neck. Knuckles came into view.

"Hey. How you doing?"

I couldn't believe the question, like I'd been in a car wreck.

"How am I doing? *How am I doing*? You fuck! I'm going to kill every single one of you son of a bitches! Let me go right now!"

He sat down on the single metal chair in the room. "Look around you. What do you see?"

I did as he asked. I saw rough brick walls and two cameras in the corners, both with open wires running down the walls and out the door. Which meant this place had been hastily established. A hide site built on existing architecture.

He said, "The cameras don't have audio. Only video."

"Why should I give a shit about that? Where's Jennifer?"

He stood up. "She's two floors up. And she's in danger. They're going to move her in a couple of hours. They were just waiting on your anesthesia to wear off." He smiled. "Radcliffe was a little worried about your superhuman capabilities. He gave you twice as much juice as was required."

I asked, "How long have I been out?"

"Over twenty-four hours. It got so bad that they were talking about moving you to a hospital. Apparently your breathing became pretty damn shallow."

I said, "Is Jennifer okay? What did the drugs do to *her*?"

He said, "She's fine. She woke up twelve hours ago. She's absolutely fine."

I sagged back onto the bed. "I'm not even going to ask why you're doing this. Just get out of my room."

He said, "Pike, they're going to take her to DC. They think she's got the virus. That she's a threat."

The statement caused another ripple of anger. I jerked against the bonds and screamed, "She's not sick, you dumbass! We had the guy who's going to kill half the fucking world, and you idiots chased us!"

His next words gave me pause.

"I know. Pike, I was wrong. The Oversight Council doesn't know it, but Kurt's still in charge. Well, in charge of some."

I simply looked at him, waiting to see where this was going. He walked up to me, blocking the view of the cameras. He dropped a set of keys into my hand.

"I'm going to walk away from you and face the wall. You need to make this look real. Choke me out. Once you do so, the clock will be ticking. Jennifer's two flights up, in a room like yours."

"What am I facing?"

He smiled. "Nothing much. Two Taskforce teams, one of them Turbo's. By the way, that guy really hates you."

"Where am I?"

"Hell's Kitchen. You never left Manhattan."

He turned away and walked to the other side of the room, ostensibly still talking. I worked the cuffs as fast as I could, trying to shield the fact that I had a key, wanting to delay any alert. I knew that they'd figure out where the key came from later. So did Knuckles, but what mattered was now. I needed to make it look real.

I broke free and sprang out of the bed. I advanced on Knuckles—my teammate and my friend—and circled my arm around his neck gently, preparing to cinch it down.

He jerked out, whirled, and popped me in the mouth with a palm strike, shouting, "You call that realistic? Jesus. This needs to look *good*!"

Shocked, I raised my hands into a fighting stance and said, "What the hell are you doing? Turn around, damn it! Let me choke you out!"

He shook his head in exasperation, then swung a ridiculous cross, leaving himself open.

That'll look good on tape.

I blocked it, redirecting his energy against him by rotating him around. He, of course, let it happen. I slipped inside his reach and closed on his neck, wrapping my arm around and cinching his carotid arteries closed. He passed out and I lowered him to the floor.

I went to the door and listened for a second, now regretting that I hadn't asked Knuckles any questions about a floor plan.

I heard nothing and entered the hallway, which ended up being a balcony four floors above the ground, the railing running left and right down the corridor. I was in an abandoned pseudo apartment complex/firehouse that looked just like the headquarters from the *Ghostbusters* movies. I ran to the end of the hall, figuring that's where the stairs would be and hearing people shouting on the ground floor below.

I found a stairwell and took them two at a time, skipping the floor between and praying that Knuckles hadn't given me bad information. I cracked the door and saw a hallway without a balcony. A straight shot with nothing in the way. No guards, no security.

I sprinted out and went to the first door, jerking it open. Inside were the seven police officers who were involved in our arrest, sitting around a table and looking bored. Until I opened the door.

I slammed it closed and kept moving before they could recognize me. *Wow. They've got them in quarantine because of Jennifer. Wonder what they did with the horses.*

The hall ended at a T intersection, running both left and right. Outside of the police, I'd found nothing but empty rooms and broom closets, feeling the time slipping away. Knuckles had given me an edge, and I was wasting it searching.

I heard voices to the left and pressed against the wall, listening.

"I don't know, man. Word on the street is she broke your arm."

"She didn't break my fucking arm! She tricked me during assessment. She should've never been there. Which is why she's here now."

Radcliffe.

I poked my head around the corner and saw Radcliffe

in front of a door, looming over another guy who had his hands up, smiling.

"Whoa, man, back off. It's a joke."

Radcliffe said, "I don't find it funny. I'm sick of hearing about it. I'll tell you this right now: She ends up not being sick, and I'm going to teach her a lesson she'll never forget. Along with that asshole Pike."

Well, no time like the present.

I thought about stepping out and saying something appropriately badass like "You want a piece of me?" or "Bring it on!" but knew I was facing two highly trained fighters. I settled on a sprint.

Radcliffe heard the footsteps while I was still fifteen yards out. Looking over the shoulder of the other man, I saw his eyes widen. The second guy was between me and Radcliffe, his back facing me. I decided to take him first.

He began to turn just as I reached him. I hopped lightly and hammered my fist into his right kidney, with all of my weight behind it, hard enough to make him piss blood for a month. He shrieked as I wrapped my left hand in his hair and slammed his head into the wall. The scream was abruptly cut off, and he slid to the ground.

Radcliffe assaulted simultaneously, clocking me on the temple hard enough to make me see stars. I covered up my head and attempted to break contact, stepping back to get space between us and give me a chance to regain the initiative. He wrapped his arms around my body and rotated backward, lifting me off of my feet and driving me headfirst into the floor.

I took the brunt of the fall on my left shoulder, sparing my skull the full impact, but it was enough to stun me. I was losing control of the fight. Handing all momentum to Radcliffe, something that would guarantee I would fail. Giving him *any* edge was suicide.

The force of the fall broke his hold, and I rotated away, kicking back and connecting with something. He leapt at me, intent on keeping the initiative, landing on my back and slamming me into the door he had been standing in front of. He wrapped his arm around my neck, and I knew I was in trouble. I speared his ribs with two elbow strikes, getting some breathing room, but not much.

He cinched the hold, but not before I swam a hand under his arm, slowing the process of losing the blood-flow to my brain. I speared him again, but with little effect. He bucked forward, pounding my head into the door. I blindly reached up and unlatched it. He bucked again, using my skull as a battering ram, and it flung open. He squeezed harder, and I thought my eyes were going to pop out of my head. His hold wasn't perfect, and he was cutting off my windpipe. I saw my salvation thirty feet into the room.

I grunted, "Jennifer . . ."

For a split second, she looked shocked. I saw her eyes narrow, and she sprang off the bed. Then my vision tunneled.

But not for long.

Radcliffe saw Jennifer barreling down on him and now

had a choice: Lock me down and remain defenseless against Jennifer, or release me to take her out. If he was smart, he'd have put me out of the fight first, knowing he could take whatever she could dish out for a few seconds.

He must have remembered what Jennifer had done to his arm. Or he wasn't smart.

He let me go.

66

Jennifer launched herself into the air, and Radcliffe tucked. She wrapped herself around him, putting him in the same choke he had on me. His face showed surprise, like he'd expected her to try to claw his eyes with her nails.

He pummeled her ribs with his elbows, repeating what I had done, but much more successfully. Jennifer lost her hold and he reached behind, bodily ripping her over his head and into the wall.

I sprang to my knees and whipped an uppercut straight into his balls, taking the wind out of him. He doubled over and Jennifer picked herself off the ground, lining up her shot. She danced forward and delivered a snap kick straight into his chin, like she was punting a football, knocking him out cold.

Breathing heavily, she tapped his unconscious form with a toe and said, "Piece of shit."

"Damn, woman!" I said. "What the hell were you waiting on? Couldn't you hear me out here?"

"You mean hear him using your head as a door

knocker? As he mopped up the floor with you? No. I didn't hear that. Sorry."

I stood up and smiled. "Touché."

The radio on Radcliffe's belt started beeping, then squawked, "Pike's out. Pike's out. Current location unknown. Acknowledge."

"Let's get out of here before they figure out we're both jailbreaks."

We raced to the end of the hallway, bounding down the stairs until we reached the bottom floor. Leaving the stairwell, we found ourselves in a large warehouse-type structure that looked like the Ghostbusters' receptionist area. Old, made of stone, with desks scattered haphazardly and debris all around. Jennifer saw an exit sign and pointed toward a hallway. We entered and found ourselves facing Turbo and another man. Both with Glocks in their hands.

We slid to a stop, and I began backing up the way we'd come, both hands in the air.

Turbo sighted down the slide, putting a laser on my chest. He said, "Stop. Don't move."

I did as he asked, saying, "You going to shoot me? Shoot a damn teammate?"

"I'm following orders. Why don't you do the same? It's your choice. Not mine. Don't push it. I'm not bluffing."

"Turbo, listen—this is a mistake. We're wasting time. You guys should be focused on the location of the general."

He motioned with the pistol. "Get on your knees, your hands behind your back."

I said, "No. I'm not getting locked up again. You people are fixated on the wrong threat."

I started to back up again and heard feet behind me. I turned and saw Retro and Decoy now blocking my exit, also with Glocks drawn.

Jesus. My own team.

Turbo said, "Look, you're not going anywhere. Get on your knees. Now."

I stared at Decoy, wanting to punch him. He lowered his Glock and said, "Come on through."

Jennifer, much quicker on the uptake, began backing up, hands still in the air. Turbo shouted again and centered the laser on her chest. Retro stepped in front, the laser now on him.

"You going to shoot me too? Put the weapon down."

I backed up as well, the other man's laser blocked when Decoy stepped in front of me. Turbo shouted, "What the hell are you doing? I knew putting Knuckles's team on this was a mistake."

Decoy glanced back at me and said, "What are you waiting on? Someone to carry you? Get the hell out of here."

Not needing a second invitation, I grabbed Jennifer's hand and sprinted back the way we'd come, running through the warehouse section to another exit. We jogged east down Forty-Second Street, hitting Times Square. We went into the subway, getting off at Grand

Central Terminal. Seeing the crowds wash around us, I relaxed. We were safe for the time being.

Jennifer said, "What now?"

"I don't know. First thing we need to do is call Kurt. Figure out the status of things." Clearly, the Taskforce was split on what was going down, and I wanted to know the exact state of play, along with any leads that might have popped up during our pleasant stay at Hotel Ghostbuster.

She said, "You think that's smart?"

"Yeah. I think we can trust him. He called to warn us in the first place."

She saw a Verizon store and said, "You got a preference on phones?"

"Yeah. No iPhone 5. I'm not paying out the nose for this."

"I'm famished. Go get me a hamburger. I'll meet you in the food concourse."

Twenty minutes later, because she's a smartass, Jennifer returned with two iPhone 4s. I fired mine up and immediately went to the settings to ensure any location-finding features were turned off. Scrolling through the various tabs, I saw something called "Find my iPhone."

The only Apple products I'd ever owned were counterfeit ones the Taskforce made, full of top-secret bullshit buried under a layer of false apps. I showed the toggle to Jennifer and said, "What's this?"

"It's an Apple thing. You open an iCloud account, turn that on, and you can lock, track, or wipe your phone if it's stolen."

"Jesus. That's better than the Taskforce apps."

"Yeah, I know. It works on Mac laptops and iPads too."

Her words sank in and I dropped my hamburger into its basket, dialing the phone.

"What?" she said. "What did I say?"

"Remember following Ernie in Singapore? Where did he go after getting the phones in Sin Tat Plaza?"

She thought for a second, and it hit home, her eyes becoming animated. "The Apple store. He bought an iPad."

67

Chip Dekkard waited to get cleared into the White House, worried about what he would hear from President Warren. He'd overstepped his bounds on the Oversight Council, and he knew it. Luckily, nobody else on the council felt that way. They'd stood by him, and he'd appreciated it. But he knew they were doing it out of ignorance. They were afraid of the genetically altered avian flu, and rightly so, but they had no idea that he was the sole cause of the threat. The thought of their finding out was terrifying.

He'd spent the last three days erasing his personal tracks with the company in Singapore, doing whatever he could to wipe the stain away from his holdings. He knew he couldn't cut his ties completely, so he went for the less optimal choice of building a firewall between himself and the company, data-mining multiple servers and destroying all communications that indicated he had any idea of the ongoing experiments.

If necessary, he would sacrifice the businessmen who had broached the idea in the first place, expressing surprise at the "riskiness" of the idea and jumping on the bandwagon with everyone else about bringing them to justice. He'd already begun building his evidence, sprinkling e-mails with disinformation in them, damning the company and leaving him in the clear.

He felt pretty good about surviving any follow-on investigation. It was unfortunate that he had been forced to turn on his people, but thinking logically, the punishment they received would be meted out whether he joined them or not, and localizing the damage would prevent a catastrophic loss of his conglomerate's trading value—in effect, protecting innocent stockholders who had nothing to do with the calamity. It might seem brutal, but it was for the best.

Like the saying goes, it's not "show friends," it's "show business."

He heard his name called and saw Alexander Palmer entering the West Wing foyer. Palmer handed him a visitor's badge that said ESCORT ONLY and said, "Come on. You're the last one here."

Being led at a brisk pace through the narrow hallways, Chip said, "What's going on?"

"President Warren wants an update. He's called the principals of the Oversight Council."

"I'm not a principal."

"Yeah, but you know more about this virus than anyone else."

Chip simply nodded, wondering if the president would ask for the "research" he was supposed to have done on the company. He was close but not yet ready to provide it. Trigger an investigation too early, and he'd be caught in the net.

Passing through the center hall of the main building, they took the stairs to the residence on the second floor.

Palmer said, "They've got him in the Lincoln Bedroom. Turned it into a mini-hospital. The doctor's cleared him for one meeting a day, and today, it's us."

The Secret Service protective detail opened the door, and he saw the president on a canopied bed, surrounded by three other men, intravenous lines running into both arms, a plethora of monitors bleeping around him. And looking pissed.

"Whose bright idea was it to divert a Taskforce team to chase another Taskforce team?"

Vice President Hannister said, "It was a collective decision, but ultimately my call."

"And Kurt went along with it? Did he go as batshit crazy as the rest of you?"

The men shuffled back and forth. Palmer cleared his throat, getting the president's attention.

"Sir, he . . . uh . . . resigned. So did George Wolffe. We had Lieutenant Colonel Blaine Alexander running the operation against Pike and Jennifer."

President Warren looked like he was going to explode. A monitor began flashing and a squad of doctors and nurses barged in. He waved them away.

The lead doctor said, "Sir, you really should be resting. I'm going to have to ask these men—"

"Leave this room right now."

They began to backpedal, and he said, "Jesus, I just have the flu. You'd think I was terminal."

After the door closed again, he said, "So you've got the Taskforce chain of command on unemployment, a lieutenant colonel heading up a chase for Taskforce members instead of an Iranian general, where other Taskforce members refused to participate and let them go. Am I summing things up pretty well?"

Hannister said, "We diverted assets to track the general but failed to pick him up again. Whatever phone he was using has been dead since Pike's original sighting. We do, however, believe we have the name he's using."

"So you're on him? That would be some good news."

"No, sir. The alias took a flight to Venezuela yesterday. We believe he's no longer in the country."

He looked at the director of the CIA. "Venezuela? Why there?"

"Honestly, we don't have any idea."

"What about the carrier?"

"We never had a single hit on her. We're still looking, trying to track her down through the original source of the infection in Manhattan. If we can backtrack his movements we might get a lead."

"So you're now convinced it isn't Jennifer?"

"Well, yeah. I'm not saying going after her was wrong.

She's still a risk. Just that she couldn't be the one who caused this specific outbreak. It was too soon. If we can locate where this guy got sick, we might be able to juxtapose other intelligence for the carrier, start tracking her."

"Is he cooperating?"

"He's dead."

"Well, that's great." He turned to Chip. "What's the status of the company that started this whole mess?"

Chip said, "It's a small firm in Singapore that partnered with an American company here. I'm still trying to sort out who knew what."

"Keep working it. I want to know who to hang when this is over."

Chip felt sweat form on the back of his neck but nodded vigorously.

"Everyone else, listen up. Number one, no more Taskforce operations until I'm cleared back to work. Just put them on hold. I can't have that force running around under a lieutenant colonel, and you people showed me about as much judgment as a kindergartner."

Hannister started to protest, and President Warren cut him off with a glare.

"Number two, focus on Malik. Get whatever assets we have available in Venezuela to start working his location. Then drop everything else. I mean NSA, CIA, DIA, and any other agency that can help."

He looked at the secretary of state. "Finally, start bringing pressure on Iran. Go through the Swiss protecting powers and pass a message. Let them know we suspect what Malik's up to, and we're going to unleash holy hell if it comes to fruition. I know they'll proclaim no knowledge, but put them on notice. Scare the shit out of them, like we are right now. If we can't find Malik, maybe they'll do it for us."

The men nodded, waiting on further instructions.

President Warren said, "What the hell are you still standing here for? Get to work. The next time we talk, I want some good news."

As they began to leave, President Warren pulled Alexander Palmer's sleeve. "Alex, hold up."

"Yes, sir?"

"Find Kurt Hale. I want to talk to him. Immediately."

"He's not going to be able to do anything more than what you've outlined."

"Bullshit. Right now I feel like all we're doing is talking. The carrier is real, and she doesn't give a damn about anything I just said. I'd like to change that, and he's got the men who can do it."

68

The sun crested the bow of the boat, hitting Malik in the face. He groaned and rolled over, feeling the crust from his vomit on the small aft cushion someone had told him was a bed.

The captain tapped his leg and said, "Come on. Get up. Calmer seas today, I promise. We've taken on fuel and are ready to go. Only about ten more hours."

The very thought of ten hours on the open ocean turned Malik's stomach. Just sleeping on board with the gentle rocking of the marina had caused him to throw up most of the night.

He'd arrived in Caracas, Venezuela, in the late afternoon two days ago, getting picked up by his contact—the man who would build the martyr vest. They had driven down the coast for four hours, then transferred to a boat bound for a marina on Margarita Island. It was an indicator of what was to come, bouncing across the water in the dead of night.

That trip had been short enough to prevent any discomfort, and Malik had the misconception that the boat taking him to meet the Black Widow would be some grand ship, a large fishing trawler or the equivalent.

Arriving at the marina, he'd met the two-man crew and was shown the boat. Something much, much smaller than he'd had in his mind's eye.

"This will take us across the ocean?"

The captain had said, "Yes, of course. It's a Bertram Thirty-Eight Special. Twenty-six knots and really good range."

Having grown up in the desert, the words meant absolutely nothing to him. What he saw was a boat barely forty feet long, and he knew how far they had to go. He told them the destination, praying they'd take him to another boat when they realized the distance. They didn't. Completely unfazed, the two talked among themselves for a couple of minutes until Malik interrupted.

"Can you do it? How long will it take?"

"Yes, of course we can. Two days. We leave tomorrow morning and drive hard to Dominica. We get there, get fuel and spend the night, then complete the journey."

Something else he hadn't factored in. The distance was only about five hundred miles as the bird flew, and he'd figured that's exactly what the boat would do, getting there in one day.

"We can't make it in a single day?"

"No, no. Much too dangerous. We'll hug the islands, stopping for fuel."

He'd said, "Two days is the absolute maximum time. I have a meeting in three days."

The next morning they had set out, him, the two-man crew, and the bomb builder. At first, he had spent his time ensuring the vest was constructed correctly, wanting to prevent the man from attempting to build a device that was designed to kill by itself, using a large explosive charge and nails or ball bearings. He wanted something to spread the virus, period, under a charade of an attack.

Two hours into the trip, he had thrown up for the first time, much to the crew's amusement. He spent the rest of the trip in utter misery, vomiting over and over again until his body was as weak as a newborn kitten.

With today's journey in front of him, he was unsure if he would survive.

At least the vest is complete.

He pulled out his smartphone and turned it on. Not wanting to waste the battery power on the open ocean devoid of cell towers, he'd shut it off after they'd left, then had been too miserable to turn it back on when they'd docked the night before.

Five minutes later, it vibrated with no less than five missed calls. From the cleric.

He got the captain's attention, pointed at his phone, and said, "Don't leave yet."

Knowing it wouldn't be good news, he considered simply ignoring the calls, but, while the odds weren't that great, it could have been intelligence he needed to accomplish the mission.

The cleric answered and Malik began relaying his status, only to be interrupted.

"The mission has changed. We no longer want to attack. The United States is aware of the virus and our role in it."

Malik squeezed his eyes shut, hearing the very last thing he wanted. "How do you know? We are too close to stop because someone is getting skittish."

"Malik, they named you, along with your position in the Pasdaran Quds. They know the carrier is a woman. They know the alias name you're using. And those are just the things they told us. They don't *suspect,* they *know,* and that was the one thing we couldn't have. We couldn't give them any reason to retaliate."

They know my name? Then they know I flew to Venezuela. The mission was going to be very, very close. He would need to erase the crew members and the bomb maker.

"We can still go ahead. They won't attack us and risk losing the vaccine. We should continue, and when they rattle their sabers, feign innocence and offer them the vaccine. We will accomplish much even if they manage to stop the pandemic."

Malik knew he was grasping, but it was all he could think to say.

"No. We will not. They have threatened to destroy the Islamic republic, and we don't believe they are bluffing. They were more overt than we have ever seen. No hidden meanings. We want you to meet the Black Widow as you intended, but instead of giving her the explosives, draw some blood from her. Bring that home. At the least, we can use the virus as a future deterrent."

Malik knew he would never convince the cleric and gave up. "What do you want me to do with the Widow?"

"Kill her on the ocean. Make sure she cannot contaminate anyone."

The comment sank in, and Malik knew the cleric had lost his way. Perhaps the regime as well. Fear of repercussions alone ruled their response. It was not what the revolution was founded upon, when a small band of students overcame a tyrant and thereby set about altering the course of the Islamic world. He remembered his friends tortured to death by the shah's SAVAK, wondering if the cleric knew of such sacrifice. Men who willingly embraced the repercussions of the revolution.

The Black Widow had volunteered for this mission, much like Malik had in 1979, fully willing to give her life for a greater cause, and Malik would not simply toss her in the ocean so that the cowardly people in charge would have a "deterrent." She was better than all of them and deserved to achieve the martyrdom she had striven for.

He closed his eyes and went back to those days, remembering the heady success of the revolution. When everything had been clear-cut, before the Islamic republic began straying from the pure path and fighting among themselves. Politics had superseded the revolution, with President Ahmadinejad spending his final months in power fighting the clerics over petty things. It sickened him.

Malik said, "I understand. I will be home in less than four days."

He hung up to find the bomb maker standing in the galley. "Bad news?"

"Only if one chooses to listen to it. Tell the captain to cast off."

69

Jennifer said, "This has got to be a mistake. We're missing something."

Driving down the spit of land known as Cocoa Beach, I was with her, absolutely confused as to why the iPad trace had landed here. There was nothing but third-tier vacation rentals and cheap surf shops. Certainly nothing that would be worthy of releasing the virus.

Why would you drive out of Manhattan, one of the most densely populated cities in the United States, to come here?

It had to be a way station. Something picked because of an ease of use to segue into something else.

But what?

Yeah, Cape Canaveral was here, along with the Kennedy Space Center, but why on earth would that be a target? Was Iran's intel so pathetic they thought attack planning against them happened here? In some secret basement? *Maybe.* You never could predict what the other guy believed. Trust me—I'd seen enough bad intelligence over the years to know even the greatest superpower on earth sometimes ends up chasing a rabbit down the hole.

I said, "Let's get to the hotel and check it out. At least we can eliminate it as a location. Somebody will either recognize your sketch or not."

We'd called Kurt within minutes of getting out of the Ghostbusters Hotel, and, luckily, he'd proven to be on our side. Unlike the other jackasses at the Oversight Council, he'd coordinated to get us to a professional law enforcement sketch artist. I don't know how he did it, but it was the first bit of common sense that I'd heard in days. Well, other than Knuckles and his team getting us out. Now we had a sketch of the woman, which, along with her accent, would help neck things down.

Getting a start point to even show the sketch had taken more time than I would have liked. Turns out, you *can* track an individual iPad, but only if the owner signs up for an account called iCloud, thereby registering something called a MAC address. The MAC, or Media Access Control, was a numerical identification for the magic widget in the iPad that communicated with a Wi-Fi hotspot, which left us with two problems. One, the carrier had never initiated an iCloud account, and two, we had no idea of the MAC address. But we did know where her iPad had been bought.

After some wheedling with Kurt, he'd agreed to authorize the penetration of the Apple store in Hong Kong through the hacking cell. I had the date, time, and location of the purchase; all they needed to do was get the serial number of the iPad. From there, further exploration would give us the specifications of that particular iPad, to include the MAC address.

I had no idea how he accomplished it, since he'd officially resigned. Well, actually, I did. He was a commander that people followed because of his personality, not his rank. He'd probably just walked into the building and started issuing orders. Nobody there would have questioned him, including LTC Alexander.

We got the MAC, only to run into the iCloud problem. Now I was not only asking for the penetration of Apple computing but also the manipulation of its systems, because we needed to create a fake iCloud account and feed it the MAC address, tricking the software into thinking the "find me" feature was active in the iPad. Something that was way, way outside of our mandate— even in normal times, when Kurt was officially in charge. Now it was impossible. Kurt had shut me down. For one night, anyway.

Yesterday, I'd woken up to my phone ringing. Kurt had apparently been contacted by the president, and the world was decidedly different from just eight hours before. Nothing was off the table, and he had the trace of the iPad. I didn't ask any questions.

Now I wasn't sure if we were too late. The trace was two days old, and we had no idea if the carrier was still here. Two days of wasted time.

We pulled into the Marriott and parked in back, away from the entrance. I left Jennifer in the car and took her sketch into the hotel. I didn't want to risk her bumping into the carrier if she happened to be getting coffee in the lobby, so Jennifer would stay outside in the heat, sweating.

I asked for a manager and stated I was conducting an investigation, using a phony badge provided by the Taskforce. In fine print it said something stupid like "Investigator of the Paranormal." Well, not that bad, but it wouldn't stand up to any scrutiny.

Luckily, the badge did its job. I got the staff into a room and passed the sketch around, giving a story about trying to find a runaway.

Nobody recognized the drawing. I said, "She would have checked in during the last week. We know she was here two days ago."

The manager said, "This sketch isn't that great. We see hundreds of people a day. Do you have a name?"

"No. Believe me, I wish I did, but I don't. I have no idea what name she's using. She has an accent, though. Sounds like an Eastern European."

He laughed. "Do you know how many foreigners come through here? We make our money on cruise ship stopovers. We get more foreigners here than Washington, DC." My face went sour, and he said, "Hey, you can hang around for another twenty minutes. The other shift will come on and maybe they'll have seen her, but I wouldn't hold my breath."

I left the hotel and found Jennifer on the phone. I said, "Who are you talking to?"

She held up a finger, saying, "Yes, alpha, six, alpha. That's right."

I patiently waited, and she started writing in the air. I looked at her like she'd lost her mind and she hissed, "Get me a something to write with!"

Ripping through the seat cushions of our rental, I found a broken pencil and handed it to her, along with a napkin from our last stop. She scribbled something down and hung up.

"What was that all about?"

"I got sick of waiting around in the car, so I trolled the parking lot. I found five cars with New York license plates. One is from a rental car company at JFK driven by a woman from Latvia. Named Elina Maskhadov."

When I didn't respond, Jennifer said, "You trying to catch flies with that open mouth? It wasn't rocket science. The car in question is hidden by a Dumpster."

I snapped my mouth closed, then said, "Holy shit, you are the heat! That's the smartest thing I've seen in years! So we know she's still here, and we have a name."

Her eyes widened at my accolades, completely oblivious that what she had done was outside the box and something very few would have thought of. But only for a second. She grinned and said, "Don't get worked up. Me being the heat doesn't get you any closer to the flame. You want to go back in and see if this helps?"

I felt an irrational pull to lean in and kiss her. I didn't. Maybe, given what was coming, it would have helped, but at that moment I was sure it was the wrong time and wrong place. I was never a good judge of that.

I snatched the name out of her hand and said, "Get a

beacon out of our kit and put it on the car. If this doesn't pan out, we might get something from tracking its movements."

I jogged back into the hotel lobby, getting the manager. He had already passed my sketch to the oncoming crew, who were now talking among themselves. The manager ran the name, and sure enough, it came up; she had checked out two days ago.

I said, "But her car is still here. Why would that be?"

Before the manager could answer, one woman on the new shift said, "I think I know who this is. She had a strong accent, but she didn't spend any time walking around. Stayed in her room for most of her stay. She didn't really use the bar or pool."

"You're sure that's the girl?"

"No. I can't be sure. The eyes are right, and she did have an accent, but the woman I'm thinking of always wore a mask. You know, like a doctor's mask?"

Bingo.

"You remember her checking out?"

"Yeah, sure. She left with everyone else on the cruise."

70

Elina was shocked at the number of people trying to leave the ship, all at the same time. She was on the eighth deck, and each of the six elevators had shown up full, packed with kids and parents moving to the lobby.

She patiently waited, then crammed into the small elevator with six other people, wanting to hold her breath. Since boarding, she'd spent just about every waking moment inside her cubicle, living on room service and only traveling out during darkness, when the decks were much less crowded. She steered clear of any of the onboard entertainment, such as the casino, because she'd taken to not wearing the hospital mask.

Initially after boarding, walking to her berth, she'd been questioned by a crew member who happened to work in the infirmary, and the encounter had not been pleasant. Apparently, sickness on board was something they continually fought, and they didn't want anyone contagious mingling with the other passengers. It had almost come to her ordering Elina to the infirmary for tests.

Eventually the woman had relented, but Elina had left

the mask behind after that. Now, crammed together with a thousand other people all waiting to exit the massive ship, she struggled to avoid personal contact.

Not that she was sure it mattered. Today was the meeting with Malik, which surely meant an endgame. If somebody got infected now it would just mean they were ahead of the curve by hours.

She shuffled forward, watching the procedures for leaving the ship. Apparently, it only consisted of showing the identification card she'd been issued upon boarding. The crew member slid it through a magnetic reader and handed it back.

She saw signs saying all bags would be searched upon reentry and listing the proscriptions against bringing unauthorized alcohol on board. With gallows humor, she reflected that it didn't say anything about explosives. She had no bag to be searched and was wearing a loose-fitting sundress/shawl combination that would camouflage the vest.

Ahead of her, someone shouted, "Hey! Hey you!" Several people turned to see who was yelling, including Elina. She instantly wished she hadn't.

It was the obese man from the hotel bar, and he was waving at her.

"Where you been? I haven't seen you the entire cruise."

She smiled weakly but said nothing. He reached the crew member taking IDs and said, "I'll wait for you outside."

He disappeared through the gangway, and she began looking for some other exit. Some way to get off the boat without going by him. She saw it was futile. There was only one line and one gangway.

Now what? I can't have him follow me.

She passed through the portal and saw him standing on the dock wearing a pair of board shorts that ended just above the knees and a T-shirt from the Atlantis resort in the Bahamas, the first place the cruise had stopped.

She reached him and he said, "What are you doing this morning? My buddies are going on a snorkeling trip to the French side of the island later this afternoon, but right now they're sleeping off a hangover."

She said, "Look, I'm just doing some souvenir shopping. I don't have any plans."

"Hey, me too! I'm killing time until those deadbeats wake up. We have to meet our snorkeling boat right here at eleven. Want some company?"

Despite herself, she found him charming in a bumbling sort of way and didn't want to hurt him. "No. I really don't. I took this cruise to get away, not to socialize. I'm sorry."

His face fell, and he said, "Okay. I get it."

He turned to walk away, and for reasons she couldn't explain, she said, "Maybe we can have lunch or dinner. What's your room number? I'll call you."

He brightened and said, "Twenty-three sixty-three. In the bowels of the ship. What's yours?"

She smiled and said, "I'll call *you*, not the other way around."

He nodded over and over, like a puppy, and she walked

away, wondering why she had done that. She tried to convince herself that she needed someone knowledgeable about the ship. Someone who could tell her where it was most crowded and at what time, so she could infect the greatest number possible. But she knew it wasn't true.

She simply wanted a touch of human companionship before she blew herself apart. One last chance to talk to another person who wasn't out to kill her or directing her to kill others.

She walked through the small customs facility, showing her cruise identification and getting waved past. Immediately assaulted by taxi drivers, she ignored them and continued walking out of the cruise terminal, replete with a plethora of souvenir shops, until she reached the road fronting the port.

As instructed, she traveled north on the narrow, cracked sidewalk until she passed a marina called Dock Maarten.

First checkpoint.

Relieved to see the sign, now confident, she picked up her pace. She passed a restaurant called Chesterfields and turned left, heading toward the bay and the sailboats anchored there. She walked past an empty customs house and onto the docks, searching for her signal.

She saw it two docks over. A Chechen-separatist flag, green with red and white stripes, floating in the breeze aboard what looked like a sportfishing boat.

She went to it, unsure how to proceed. She settled on saying, "Hello?"

A man she didn't know poked his head out, then disappeared just as quickly. She waited, then heard a voice she recognized.

"Come in, Widow, come in."

Malik.

She went down the steps into the galley and saw him sitting on a makeshift bed, his back against the bulkhead. And he looked awful. For a horrible moment, she thought he'd contracted the virus.

"What happened to you?"

He barked a short laugh devoid of humor and said, "It appears the ocean and I don't get along. Nothing to worry about. Have a seat."

While she did, he brought out a box.

"Open it."

Inside was her method of destruction. A vest laced with explosives. She looked closer and saw it was different from the other vests she'd trained with. For one, there was much less explosive. For another, the charges seemed to spiral down the vest, like a Slinky, with what looked like a sleeve of sausage hanging off the bottom.

Malik said, "It fits just under your chest and goes to just above your pelvis. That last piece goes between your legs and fastens in the back. The explosive charge is designed to cut."

She looked him in the eye and said, "You mean cut *me*. Slice me into pieces and fling me out."

She spat it as a statement, not a question. Malik, originally proud of the construction, realized the callousness of what he had said.

"Yes. I'm sorry. I just wanted to ensure you wore it correctly. I didn't mean to belittle your sacrifice."

She said nothing.

He continued. "You'll need to wear it to get back on the boat, but you shouldn't have any trouble. Sint Maarten is your last stop, yes? You head back to the United States tonight?"

"Yes. We have two full days at sea."

"Do not conduct the mission until tomorrow midday at the earliest. Midnight at the latest. We need to hit a balance where we have enough time for the virus to spread but the ship is far enough out to sea that it will continue on instead of turning back."

"Because of my explosion?"

"Yes. They won't know what to make of it, and I want them to simply clean it up and decide to proceed, allowing everyone on board the chance to become infected. To that end, it would be helpful if you executed near a food-serving area."

She nodded, the final plan becoming clear. "And once we—I mean they—dock in America, they'll travel back to wherever they came from, not showing signs of the illness for another day or two. So you get your multiple infection points. Multiple outbreaks all over the United States."

"Exactly."

She changed the subject. "You don't appear too worried about catching the virus. I expected to talk to you through a wall."

His answer surprised her. "I'm afraid that I'm a martyr too. By passing you this vest, I have sealed my fate. Truthfully, the virus might be an easier way to go."

She thought to ask what he meant but let it lie, assuming the Americans were closing in. The fact that he was willing to die for this mission meant a great deal to her. Gave her strength about the path she was on.

She stood up, removed the shawl, and dropped the sundress to her feet. He recoiled, his eyes growing wide. "What are you doing?"

"Putting on the vest."

He leapt up, the image of her standing in nothing but a bra and panties causing his face to turn crimson. "Let me give you privacy."

Elina laughed. "You have no fear of the virus but run at the sight of my body? Why? I'm nothing more than a tool. Just like the vest in that box."

He turned his back, saying, "Make this fast, please."

She cinched the vest in place, bringing it just below the swell of her breasts before affixing the Velcro in front, then sliding the tail of explosives between her legs, contacting the Velcro on her back. She tucked the two wire leads, connected to a blasting cap on her waist, into the Velcro. Lastly, she pulled the detonator out of the box, a simple one-button affair about the size of a pack of gum, and tucked it into the Velcro on the opposite side.

She pulled up her sundress and said, "How does it look?"

He turned around and studied her for a moment, then said, "There are some lumps, but not too bad."

She unfurled the shawl and laid it across her shoulders so it draped in back, the two ends hanging down the front.

"Better?"

"Much better. Now get back to the boat. Remember what I said. No earlier than noon tomorrow."

She was halfway up the steps when Malik said, "Elina?"

She looked at him and saw sadness on his face.

"You are very, very brave. You will be remembered for eternity. You are not a tool to be used. Don't ever think that."

She felt tears well up in her eyes. She nodded and continued up the stairs, marching to her destiny.

71

We bounced into the runway and then were jerked forward as the MC-130's turboprops reversed. After a brief taxi, the engines shut down and the ramp began to lower, the humid breath of Puerto Rico competing with the stale air from the blowers of the aircraft AC, causing fog to stream out of the vents. The sun had just crested the horizon, and it would have looked like a vacation photo, with the palm trees waving around and the ocean in the distance. Would have except for the loadmaster in an Air Force flight suit and the Coast Guard pilot on the tarmac waving us off, a not-so-subtle reminder of why we were here.

Vacation photo from Stephen King.

Knuckles pulled out his earplugs and said, "If I knew I'd be getting dropped into a ship full of walking dead, I would have just left you locked up."

One of the doctors heard him and looked like he was going to throw up.

I said, "Cut the chatter. They're nervous enough as it

is. Get the kit offloaded. I'm going to find the coastie in charge of our helicopters."

Decoy, Retro, and the rest of the team began offloading black bags that looked exactly like the bags of the five-man team from the Centers for Disease Control and Prevention. As far as the Air Force and Coast Guard knew, we were all members of the CDC. They'd get a shock if they opened one of our team bags, though. Probably would want to know what an H&K submachine gun had to do with viruses.

Everyone involved in this charade thought we were investigating some strange disease on a cruise ship. Including the crew of the ship itself. Nobody knew of the terrorist aboard, except for my team, the captain of the ship, and the real CDC crew, which is why they were nervous. From what I'd been told, each one of them had accomplished some pretty heroic stuff, from fighting Marburg and Ebola in Africa to the avian flu in Thailand, Indonesia, and Hong Kong, but mention a terrorist and everyone gets skittish.

After discovering the name of the carrier, it had taken very little work for Kurt to locate which cruise she was on, but we were still too late for the easy fix of simply telling the boat to wait for our arrival at the island of Sint Maarten.

It had left last night and had spent the last twelve hours steaming home to America, putting it out in the middle of the Caribbean Sea. From the captain we'd learned that nobody had become sick—yet—which had us breathing a sigh of relief. Analyzing what the carrier was trying to accomplish, it appeared she wanted to get the whole damn boat infected, but it wouldn't do any good to have anyone showing the illness before it reached American shores. From what the CDC said, they'd never let it dock. So, she was waiting, knowing it took three days for the virus to appear. Which meant she was probably sneezing in the salad line right this very moment. Something that gave everyone pause, and why Knuckles had made the comment about "walking dead."

Unless, of course, she'd been spitting in everyone's food since she'd hit American shores and it hadn't infected anyone. The doctors were arguing like crazy over how communicable she was, with some saying the vaccine was a hoax and she was just as deadly as anyone who contracted the disease, and others saying sneezing and spitting wouldn't cut it—that she'd have to really slobber over something you put directly into your mouth for her to be contagious.

There was evidence supporting both sides, with six dead in New York after we knew she had been there, but *nobody else* sick even though she'd driven the length of the Eastern Seaboard. Truthfully, I was shocked at the two sides, figuring this would have been a little bit of an open-and-shut discussion, like gravity. Drop a rock, and it falls to earth. Apparently, viruses don't work that way, and doctors spend a great deal of time trying to find the reason as to why some become pandemics and others fade away. In the end, nobody knew what the truth was, so my team, along with our intrepid CDC crew, had been given my favorite order: Go figure it out.

I found the guy who'd been waving us off the MC-130 and was surprised to see he was a full colonel—or captain, in people-who-deal-with-water speak.

"I'm Captain Franke. Welcome to Air Station Borinquen."

I shook his hand. "Pike Logan, Centers for Disease Control, and I don't really have the time to enjoy your post. You got the word we were coming?"

"Yes. You need transport to a cruise ship; is that right?"

"Like yesterday."

We walked into a hangar and he pointed at a group of sleek orange and white helicopters, with a unique embedded tail rotor. "We're tracking its location, and I've got four Dolphins, three fully mission capable."

"Perfect. The boat has no landing pad, so we'll need to rope in. These outfitted for that?"

"Rope? What do you mean?"

Uh-oh.

"You know, fast rope? Like Call of Duty?"

He looked at me like I was speaking Swahili. I gave up.

"How will we get on board the ship?"

He pointed at a basket and said, "You'll get lowered in that."

Boy, that's going to be real speedy. Knuckles is going to shit.

Speaking of the devil, Knuckles and Jennifer walked

up, with him asking, "Did I just hear what I thought I did?"

"Don't even start. Get our kit loaded. Docs in one bird, our team in another. We'll develop the situation first, then call them in."

72

Elina turned off the small television above her bed, sick of seeing the exact same movie for what could have been the tenth time. She closed the drapes to her stateroom and laid out the vest, staring at it.

It was time. Twelve o'clock.

She cinched it on, slowly ensuring everything was perfectly in place, taking much longer than was necessary. Satisfied at the fit, she joined the loose wires from the blasting cap to the detonator, ensured a solid connection, then slid the assembly into the Velcro fabric just underneath her left armpit, trapping it between her dress and the vest.

She sat on the bed, debating, then decided to call. She had earned one final meal with actual silverware, where she could drink from a glass instead of a water bottle.

And a final bit of companionship from another human being.

The man answered the phone, and she said, "You still want lunch?"

*   *   *

I saw the ship in the distance, a speck that grew larger by the second. I could hear the pilot talking to the bridge, letting them know we were inbound and to slow the engines, making it easier to transfer us with the basket— what Knuckles now referred to as "putting on the training wheels."

Even though it didn't matter, I held up a finger and shouted, "One minute!"

Everyone else echoed the command, checking that their weapons were concealed and touching other pieces of kit. Knuckles just rolled his eyes.

We drew into a hover over a basketball court, four crew members below to assist in the transfer and others keeping a crowd off of the deck. Decoy and I went out first, and I had to admit I felt a little bit like a pussy as the basket lowered onto the deck, slow as molasses.

A full fifteen minutes later, we were assembled and the helo had pulled off enough to allow us to talk without a gale-force wind.

I pulled the captain aside, out of earshot, and said, "Room number?"

He gave it to me and said, "What are you going to do if she's not there?"

"I'm going to find her."

The primary plan was to go to her stateroom and see if she was inside. If she was, we were simply going to barricade the door, locking her in, then bring in CDC to assess any damage. She couldn't get out through the miniature window of her room.

The captain said, "What should I be doing?"

"Nothing. Whatever you do, keep to the story you've been told. We get a panic on this boat and there's not enough people on the island of Puerto Rico to contain it."

He gave me several copies of a map of the boat and a passkey, then said, "Good luck."

They left the deck and I handed out the maps. The place was a damn maze, and it was huge. "Man," I said. "If she's not in the room, we're in real trouble."

Decoy said, "I always hated ship takedowns. They are the fucking worst."

Having done one or two during training, I couldn't have agreed more, but I had been ordered into it as a "force enhancer" because I was in the Army. Hearing him say it was ridiculous.

I said, "You're a damn SEAL. This is what you do."

"Doesn't mean I have to like it."

I glanced at Knuckles, the other SEAL, and said, "I've never met a squid who hated boats more than him."

I raised my voice. "Everyone, remember, we only have about thirty minutes of on-station time for the helos. We don't find her in under thirty, and we're stuck on the boat without the CDC help until they can do a revolution back to base for fuel. No change to the plan. Room first, then we start our search grid. Jennifer and I take the most likely, because she knows her on sight. Questions?"

Retro said, "We never finalized rules of engagement. I see her, what do you want me to do?"

I knew what he was asking. He could take her down

with little effort, but he'd be dealing with a death machine. He wanted to know if he was supposed to risk his
life. All it would take was her biting or spitting on him.

"Stay in pairs. You find her, get guns out. Screw the
CDC cover. Get her on the ground. Be prepared for her
to run—remember, she has nothing to lose. She tries,
shoot to kill. But only as a last resort. You spill her
blood, and that place becomes ground zero of virus
land."

The team's humor wilted at my statement, all realizing
how deadly this had become. Unlike the CDC doctors,
we were used to the threat of conventional attacks. What
frightened them was old hat to us. Facing a mindless virus
that would rip a body apart from the inside out scared all
of us more than anything we had ever seen.

Knuckles said, "That happens, what are our odds of
getting out clean? No bullshit. You're the guy that talked
to the doctor who made this thing."

I took a breath and let it out. "I don't know. We've
been vaccinated, but the doctor never got to test the version we used. He seemed to think it would work, but
there's really no way to tell. We've all been pumped full
of Tamiflu, and that's supposed to help. The doctor
couldn't predict, but he did say he thought we'd be good
as long as we didn't get any bodily fluids on us."

Nobody said anything for a second, then Retro whispered, "Head shots only. Stop her in her tracks."

*   *   *

ELINA MET HIM in the aft dining room on the lobby level, her first time there. In fact, her first time in any of the multitude of restaurants on the boat, and she was enjoying it immensely. The thought of eating with real silverware on a real plate, drinking out of a real glass, was almost overwhelming, causing her to forget for a moment what was to come.

After leaving her room, strangely giddy at the prospect of talking to someone, she'd had a little bit of a delay as the ship stopped its forward movement and prevented any travel from bow to stern. She'd asked what was going on and had been told someone very sick was being flown off of the boat by helicopter. She'd nodded, wondering if somehow she'd slipped up.

Eventually, she'd made it to the dining room and was met by her suitor, now wearing a coat and tie and looking somewhat decent. Even attractive. He pulled out her chair and she sat down, saying, "I didn't know they even had restaurants like this on the boat."

"Yeah, it's the best place to come because you have to wear regular clothes and they take your order. Most on a cruise don't want to waste their time, so they all go to the hog-trough buffet on the Lido deck. That place is always jam-packed."

Elina filed that away. She said, "You never told me your name."

"It's Jared. Jared Bonaparte. I'm from Louisiana. What about you?"

"I'm Elina. I live in Latvia. You know it?"

He surprised her. "Yeah, actually I do. I was in the Army in the eighties. I served in Berlin. After the wall fell, my buddies and I traveled around over there, hitting up all the new countries that used to be the Soviet Union. We never made it to Latvia, but I know where it is."

She said, "You went to Prague, didn't you?"

He laughed and said, "I did. How did you know?"

"That's where all the Westerners go. Have you ever heard of Chechnya?"

The waiter arrived, interrupting the conversation. Elina showed confusion, and Jared helped her out. "Order whatever is on the menu. It's free. Part of your ticket."

She did so, and the man left.

He said, "You were asking about Chechnya, and yeah, I've heard of it. Sometimes I wonder about where the world is going. I 'fought,' if you can call it that, against the Soviet Union, and now they're our friends, but they're doing the same damn things they did when they were our enemies."

She took that in and said, "But they're all Muslims."

He looked at her in confusion and said, "What the hell does that have to do with anything?"

She felt her foundation shift. The reason for the attack beginning to slide. She said, "Jared, whatever you do, after today, go to your room and stay there. Leave here and get enough bottled water to last until you dock. No matter what anyone says, don't open your door."

"What are you talking about? Are you nuts? Muslims, hide in the room—really?"

He was looking at her like she was insane, and she realized how ridiculous she sounded. She reached across and put her hand over his, saying, "Sorry. It has been a rough couple of months for me. And I don't speak English that well."

He relaxed, and Elina pulled her hand away. He said, "I know what you mean. I just got divorced after twenty years. Wife was sleeping around on me. Completely shattered my entire life."

She started to respond when she saw a woman enter the dining room with a man, both searching about as if trying to find someone who was waiting on them. The female looked vaguely familiar.

She searched her memory, then felt a jolt of fear straight to her core. The woman's hair had a different color and was shorter, but there was no doubt.

It was her pursuer from Macau.

73

The room check had proven to be a bust, with the carrier out and about somewhere on the massive ship. The cubicle looked like the den of an animal, with Styrofoam room-service boxes stacked all over the place. We'd searched it, picking up items with coat hangers and ridiculously holding our breath, and found nothing but her clothes, a packet of disposable hospital masks, and a garbage can full of plastic water bottles. Which meant she was taking precautions, something I read as a good sign.

She hasn't been spitting in the salad bowl for the past week if she's only eating room service, drinking bottled water, and running around like she's in the ER.

The bad news was she wasn't there, which meant she was potentially at an endgame, doing whatever it was to infect the boat. Everyone saw the reality in the empty space, but nobody could figure out the method.

Retro said, "What now? How is she going to hit this place?"

"I don't know, but it's coming soon. We need to find her before she triggers."

Decoy said, "Maybe she's filled up a bunch of water balloons with her urine, and she's going to start lobbing them at the pool during the limbo competition."

Jennifer snorted in disgust and glared at him. I split up the crew into teams of two, giving us three separate search teams. We spent a second dissecting the boat, then I divvied up assignments, focusing primarily on the dining areas, since it was lunchtime. The biggest problem we had was that nobody but Jennifer had actually seen her. Everyone else was working off of the sketch.

"Look for a woman alone. On this boat, that's going to stand out. See that, then compare to the sketch. Worst case, remember, she doesn't know you. Ask her for the time. If she's got a Russian-sounding accent, take her down. We'll sort out the due-process bullshit later. Better to ask for forgiveness on this one."

There were four separate dining rooms, but only two were open for lunch. Jennifer and I took the one at the lobby level, Decoy and Retro went to the casino, and Knuckles and Blood went to the Lido deck to the buffet and assorted hamburger stations.

We arrived at the lobby level, only to find you couldn't reach the restaurant by going straight to it. You had to go up one deck and over, then down again. *What a damn maze.*

Cutting through a children's arcade, Jennifer grabbed

my arm, pointing at a woman disappearing through a hatch.

"That looked like her."

We picked up our pace, only to see the woman snag a little boy and begin scolding him.

We're never going to find her on this boat. I began thinking about drastic action. Calling an emergency lifeboat drill or something, just to get everyone locked up in certain locations. The problem was the chaos might actually help her achieve whatever she was planning, and there was no way I could trust that she'd pay attention to the commands and go to her designated area.

We searched the first level of the dining room and came up empty. We wound our way down the circular staircase and began searching the bottom floor. We'd walked only about six feet when Jennifer did a double take on a woman sitting with a man. Someone I'd initially ignored because she wasn't alone.

"That's the carrier."

I started to ask if she was sure when the woman stood up and began walking at a fast pace to a side stairwell.

I keyed my radio as we both broke into a jog. "We have the carrier. Aft dining room. Going up the stairs. We're compromised."

We ran by her companion, who shouted, "Hey, what the hell's going on?"

Hitting the stairwell, we both started to run, taking the steps two at a time, hearing her just above us.

*   *   *

ELINA FELT HER lungs screaming and ran on, weaving up the stairwell, one thought pulsing in her: *Lido deck. Get to the Lido deck.*

She passed the seventh deck, her legs beginning to feel like rubber. She slowed and heard the pounding just below her. She staggered on. Hitting the eighth deck, where her room was located, she knew they were going to catch her before she reached the Lido deck at level ten. She left the stairwell, racing down the narrow hallway of staterooms, taking a left in a corridor to get to the port side, then ran backward to another stairwell and continued on, hoping she'd gained some time.

She broke out on level ten right outside the swimming pool, dazzled by the sunlight. She saw the entrance to the buffet a few feet on the other side of the pool, a long line snaking out of the doors almost reaching the edge of the water. She took two ragged breaths and began to jog forward, ignoring the stares of people sunbathing in the lounge chairs.

She had reached the edge of the line when she saw a commotion coming from the opposite direction. Two men bulling their way through the crowd, drawing curses. She heard someone say, "He's got a gun!"

And knew who they were.

She turned around and ran on the edge of the pool, trying to reach the second entrance on the starboard side,

leaping over people lying out sunning. She reached the
stretch of deck leading to the second buffet line and saw
another man holding an assault rifle with a folding stock.
She stopped moving, and he swiveled his head back and
forth, going right over her.

He doesn't recognize me.

She began to backtrack, intent on getting back into
the stairwell she had come from, now certain the team
hunting her did not know what she looked like. She
moved slowly so as not to draw attention. She had
reached the far side of the pool, the stairwell directly in
front of her, when the door opened.

74

Knuckles radioed that they had cleared the buffet and it was a dry hole. I directed him up to the final level, to the water slides, in the hopes that she was now simply trying to hide. I was a step behind Jennifer exiting onto the Lido deck, the heat and glare of the sun overpowering, blinding me. I saw Jennifer draw up short and followed her gaze.

She shouted, "Elina!"

And the carrier turned and ran, toward the railing of the boat, near a Ping Pong table with a multitude of kids playing around it and two women asleep on adjacent lounge chairs. She sprinted around the table and glanced over the railing, now hemmed in by the bulkhead of the boat and the open ocean. The only way out was through us.

Jennifer closed the distance, her H&K UMP at her side, nonthreatening, getting thirty feet away. I stayed on the far side, preventing the carrier from squirting back to the stairwell.

I put my red dot on her eye orbit and said, "Jennifer,

don't get any closer. Get your weapon up. Get her on the ground."

The crowd behind us began to gather, some shouting. A few of the kids scampered away, others hid under the table or simply sat down and began crying.

Jennifer said, "Elina, it's over. We don't want to hurt you, and you don't want to harm these children."

The carrier said nothing. She simply stared at Jennifer.

"Come on. Please. Get on your knees. Don't make us hurt you. I know you don't want to do this. I *know*."

She spoke for the first time. "You shoot me, you release the virus."

"I can't let you go. I can't let you infect this ship."

She said, "Maybe I already have."

"Maybe, but I don't think so. We saw your room. And I saw you eating lunch with the man. You weren't going to harm him. I watched you smile. Please. Lie on the ground."

I wondered if this was stupid. If we just shouldn't put a bullet in her head, because it would probably end up that way anyway. But that would release the virus, so I let Jennifer run.

The carrier shook her head and gazed out into the ocean. "It doesn't matter now. You have to kill me. I'm a Black Widow. I can't go back. I can't go forward. I can't do anything but die. It's my destiny."

Something she said tickled the back of my brain, telling me it was important. Deadly important.

Jennifer said, "You *can* go forward. We can help you. Please."

She began to fiddle with her sundress, just under her armpit. She said, "You're kind. Not like the ones who hate my people. More like the man downstairs. Please, make sure he is okay after this. Make sure he stays in his room."

Jennifer said, "You can do that yourself. Come on. This is *your* choice. Don't make me harm you."

The carrier smiled, a ravaged look that held no joy, a glimpse into a pit that conveyed nothing but pain. She said, "It is I who will give *you* the choice. Shoot me now and save yourself. I'll give you that for your kindness."

"Elina, just get on your knees. There's nowhere for you to go, and I *will* do it. I can't let you infect the ship."

She reached her hand inside her dress, pulling something out.

"You can't stop me."

What she'd called herself earlier finally broke the surface of my memory like the fin of a shark, the intelligence reports springing forth. *Black Widow.*

And what she intended became crystal clear.

I snapped my weapon tight into my shoulder, centered the dot, and squeezed the trigger. A shape slammed into me, causing the round to burrow harmlessly into the wood deck. I whirled back, raising my weapon, only to see her lunch partner from downstairs in front of her, blocking my shot and screaming.

"What the hell is going on? Put those guns down. Someone call the crew!"

"Get out of the way! Jennifer, take the shot. She's wearing a vest!"

Jennifer whipped her weapon to her shoulder, and I heard a sharp crack, like a tree splitting in two. I flung myself backward, trying to escape the blast.

I rolled over twice, losing my weapon. Sitting up, I heard screaming from the people around the pool and smelled the acrid burn of the explosives. In front of me the carrier had disintegrated, her body parts flung in all directions, her head lying intact on the ground.

The walls were splattered in blood, like someone had sloshed a paint bucket. The two sunbathers were awake and screaming, both with parts of the carrier on them, grisly beige lumps mixed with red. One passed out at the sight. The other continued to wail, staring at her arms and stomach, once a healthy tan, now covered in offal. Two of the children looked like they'd been killed or knocked out in the blast. Two more were wailing, holding their arms out, also covered in the dripping, stringy remains of something once alive. One pointed at the head of the carrier, cocked sideways on the deck with her eyes open, and began to shriek as if he were looking into hell itself.

I frantically scanned my body to see if I had any fluids on me, then shouted at Jennifer. She stood up in a daze, staring uncomprehendingly at the carnage.

I heard a low groan that grew into a keening wail and

saw the carrier's lunch partner rise from the ground, holding his hands out in shock. The back of his head was singed and smoking; the rest of him was covered in what was left of her, bits and pieces of flesh clinging to him.

He blocked the blast.

He took a step forward, then another, then began running, his lonesome wail growing louder.

Jesus Christ. He's now a carrier.

I scrambled to raise my weapon, and he was by me, staggering in a drunken jog straight at Jennifer, the panicking crowd next to the pool running amok in between him and me.

"Jennifer! Stop him! He's going to infect the ship!"

She raised her weapon and said, "Stop! Get on your knees! Halt right there."

He kept coming, moaning, clearly not in his right mind, and she began backing up, reaching the edge of the crowd.

"Shoot him!"

And she did, splitting his head open.

He fell to the deck, and the crowd began to go crazy, running in all directions. I saw a man dart out of the pack, moving toward the shrieking child, shouting a name. I yelled at him to stop, but he ignored me, scooping up the child and brushing the blood off of him. He turned to leave and I shouted, "Sit down. Right there. Help is on the way."

He stared at the charnel for a second, his eyes panicked, then said, "I've got to get him to a doctor."

He made like he was going to run, and I raised my weapon. "Stop. Right. There."

He looked over at the carrier's lunch partner, the blood spilling onto the deck from his head wound, then sat heavily on a lounge chair, going into emotional shock, the child still screaming.

I keyed my radio and said, "All elements get to the Lido deck ASAP. We need crowd control. And get the CDC crew on board. We have some cleanup."

"What's the situation?"

I saw Jennifer begin to stagger toward me, her eyes locked on the corpse of the man she'd just killed. I said, "Just get here. Trust me—it's bad."

She reached my side and I saw absolute fear. A terror from deep inside.

I looked her up and down, seeing no blood, and asked, "You get any on you?"

Her arms were trembling, and I thought it was because of a dread of getting the virus. I was wrong.

"What if she's not really a carrier?"

She dropped her weapon as if it too might be poison.

"What if I just killed an innocent man?"

75

Malik had begun to feel like Elina, having spent the last two days sitting in his hotel room in Caracas doing nothing but watching the news. He knew that there more than likely wouldn't be a story on her attack as soon as it happened, given the boat was still out at sea, but he watched anyway.

Now he was intently studying the only English channel he could find in Venezuela, his watch telling him the boat should have docked. Sooner or later, there would be a story.

The screen flashed a stock photo of a cruise ship, and he turned the sound up. The announcer switched to footage of a helicopter circling a ship, and he recognized Elina's cruise, still out at sea, the coast of Florida barely in the camera's range. The announcer said reports were sketchy, but the cruise ship apparently had a rare disease on board and was being quarantined before being allowed to dock. The rest of the story discussed the rights of the passengers, along with the ubiquitous lawyer discussing lawsuits against the cruise line. There was no mention of a suicide bomber.

Quarantined?

So she'd failed. Someone must have gotten the virus early, before she could execute her mission, making her sacrifice worthless. He supposed he should have been curious as to what had occurred, but he wasn't. It didn't really matter. Her failure was his failure. He wondered if she was still alive and thought about sending her a message through their Yahoo! account.

Maybe later.

He was tired. More than he could ever remember. The mission, dealing with the cowards of the ruling theocracy while working with Elina's pure sacrifice, had taxed his beliefs to the limit. He realized he'd lost faith. He no longer believed in the same thing that the republic believed. He still held the revolution as pure. They had evolved into something resembling the Great Satan itself. Worried more about their own survival than the very precepts they claimed to hold dear.

He was done. He considered flying home to Tehran but decided not to. He knew they'd kill him for his failure, but that wasn't driving him. It wasn't death. He had no fear of that. It was the fact that they weren't worthy of killing him.

He had many ways to disappear, and maybe, after a few years, he could connect with others who understood. He packed up his small suitcase, went online, and checked for flights out. Finding one, he made a reservation, then took one last look around the room. In the corner was the small Chechen flag he'd used to signal Elina at the marina. He smiled and picked it up, thinking again of her. Of her willingness to sacrifice.

Others could learn from her. She should have songs made about her, just as the revolutionaries before her.

He left the room, walking slowly to the elevator. The doors opened on the ground floor, and he saw the cleric sitting in a lobby chair. Flanked by two men he recognized as Quds enforcers.

The cleric said, "Hello, General. I'm here to take you home. To answer for your crimes."

76

Chip Dekkard waited patiently outside the Oval Office, ready to present his report to President Warren. It was very thorough—damning in its evidence against Cailleach Laboratories. He was up front with his connection to the firm, knowing that was the best way to defuse any implication of guilt. He'd made sure to get a little egg on his face as someone who should have known but just didn't. Dispelling any accusation that he was conducting a cover-up. He'd already rehearsed his lines. *"Sir, I know I screwed up, but I can't possibly be aware of everything that goes on in my conglomerate. It's just impossible."*

He'd show suitable remorse, offer to resign or take whatever punishment the president felt prudent, all the while subtly reminding him of the work he had done, both to get him elected and to stop this current threat.

The one fly in the ointment was the board of directors of the laboratory. Of course, eventually they had discovered they were being hung out to dry as scapegoats and had immediately begun threatening to tell all they knew, using e-mails and reports he'd signed to prove their case.

Careful of his words, knowing they were probably recording the discussion, he'd stated he had no idea what they were talking about and that they'd be well-advised to get criminal defense attorneys.

He smiled at the thought of their attempting to build their case, only to find the e-mails and reports inexplicably gone. Nothing but his word against theirs, and his word was gold when it came to the president of the United States.

The door opened, and Alexander Palmer waved him in. He entered, seeing two men with military haircuts and business suits sitting on the far couch. In front of the president's desk was a distinguished-looking man he recognized.

President Warren said, "Come on in, Chip. This is Andy Barksdale. I'm not sure you've ever met before."

Internally taken aback, Chip said, "Yes, of course, the attorney general. No, we've never met, unless you count watching testimony in front of Congress."

He drew polite laughter and wondered what the AG was doing here. He wasn't read on to Taskforce activities, and that fact gave him a little alarm.

Then again, he was about to report criminal malfeasance, so maybe the AG was simply here to take his report and do whatever they needed to bring the laboratory to justice.

They had to come into play sooner or later.

President Warren said, "Well, what do you have?"

Chip laid out his case, presenting the doctored e-mails,

forged reports, and other damning evidence, concluding that the laboratory had willfully risked great harm in order to make profits. All in all, the briefing took thirty minutes, with the president asking no questions.

Chip ended with his own culpability and delivered his rehearsed lines about accepting responsibility. The president's answer was not what he had expected.

"I'm glad you're willing to accept responsibility. Do you know how many people are going to die on the cruise ship?"

"Uhh . . . no, sir."

"Well, it's day three, and we have twenty-three cases. So far. With a seventy percent mortality rate, sixteen are going to die. That's on top of the six who died in New York. You state you should have known, and I agree. If you'd had that knowledge, we would have known immediately what this was about the minute the doctor's son from Cailleach Laboratories was kidnapped. We could have stopped this before it even began."

Where is this going? "Yes, and as I said, I regret that immensely, but I can't possibly know every single thing that goes on in every firm in my portfolio."

President Warren said, "The Cailleach people reached out to Justice today. They claim you *did* know."

The conversation not going the way he thought, Chip became slightly belligerent, puffing up his anger at the slander. "Of course they're saying that. They're doing whatever they can to spare themselves. They know we're friends and are hoping a political taint from dragging me into this will cause you to sweep it under the rug."

"Are you hoping for the same thing? That our friendship will cause me to sweep this under the rug?"

"No! I told you I accept limited responsibility already."

"Chip, what would we have done if the carrier's plan had worked? If the boat had reached American shores and released the passengers? It would have been the end of our way of life, all over a little greed. Don't you agree?"

"Yes. Of course I agree. I'm not sure why you're asking. It's horrible, and I'm glad we stopped it in time."

"'In time.' Funny choice of words."

President Warren leaned forward and pressed a button on a laptop. Chip heard his own voice and felt his world dissolve.

"What the hell do you mean a lab tech died? You guys assured me you could get this done in accordance with all applicable regulations."

The tape droned on, Chip hearing the lab tech describing again the initial death at the makeshift biosafety facility in Singapore and his rejoinder to shut the entire project down.

President Warren said, "That was recorded before we knew about Cailleach Laboratories. Before we learned of the doctor's son."

Chip switched gears. "Yes, yes, now I remember. You heard me tell them to shut it down. That's why I didn't bring it up when I found out about Cailleach's involvement. I *ordered* them to quit the project. *They're* the ones who kept the virus. Against my orders. I was going—"

The attorney general held up a hand, cutting him off. "Stop. These two men are special agents of the Federal Bureau of Investigation, and you have the right to remain silent."

They both stood, flanking him, and Chip played the only card he had left. "Sir, you don't want to do this. I know how the virus was stopped. I know about who did it."

He saw the attorney general get a curious look on his face and hoped it would be enough.

It wasn't.

President Warren turned red, but it was Alexander Palmer who spoke first. "Remember what Kurt told you about Pike? About what would happen if you went after him? Well, so far he doesn't know who caused that pain. But I do. Remember that, because if it were to leak, the only place you'd be safe is a federal prison."

Chip assimilated the words and began to tremble. He'd seen enough Taskforce activities to know Palmer was telling the truth. Losing his strength, he sank to his knees, placing his head in his hands on the floor of the most powerful man on earth.

77

Day four of the quarantine, and I was going a little stir-crazy. The room I was in was the size of a closet, and I hadn't been allowed to leave for a single moment. I was visited twice a day by some CDC turd in a moon suit who'd take a vial of blood and leave me some food. None of which was cooked. I'd been living on peanuts, beef jerky, and bottled water, staring at the mirror every five minutes to see if I was going bloodshot.

The anxiety was incredible, wondering if the next knock on the door would be the one where I transferred rooms to what they called the "hot zone." They'd moved at least five people on my floor so far, some going kicking and screaming, knowing it meant they were infected. I hadn't been moved, which led me to believe the vaccine had utterly failed because I hadn't come up hot immediately on an antibodies test. Well, failed in the men. A small comfort now, although I was glad I didn't know it when we hit the deck of the ship.

It was made worse because I had no idea of the status of my team, especially Jennifer. All of us had been locked up, but she had been the closest to the carrier. The most likely to be sick. I couldn't imagine what some mother or father was feeling right now, separated from their loved ones, not knowing if they were alive or dead. Especially since I knew for a fact at least four children wouldn't be going home. Four sets of parents who would get the news.

I heard a knock on my door, and my apprehension skyrocketed. It wasn't blood-vial feeding time.

I opened it to see another moon suit. "Yes?"

"Jesus, this place stinks."

Huh? He can't smell anything in that suit. I peered closer to the flow hood and saw Kurt inside, smiling.

"You ready to leave?"

"Hell yeah!"

"Come on. You're clear, and we want to get you guys off before anyone asks any questions. Put this on. You'll go out as CDC personnel."

He handed me my own moon suit, and soon enough we were out of the confines of the ship and on the basketball court. I counted four other moon suits. Which meant someone was missing.

"Who's not here?"

Kurt said, "Jennifer."

That one word was a hammer blow, almost bringing me to my knees. Kurt quickly put his hand on my arm.

"She hasn't come up hot. Not yet anyway, but they can't trust the vaccine. They just want to make sure she's not a carrier."

"How much longer?"

"Another day. Maybe two."

I saw a Dolphin helicopter in the distance and knew I wouldn't have much more time to talk before we were in its rotor wash.

"What's the fallout?"

"There's thirty confirmed on the boat. In the running around after the body bomb, somebody spread the virus, but they think it's contained at this point. They'll dock the boat today or tomorrow and let everyone off. Everyone except the ones infected."

"What about them? Any hope?"

"Not really. They're getting the best treatment available. Shit, better than what they'd get at a hospital. The top doctors in the country are on this boat, and they've turned the hot zone into a floating hospital. Even with all that, most will die."

"What about Iran? Did we nuke them or something?"

Kurt laughed, the sound muffled by the flow-hood speaker. "No. They claimed it was a rogue Quds general and that they've inflicted the appropriate punishment."

"And we believe that shit? Really?"

"They sent a video through a back channel. It was Malik getting hanged. Honestly, most of the administration's national security team thinks they might be telling the truth. There was no way for them to protect their own country from the virus, and it just never made any sense for them to use it. *Threaten* use, maybe, as a last-ditch effort should we attack them, but come right out and use it?"

"You believe that?"

"I don't know. I just don't know."

The helicopter pulled overhead, and the basket began to lower. Knuckles walked up to me and said, "Here we go again. Riding like a bitch."

I didn't smile, and he said, "Hey, don't worry. It's going to be okay. You'll see her in a couple of days."

78

Jennifer was awakened by a scream. A wail of suffering that permeated the confines of her stateroom like a gangrenous fog, reminding her of what her future held.

Someone looked in a mirror.

Someone had learned the awful truth about his or her fate. A fate that was particularly disturbing in its pernicious timeline. There was no executioner to flick a switch and be done, nor was it a six-year battle against some other, more forgiving invader. The former gave the benefit of being over instantaneously, while the latter afforded hope and the chance to prepare. This fate allowed neither. It would be a torturous demise spanning four days of agony.

She wondered if she would scream when she found out.

She had been placed in her original quarantine room for a mere six hours, then had been hustled to the aft section of the ship based on the results of her initial tests. To the hot zone. She held a thin hope that it was because of the vaccine she'd taken and that the doctors were simply not taking any chances, but she had mentally begun to prepare herself for the worst. After the initial twenty-four hours she had steeled herself and looked in the mirror for the first time. Her eyes had remained clear. No crisscrossing of blood signaling the sickness inside her.

In truth, she knew she was unique because of the vaccine. The virus wouldn't eat her whole as it would everyone else it contacted, but she would become a walking time bomb. A modern-day Typhoid Mary who wouldn't—couldn't—be allowed to set foot again in the outside world.

Sitting alone with her thoughts, she had clinically considered taking her own life, should the mirror speak. She had heard others in the hot zone do it already. A muffled, panicky stampede of doctors in the narrow hallway and snatches of conversation bringing to light the decision.

She knew she couldn't spend eternity locked in hospital quarantine.

She thought of Elina and how calm she had been. How she had sacrificed her life with a surreal devotion. In the end, Jennifer wasn't sure she held the same iron strength. A part of her felt it was just punishment for the man she had killed.

The death of Elina's protector had haunted her almost as much as the wails of the sick. Him staggering toward her like something out of a zombie apocalypse, his body coated in the remains of Elina. Her begging him to stop, then squeezing the trigger. His head snapping back in a spray of gore. Him lying on the deck, his clean blood mingling with the ravaged blood of the person he had tried to save.

Her greatest fear had been that Elina wasn't infected and that she'd killed a man for no reason. She had drawn a small bit of comfort from the contagion sweeping the ship, a twisted blessing that had alleviated some of her pain, but she couldn't get over the fact that he only *might* have died had she done nothing. Instead, she had ensured it.

In the end, she knew she had made the right call but desperately wished she had shot him in the legs or stomach or anywhere that a doctor could have helped. A nonlethal location, so that if he was to die, it would have been because of the virus. Because of Elina and not her. A rational part of her understood that that was just selfish wishful thinking to alleviate the mental cost of the decision she had made. There was no way the CDC team could have treated him in the middle of a hot zone, and he would have died just as easily from the wounds she had created. A slow death much like the virus.

The edges of her room gradually appeared in the thin reed of light penetrating her small porthole window, signaling the start of a new day. Signaling another visit.

The doctors will be here soon.

They came twice a day delivering awful food and bottled water, one set clinically dispassionate and the other almost fawning underneath the biohazard suits, desperately trying to salve the worry. She wondered which set would show up this morning. She glanced at her forearm; the needle tracks in it made her look like a heroin addict.

Each time they came, they drew blood and gave her an update on her status, which to this point had been inconclusive. She hoped if she came up hot, it would be the clinical ones who told her. She couldn't take the pity from the other team.

She sat up and felt an ache in her head. A small bit of pressure right between her eyes. A symptom that could have just been her imagination. She felt the fear of her neighbor invade her. She felt like screaming.

She stood and went to the small sink, leaning into the mirror, afraid of what she would find. Afraid of what the mirror would tell her.

She couldn't see in the darkened room and fumbled for the switch with a trembling hand. She flicked it up, blazing the room with light.

And the mirror spoke.

79

Exactly three days after I was hoisted off of the ship ingloriously in a basket, I stood outside the port of Cape Canaveral with about five hundred other people waiting to see who would get off the boat. The difference was that everyone else had a name on a manifest. All I had was the word of the Taskforce that Jennifer had been cleared and would be exiting with the rest of the passengers.

The entire affair had been horrific, with the boat devolving into some sewer existence reminiscent of the worst of Charles Dickens. The government had done what they could, but the ship just wasn't designed to house so many people without the ability to service them. Every crew member who'd had the job of keeping it functioning had been quarantined.

The government had done an admirable job on the medical front but had trouble finding enough people qualified to do the mundane work of keeping the boat functioning. I couldn't blame them. How would you react if someone said, "We need you to help out on a cruise ship because of your special skills. By the way, it's a floating death trap. You might die just by showing up. Did I mention you'd have to spend every waking moment in a moon suit?"

Surprisingly, they'd found enough dumbasses to show up. And now we waited. For the first time, I felt a little bit of what my family had when I deployed. This time it was me waiting on the steps to see the loved one coming home. Only I had the added angst of not being really sure she'd step off.

Kurt had said he "thought" she was cleared and that he was "sure" she'd be on the dock, but he'd also said the communication to the CDC was convoluted, something I'd seen on the news with my own eyes. Everyone was screaming about the lack of information, which, given what had occurred and what the administration was trying to keep hidden, was to be expected.

I was a little pissed that they couldn't find out about Jennifer, though. After all, she was the person who had stopped every damn one of them from getting sick. But I understood why. My team had been evacuated before the press started really going into a frenzy, looking for the government cover-up, so we no longer existed for them to find. Pushing too hard into Jennifer's status might have caused questions.

My eyes were drawn to a television set on a pole, much like you see at airport departure gates. A crowd was forming around it, and I followed, recognizing the presidential podium from the White House briefing room.

President Payton Warren arrived on-screen, and the crowd around me began making shushing noises. He looked particularly somber, which, given the circumstances, was probably not an act. He gave a prepared statement, blending fact with fiction, stating a terrorist strike with a biological weapon had been averted, but making no mention whatsoever of Iran's being behind it. He left it as a "Chechen separatist" event, keeping us out of a full-scale war.

It was a skillful display, as he walked the line of what to give out based on what he knew would leak, starting with the deaths in New York City and ending with the numerous witnesses to Elina's death on the boat. When he was done, he opened the floor to questions.

The first, of course, had to do with who had stopped the attack. The press and the American public routinely slobbered at the mouth for stuff like this, spinning themselves into the ground trying to find the super-secret SEAL team, the Special Forces killer-commandos, or the Impossible Mission Force that operated beyond the usual classified units. Trying mightily to penetrate the facade to find a unit that didn't exist in the real world. Except in this case, there actually *was* one. I leaned in to hear his answer.

"A combination of indicators from our intelligence community led to the threat being exposed. Once we had actionable intelligence we initiated a direct-action operation utilizing Special Operations forces. Unfortunately, during the interdiction, the terrorist initiated her suicide device, precluding a perfect outcome."

A clamoring of voices emerged, all shouting essentially the same question: "What do you mean, Special Operations forces? What unit? Who was it?"

I smirked at that. Like it made a bit of difference who actually executed the mission. All that mattered was the outcome. But the press would not be denied.

President Warren said, "I'm not going to divulge which unit for both the protection of our capabilities and the safety of our forces."

A perfect answer.

Another reporter chimed in: "Were there any casualties from the team?"

Smart journalist. He was going to try to locate the unit by walking up the thread of a casualty list from the Department of Defense. Except he'd get nowhere with this one, because even if there had been a major casualty from the Taskforce—which there wasn't—it would never enter into the Department of Defense database.

The president's answer shook me to my core.

"Yes, but I'm not going to get into the nature of the injuries or the status. I'm not going to talk about the team in any way. Next question."

Who is he talking about? Was it Blood's gunshot wound? Knuckles's almost getting beaten to death in prison? *Jesus, is it Jennifer?*

80

The press conference droned on, but I heard nothing, my mind numb to the possibility that when the boat emptied, I'd be standing there alone. Waiting on someone who wasn't coming.

The gangway door to our right opened and a trickle of passengers began to flow out, rapidly increasing to a flood, with all of them running through the terminal doors, some kissing the ground as soon as they exited. The crowd around the television broke free and rushed to the ropes separating the waiting from the arriving.

Families began waving flags as if the boat had just returned from Normandy in World War II, the crowds beginning to overwhelm the security force on the ground. And starting to piss me off because they were blocking my view.

I was jostled to the left and turned to the man who'd done it, glaring. An idiot wearing a torn-up ball cap, the man tried to push past me, and I shoved him back.

"Wait your damn turn."

He raised his hands as if he wanted to fight, then began tearing up. His fists clenched, he stared at me, then said, "My wife is coming off that boat. Without my kids. They're dead. Get the hell out of my way."

He began to cry, and I remembered the blood-covered children. Realizing I was standing next to ground zero of the tragedy. His face held so much pain I didn't know what to do. I didn't know what to say.

He choked out, "They went on her family reunion. I had to work. I told her it was too expensive. Now . . . now . . ."

A woman screamed near us, and he broke free, dipping under the cordoned-off lines and running to her. Security closed around him, demanding he fall back behind the rope. The argument devolved into a fistfight. I felt sick.

I returned to staring at the doorway in front of the terminal escalator, straining to see any sign of Jennifer. I stood for thirty minutes. Then forty-five. The exiting flow of the passengers began to slow, the flood becoming a trickle. I thought about calling Kurt. Calling anyone who could tell me what the situation was. Wanting the reassurance I'd had when I'd come here instead of the words of the president echoing in my head.

I pulled out my phone and saw Jennifer through the glass. Looking morose and riding down all by herself.

She reached the bottom and exited through the double doors, fighting her way through the people. I shouted her name, but she couldn't hear me. She stood for a second and started walking away. I pushed my way through the crowd, shouting like an idiot until I got her attention.

She turned and broke into a smile, sprinting toward me, only to be stopped by security at the receiving line. I pointed to the left and took off running, meeting her outside the ropes.

She literally jumped on me, wrapping her legs around me and squeezing like a python.

I squeezed back, saying, "It's all right. We're okay."

She dropped to the ground, her eyes alight. "They wouldn't tell me if you were okay. Nobody would tell me."

I said, "Same here. I wasn't sure if you were coming out. Where's your luggage?"

She squinted, and I held up my hands. "Just a joke."

We began walking to my rental, no words spoken. I was content just to be near her, but I could sense this wasn't a perfect homecoming. It wasn't a movie, where we'd ride off into the sunset, because the endgame had been horrific, and she'd had to live with it by herself for days.

Truthfully, I had been kicking myself for not simply putting a bullet into the Black Widow's head instead of letting Jennifer try to talk her off the ledge. But that was all hindsight. Something others could second-guess—but not to my face. Not if they wanted to remain standing. We'd both made the right call, given what we knew.

We continued walking in silence. Eventually, she said, "How are you doing?"

I clasped her hand and said, "I'm good. The team is good. Nobody we know was killed."

She stopped and looked me in the eye. "A lot of people are dead."

"I know. Trust me, I know."

"I thought *I* was dead. Yesterday morning, I had a headache. I looked in the mirror, knowing I was going to see bloodshot eyes. It was the worst day of my life."

I wasn't sure how to make that better. I said, "I know. I waited for the same thing. A lot of people on my floor were taken way. But some of them made it. Not all of them died."

Her face sparked pain, and I knew I'd said the wrong thing.

"Pike, I killed one of them. *He* might have lived."

"Don't ever say that. You can't carry that. Yeah, he might have lived, but he would have infected anyone he touched. The odds are he would have killed many, many more people."

She let go of my hand. "I know. In my head, I know. He had to go down, but it doesn't feel right. He wasn't a terrorist. Maybe I should have . . . I don't know . . . I just wonder if I did the right thing."

"Jennifer, it *was right*. You made the correct call. Don't blame yourself. *You* didn't ask for Elina to get on that boat. You didn't ask for that guy to interfere. You can only do what you can do, and that was the right call. It's like being a firefighter and blaming yourself because you could only save one child in a burning building."

She leaned into me, putting her arms around my waist. I did the same and then felt her begin to cry, wracking sobs that went on forever. Eventually she stopped and looked up at me.

She wiped her eyes and said, "You're a good man. I don't think I've ever told you that."

I smiled and said, "Yeah, you did once. In Bosnia, when I wouldn't get in bed with you."

She remembered the conversation and turned red. "I mean when I wasn't screwed up by a near-death experience. When I could think straight."

I said, "You mean like right now?"

She broke free and punched me in the shoulder. "Jesus, you can be an ass."

I laughed and said, "Come on. I've got a pretty good hotel room, although it's a little bit of a drive out of this place."

"Better than the suite in Singapore?"

"Uh, no, but it's got something that one didn't."

"What? The Marina Bay Sands room was a Taj Mahal."

"A hot tub. You promised if I didn't drop you in Singapore, you'd get in one without a harness on."

She gave me a hesitant grin and said, "You sure you want to do that? I could be contagious."

"If I were you I'd be a little more worried about your kissing ability. The last time I tried to get infected it was like fighting a baboon for a piece of bacon."

She squeezed my hand, her face splitting into a smile that finally touched her eyes.

And I knew we'd be okay.

ACKNOWLEDGMENTS

I had already written my acknowledgments for this manuscript, thanking all the wonderful people who have helped me, when something terrible happened. In between turning in my draft and getting back the final revisions, a soldier I served with, and a close friend, was killed in action in Afghanistan.

His callsign was Taz, and he was hit repelling a synchronized suicide attack on a combat outpost in Jalalabad. I won't use his real name because when he died he was no longer in the military and is now represented by a simple black star set into a white marble wall.

Anytime I'm asked who Pike represents, I state that he's a composition of many men I've known, and that's true, up to a point. If there was a way to split up Pike and specifically define him, many people could claim a piece, but only one would be the heart, and that was Taz.

Readers sometimes chide me about the "miracles" that I have Pike survive, saying they're far-fetched, and I just nod. Inside, I'm smiling at a private joke, thinking about Taz and the real-world miracles I witnessed him accomplish in the defense of our nation. Miracles that eventually ran out. Pike *is* fictional, but he represents something real. Something tangible. More so than anyone else, he represented Taz.

I learned more about combat skill just watching him than people could possibly understand, and yet he will remain a complete unknown to the American public. No flags, no parades, no Kathryn Bigelow movies made about any of his exploits. Just a black star on a wall few are allowed to see and a granite stone at Arlington.

In the end, he died valiantly saving the lives of others, and some would say he was killed doing what he loved, which should be of some comfort. I wish that were an absolute because it would make the pain less, but I've watched him with his family, and I know what was the greater love.

Like them, I miss him every day.

PIKE LOGAN FACES HIS MOST
CHALLENGING MISSION YET:
A TASKFORCE MEMBER GONE ROGUE.

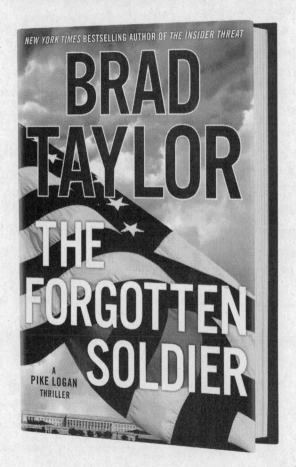

NEW YORK TIMES BESTSELLING AUTHOR OF *THE INSIDER THREAT*

BRAD
TAYLOR

THE
FORGOTTEN
SOLDIER

A
PIKE LOGAN
THRILLER

TURN THE PAGE FOR AN EXCERPT

1

The box arrived at the front door like any other delivery. It had nothing on the outside detailing what it held. Nothing to show that what was inside was anything other than an online order. Just a FedEx label on brown cardboard. Maybe a fantasy kit inspired by *Fifty Shades of Grey*. Or maybe not. Treating this like every other delivery, the FedEx driver ringing the bell had no idea that what it contained were the final vestiges of a man who'd given his life fighting in a land far, far away. A land that most of America had forgotten. Precisely because the sacrifices represented by the contents of the box allowed them to do so.

Putting on a plain oxford shirt, Guy George heard the bell and was surprised. He wasn't expecting anyone, and he was more worried about a meeting he had to attend in forty-five minutes. A meeting he knew would be crucial to his future. He didn't have time for someone selling Girl Scout cookies.

Tucking in his shirt, he padded to the front door in his socks, a little bewildered that someone would bother him here—in his condominium, behind the gate of security at the building's entrance. He put his eye to the peephole, expecting to see a mother who lived in his tower, a child in tow, exploiting her ability to penetrate security to sell raffle tickets or something else. What he saw was a FedEx man, and he felt his stomach clench.

He knew what the man held. It had arrived days earlier than he expected, but he knew.

Usually, FedEx deliveries were dropped off downstairs, but he'd told the management of the tower he lived in that this box was special and that he would sign for it personally. It wasn't outside of the ordinary, given his job. At least, given the job the management thought he held. There had been more than one box that had come to his door, all having to be signed for personally. It came with the territory, so much so that he knew the FedEx man by name.

He opened the door and said, "Hey, Carl."

"Got another one for you. You must have some pull. You're the only apartment they let me up for."

Guy smiled, feeling ill, and said, "Not really. That's for me?"

"Yeah. I haven't had a delivery for your roommate in over a year. He must be on the shit list."

Carl grinned at his joke, and Guy felt like punching him for no reason whatsoever. It wasn't Carl's fault. He couldn't possibly understand the sore he was poking with that statement, especially today. Truthfully, Guy should have moved out a year ago, precisely to prevent such questions, because Guy's roommate was dead. Just like the man represented by the contents of the box Carl held.

Carl sensed a shift and said, "Welp, just sign here and it's yours. Not nearly as heavy as some other stuff I've delivered."

Guy thought about signing his brother's name. Just as a memory. But didn't.

Guy waved at Carl and shut the door, grasping the box in his hands like it held a secret truth. He knew that was stupid. He'd done inventories for the very reasons this box held, more times than he wanted to remember. He just didn't know, in this case, that the box *did* hold a truth, and it was dark.

He went back into the living room, glancing at the other bedroom. The empty one. He remembered inventorying everything in it as if he'd done it yesterday. The pictures and notes. The flotsam and jetsam accumulated in life that seemed like trash but took on a special meaning when the person they were attached to never returned.

Putting them all in a box like the one in his hands.

He placed the package reverently on the floor, then glanced at his watch, one eye on the cardboard as if it would do something. He was running out of time, and the boss didn't take kindly to being late. But he might for this.

He pulled out an auto-opening knife from the inside of his waistband and flicked it, the black steel of the blade looking for something to bite. He took a knee. He sliced the tape, the blade moving as easily as if it was touching air. He methodically went through every joint the tape touched, not pulling. Only slicing. Delaying the inevitable. Eventually, there was nothing left to cut.

He sat for a moment, then opened the box.

The first thing he saw was a sterile, US Army bureaucratic inventory sheet detailing what was inside. He knew it wouldn't be accurate, because he'd made a call. He set it aside and saw the MultiCam uniform. He pulled it out and took in the damage. The ragged tears and burned edges. The blood.

He squeezed his eyes shut, fighting for control, wondering if he'd made a mistake in his request.

His brother, Sergeant First Class Timothy George, had been killed in a mechanical ambush in Afghanistan. Hunting a new threat of the Islamic State infiltrating the area, he'd located the leader of the nascent movement and had gained a hard-fought concurrence for a unilateral US mission. Such things were no longer allowed in the Graveyard of Empires, but this threat had been deemed worthy. The Taliban was an Afghan Army mission, but this was something else.

And he'd died, along with most of his team.

When Guy had heard of the casualties, he'd made some calls to friends in Special Operations. Telling them, first, not to mail the box to his parents. To mail it to him. And second, not to sterilize the contents. Give him everything.

Ordinarily, when a service member died, the inventory was conducted with one thing in mind: Protect the memory for a grieving family. Give the family everything they deserved, but remove anything that would be embarrassing. Porno magazines, unmailed letters of hatred, evidence of infidelity or anything else that would cause the family grief. First on the list was the uniform the deceased wore the night he died. That was usually burned.

But not this time. And Guy was regretting it.

He put the uniform aside and found his brother's cell phone. The same one Tim had used Apple iMessage to text from while he'd been deployed. The same one he'd used to send a last message, talking about his final mission. No specifics, just that he was doing good work and taking it to the enemy.

Only the enemy took it to him.

Guy turned the phone on, surprised to see it had a charge. The screen appeared, and he saw the Pandora app. He clicked on it, not wanting to, but wanting to. He found the channel his brother had talked about the night he'd died, telling him it was the perfect one for the warrior. Kidding him about how Guy's music tastes had shifted since he'd left the Special Mission Unit. Ribbing Guy for no longer being in the fight.

But his brother didn't know what Guy did now.

The app engaged, and the music softly floated out. Guy shut it off, staring at the screen. Wondering if Pandora understood the significance of a music channel from beyond the grave, his brother working laboriously to thumbs up and thumbs down songs until he thought it was perfect.

He put the phone aside and pulled out an armband, not unlike what NFL quarterbacks wore detailing plays. About four inches long, with Velcro straps to cinch it to the forearm, it was the last target his brother had chased.

A bit of history that nobody outside of Afghanistan should see.

Four pictures with Arabic names were under the plastic, followed by radio callsigns, medevac frequencies, and other coordination measures. Guy was surprised it had been included. He wanted the essence of his brother but not what his brother was chasing. He understood operational security. Understood that his brother's target wasn't in the equation. Soldiers died all the time. Some valiantly, others because they happened to drive down the wrong road at the wrong time.

And then he found himself staring at the pictures on the armband. Thinking. Wondering.

Hating.

2

Even though he was late, Guy chose to walk the short distance to the office. Inside a building a block long, the only thing indicating what was within was a small brass plaque proclaiming Blaisdell Consulting. Behind those doors was anything but a consulting firm.

He could have driven, as his office building had an underground garage, but that would have taken just as long, if not longer, since his high-rise in Clarendon, Virginia, was only a quarter of a mile away as the crow flies but probably three using all of the one-way surface streets in a car.

And he wanted the time to think.

He put in his earbuds and brought up his Pandora app, signing in as his brother. He'd managed to manipulate the login on his brother's phone and now could listen to the channel on his own device. The music came through, and he began rehearsing his speech. The one he was going to use on his boss.

The meeting was supposed to be for coordination about some ridiculous award he was getting for his actions on a target in Dubrovnik, Croatia, but the request had been a little odd. The boss didn't usually schedule pre-meetings for awardees in his office. Everyone knew the awards were bullshit anyway, given out to keep them competitive with their military peers. Men who weren't buried in an organization so secret it didn't even have a name.

Guy, like everyone he worked with, lived a dual life. While showing up at Blaisdell Consulting for his real work, he was also, ostensibly, one more military cog in the Fort Myer's motor pool, just off of Arlington Cemetery in Washington, DC. Which, given he hadn't served a day there, would be odd if you asked for a reference from the men and women who actually turned wrenches on Fort Myer. Stranger still, his rank was sergeant major. Not really cog material anymore, but he had to be sheep-dipped somewhere, and Fort Myer worked. In order to maintain the facade, his military records had to show progress, so every once in a while, he—like every other member of the Taskforce—was thrown the bone of an award.

None of the men gave a crap about them, and they understood that—while the Oversight Council presented them proudly—they were really used just to maintain the cover. But Colonel Kurt Hale, the commander of the Taskforce, understood this as well, which made the scheduled meeting odd.

He hit Arlington Boulevard in the shadow of the Iwo Jima memorial, the green carpet of Arlington directly behind, speckled with white dots. In the distance he saw a blip of brown against the green, upturned earth from a burial, and recognized it from Section 60, an area of

Arlington he knew well. The Global War on Terrorism section. It was where his brother would earn his own pile of brown. The thought brought him up short.

He ignored the honking horns and speeding Washington lobbyists and defense contractors on Arlington Boulevard, all of whom drove by this national treasure every single day, completely oblivious to the sacrifices it held while earning their living on the bodies buried within. He fixated on the piece of brown desecrating the expanse of green. He felt a darkness cloak him. A blackness blanketing his soul, and it was unsettling. He'd known many men who were killed in combat, but this was different. This was *his* blood.

He cranked the volume on his iPhone and began speed-walking down the sidewalk, rehearsing his speech.

3

Clearly irritated, Kurt Hale looked at his watch and said, "Where the hell is he?"

Johnny, Guy's team leader, said, "He's on the way. He just texted."

Kurt shook his head. "This isn't helping his case."

Johnny said, "Sir, he got the box today. Just now. Give him a break."

Kurt leaned back, taking in the words. "Bad timing. I don't think it's a discussion anymore. I no longer want to feel him out. I want him on ice, for at least a month. Get him involved in something operational, here in headquarters, but he's not deploying with you."

Axe, the second-in-command of the team, said, "Sir, wait a minute. We need him. We can't deploy without a teammate. We run bare bones as it is. Just take a look when he gets here."

Kurt said nothing. Johnny chimed in, "Sir, really, you can't give him an award and then tell him he's on ice. What signal is that sending?"

"Spare me. You and I both know how much this award

means to him. Jack squat. I can't have a guy on the edge. Especially where you're going."

George Wolffe, Kurt's deputy commander and an old CIA hand, said, "We all know the stakes, but a blanket statement is a little much. We've all lost someone along the way, and we kept fighting. We aren't talking about a Pike situation here. Let's feel him out before a decision."

Johnny nodded in appreciation. Kurt scowled at his deputy and started to respond when a shadow passed in the hallway. Guy leaned in, lightly knocking on the door-jamb.

He took in the audience and said, "Hey, sorry I'm late."

Kurt saw the emotions flit across his face, recognizing who was in the room, and knew Guy understood this was more than a coordination meeting. He said, "Come on in, Guy. Have a seat."

Guy did so, glancing at his team leader, then his 2IC. "What's up? I know this isn't about some bullshit cere-mony. If you thought I was going to embarrass the Task-force, you wouldn't have sent me to Croatia to begin with."

Kurt said, "Yes. It isn't about the ceremony. You're due to deploy tomorrow with your team, but I'm not sure you should. Make no mistake, this is my call. The men in this room feel otherwise."

He saw Guy relax, realizing it wasn't an ambush.

Guy said, "I'm good. I can operate. I'm on my game."

Despite what he said earlier, George Wolffe went into attack mode. "Good? You took Decoy's death last year pretty damn hard. You hit the bottle. Don't tell me you didn't. You were on the edge then, and you barely pulled out. You've done solid work since then, but now you've had another sacrifice. There's no shame in taking a break. None at all."

Decoy was the name of Guy's roommate, and he'd been killed in action on a mission in Istanbul. The death had been hard for everyone, but especially for Guy.

Guy said, "What do you want me to say? That my brother meant nothing? That I'm a robot? People die in combat all the time. Jesus. We'd have never left the Normandy beach if everyone who'd lost a friend was sidelined."

Kurt said, "This isn't Normandy, and you know it. We operate in a world without mistakes. Period. You fuck up, and you bring us all down. I need every man at one hundred percent."

He flicked his head toward Johnny and Axe. "They seem to think you're okay. I do not. I'm thinking you stay home for this one. Get your head on right. Axe said you weren't even going to the memorial in Montana, which raises a concern with me."

Guy said, "Sir, I can't go to the memorial. All I'll get is questions like, 'Weren't you in the military?' and 'What do you do now?' I don't need to go back to respect my brother. That's for my family. It has nothing to do with how I feel. Shit, why are you even giving me an award?"

Kurt said, "Don't go there. You earned it, even if you don't want it. Don't make this into something else. This is Taskforce business, not Oversight Council."

Guy flared. "Those fat fucks have no idea of the sacrifice. *None.* Fuck them."

The words settled, the air still. Guy shifted in his chair, but nobody else moved. Softly, Kurt said, "I think I could use you here in headquarters. Doing research. Our analysts are the best in the world, but they could use an Operator's touch. Show them what they're missing. Show them what to look for."

To Kurt's surprise, Guy leaned forward and said, "I could do that. If you let me research something specific."

Kurt looked at George, wondering where this was going. He said, "What?"

Guy pulled out the operational armband and held it up. "This. These are the fucks that killed my brother. And I want them. They're terrorists, and it *is* Taskforce business. Look, I know they aren't something that'll destroy democracy or cause the downfall of a country. They aren't high enough as a threat for the usual Taskforce envelope—but they killed my brother. Let me find them."

Axe leaned forward and took the armband, analyzing the targets on it.

Sensing buy-in with his stand-down order but wary of where it would lead, Kurt held up his hands and said, "Guy, come on. We don't do overt actions in a war zone. Yeah, you can research them, but we aren't going to hunt Taliban in Afghanistan."

Kurt saw Guy's eyes gleam and knew he'd lanced a boil, the heat coming out like a fervent missionary. Guy wanted to believe. "They aren't Taliban. Tim was hunting ISIS, and the fuckers in that target package aren't Pashtu or Uzbek or anything else in Afghanistan. They're Gulf Arabs, and they're funding the fight. It's right up our alley."

Kurt glanced again at George, his plan of sidelining Guy now taking a different turn. George said, "Guy, okay, you want to use our assets for research, that's fine. But understand we aren't going after them. A couple of Arabs in Afghanistan doesn't rise to our level. That's an Afghanistan problem. A NATO problem. Not a Task-force problem."

Guy simply looked at him. George continued. "You understand that, right? Your brother was killed in combat, but we don't react to that. We execute actions based on the national threat. Period. We aren't in the vendetta business."

Guy said, "I got that loud and clear. I understand. I'll stand down for a spell and let these guys go have the fun." He pointed at a wide-screen television behind Kurt's head, tuned to cable news. "But that fat asshole had better be at my award ceremony."

Kurt turned and saw Jonathan Billings, the secretary of state, exiting a building followed by a scrum of men dressed in traditional Gulf attire.

He rotated back around and grinned. "Yeah, that 'fat asshole' will be there. He's leaving Qatar tomorrow. He was doing something with investment in Greece. The ceremony isn't for a week. I'll make sure he's here."

Kurt should have reprimanded Guy for the slur, but

Billings *was* an asshole. Out of the thirteen members in the Oversight Council—the only people read on to Taskforce activities in the entire US government—he was the single sticking point, constantly fighting any operation solely because he was afraid of the exposure. Afraid for his own skin, regardless of the deaths that were saved by Taskforce intervention.

In truth, Kurt understood the reticence. If Taskforce activities were exposed, it would make Watergate's revelations look like they'd detailed shoplifting at the local 7-Eleven, but Billings constantly erred on the side of caution, preferring the terrorist attack to occur to prevent his own political demise. Kurt lived in the same world, and held the same fear of exposure, but he despised Billings for his willingness to sacrifice American lives. It was a fine line, and as far as Kurt was concerned, Billings was always on the wrong side.

Kurt said, "So we're good? You spend a spell here, and Johnny takes the team without you?"

Guy nodded, and Axe said, "Holy shit. Look at the guy behind Billings."

They turned, seeing a well-manicured Arab wearing traditional dress, a Rolex on his wrist, and a blazing smile. Kurt said, "What about him?"

Axe held up the armband and pointed at a picture. "It's this guy."

Guy became agitated, leaning into the TV. He said, "It *is* him. He's the one. I knew it wasn't some fleabag Taliban hit. That guy killed my brother!"

Kurt said, "Hold on. Jesus. Calm down. That guy is Haider al-Attiya. His father is a bigwig with the Qatar Investment Authority. They have nothing to do with any attacks in Afghanistan. Billings is working with them on the Greek euro crisis. The kid is a rich Gulf Arab, with a silver spoon shoved up his ass."

Guy said, "Look at him. Then look at the picture. It's him."

Kurt glanced at George, knowing he needed to stamp out wild conspiracy theories. Kurt said, "Guy. Look at me. You're giving me worry about your control. The man on TV is a respected member of the Qatari government. Don't make this into something it's not from a damn CNN clip. Don't make me doubt you."

Guy said nothing, still staring at the screen. Kurt leaned over and took the armband away from Axe. He said, "This guy's name is Abu Kamal."

A wolf smile spread across Guy's face. "Yeah, like he'd use his real name in Afghanistan. That's him. And that's his picture."

Kurt balled up the armband and said, "Don't go all Alex Jones on me here. Keep the conspiracies within the realm of the possible."

Guy leaned back and said, "All right. Okay. I'm good with sitting out the deployment. I'll stay and do a little help on the analytical side."

Kurt said, "I think it would be better if you went home. For the memorial."

"No. I already told you. Too painful. I'll help out you guys here. Even if I can't deploy. I'm good."

Kurt sized him up, trying to see if Guy was really as even-keeled as he professed. He wasn't sure, but honestly, it wasn't like the man had threatened to go postal. And he *was* a Taskforce Operator. Handpicked by Kurt himself.

Kurt said, "Okay. Then it's settled. You help on the analytical side and take some time off. But you'll see the psychs here. No questions asked. You can tell them whatever you want, but you're seeing them."

He saw Guy bristle and leaned forward, speaking barely above a whisper. "Guy. Trust me. They can help. I've walked your path. Talk to them. I don't need to lose an Operator over something that can be helped."

Guy let the words settle, then nodded. Johnny exhaled, glad it was over. He clapped Guy on the back and said, "Hey, if there's anything to the Qatar thing, Pike will find it. He drew the card for the James Bond mission."

Guy looked confused, and Johnny snapped back in embarrassment, stealing a glance at Kurt. Speaking of compartmented missions was a non-starter, and he just had. Kurt waved it off and said, "Pike's investigating some ties between Brazil and Qatar. Nothing to do with this."

Kurt saw a wicked grin slip out. Guy said, "Pike's on it? Oh yeah, if there's a connection, he'll find it. That guy's a trouble magnet."